STAR✳BEASTS

STAR✳BEASTS

WRITTEN BY
STEPHANIE YOUNG

ILLUSTRATED BY
ALLYSON LASSITER

ONI PRESS

AN ONI PRESS PUBLICATION

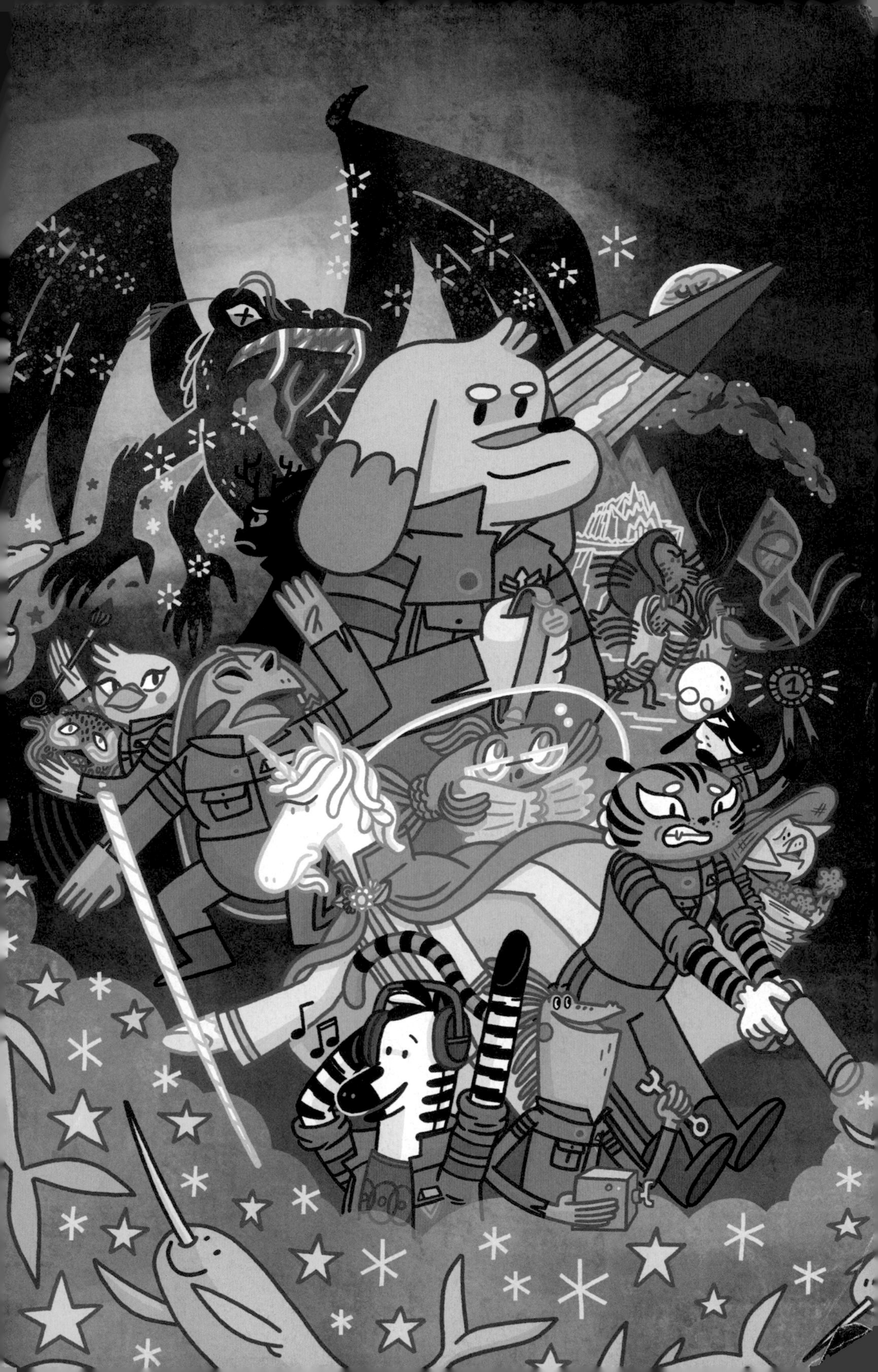

CAPTAIN BANDIT

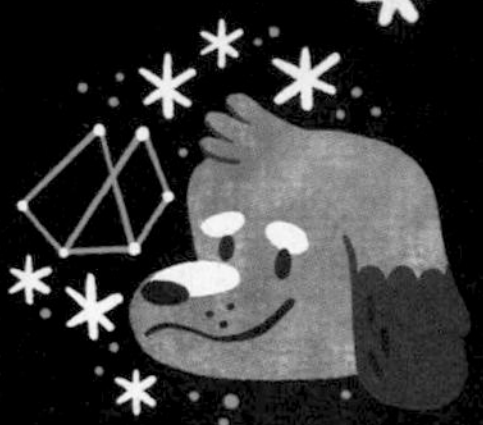

Good dog at heart
and the Star Beasts'
youngest Captain

COMMANDER FLASHTISTA

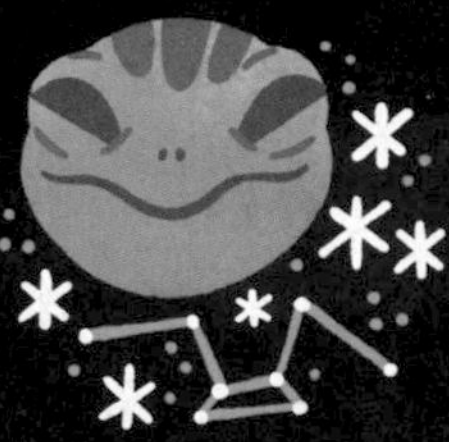

Kick-asteroid warrior
turtle and the *Condor*'s
BLAST YEAH pilot

SIR IAN MACCABRAN

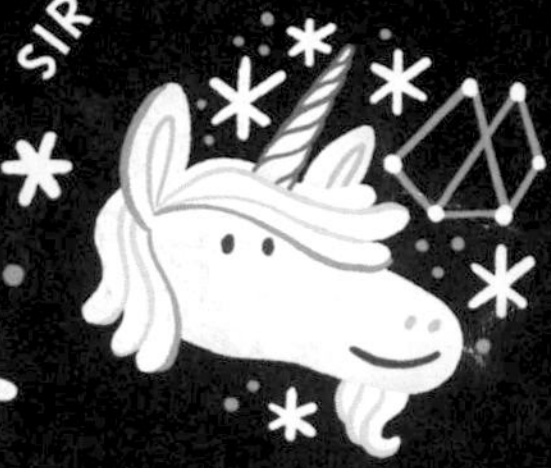

Nickname: Macca
Zoorb Councilor, Unicorn
Knight, and last of his kind

CREWCREATURE DR. MARIA CURLY

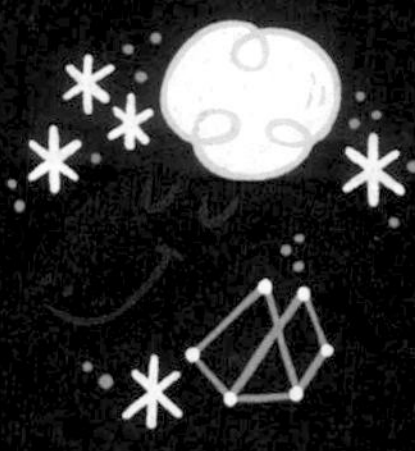

Ambitious sheep,
respected scientist,
and math wiz

LIEUTENANT KARMA JAMYANG

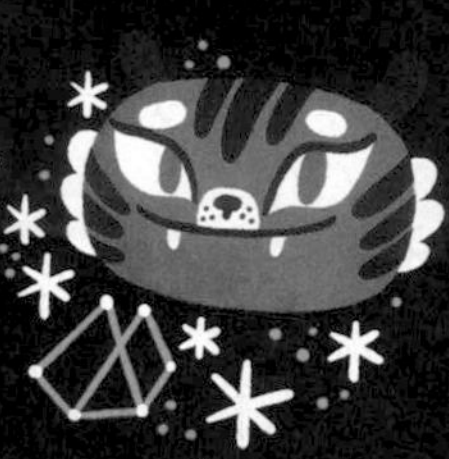

Caring healer, common-sense
medic, and peaceful tiger

ZAYD OF THE SERENGETI

Go-with-the-flow Zebra, galactic DJ, and Star Beasts Ambassador

LIEUTENANT CLIO FIN

Librarian goldfish, dedicated scholar, and swimming in historical facts

CREWCREATURE ELEANOR LA

Creative parakeet, artistic innovator, and problem-solver

CREWCREATURE SNUFFS LEWIS

Practical pig, space farmer, and grows far-out veggies

RECRUIT PEPITO

Nickname: Pep
Techie iguana, happy helper, and gadget geek

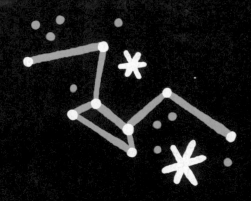

Written by STEPHANIE YOUNG

Illustrated by ALLYSON LASSITER

Colors by LISA HADLEY & ALLYSON LASSITER

Lassie Font Created by LILA SYMONS
at ALPHABETS AT WORK

Designed by SONJA SYNAK

Edited by AMANDA MEADOWS

PUBLISHED BY ONI-LION FORGE
PUBLISHING GROUP, LLC

James Lucas Jones, president & publisher
Sarah Gaydos, editor in chief • Charlie Chu,
e.v.p. of creative & business development
Brad Rooks, director of operations • Amber
O'Neill, special projects manager • Margot Wood,
director of marketing & sales • Katie Sainz,
marketing manager • Tara Lehmann, publicist
Holly Aitchison, consumer marketing manager
Troy Look, director of design & production • Kate Z.
Stone, senior graphic designer • Hilary Thompson,
graphic designer • Carey Hall, graphic designer
Sarah Rockwell, graphic designer • Angie
Knowles, digital prepress lead • Vincent Kukua,
digital prepress technician • Jasmine Amiri,
senior editor • Shawna Gore, senior editor
Amanda Meadows, senior editor • Robert Meyers,
senior editor, licensing • Desiree Rodriguez, editor
Grace Scheipeter, editor • Zack Soto, editor
Chris Cerasi, editorial coordinator • Steve
Ellis, vice president of games • Ben Eisner,
game developer • Michelle Nguyen, executive
assistant • Jung Lee, logistics coordinator

Joe Nozemack, publisher emeritus

1319 SE Martin Luther King Jr. Blvd.
Suite 240
Portland, OR 97214

ONIPRESS.COM
f @onipress
@onipress
t @onipress
@onipress

STARBEASTSCOMIC.WORDPRESS.COM
@allysonlassiter   @sfarrisyoung

First Edition: August 2021
ISBN 978-1-62010-937-3
eISBN 978-1-62010-950-2

1 2 3 4 5 6 7 8 9 10

Library of Congress Control Number
2021934310

Printed in Canada.

For Pickles
and Mr. Whiskers

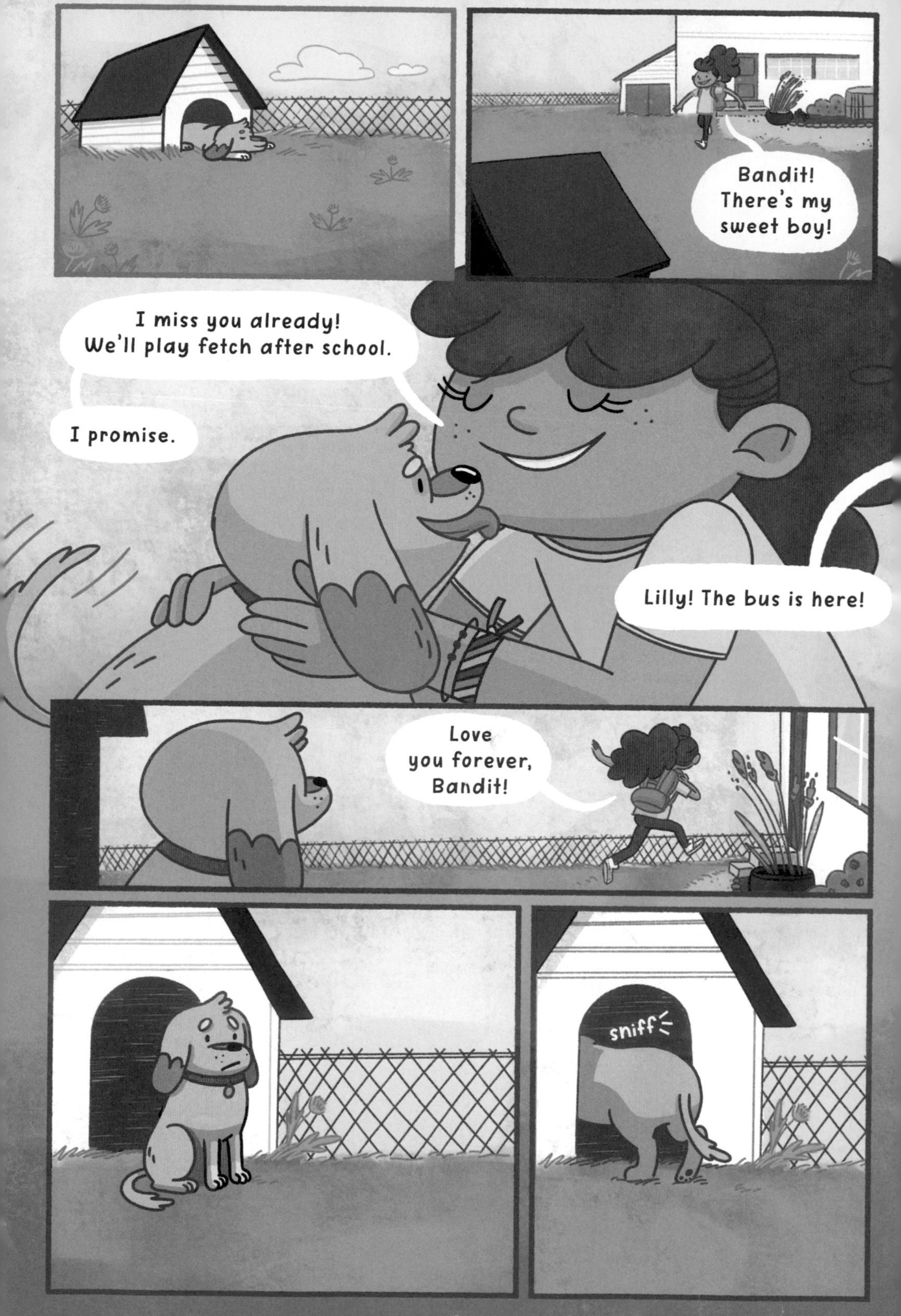
Bandit! There's my sweet boy!
I miss you already! We'll play fetch after school.
I promise.
Lilly! The bus is here!
Love you forever, Bandit!
sniff

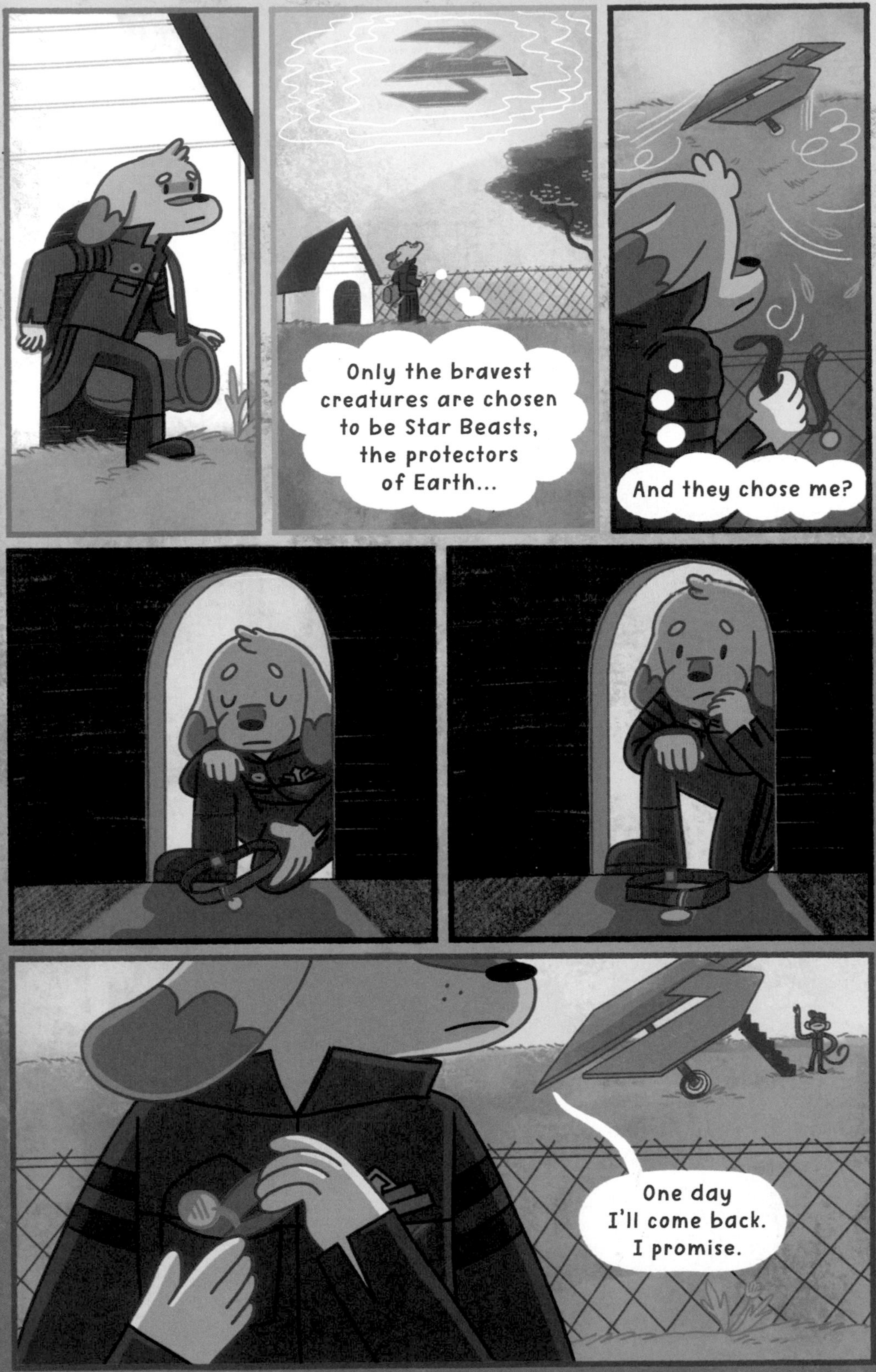
Only the bravest creatures are chosen to be Star Beasts, the protectors of Earth...
And they chose me?
One day I'll come back. I promise.

CHAPTER 1

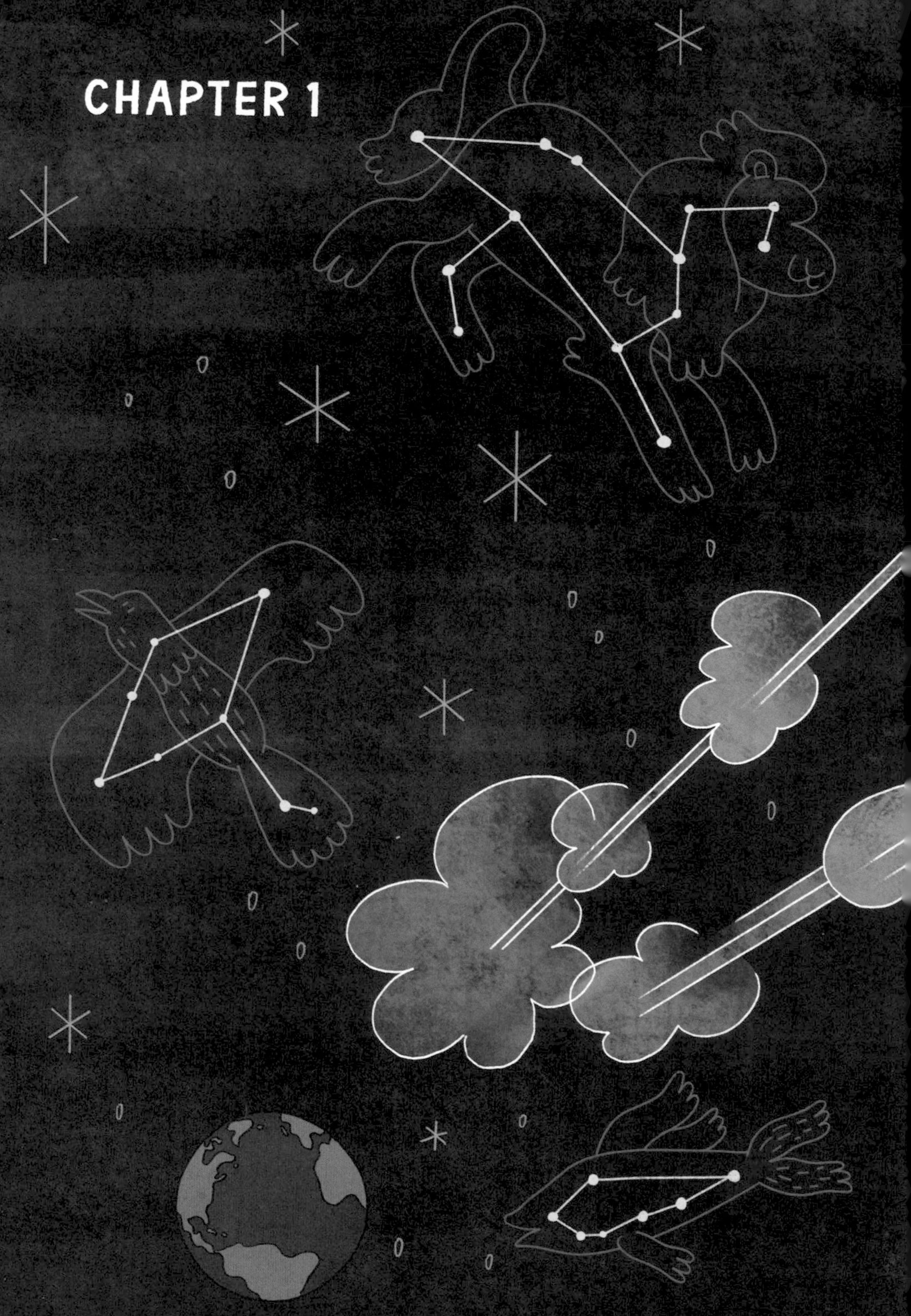

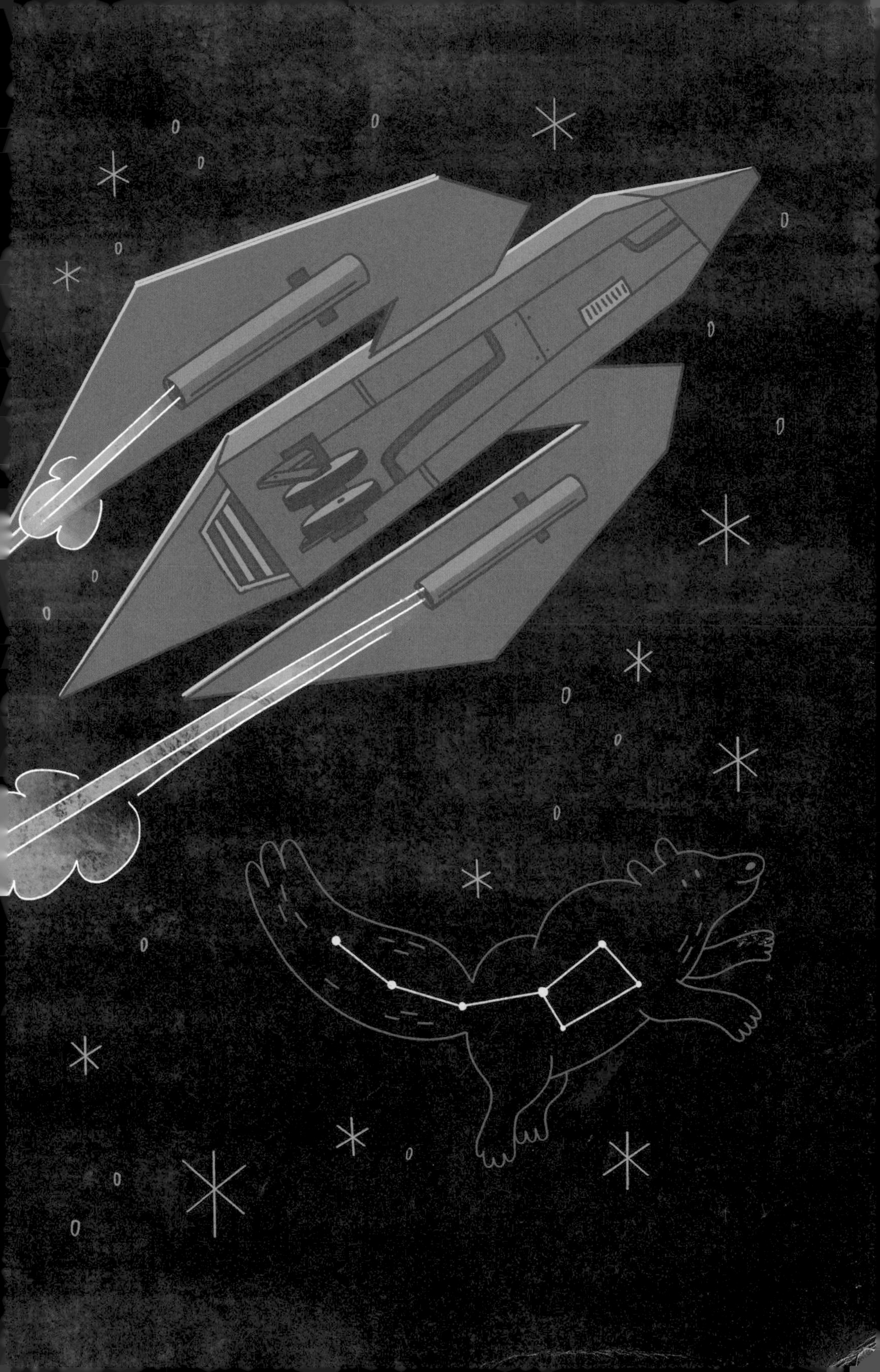

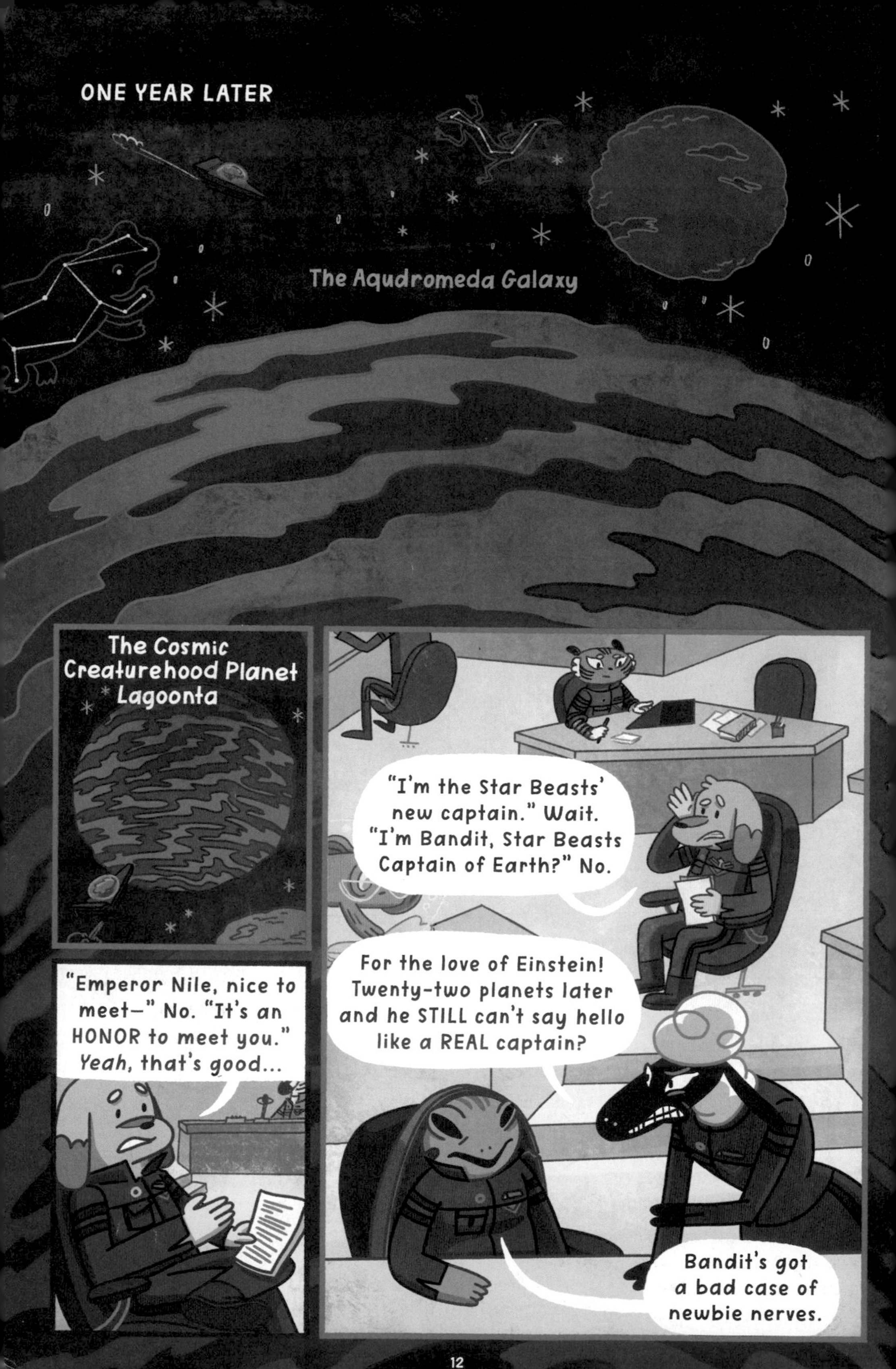
ONE YEAR LATER
The Aqudromeda Galaxy
The Cosmic Creaturehood Planet Lagoonta
"Emperor Nile, nice to meet–" No. "It's an HONOR to meet you." Yeah, that's good...
"I'm the Star Beasts' new captain." Wait. "I'm Bandit, Star Beasts Captain of Earth?" No.
For the love of Einstein! Twenty-two planets later and he STILL can't say hello like a REAL captain?
Bandit's got a bad case of newbie nerves.

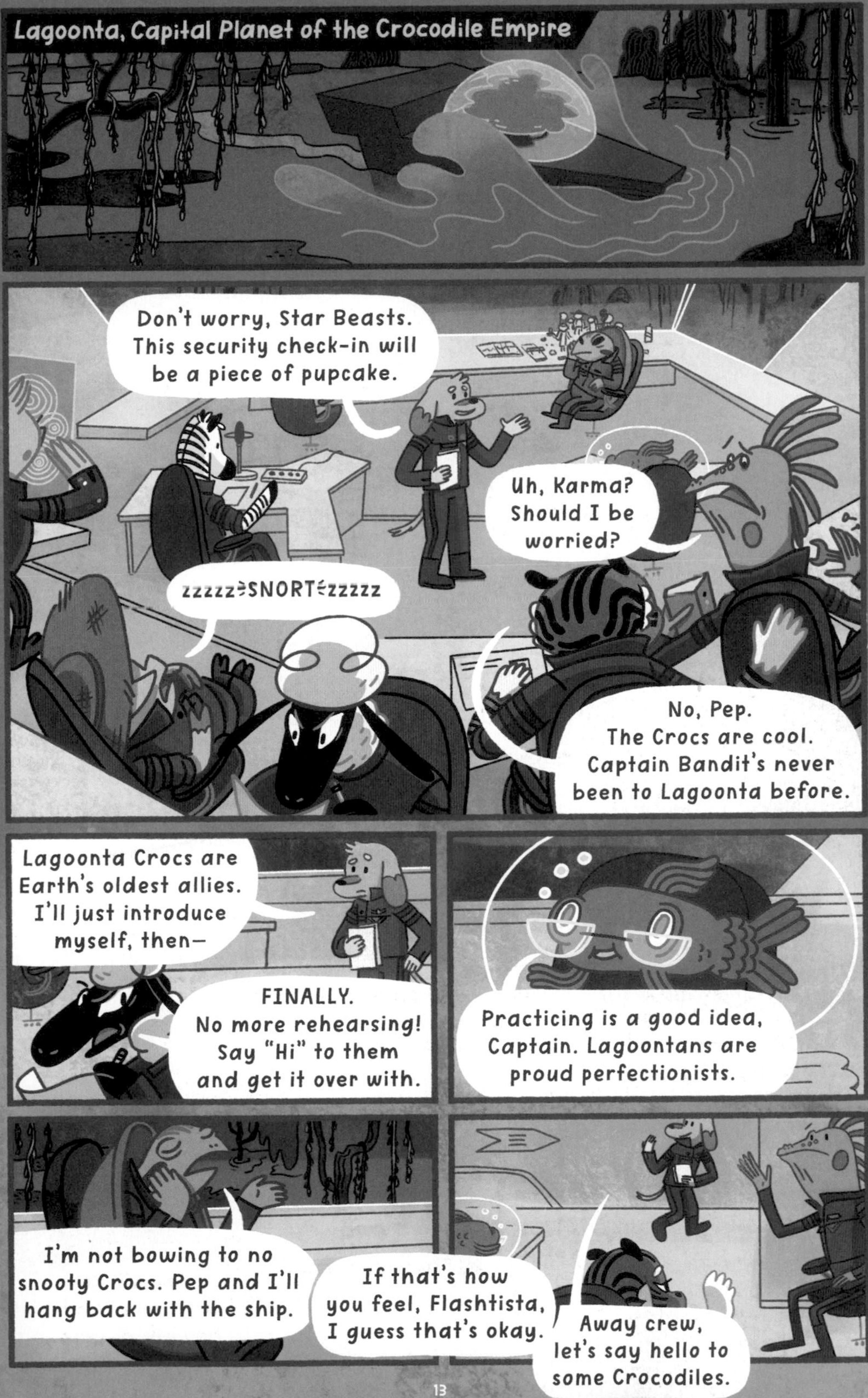

Lagoonta, Capital Planet of the Crocodile Empire
Don't worry, Star Beasts. This security check-in will be a piece of pupcake.
Uh, Karma? Should I be worried?
zzzzz⪢SNORT⪡zzzzz
No, Pep. The Crocs are cool. Captain Bandit's never been to Lagoonta before.
Lagoonta Crocs are Earth's oldest allies. I'll just introduce myself, then—
FINALLY. No more rehearsing! Say "Hi" to them and get it over with.
Practicing is a good idea, Captain. Lagoontans are proud perfectionists.
I'm not bowing to no snooty Crocs. Pep and I'll hang back with the ship.
If that's how you feel, Flashtista, I guess that's okay.
Away crew, let's say hello to some Crocodiles.

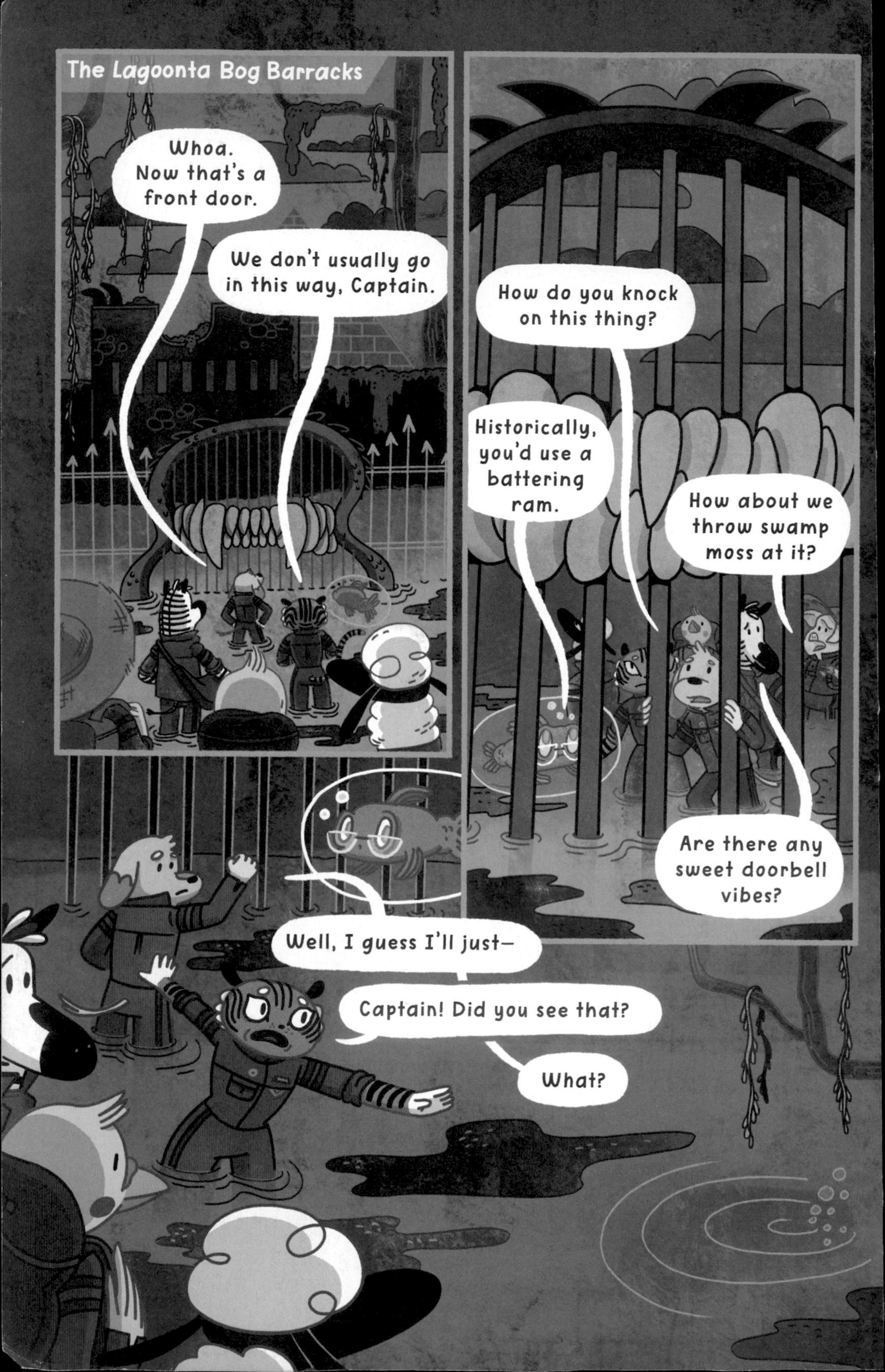
The Lagoonta Bog Barracks
Whoa. Now that's a front door.
We don't usually go in this way, Captain.
How do you knock on this thing?
Historically, you'd use a battering ram.
How about we throw swamp moss at it?
Are there any sweet doorbell vibes?
Well, I guess I'll just—
Captain! Did you see that?
What?

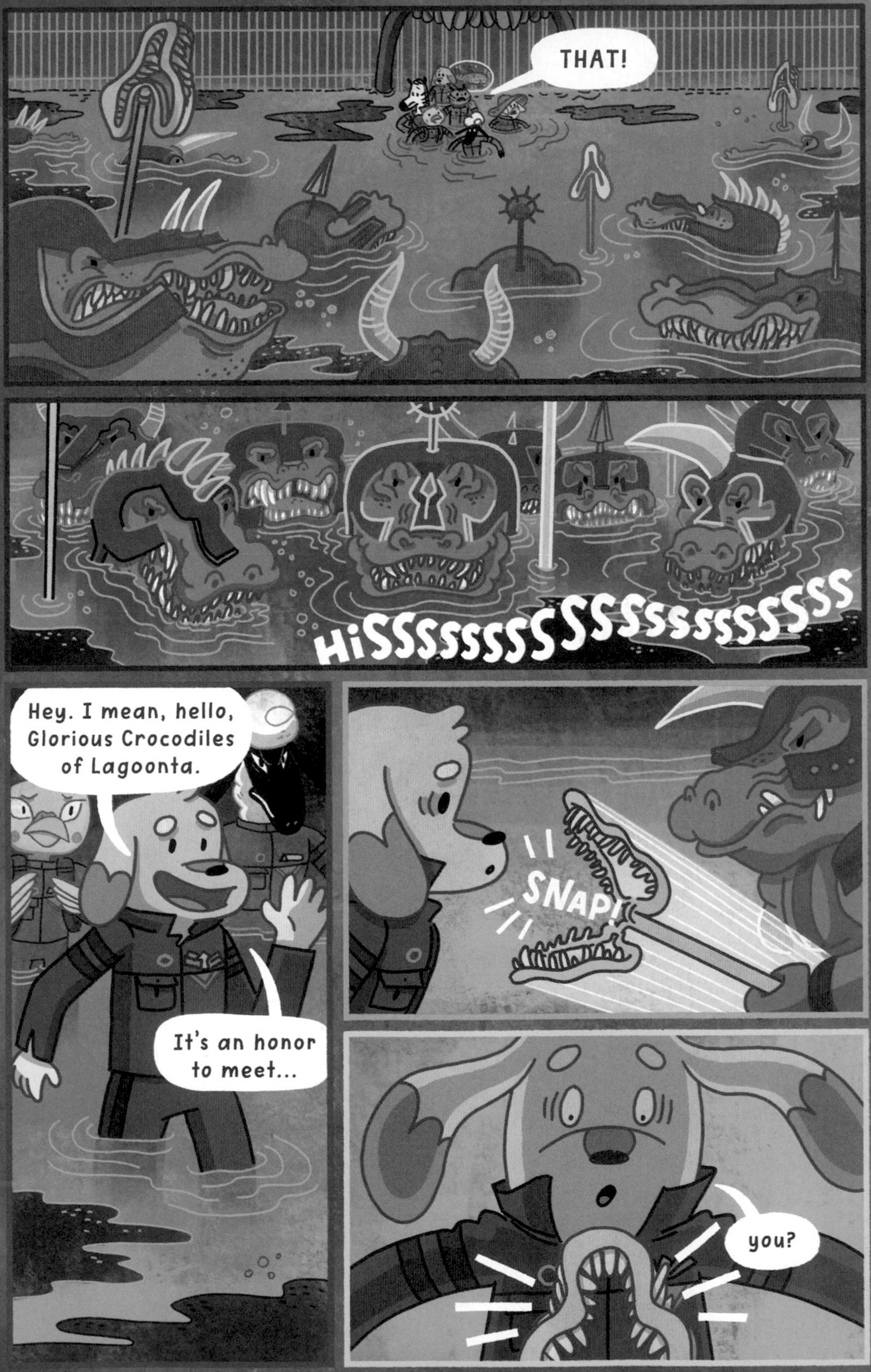
THAT!
HiSSSSSSSSSSSSSSSSSSSS
Hey. I mean, hello, Glorious Crocodiles of Lagoonta.
It's an honor to meet...
SNAP!
you?

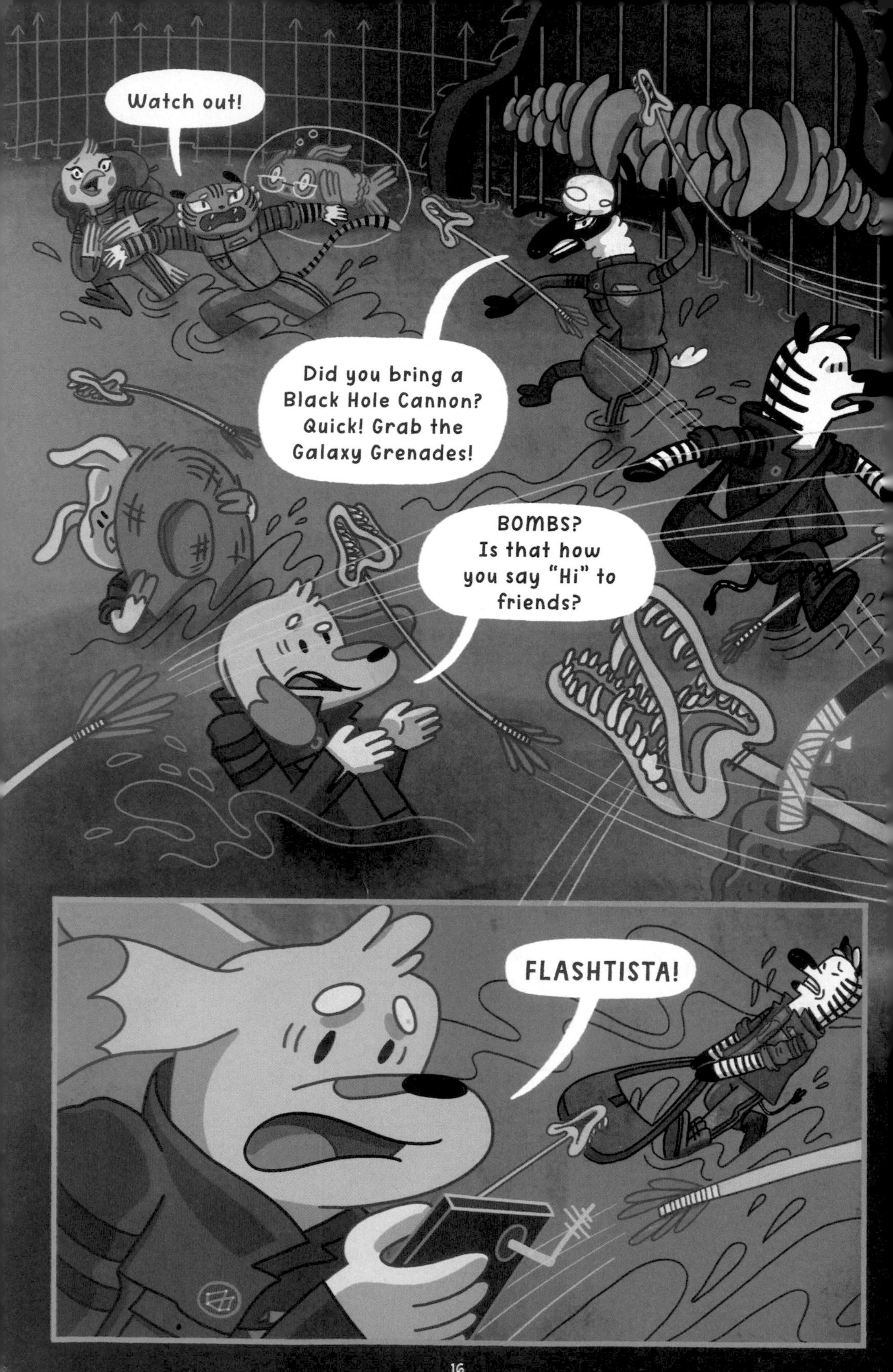
Watch out!
Did you bring a Black Hole Cannon? Quick! Grab the Galaxy Grenades!
BOMBS? Is that how you say "Hi" to friends?
FLASHTISTA!

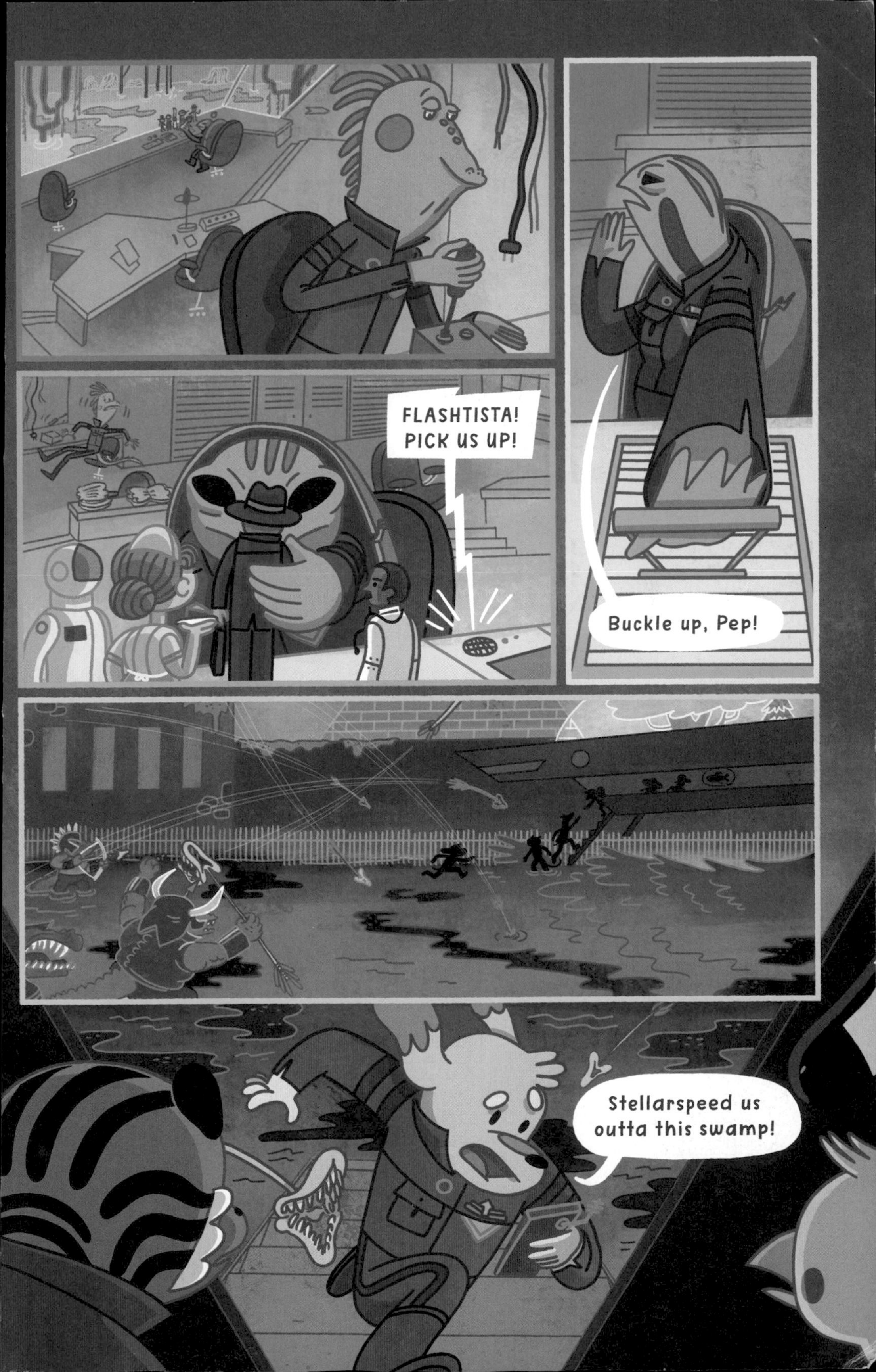
FLASHTISTA! PICK US UP!
Buckle up, Pep!
Stellarspeed us outta this swamp!

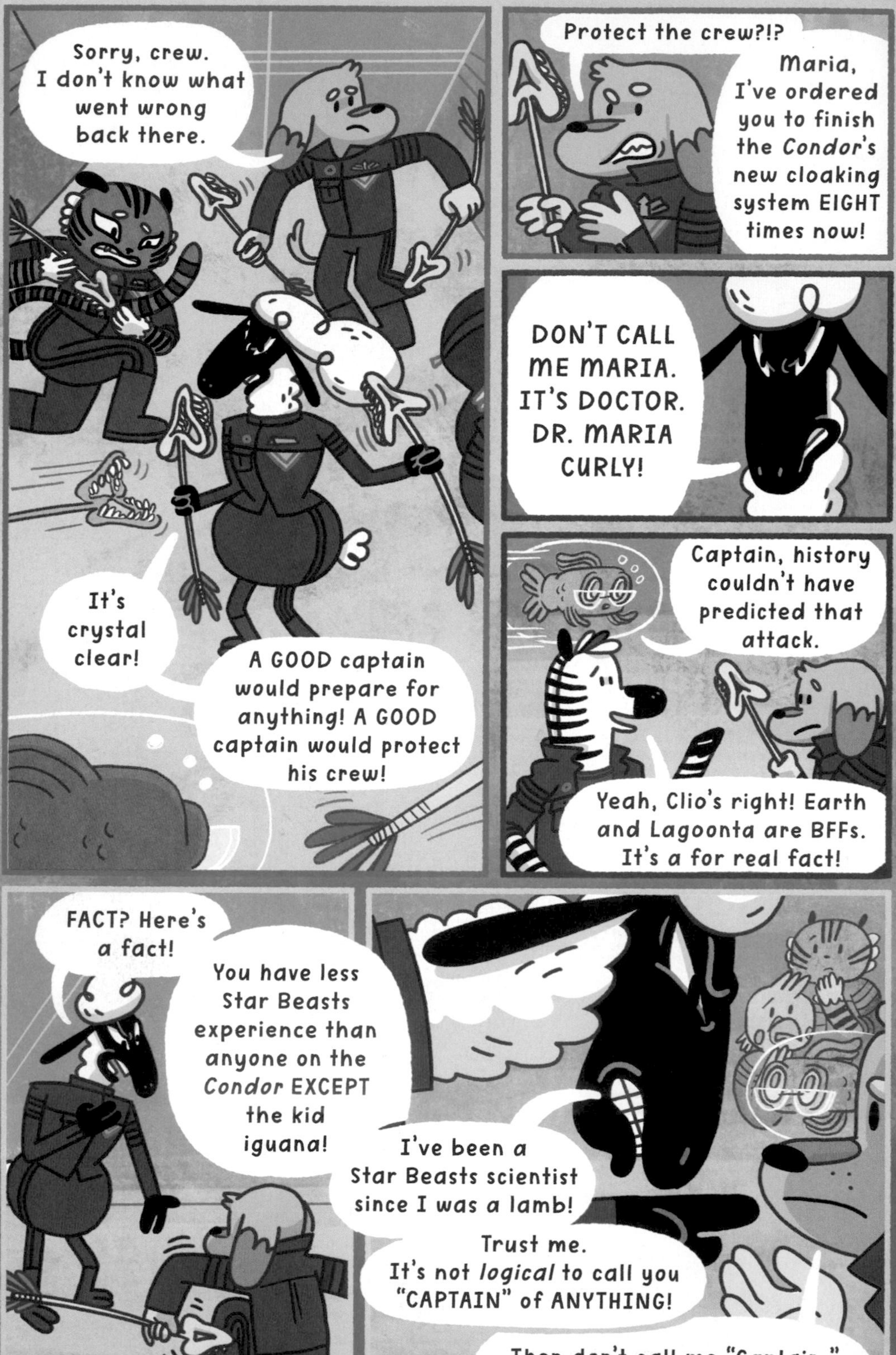
Sorry, crew. I don't know what went wrong back there.
It's crystal clear!
A GOOD captain would prepare for anything! A GOOD captain would protect his crew!
Protect the crew?!?
Maria, I've ordered you to finish the *Condor*'s new cloaking system EIGHT times now!
DON'T CALL ME MARIA. IT'S DOCTOR. DR. MARIA CURLY!
Captain, history couldn't have predicted that attack.
Yeah, Clio's right! Earth and Lagoonta are BFFs. It's a for real fact!
FACT? Here's a fact!
You have less Star Beasts experience than anyone on the *Condor* EXCEPT the kid iguana!
I've been a Star Beasts scientist since I was a lamb!
Trust me. It's not *logical* to call you "CAPTAIN" of ANYTHING!
Then don't call me "Captain." I like "Bandit" better, anyway.

CLICK. CLICKTY-CLICK. CLICK. CLICK...

CLICK. CLICK. CLICKTY...

Bandit?

Stupid space junk!

Uh... Captain?

Go ahead, Pep.

Um. I'm beaming in a video call from the, UH, Star Beasts Zoorb Council.

Councilor Thunderbird. What's the news from Earth?

It's the news from Lagoonta that concerns me.

That just happened! How did the Zoorb Council hear about it so fast?

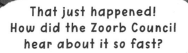

There's no time to explain. End your security tour. Bring the Star Beasts back to Earth right away!

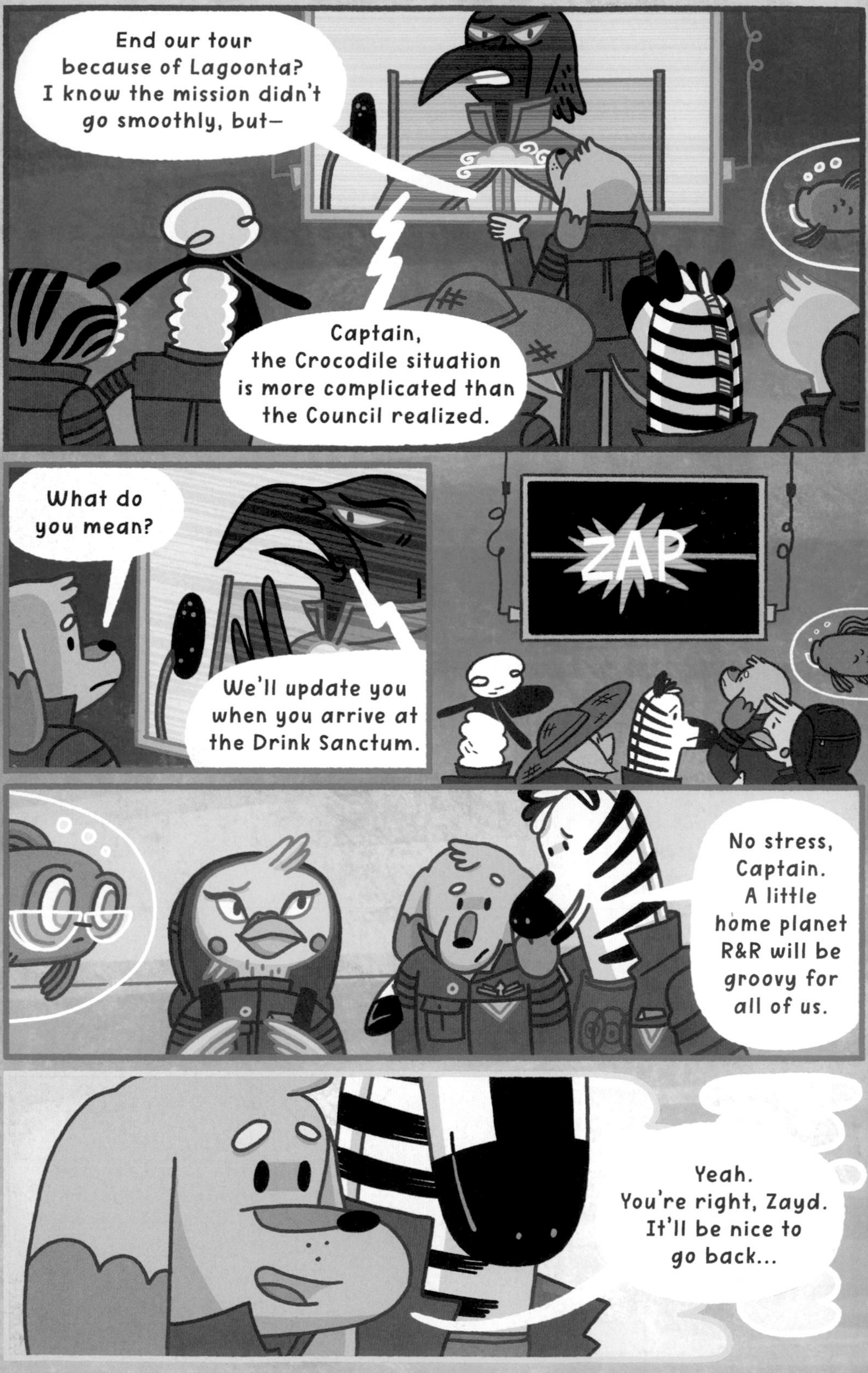
End our tour because of Lagoonta? I know the mission didn't go smoothly, but—
Captain, the Crocodile situation is more complicated than the Council realized.
What do you mean?
We'll update you when you arrive at the Drink Sanctum.
ZAP
No stress, Captain. A little home planet R&R will be groovy for all of us.
Yeah. You're right, Zayd. It'll be nice to go back...

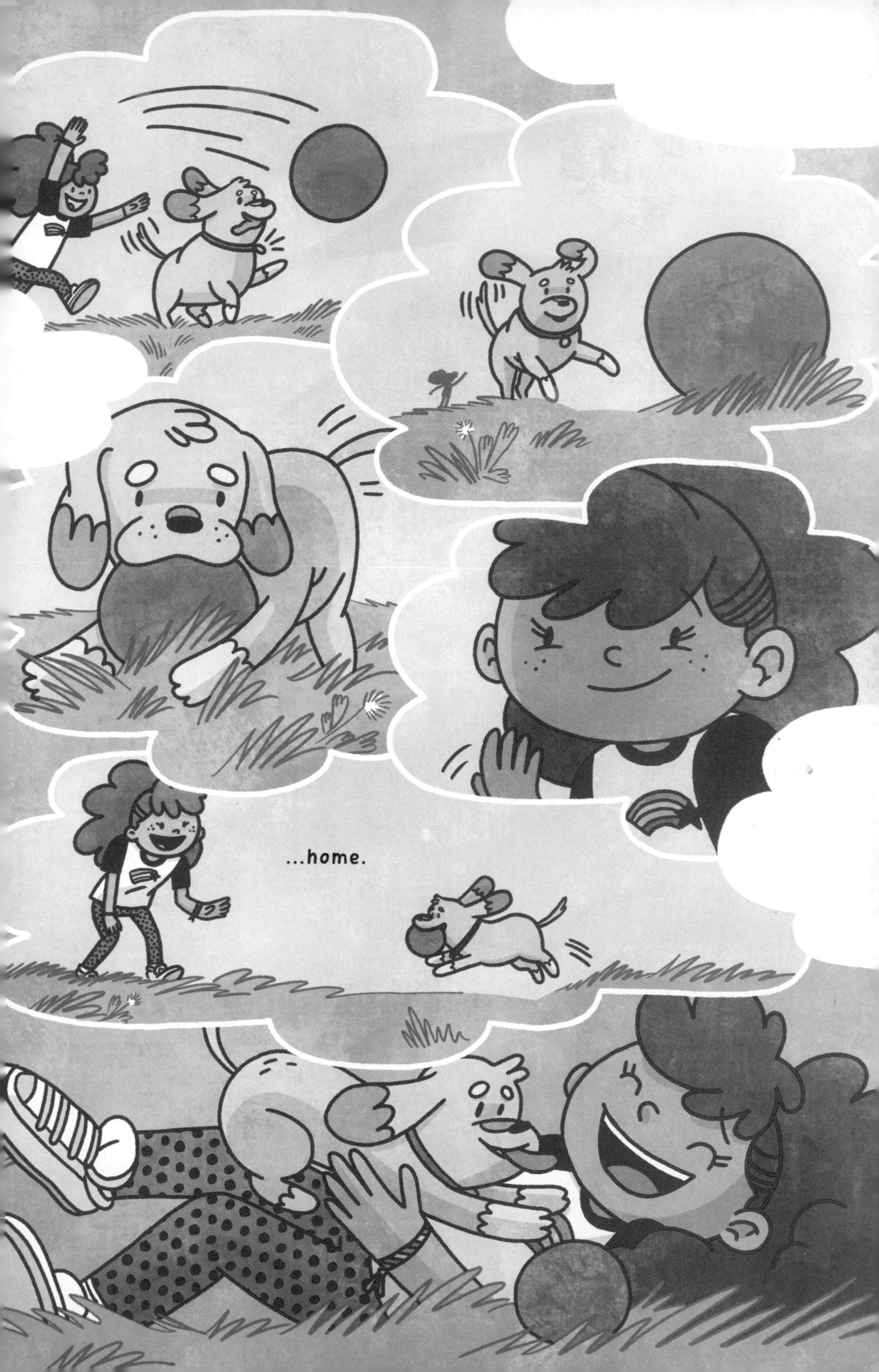
...home.

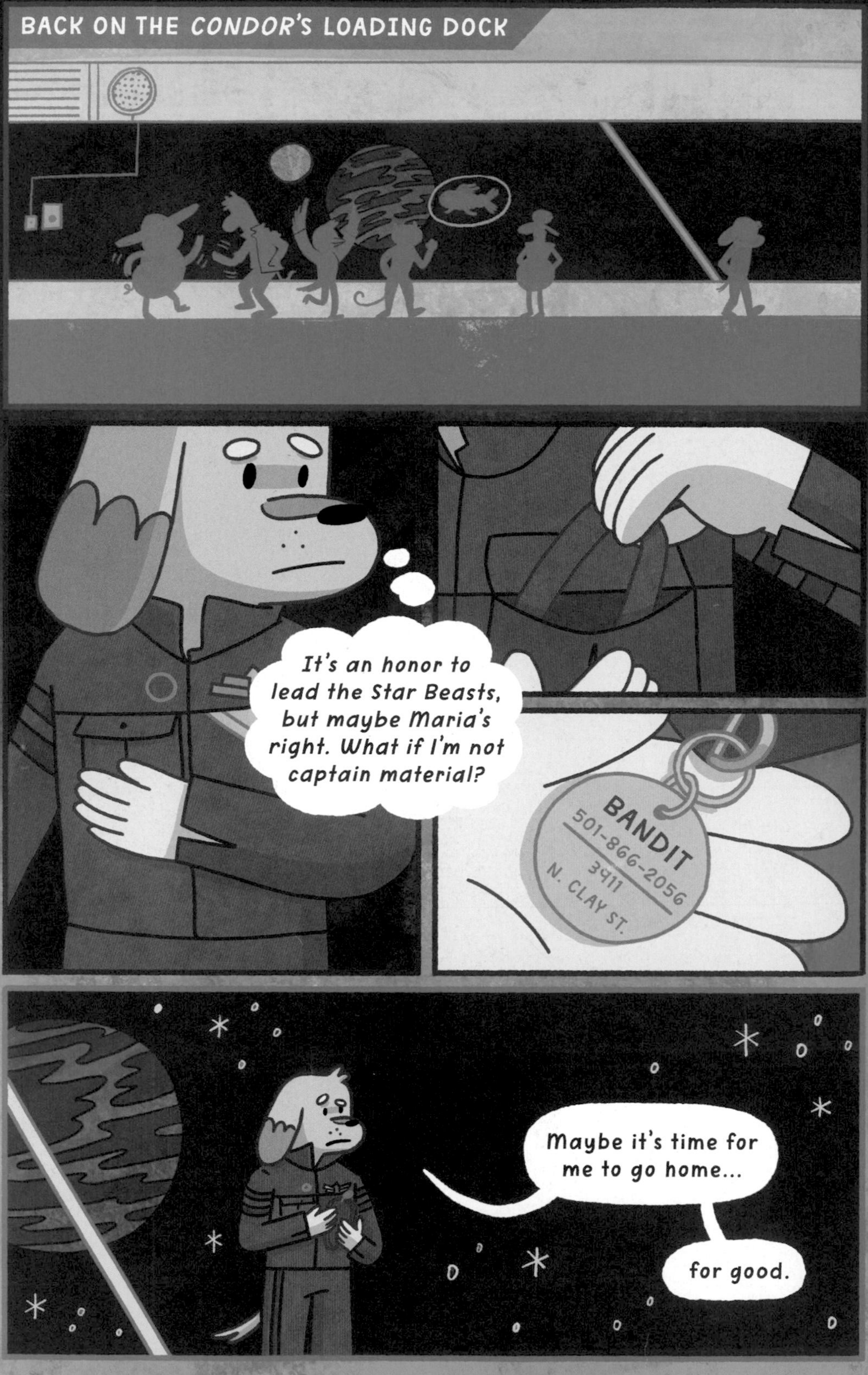
BACK ON THE *CONDOR*'S LOADING DOCK
It's an honor to lead the Star Beasts, but maybe Maria's right. What if I'm not captain material?
BANDIT
501-866-2056
3411
N. CLAY ST.
Maybe it's time for me to go home...
for good.

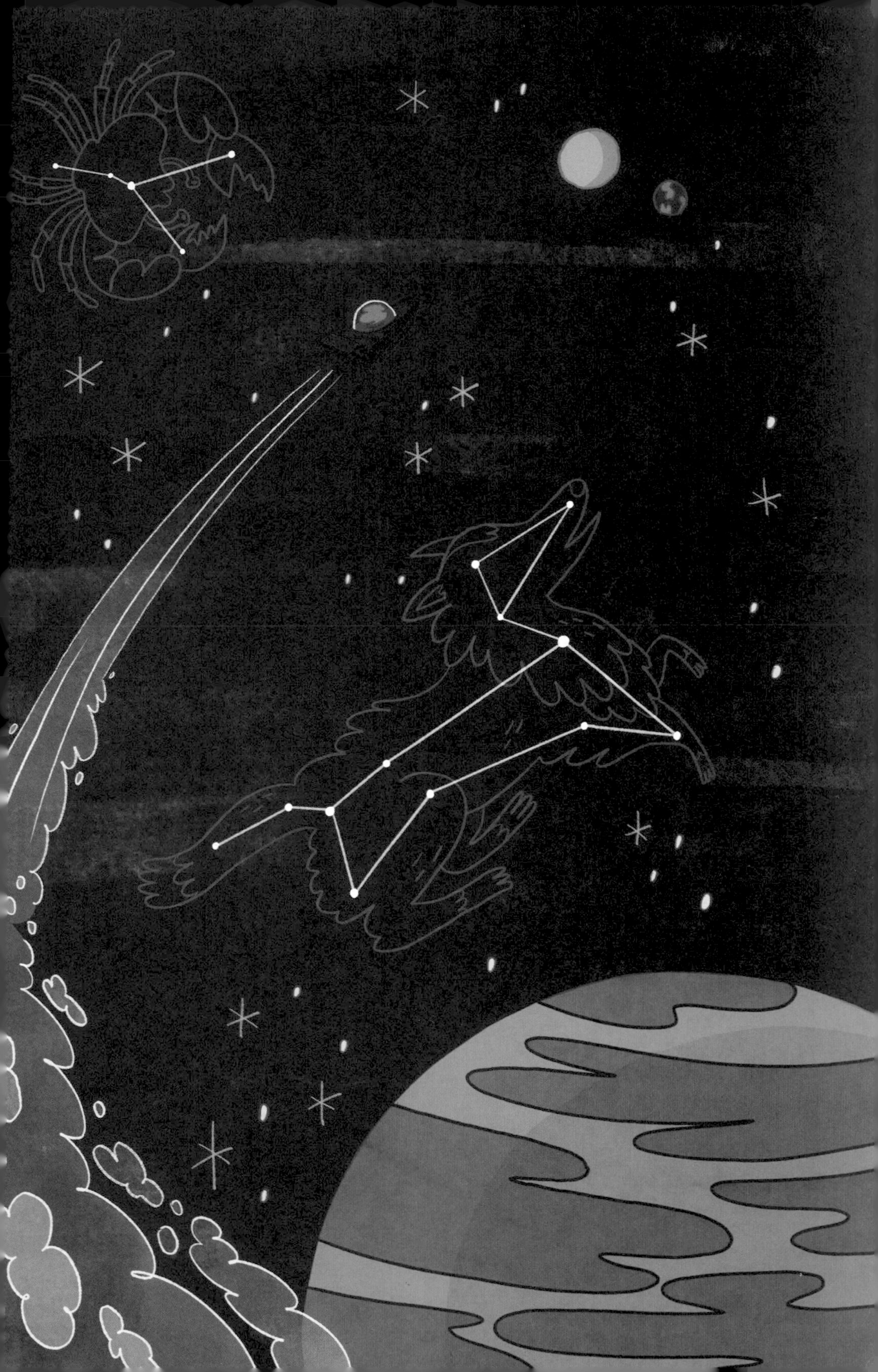

CHAPTER 2

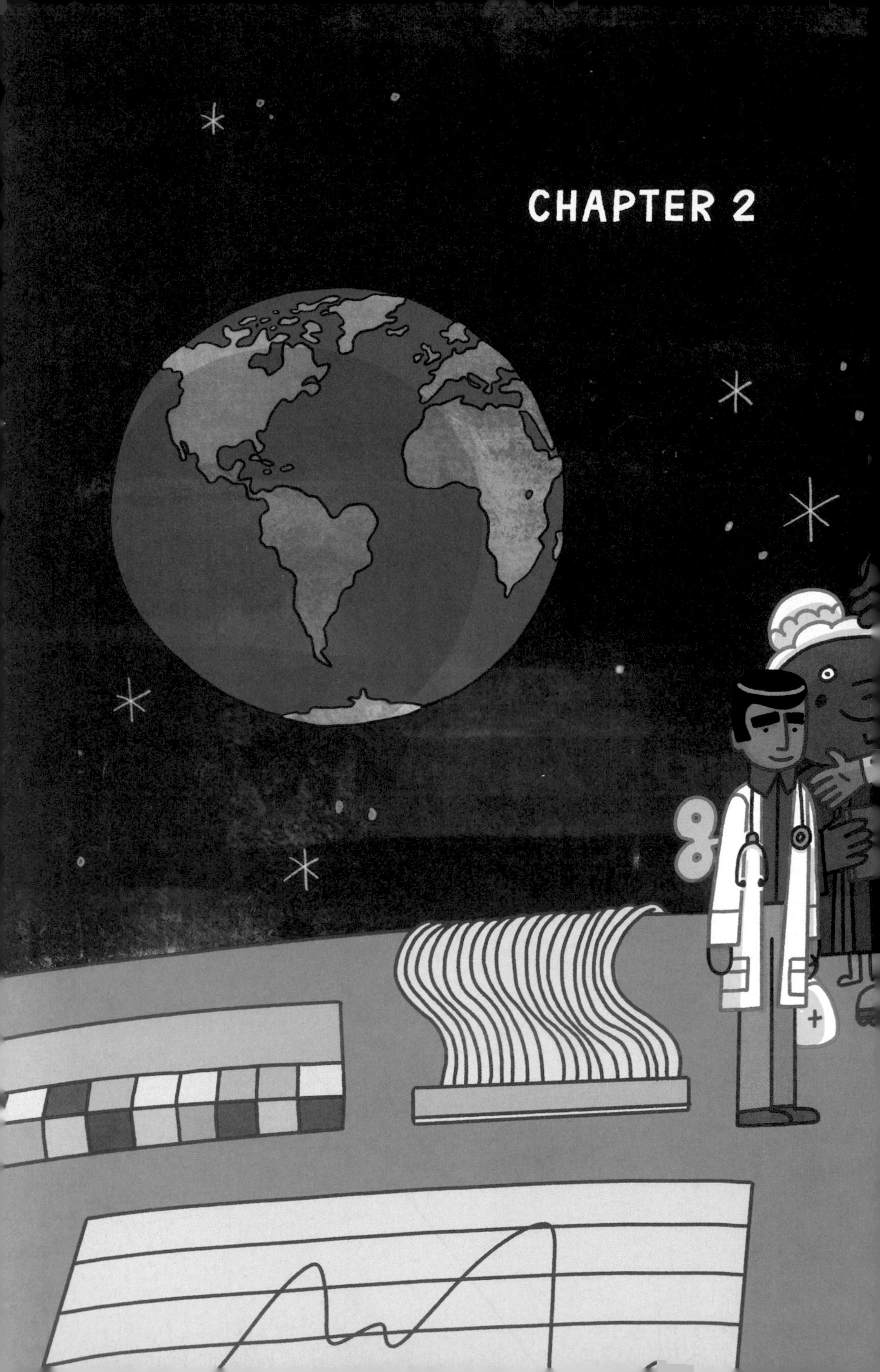

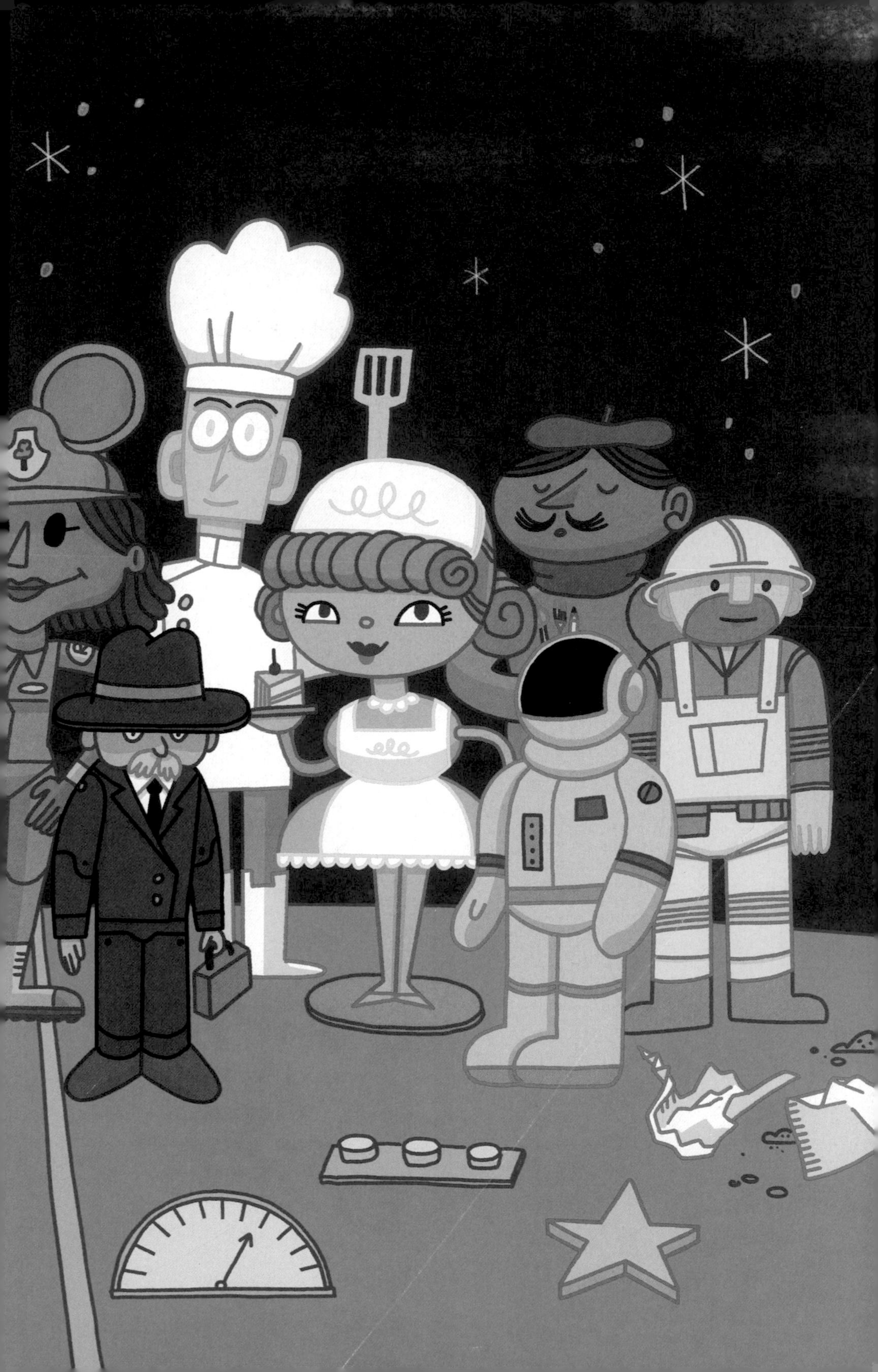

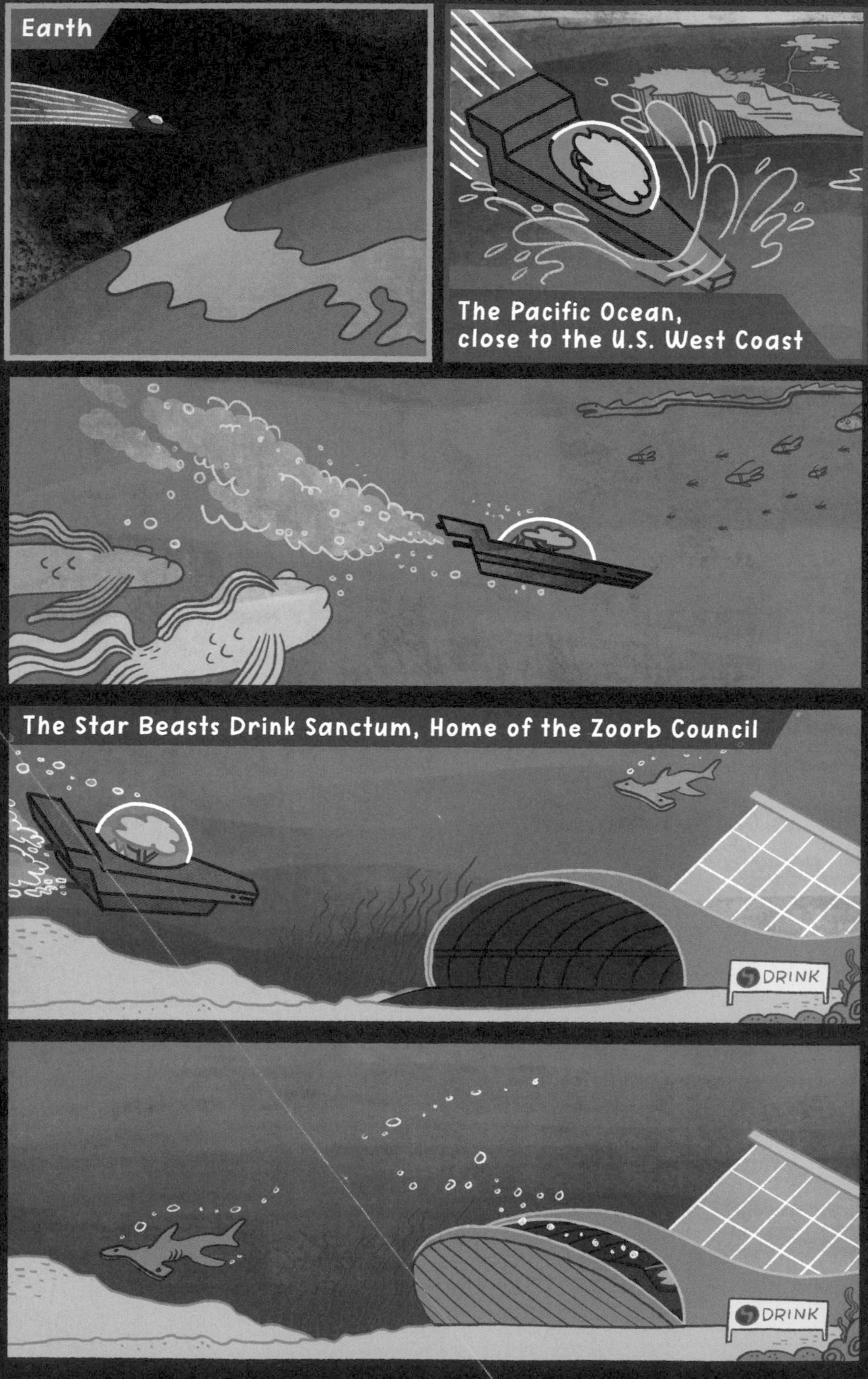
Earth
The Pacific Ocean,
close to the U.S. West Coast
The Star Beasts Drink Sanctum, Home of the Zoorb Council
DRINK
DRINK

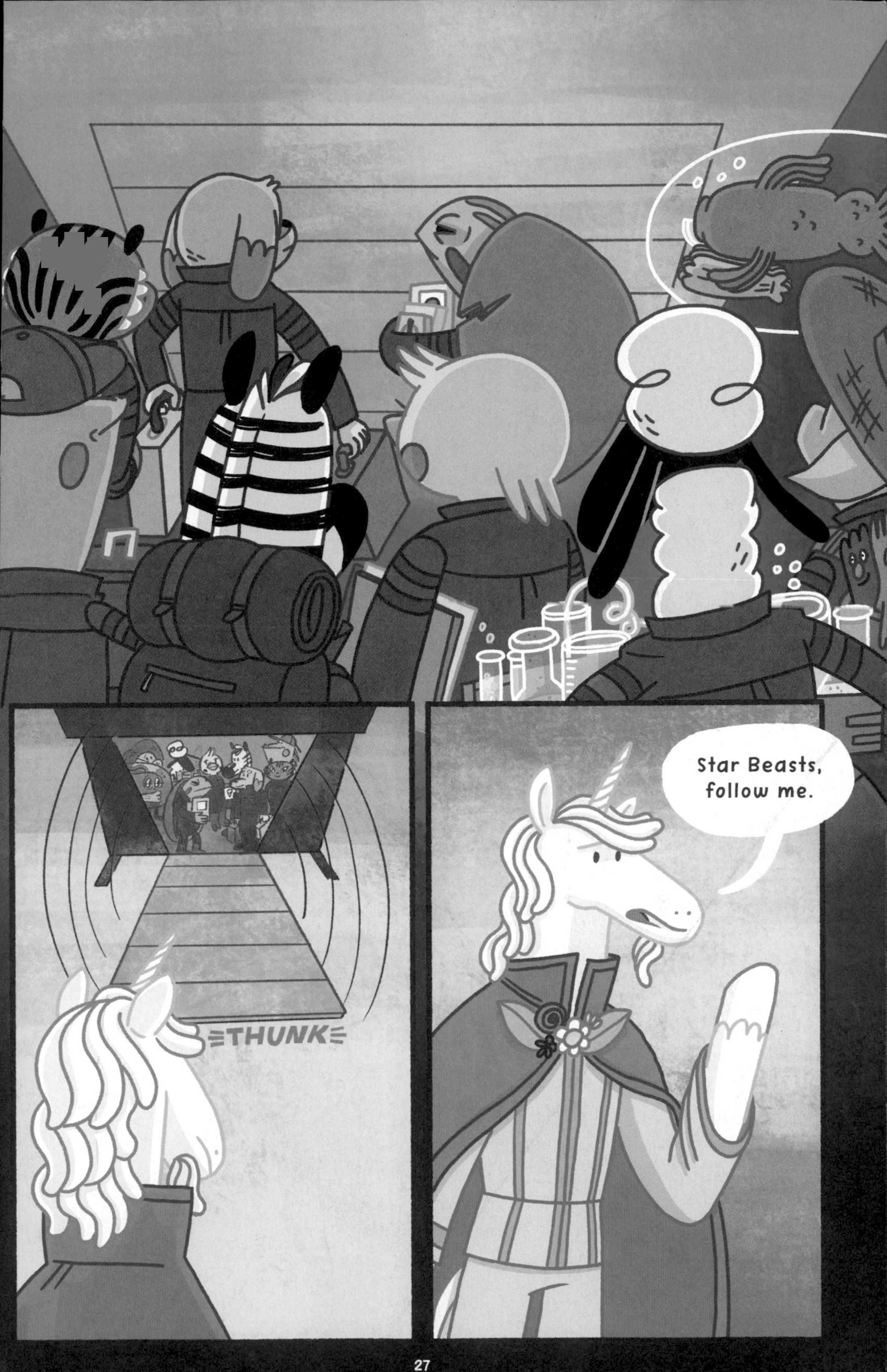
THUNK
Star Beasts, follow me.

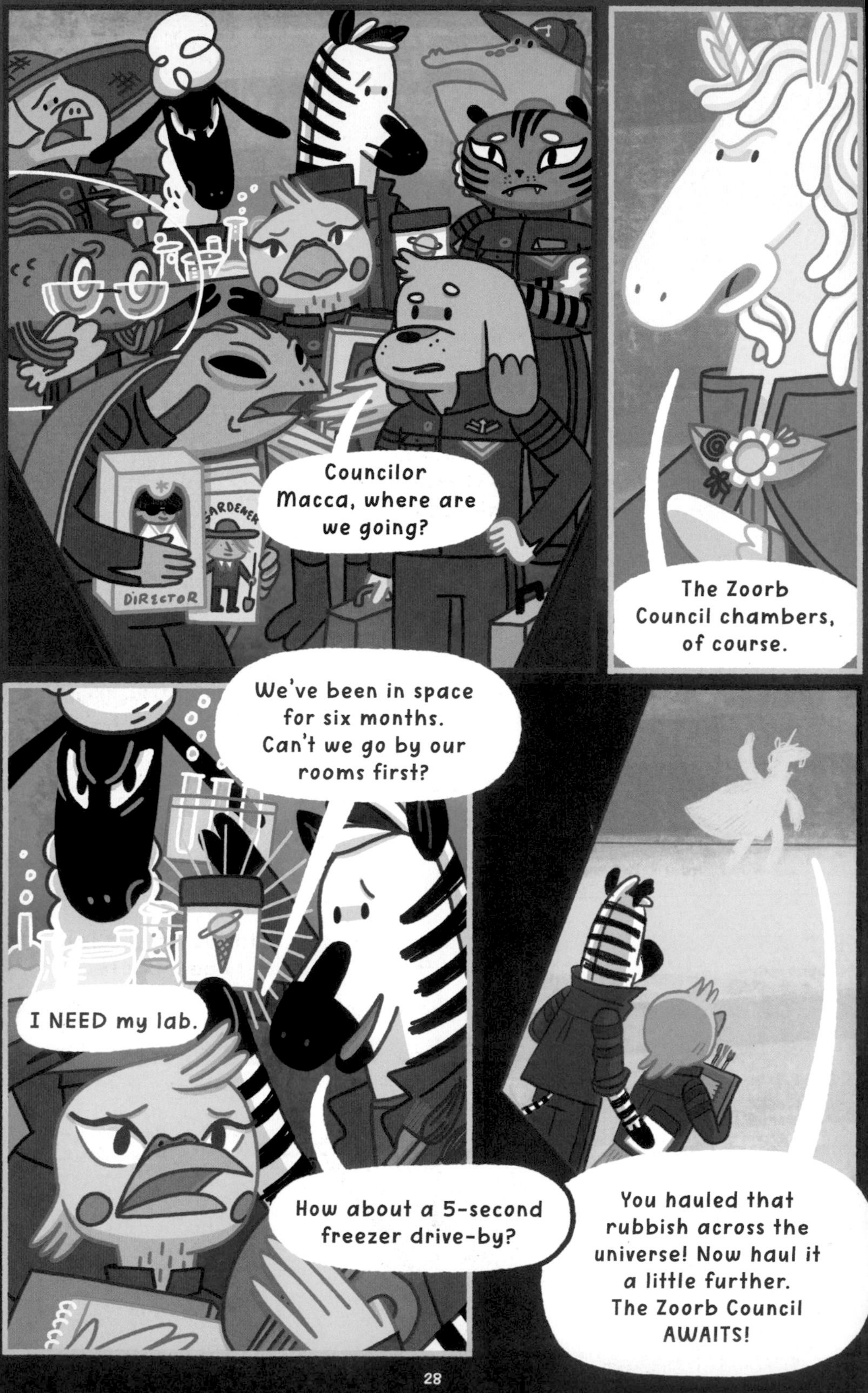
Councilor Macca, where are we going?
The Zoorb Council chambers, of course.
We've been in space for six months. Can't we go by our rooms first?
I NEED my lab.
How about a 5-second freezer drive-by?
You hauled that rubbish across the universe! Now haul it a little further. The Zoorb Council AWAITS!

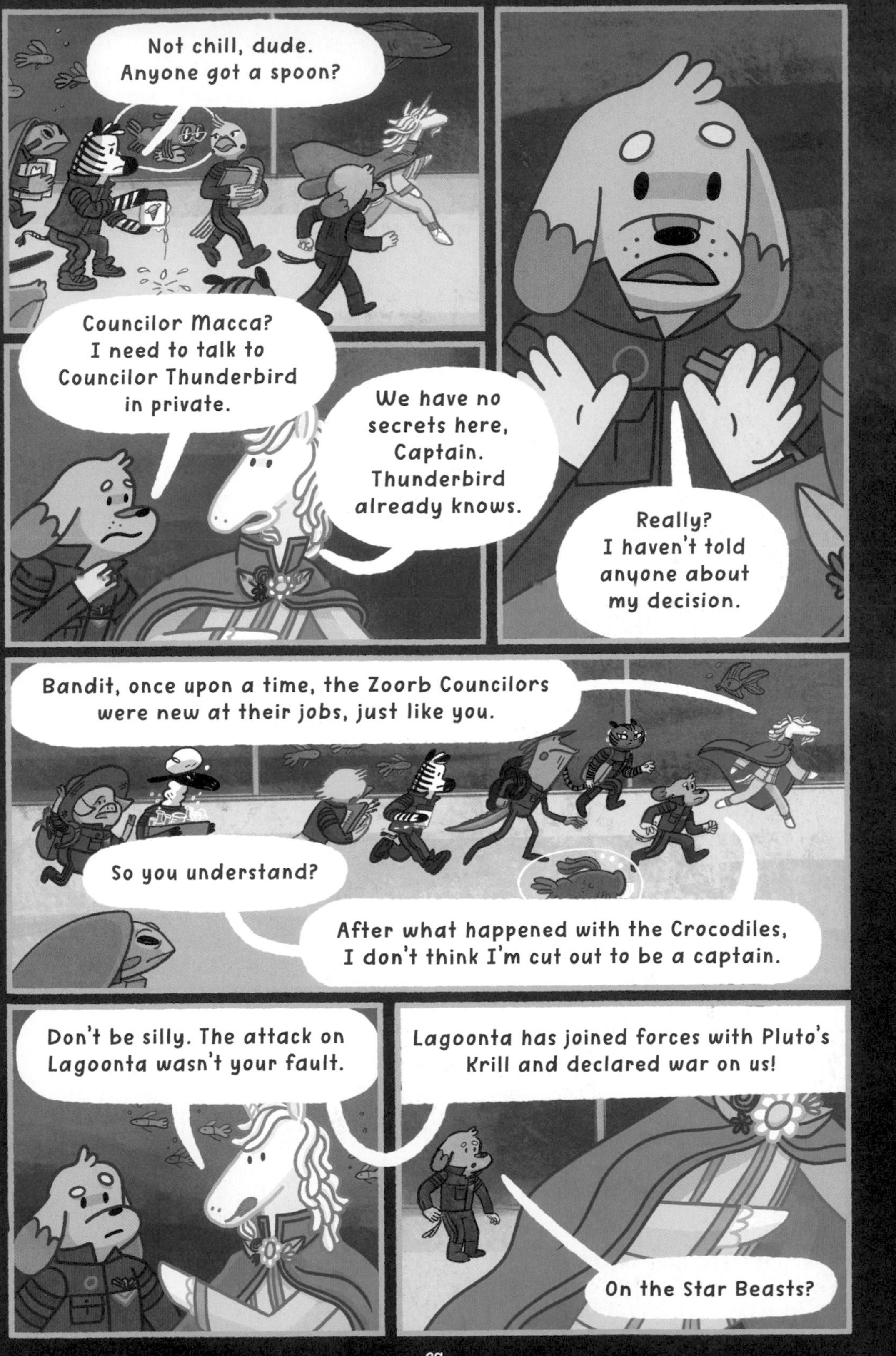

Not chill, dude. Anyone got a spoon?
Councilor Macca? I need to talk to Councilor Thunderbird in private.
We have no secrets here, Captain. Thunderbird already knows.
Really? I haven't told anyone about my decision.
Bandit, once upon a time, the Zoorb Councilors were new at their jobs, just like you.
So you understand?
After what happened with the Crocodiles, I don't think I'm cut out to be a captain.
Don't be silly. The attack on Lagoonta wasn't your fault.
Lagoonta has joined forces with Pluto's Krill and declared war on us!
On the Star Beasts?

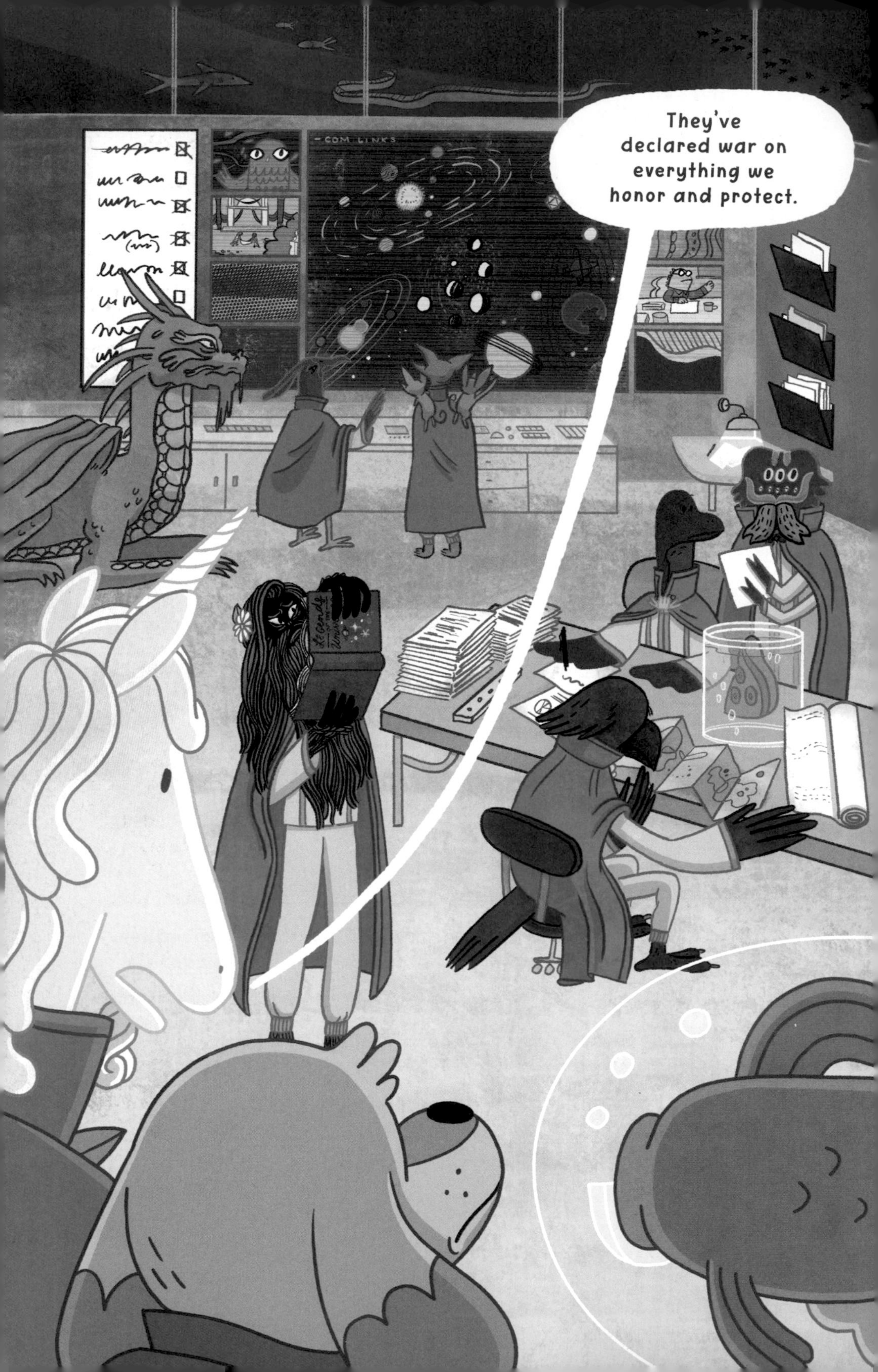
COM LINKS
They've declared war on everything we honor and protect.

The Krill are bullies. Why would the Crocs gang up with them?

As you know, in the Cosmic Creaturehood chain of command, Earth's Star Beasts outrank Pluto's Krill...

...a fact that never thrilled Pluto's leader.

CRIMES AGAINST CREATUREHOODS:

• EARTH
The Milky Way:
- Spread Frostbite V13 among humans
- Provokes shrimp boat mutinies
- Stole two of Earth's satellites
- Planned attack on Dreamy World
- Attempted North Pole invasion

• POLARD
Crystalline Galaxy:
- Alleged Assassination Attempt on Polar King of Freezemark

• SERPENTINA
The C...
- Tr...
- A... ...ltiple dens

HIGH ALERT!

KHAOS
KRILL SUPREME

DANGEROUS DICTATOR!

HOARDS OF KRILL

BRAINWASH
TECHN...

Like you said, Captain, Khaos Krill is a troublemaker.

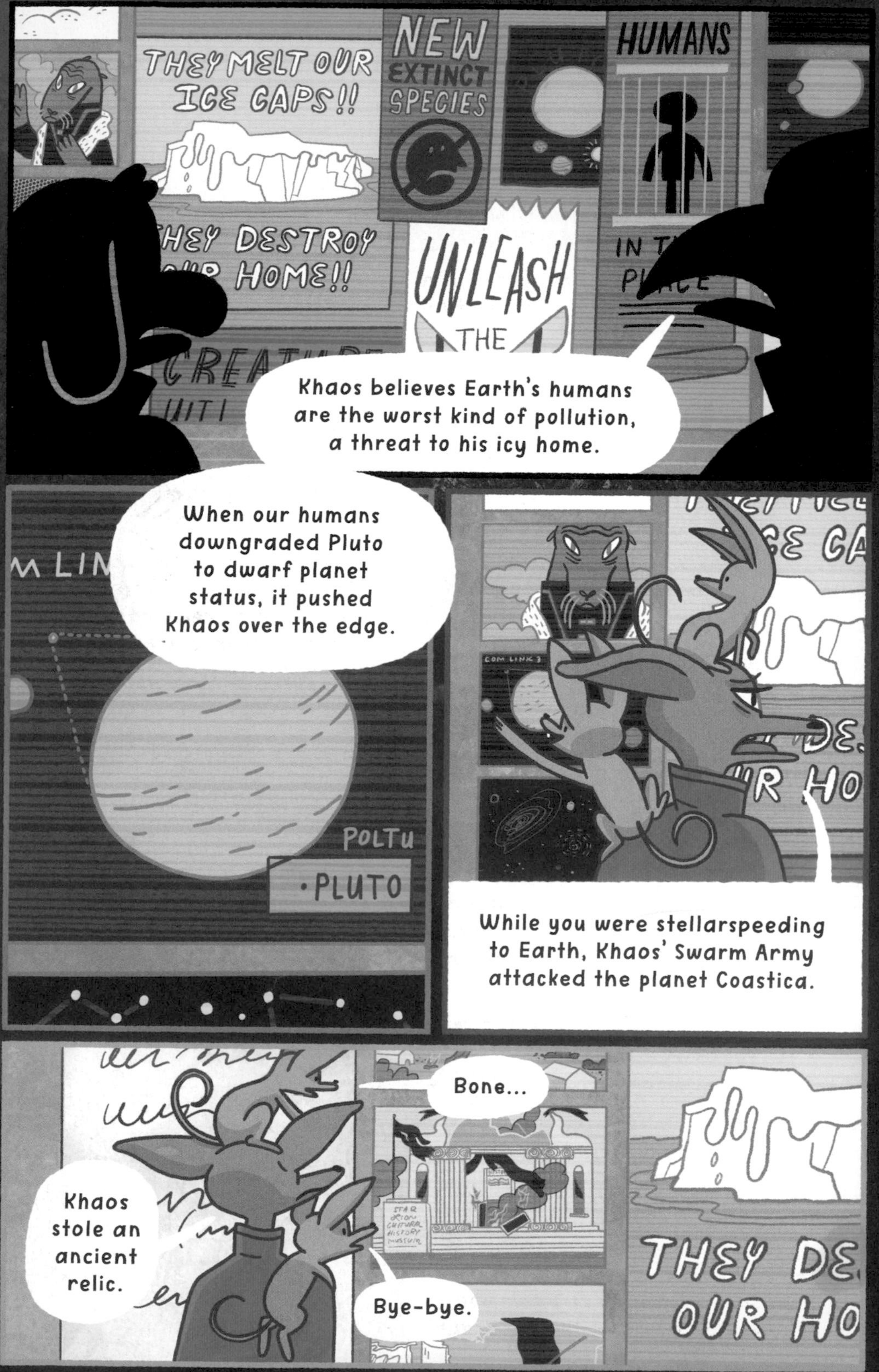
THEY MELT OUR ICE CAPS!!
NEW EXTINCT SPECIES
HUMANS
UNLEASH THE
Khaos believes Earth's humans are the worst kind of pollution, a threat to his icy home.
When our humans downgraded Pluto to dwarf planet status, it pushed Khaos over the edge.
POLTU
•PLUTO
While you were stellarspeeding to Earth, Khaos' Swarm Army attacked the planet Coastica.
Khaos stole an ancient relic.
Bone...
Bye-bye.

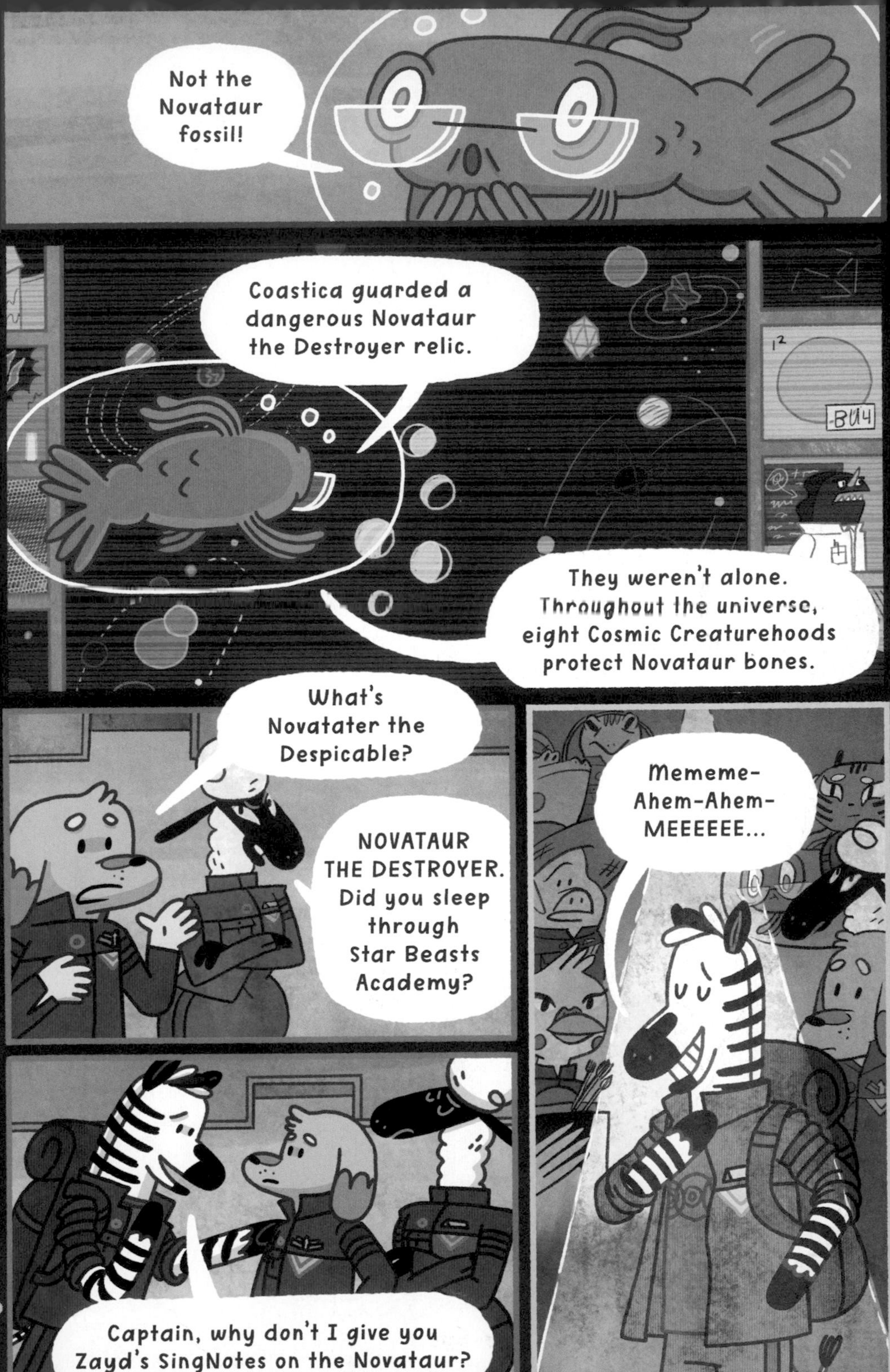
Not the Novataur fossil!
Coastica guarded a dangerous Novataur the Destroyer relic.
They weren't alone. Throughout the universe, eight Cosmic Creaturehoods protect Novataur bones.
What's Novatater the Despicable?
NOVATAUR THE DESTROYER. Did you sleep through Star Beasts Academy?
Captain, why don't I give you Zayd's SingNotes on the Novataur?
Mememe-Ahem-Ahem-MEEEEEE...

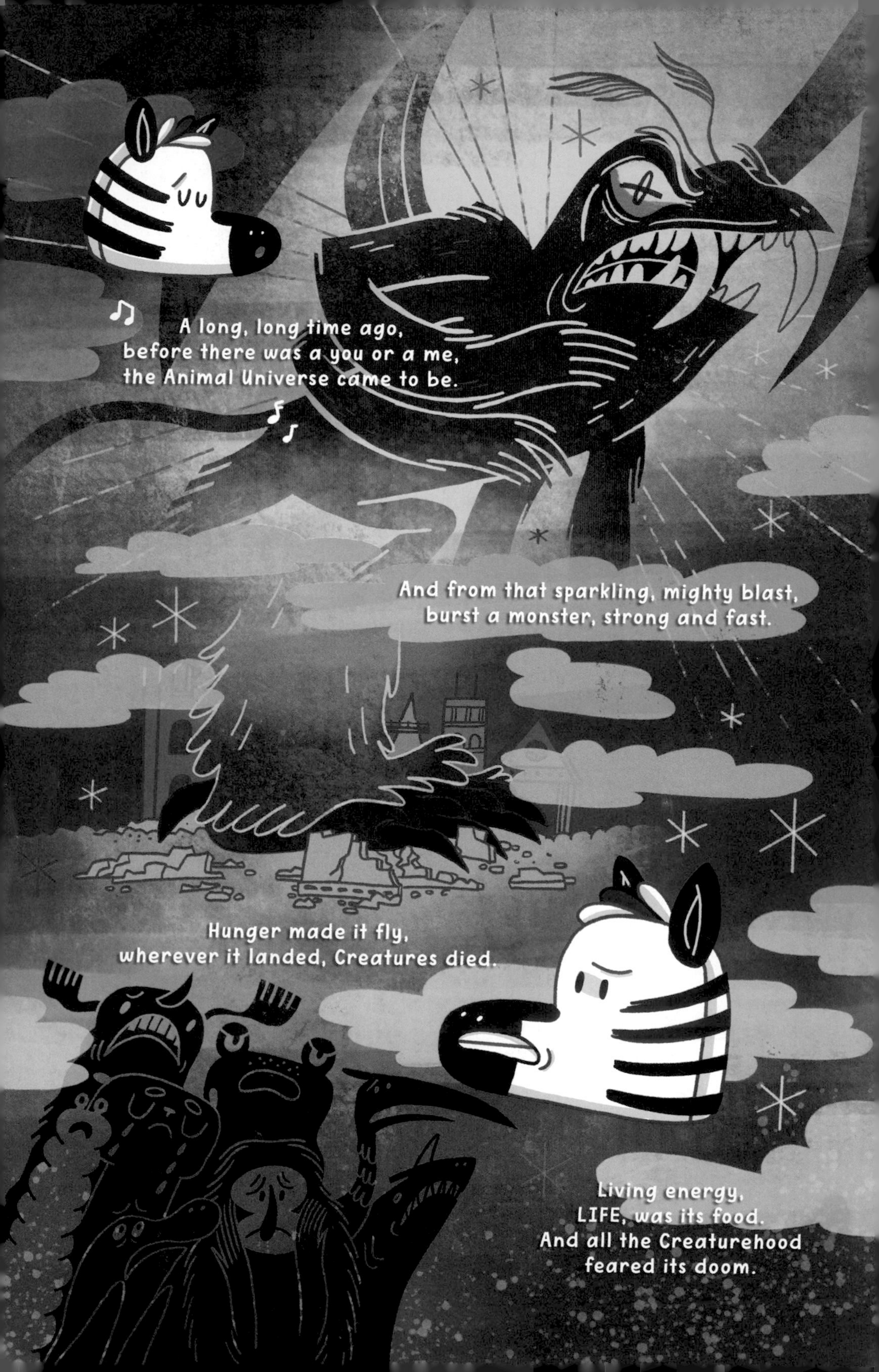
A long, long time ago,
before there was a you or a me,
the Animal Universe came to be.
And from that sparkling, mighty blast,
burst a monster, strong and fast.
Hunger made it fly,
wherever it landed, Creatures died.
Living energy,
LIFE, was its food.
And all the Creaturehood
feared its doom.

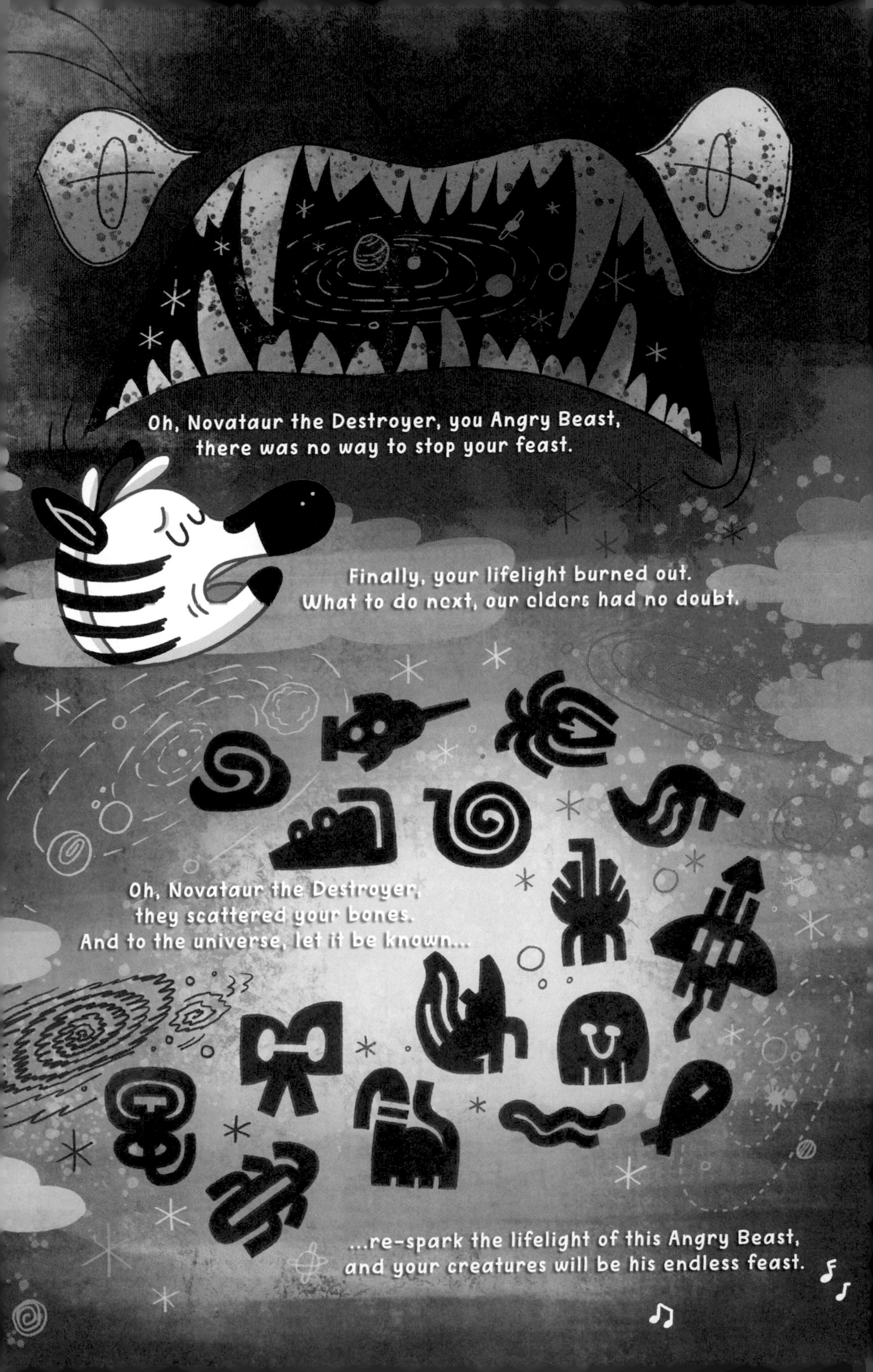
Oh, Novataur the Destroyer, you Angry Beast,
there was no way to stop your feast.
Finally, your lifelight burned out.
What to do next, our elders had no doubt.
Oh, Novataur the Destroyer,
they scattered your bones.
And to the universe, let it be known...
...re-spark the lifelight of this Angry Beast,
and your creatures will be his endless feast.

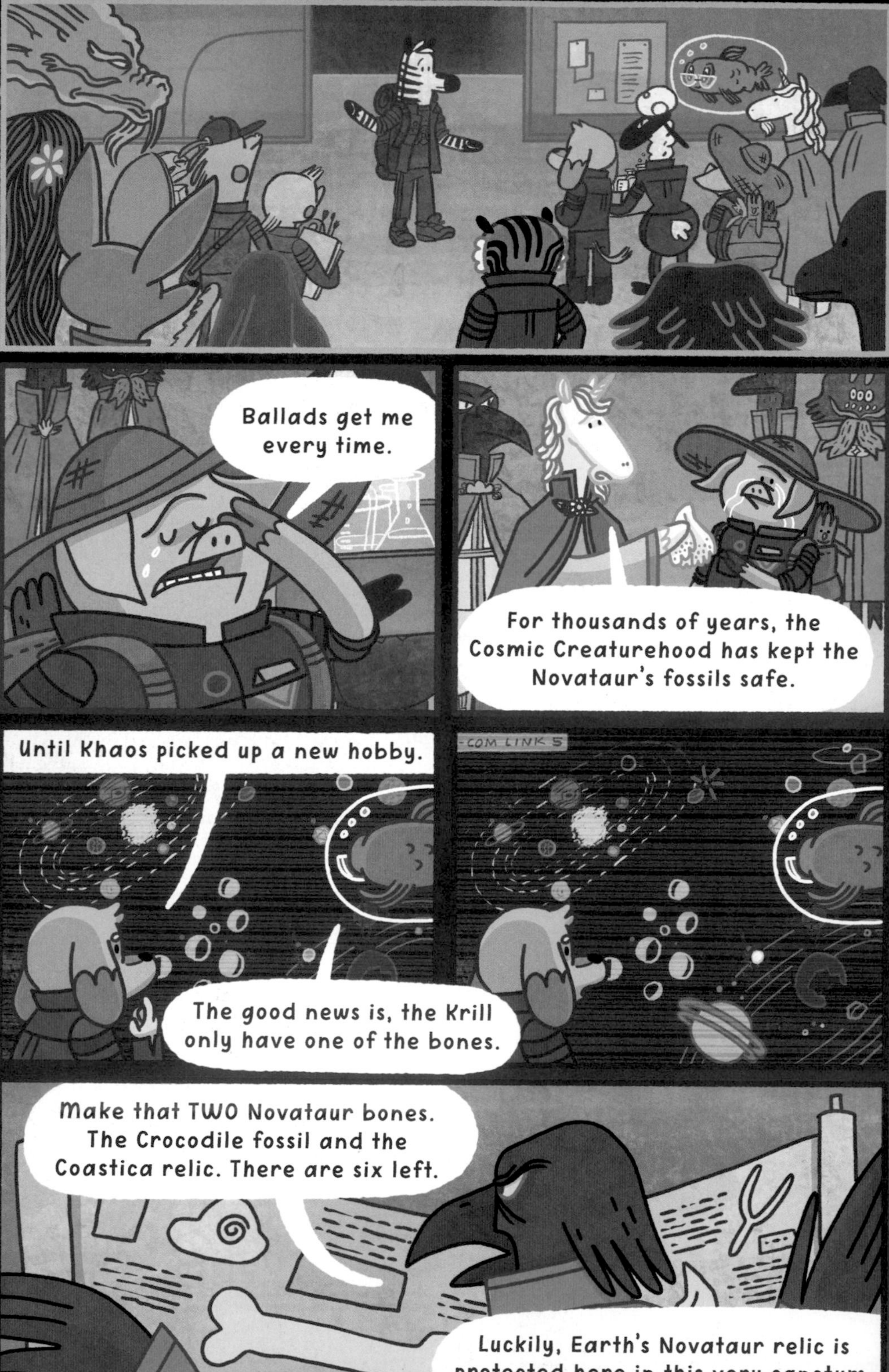
Ballads get me every time.
For thousands of years, the Cosmic Creaturehood has kept the Novataur's fossils safe.
Until Khaos picked up a new hobby.
COM LINK 5
The good news is, the Krill only have one of the bones.
Make that TWO Novataur bones. The Crocodile fossil and the Coastica relic. There are six left.
Luckily, Earth's Novataur relic is protected here in this very sanctum.

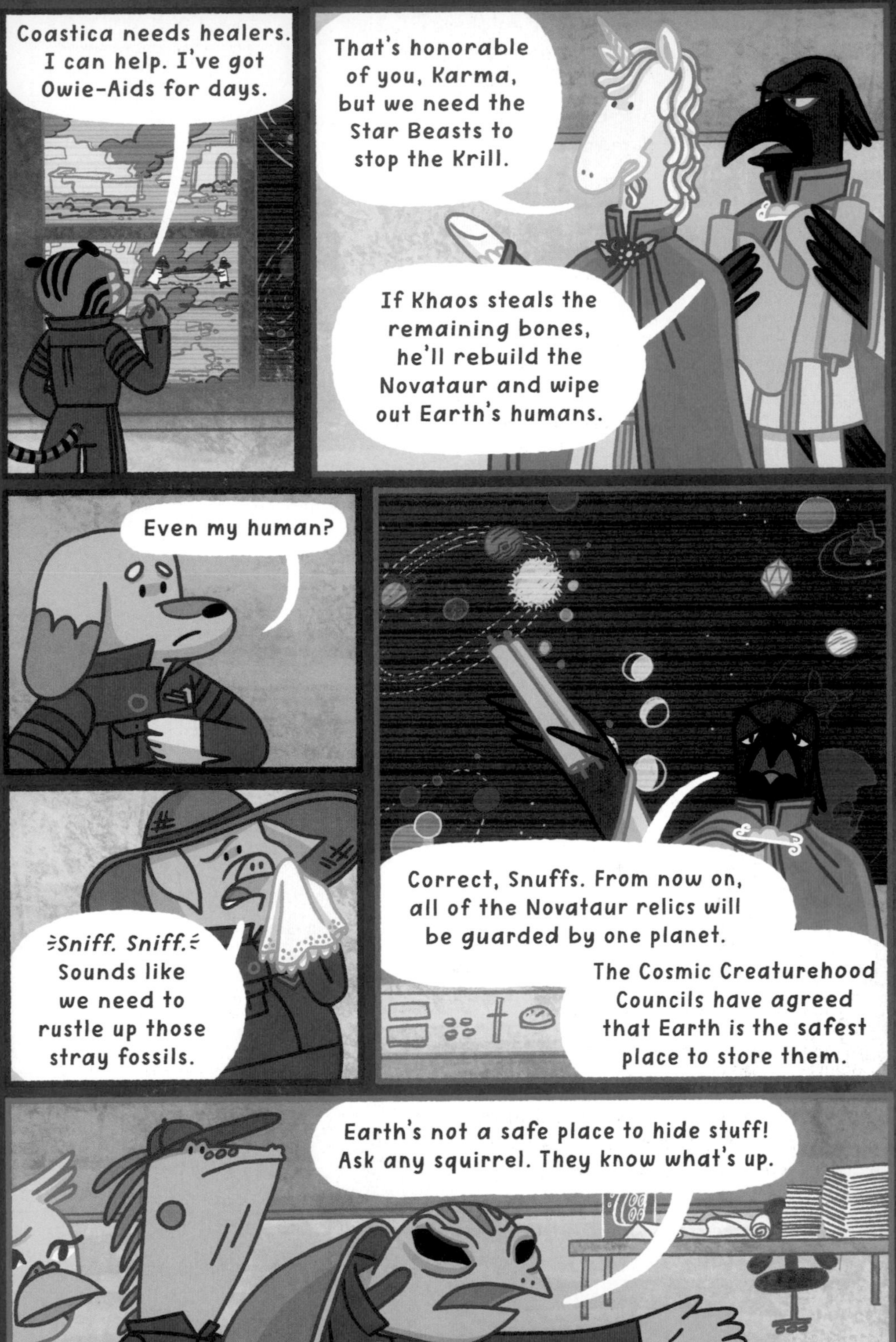
Coastica needs healers. I can help. I've got Owie-Aids for days.
That's honorable of you, Karma, but we need the Star Beasts to stop the Krill.
If Khaos steals the remaining bones, he'll rebuild the Novataur and wipe out Earth's humans.
Even my human?
Correct, Snuffs. From now on, all of the Novataur relics will be guarded by one planet.
The Cosmic Creaturehood Councils have agreed that Earth is the safest place to store them.
Sniff. Sniff. Sounds like we need to rustle up those stray fossils.
Earth's not a safe place to hide stuff! Ask any squirrel. They know what's up.

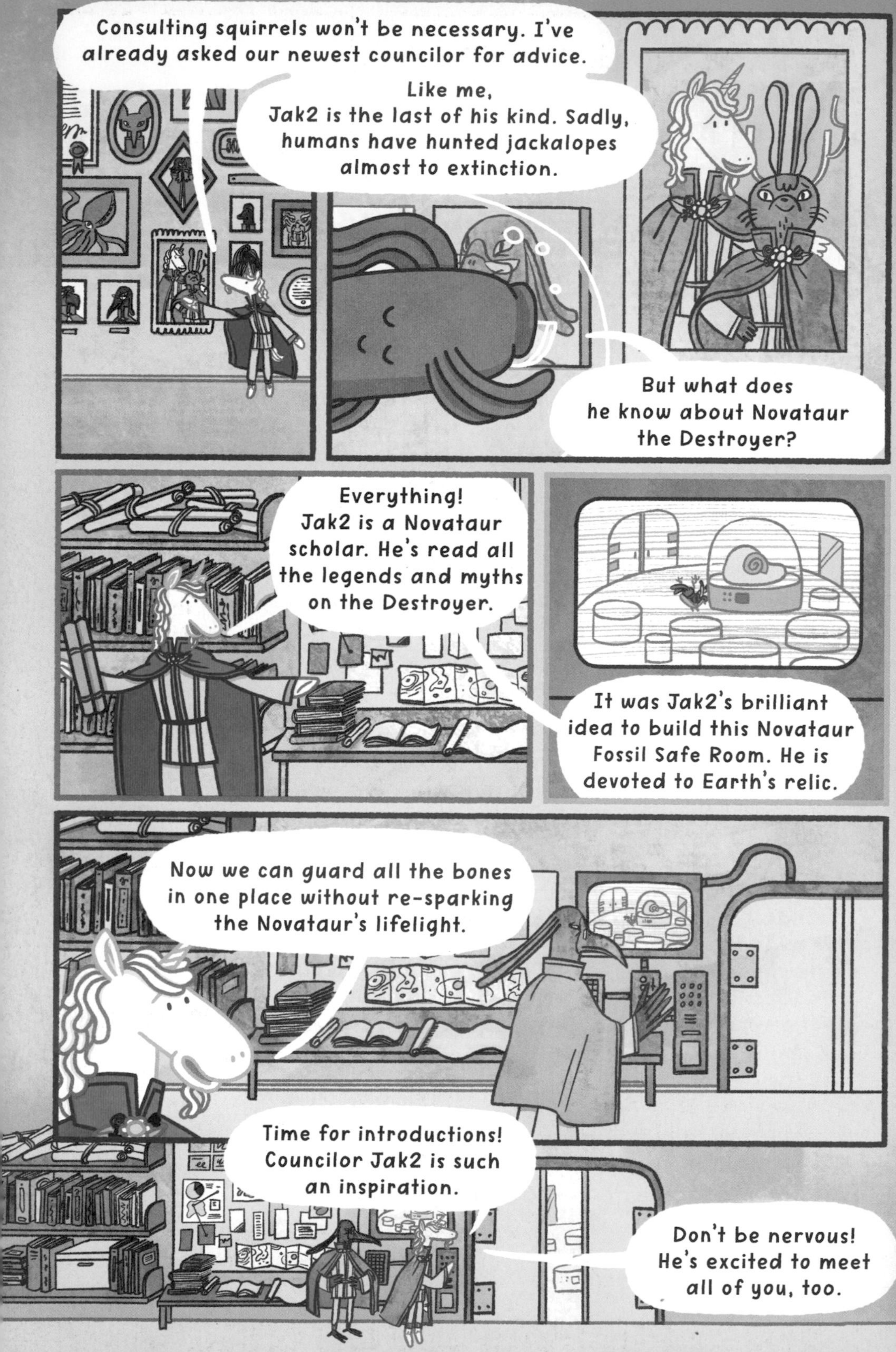
Consulting squirrels won't be necessary. I've already asked our newest councilor for advice.
Like me, Jak2 is the last of his kind. Sadly, humans have hunted jackalopes almost to extinction.
But what does he know about Novataur the Destroyer?
Everything! Jak2 is a Novataur scholar. He's read all the legends and myths on the Destroyer.
It was Jak2's brilliant idea to build this Novataur Fossil Safe Room. He is devoted to Earth's relic.
Now we can guard all the bones in one place without re-sparking the Novataur's lifelight.
Time for introductions! Councilor Jak2 is such an inspiration.
Don't be nervous! He's excited to meet all of you, too.

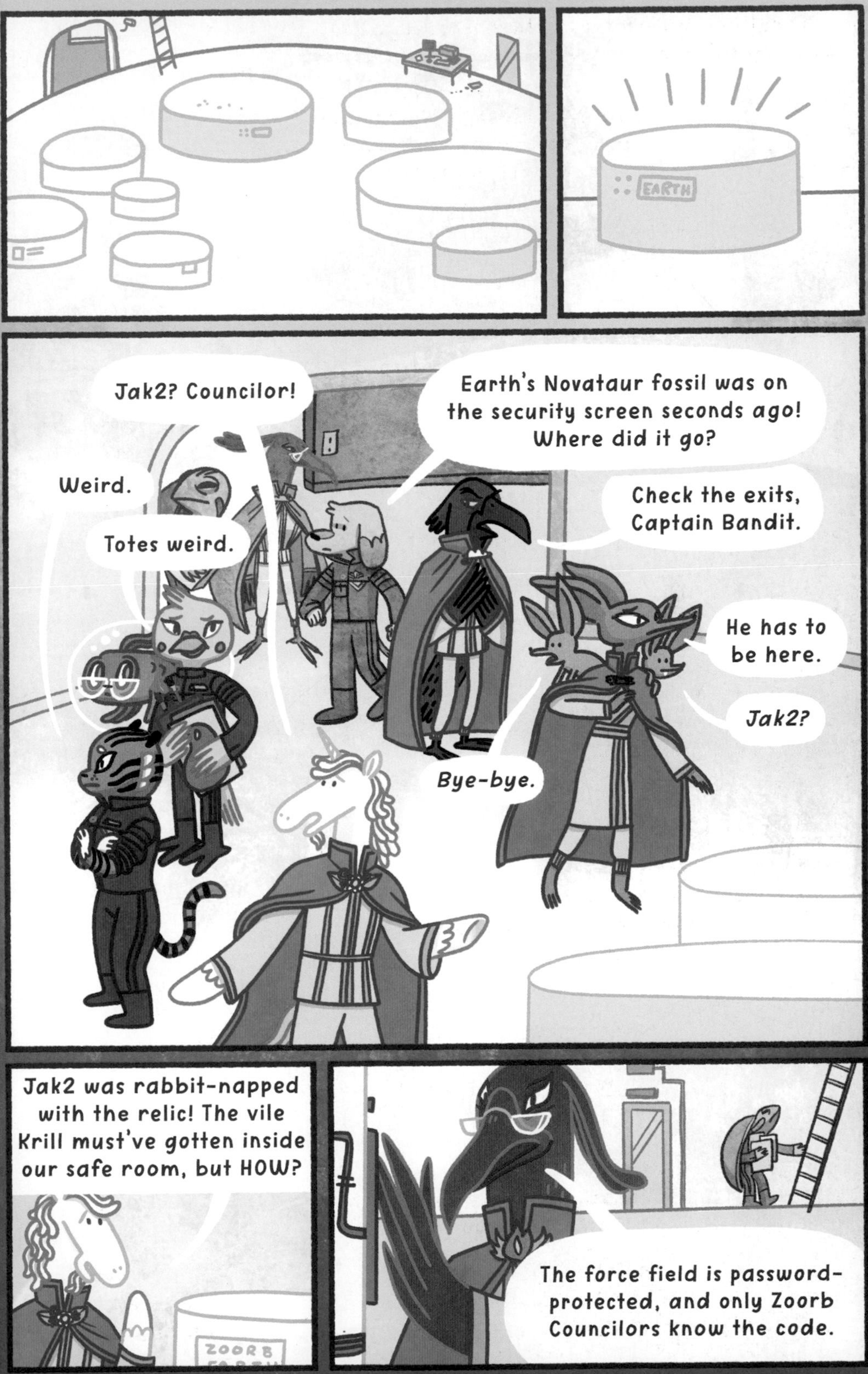
EARTH
Jak2? Councilor!
Earth's Novataur fossil was on the security screen seconds ago! Where did it go?
Weird.
Totes weird.
Check the exits, Captain Bandit.
He has to be here.
Jak2?
Bye-bye.
Jak2 was rabbit-napped with the relic! The vile Krill must've gotten inside our safe room, but HOW?
ZOORB
The force field is password-protected, and only Zoorb Councilors know the code.

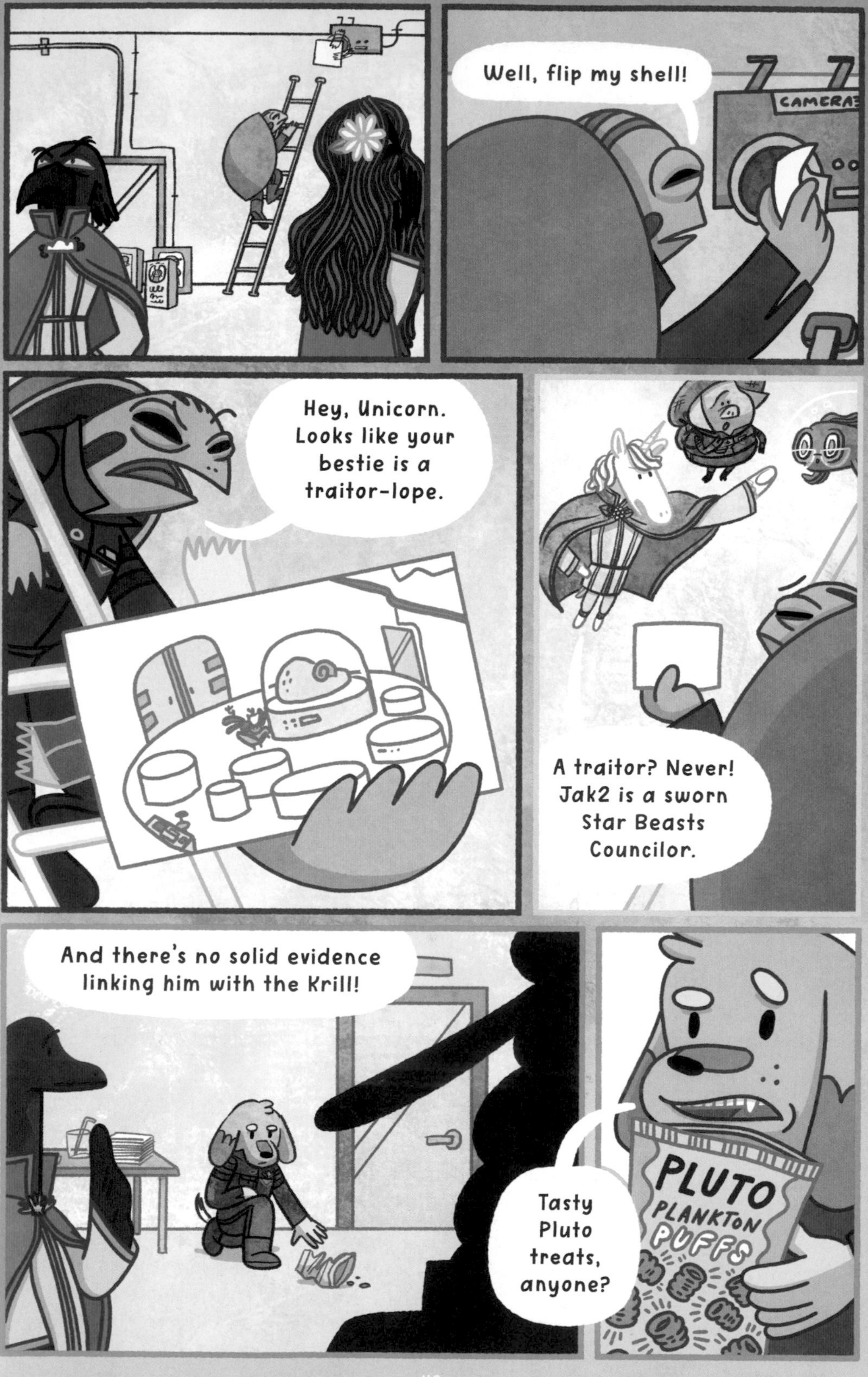
Well, flip my shell!
CAMERA3
Hey, Unicorn. Looks like your bestie is a traitor-lope.
A traitor? Never! Jak2 is a sworn Star Beasts Councilor.
And there's no solid evidence linking him with the Krill!
Tasty Pluto treats, anyone?
PLUTO PLANKTON PUFFS

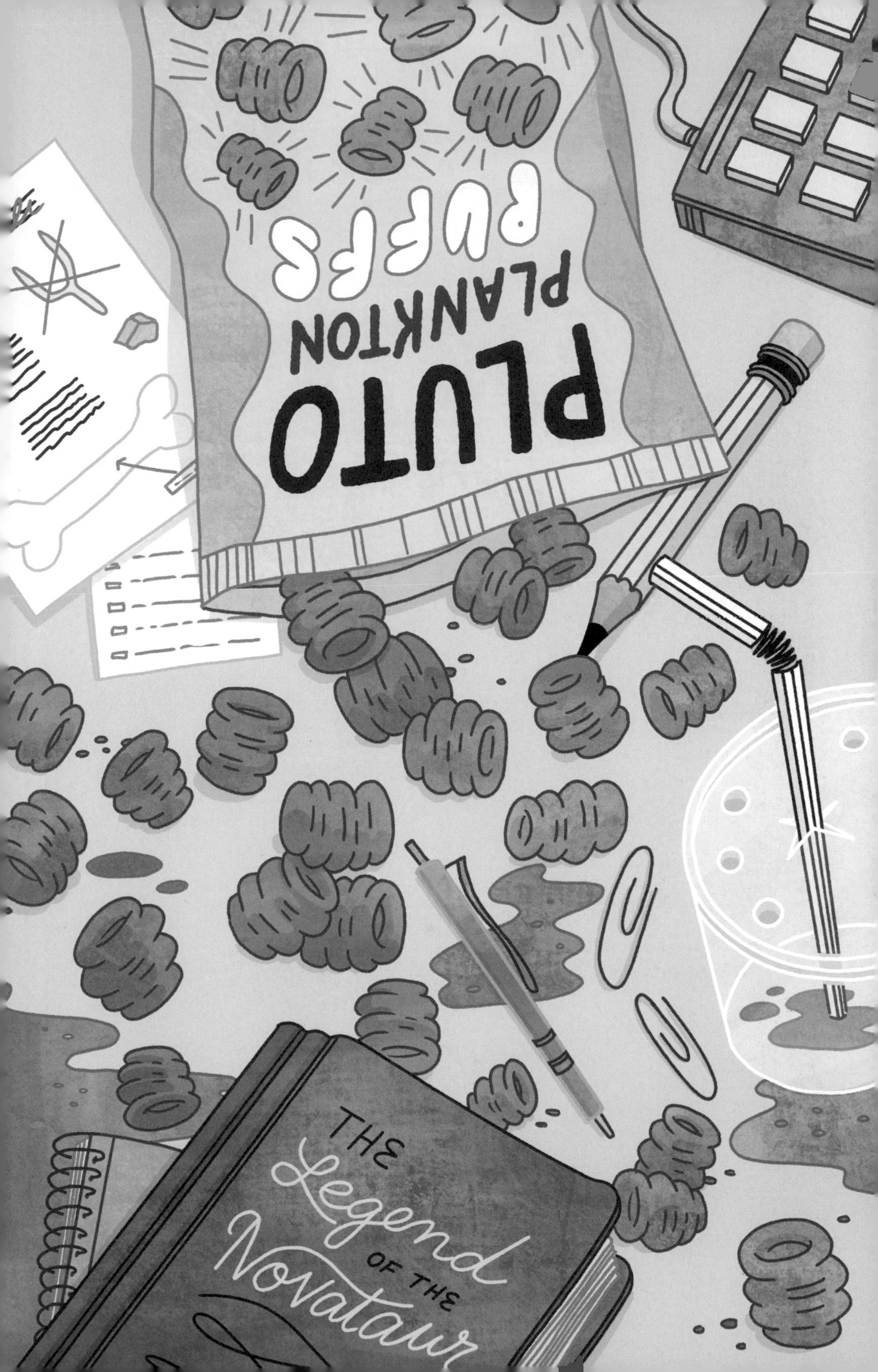
PLUTO PLANKTON PUFFS
THE Legend OF THE Novataur

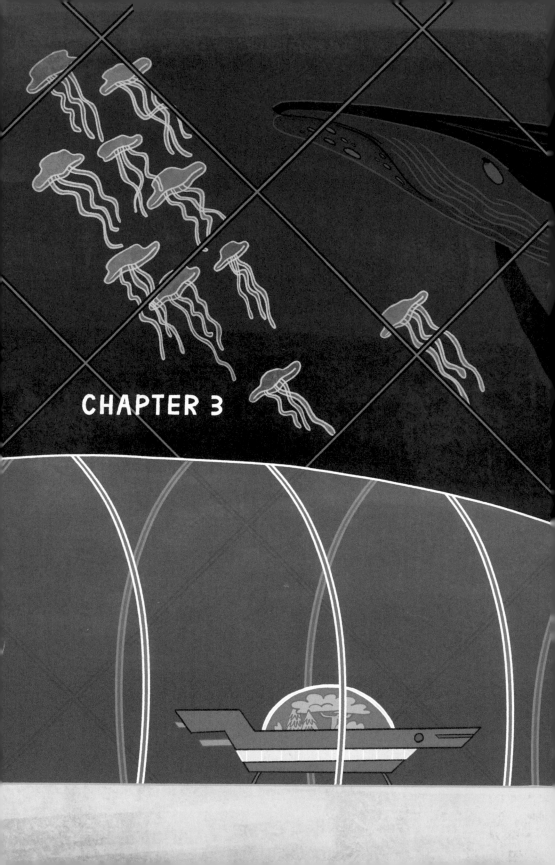

CHAPTER 3

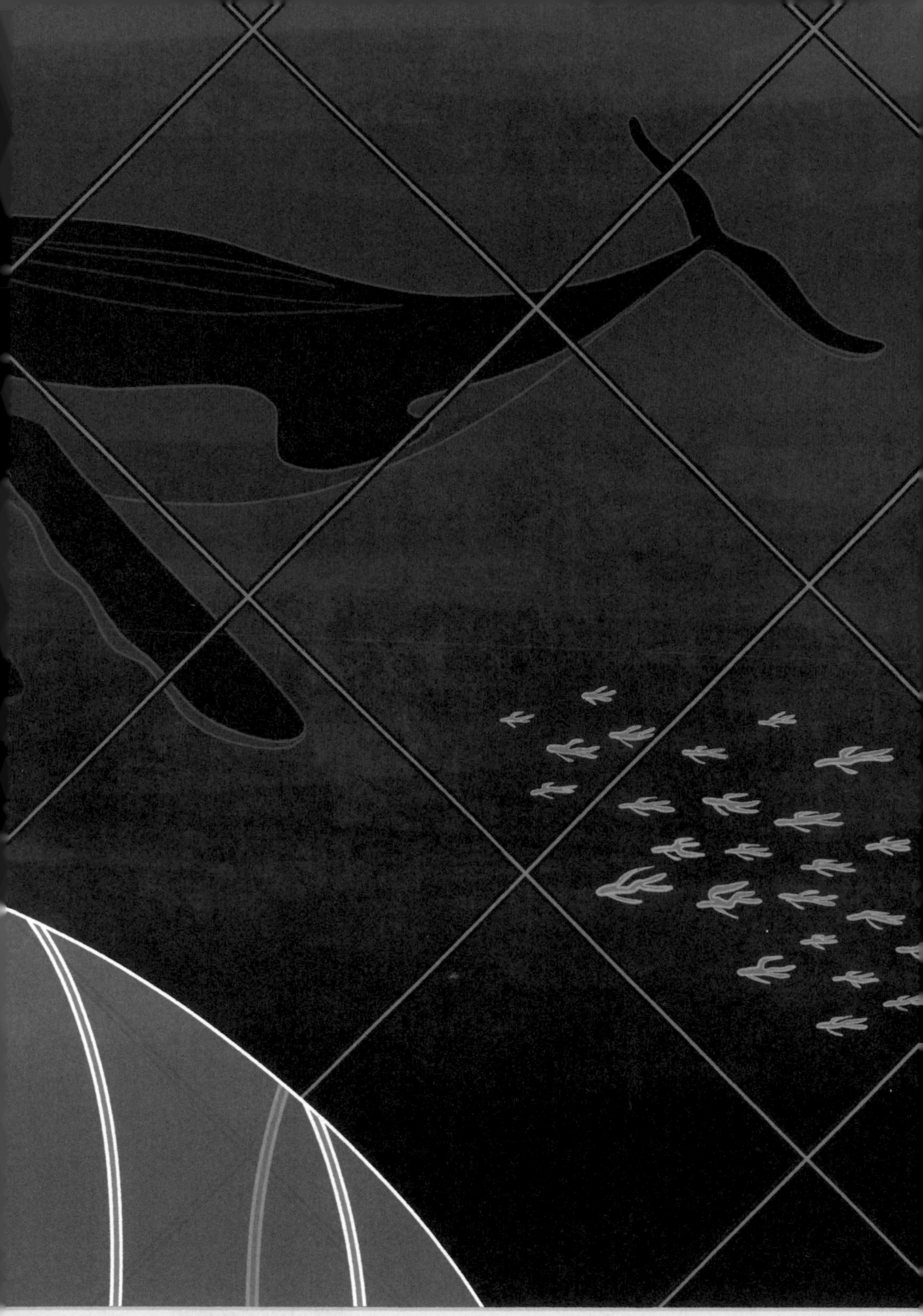

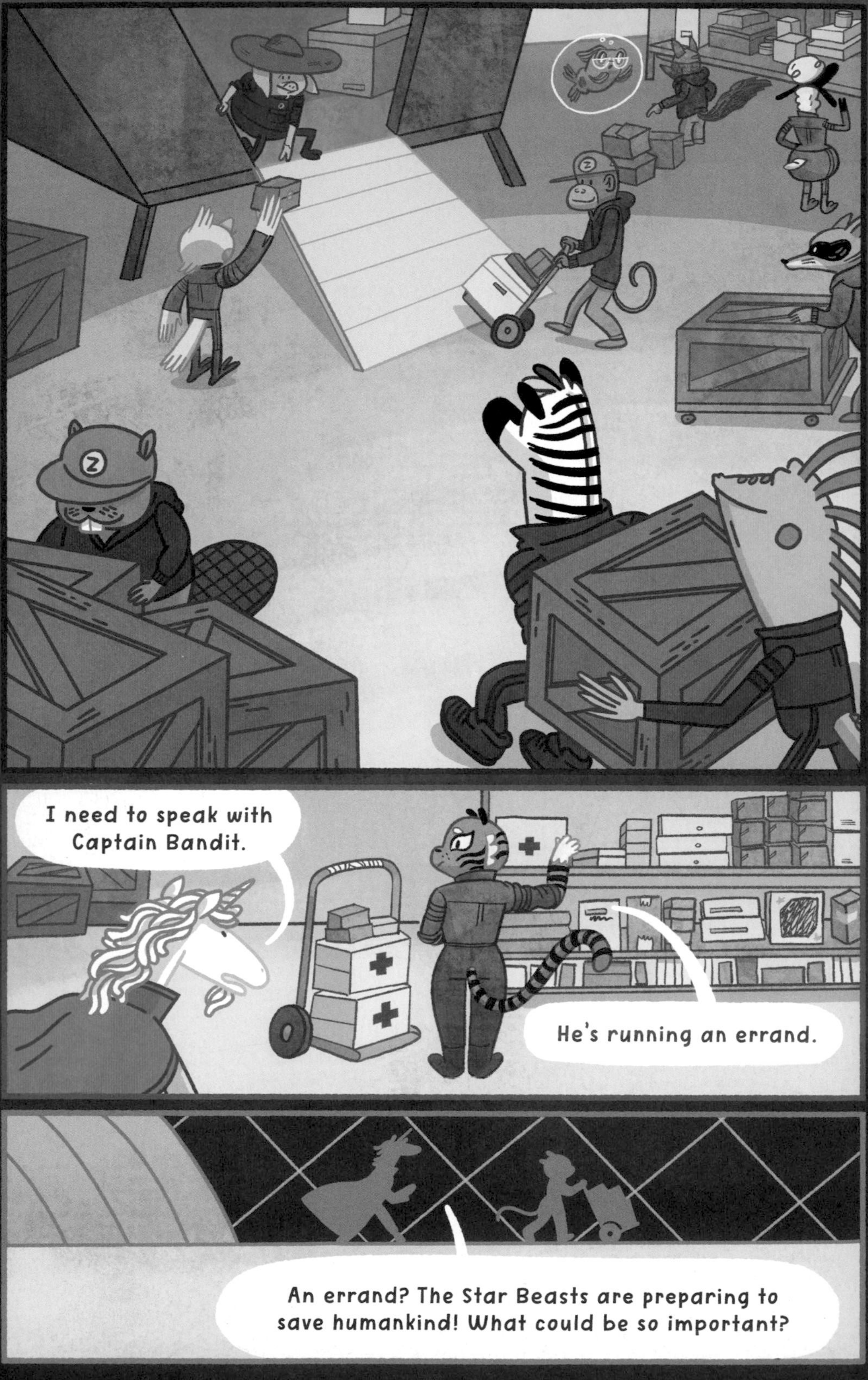
I need to speak with Captain Bandit.
He's running an errand.
An errand? The Star Beasts are preparing to save humankind! What could be so important?

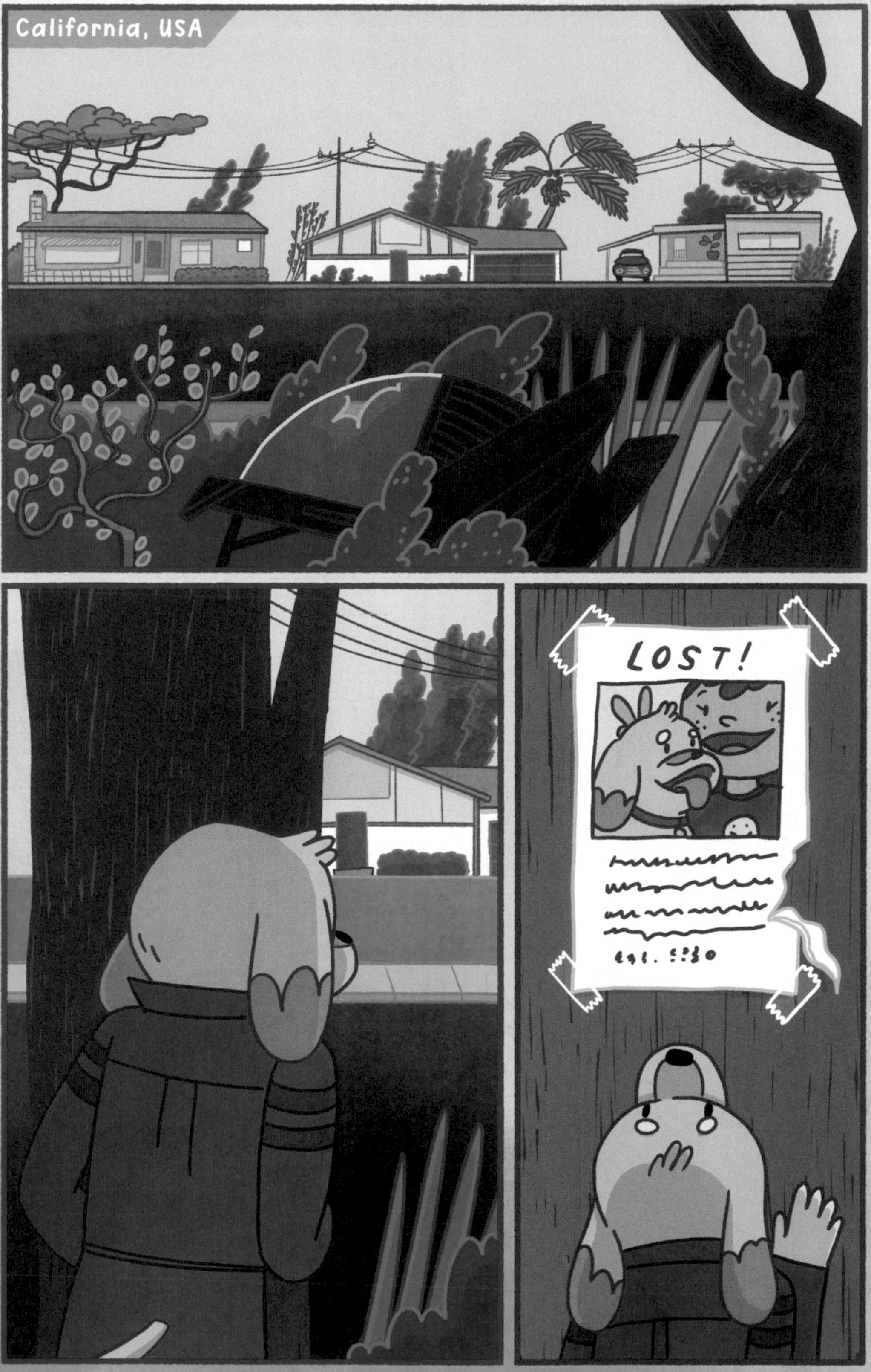
California, USA
LOST!

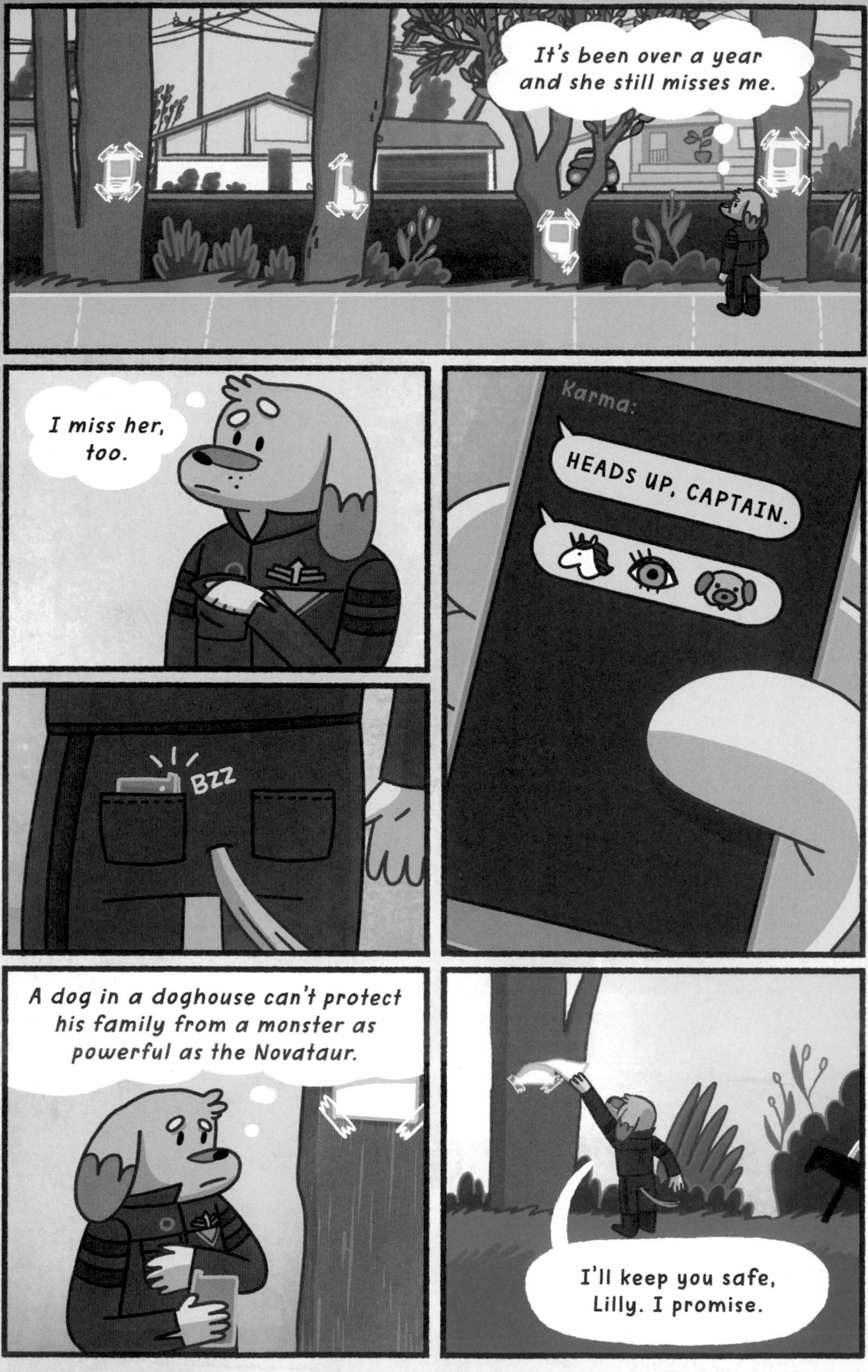
It's been over a year and she still misses me.
I miss her, too.
Karma:
HEADS UP, CAPTAIN.
BZZ
A dog in a doghouse can't protect his family from a monster as powerful as the Novataur.
I'll keep you safe, Lilly. I promise.

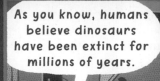

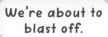

We're about to blast off.

Clio, prep us for our first relic pickup.

Sure! Soon we'll be on our way to the dinosaur planet of Mesozoic.

As you know, humans believe dinosaurs have been extinct for millions of years.

In reality, many escaped Earth.

MESOZOIC

Our dinosaur refugees live on a planet-size spaceship.

Clio! Your slideshows rock!

zzzz≋SNORT≋zzzz

These dinosaurs call themselves Sciencesaurs.

They haven't made any great discoveries like me, but they're still scientists.

Uh, thanks, Dr. Curly. Now, the—

STAR BEASTS! Our mission is to beat the Krill to this precious relic!

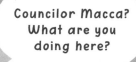

Councilor Macca? What are you doing here?

Forgive me, Captain. I've been assigned to your mission.

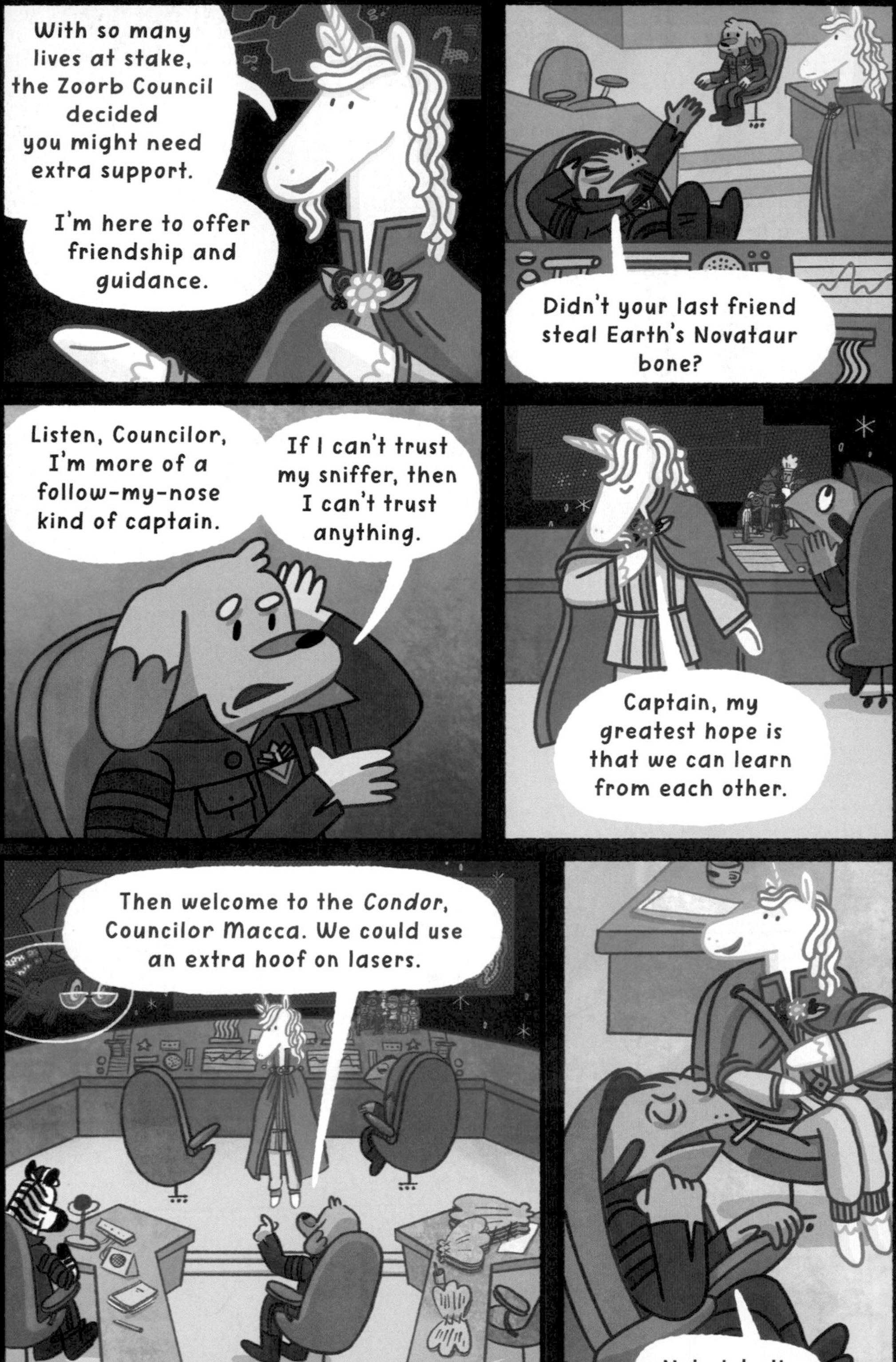
With so many lives at stake, the Zoorb Council decided you might need extra support.
I'm here to offer friendship and guidance.
Didn't your last friend steal Earth's Novataur bone?
Listen, Councilor, I'm more of a follow-my-nose kind of captain.
If I can't trust my sniffer, then I can't trust anything.
Captain, my greatest hope is that we can learn from each other.
Then welcome to the *Condor*, Councilor Macca. We could use an extra hoof on lasers.
Nebul-balls.

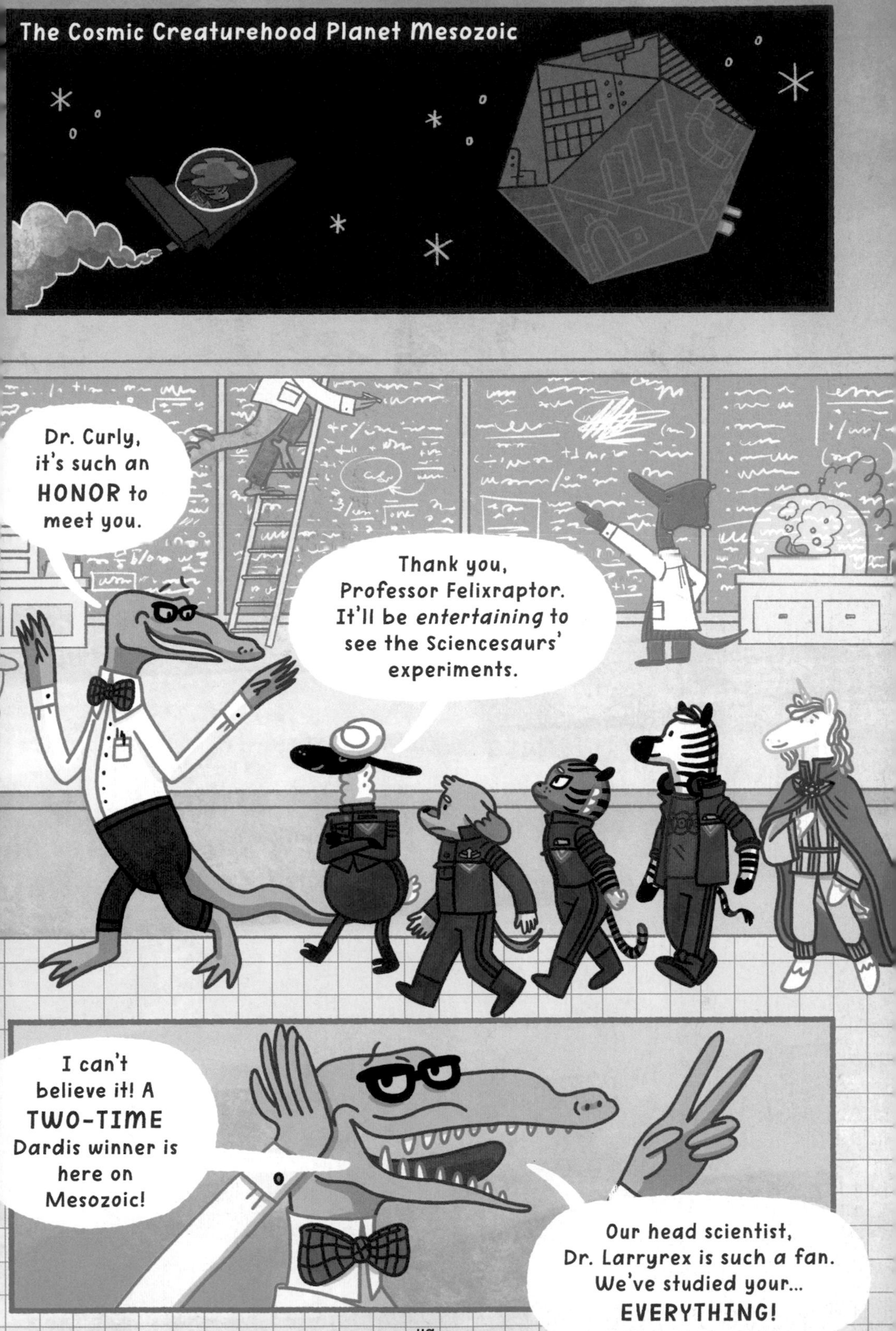
The Cosmic Creaturehood Planet Mesozoic
Dr. Curly, it's such an HONOR to meet you.
Thank you, Professor Felixraptor. It'll be *entertaining* to see the Sciencesaurs' experiments.
I can't believe it! A TWO-TIME Dardis winner is here on Mesozoic!
Our head scientist, Dr. Larryrex is such a fan. We've studied your... EVERYTHING!

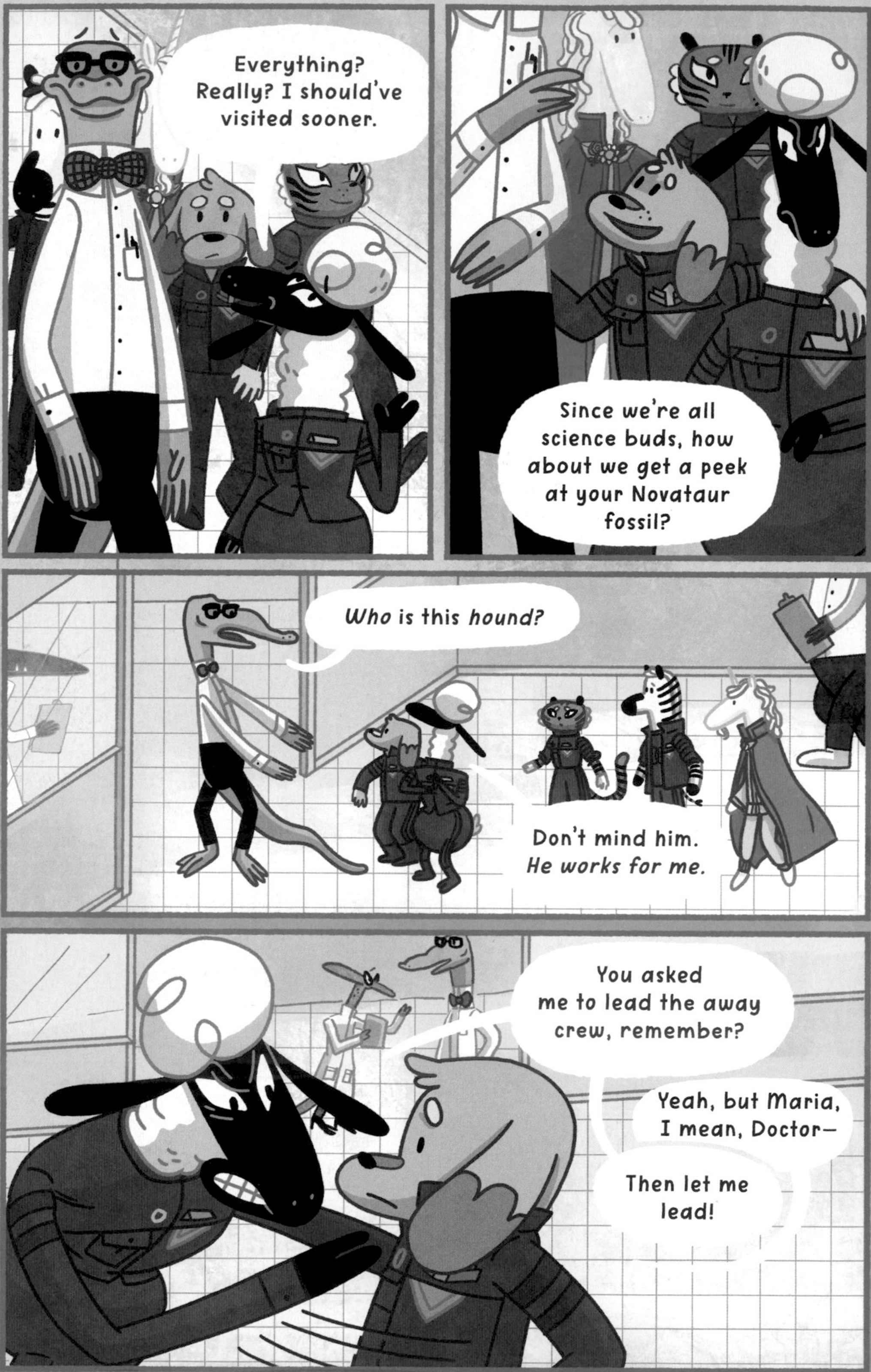
Everything? Really? I should've visited sooner.
Since we're all science buds, how about we get a peek at your Novataur fossil?
Who is this *hound?*
Don't mind him. *He works for me.*
You asked me to lead the away crew, remember?
Yeah, but Maria, I mean, Doctor—
Then let me lead!

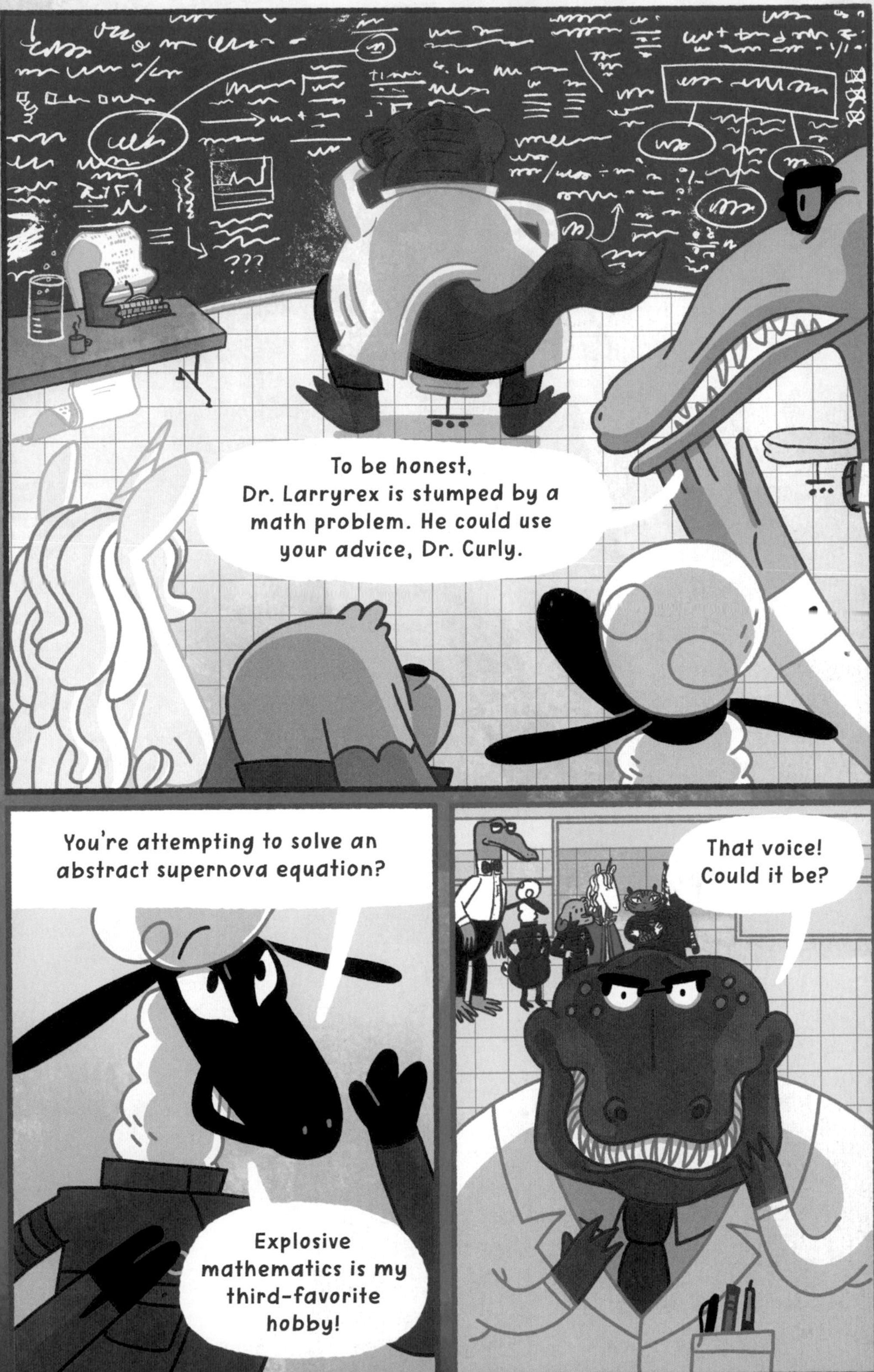
To be honest, Dr. Larryrex is stumped by a math problem. He could use your advice, Dr. Curly.
You're attempting to solve an abstract supernova equation?
Explosive mathematics is my third-favorite hobby!
That voice! Could it be?

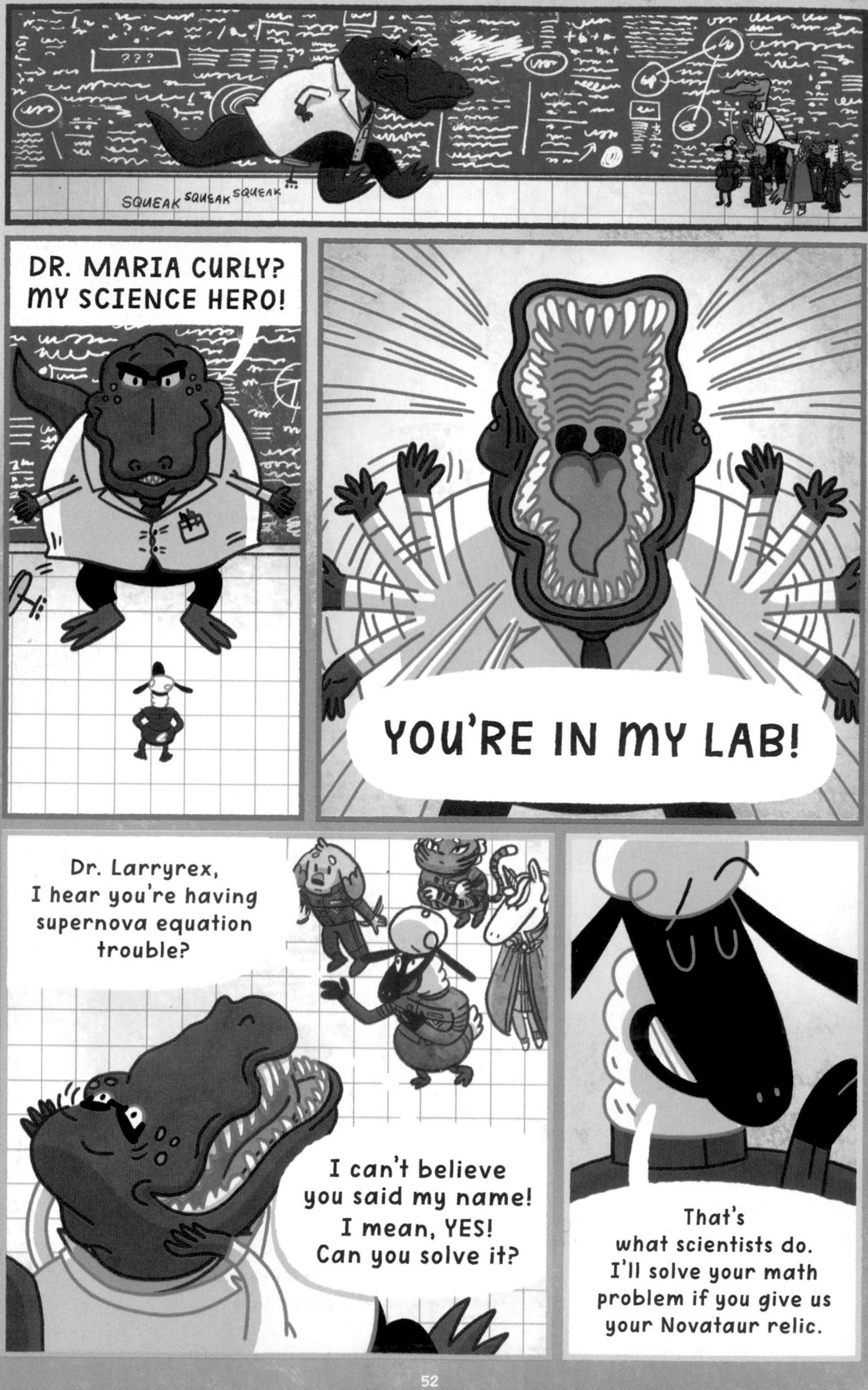

SQUEAK SQUEAK SQUEAK
DR. MARIA CURLY? MY SCIENCE HERO!
YOU'RE IN MY LAB!
Dr. Larryrex, I hear you're having supernova equation trouble?
I can't believe you said my name! I mean, YES! Can you solve it?
That's what scientists do. I'll solve your math problem if you give us your Novataur relic.

I received the Zoorb Council's urgent message about protecting the Destroyer fossils.

I thought it was a joke.

This Novataur relic is a scientific failure.

Our fossil experiments only produce these pointless sparkly sparks.

Curious... Sparkle me intrigued.

Dr. Curly, wouldn't you prefer something useful like this gravity reverser?

I'm 80 percent sure we already have a gravity refresher.

Am I right, Dr. Maria?

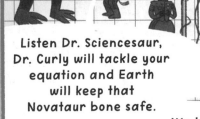

Listen Dr. Sciencesaur, Dr. Curly will tackle your equation and Earth will keep that Novataur bone safe.

We both win.

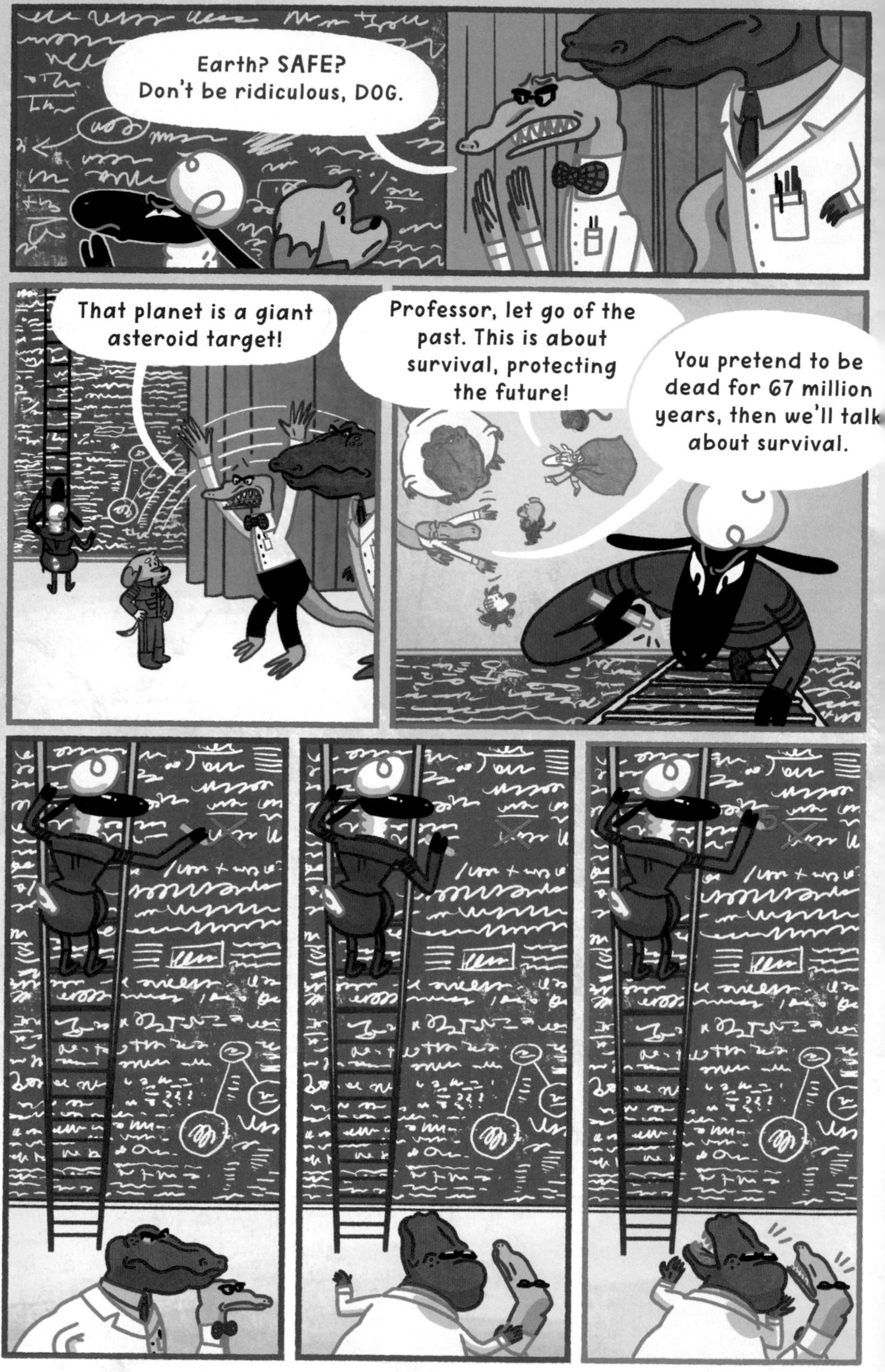
Earth? SAFE? Don't be ridiculous, DOG.
That planet is a giant asteroid target!
Professor, let go of the past. This is about survival, protecting the future!
You pretend to be dead for 67 million years, then we'll talk about survival.

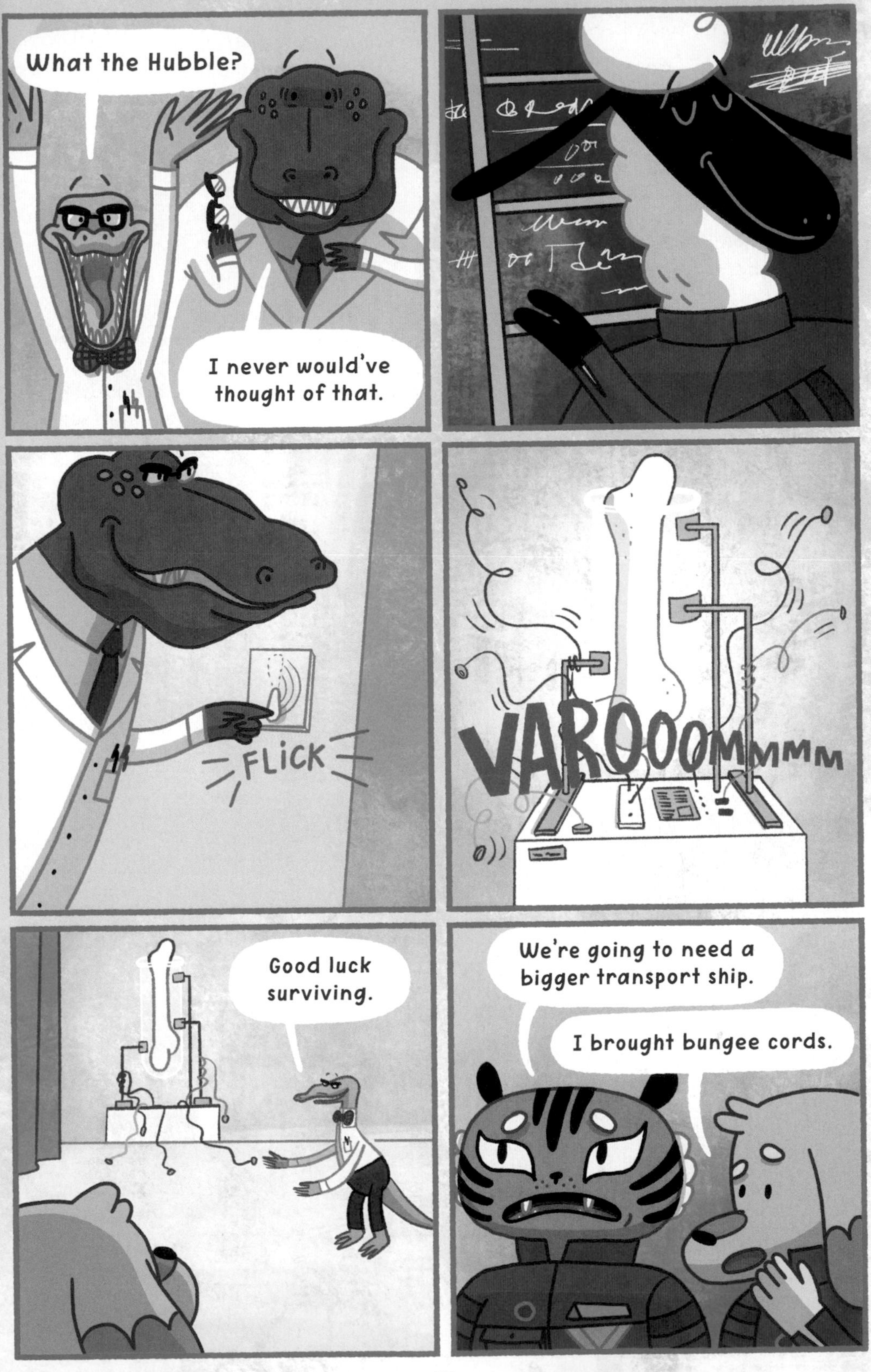
What the Hubble?
I never would've thought of that.
FLICK
VAROOOMMMMM
Good luck surviving.
We're going to need a bigger transport ship.
I brought bungee cords.

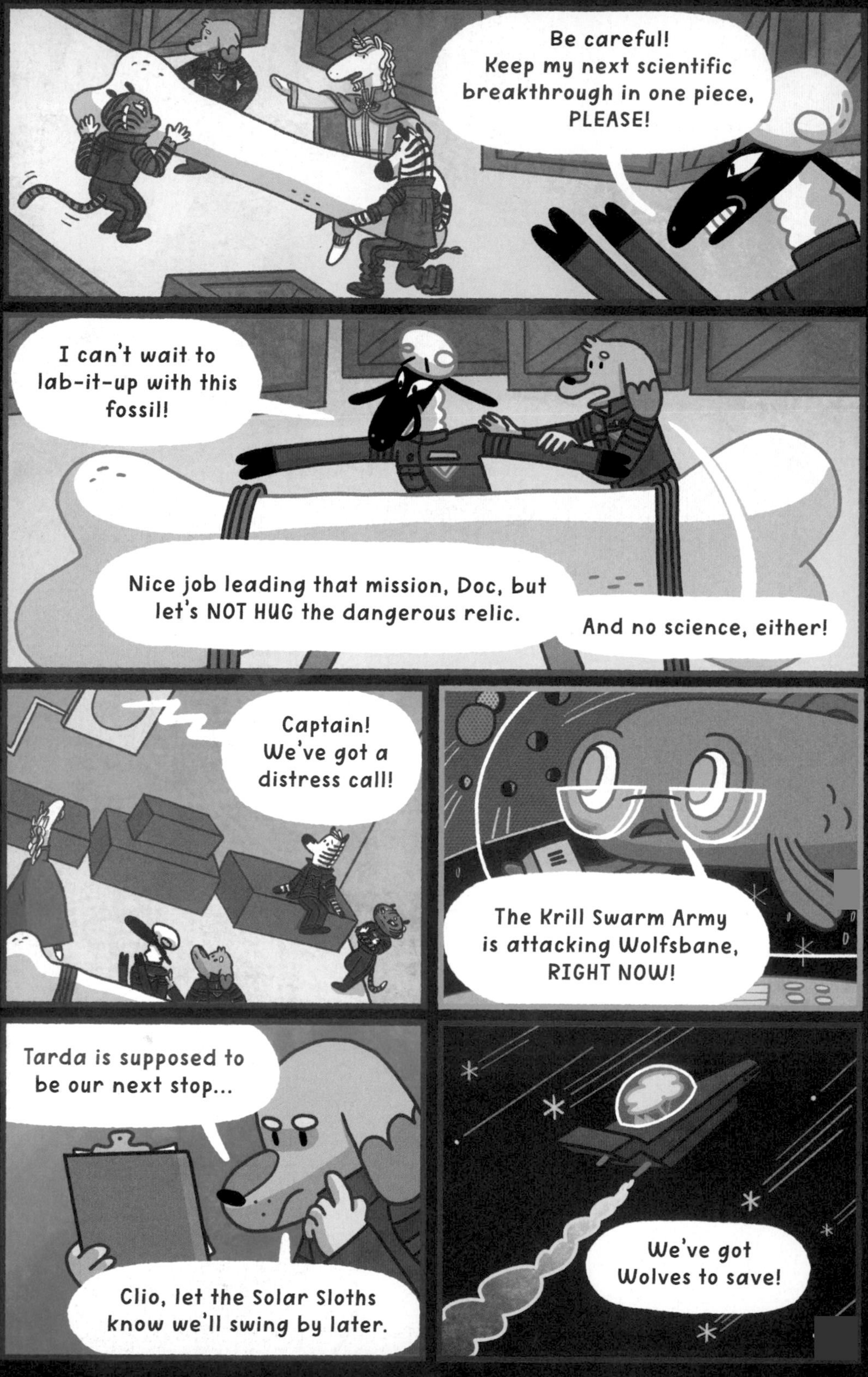
Be careful!
Keep my next scientific breakthrough in one piece, PLEASE!
I can't wait to lab-it-up with this fossil!
Nice job leading that mission, Doc, but let's NOT HUG the dangerous relic.
And no science, either!
Captain! We've got a distress call!
The Krill Swarm Army is attacking Wolfsbane, RIGHT NOW!
Tarda is supposed to be our next stop...
Clio, let the Solar Sloths know we'll swing by later.
We've got Wolves to save!

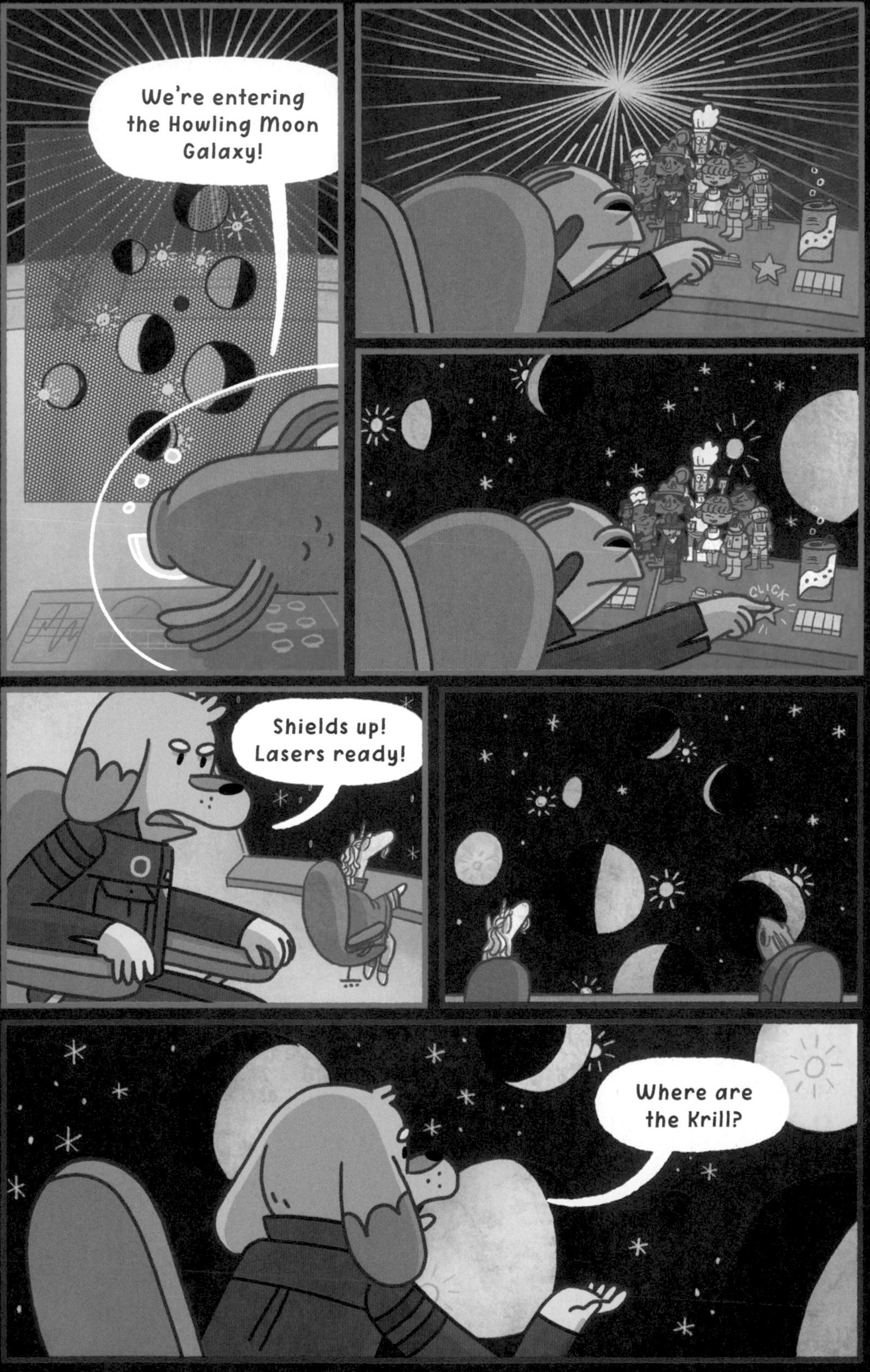
We're entering the Howling Moon Galaxy!
CLICK
Shields up! Lasers ready!
Where are the Krill?

Hey, guys? I think there's something out there.

GRRRRRRRRRR

I can't see them on the radar.

SPOTS

Where you hiding, you big, bad growlies?

GRRRRRRRRRRRRRR

Wolfsbane isn't in trouble.

WE ARE!

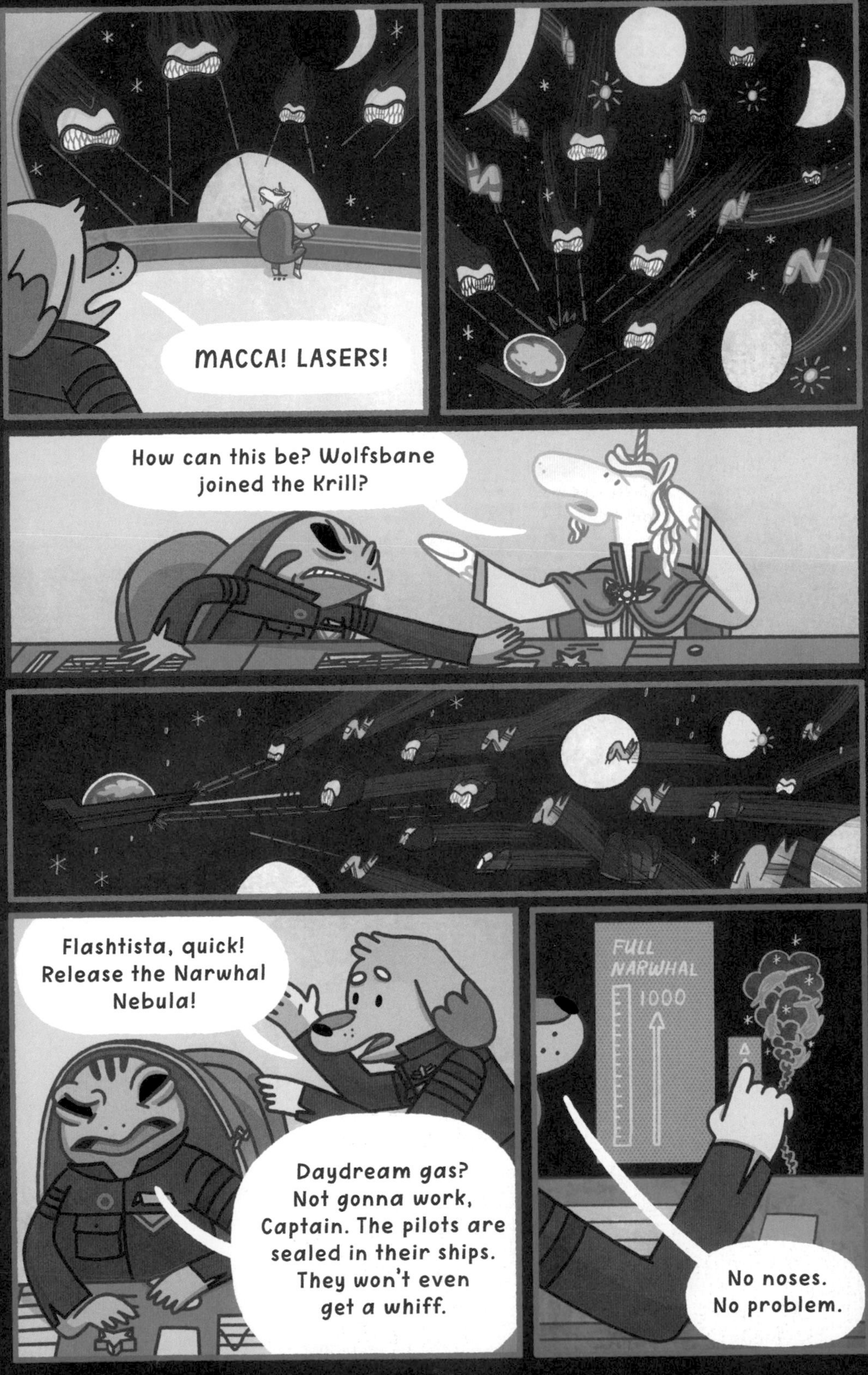
MACCA! LASERS!
How can this be? Wolfsbane joined the Krill?
Flashtista, quick! Release the Narwhal Nebula!
Daydream gas? Not gonna work, Captain. The pilots are sealed in their ships. They won't even get a whiff.
FULL NARWHAL
1000
No noses. No problem.

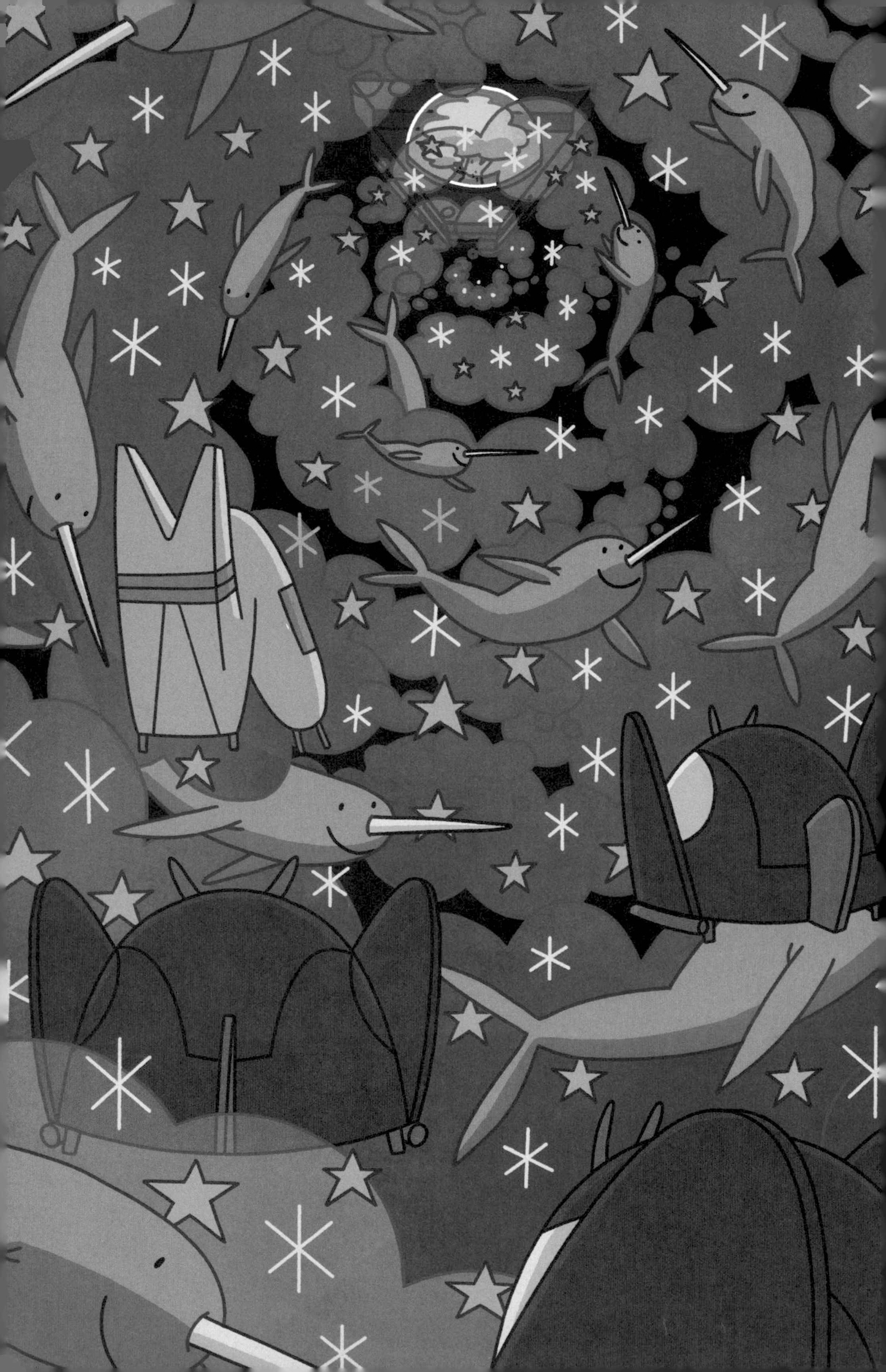

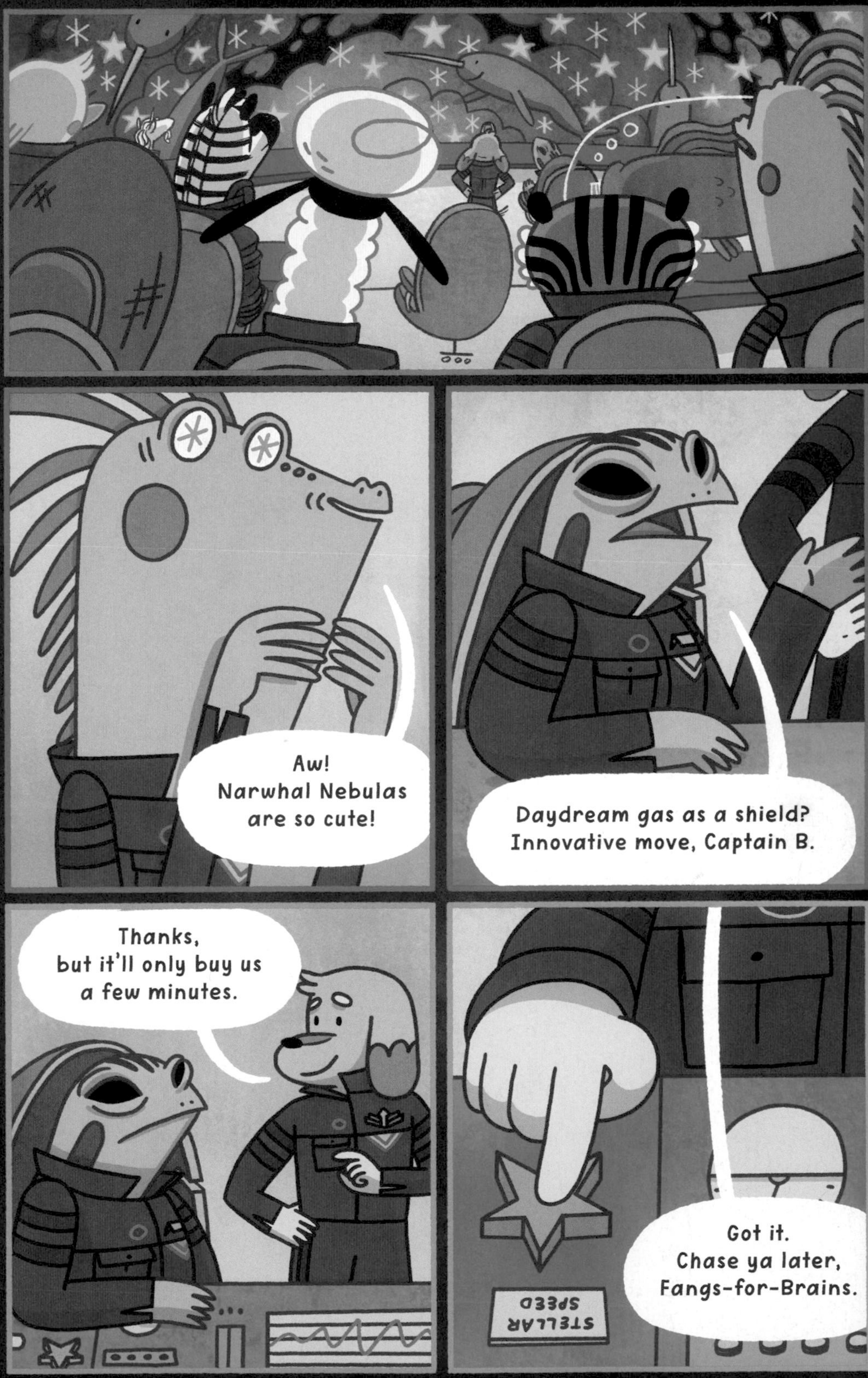
Aw! Narwhal Nebulas are so cute!
Daydream gas as a shield? Innovative move, Captain B.
Thanks, but it'll only buy us a few minutes.
Got it. Chase ya later, Fangs-for-Brains.
STELLAR SPEED

CHAPTER 4

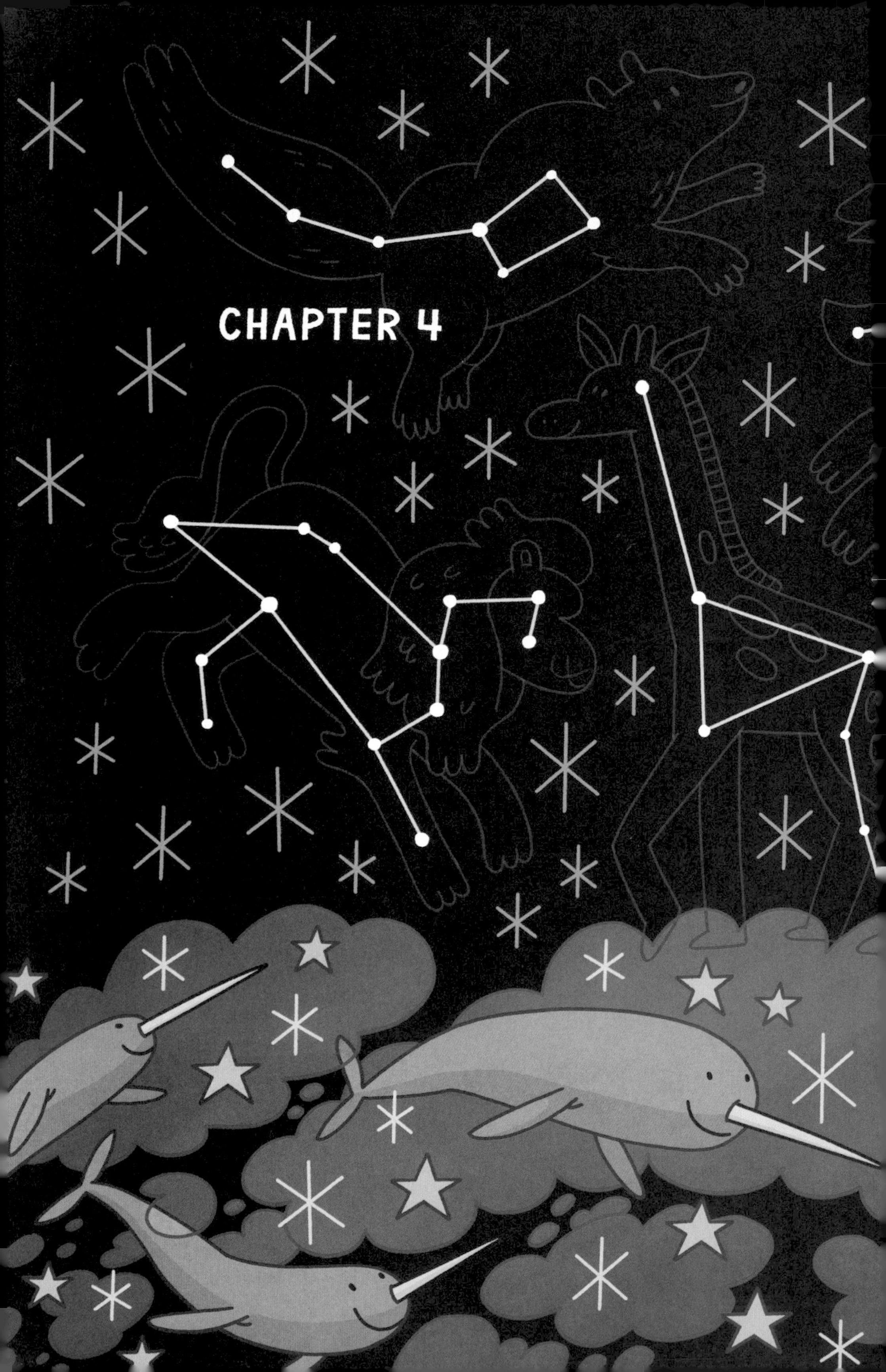

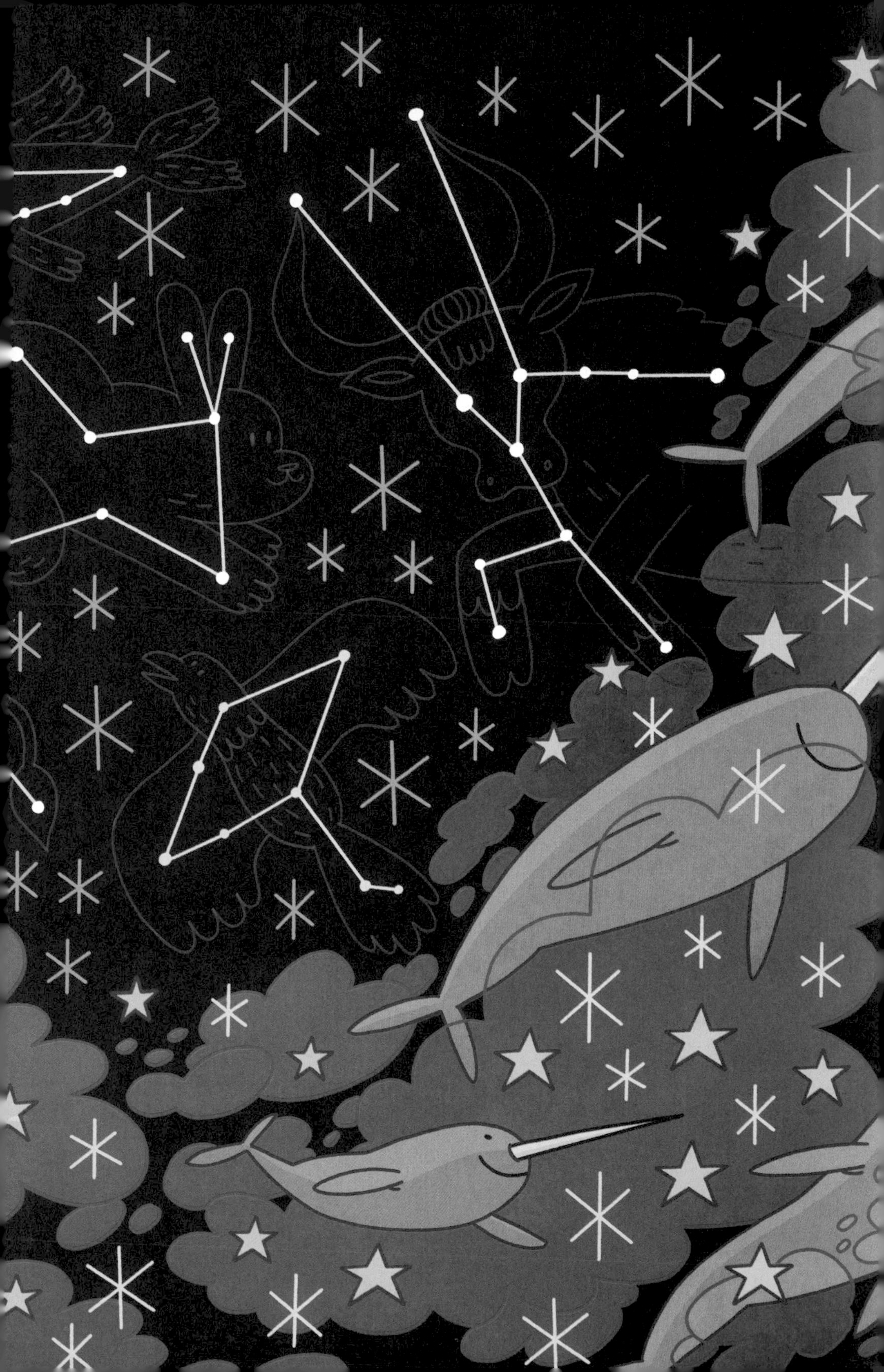

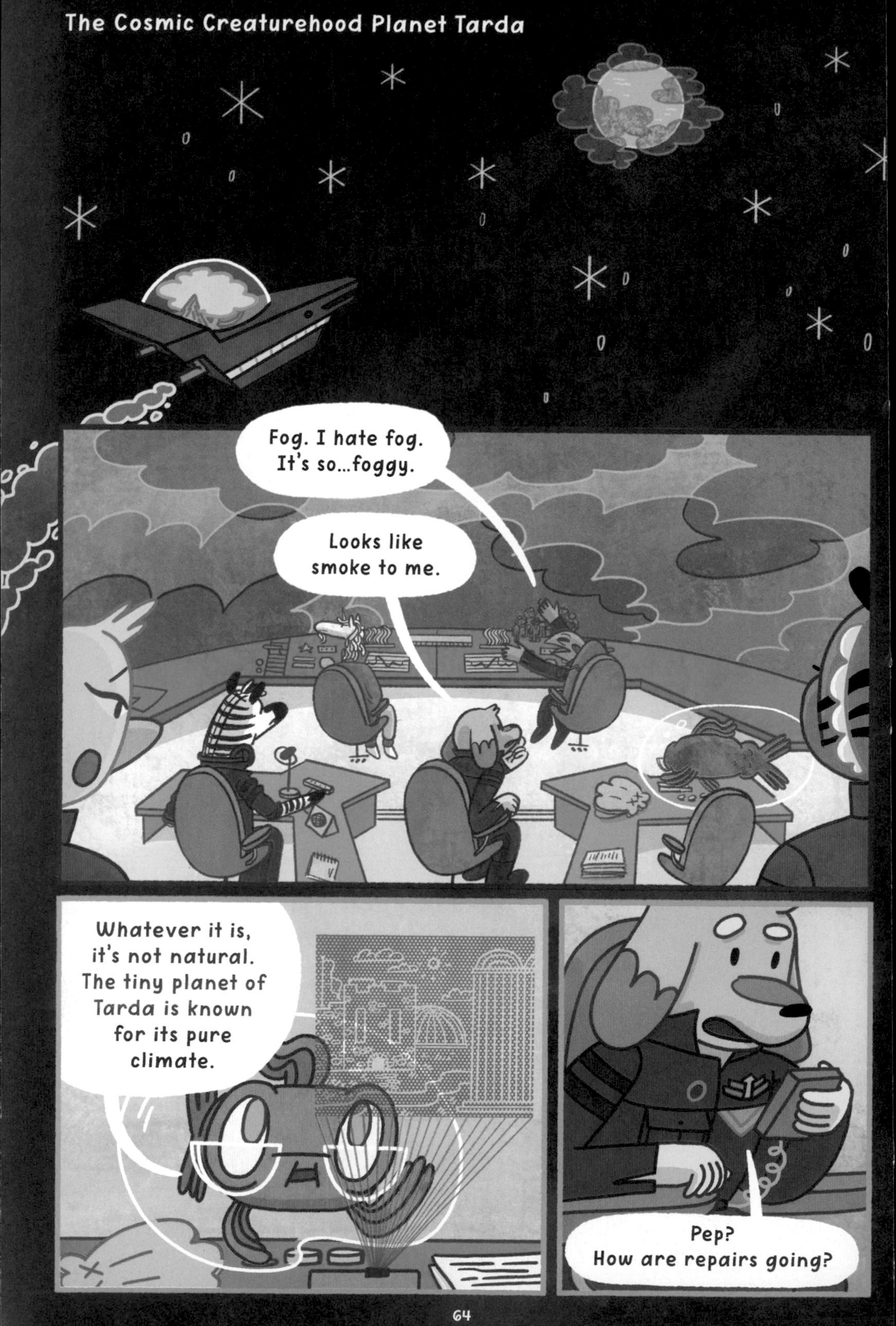
The Cosmic Creaturehood Planet Tarda
Fog. I hate fog. It's so...foggy.
Looks like smoke to me.
Whatever it is, it's not natural. The tiny planet of Tarda is known for its pure climate.
Pep? How are repairs going?

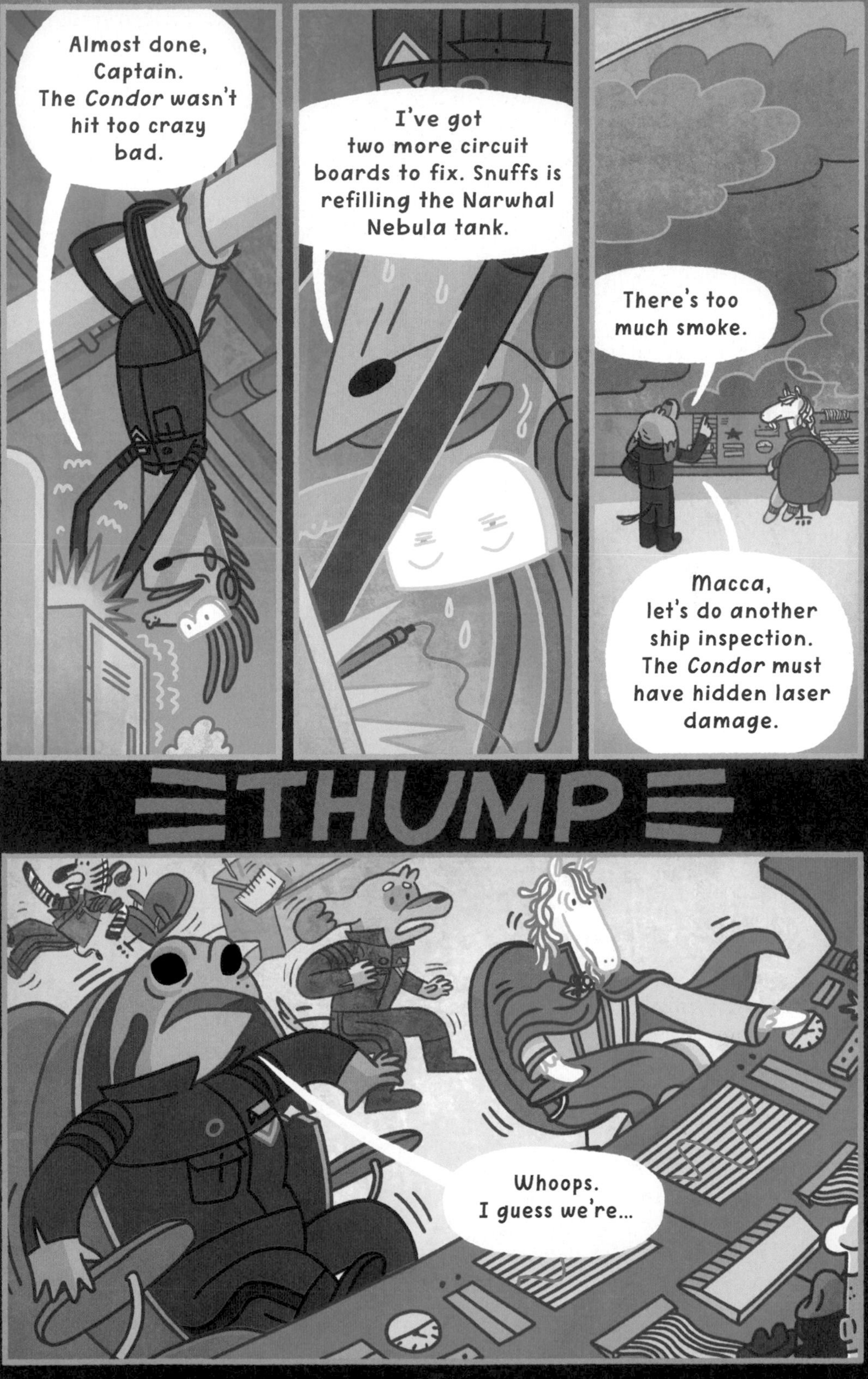
Almost done, Captain. The *Condor* wasn't hit too crazy bad.
I've got two more circuit boards to fix. Snuffs is refilling the Narwhal Nebula tank.
There's too much smoke.
Macca, let's do another ship inspection. The *Condor* must have hidden laser damage.
THUMP
Whoops. I guess we're...

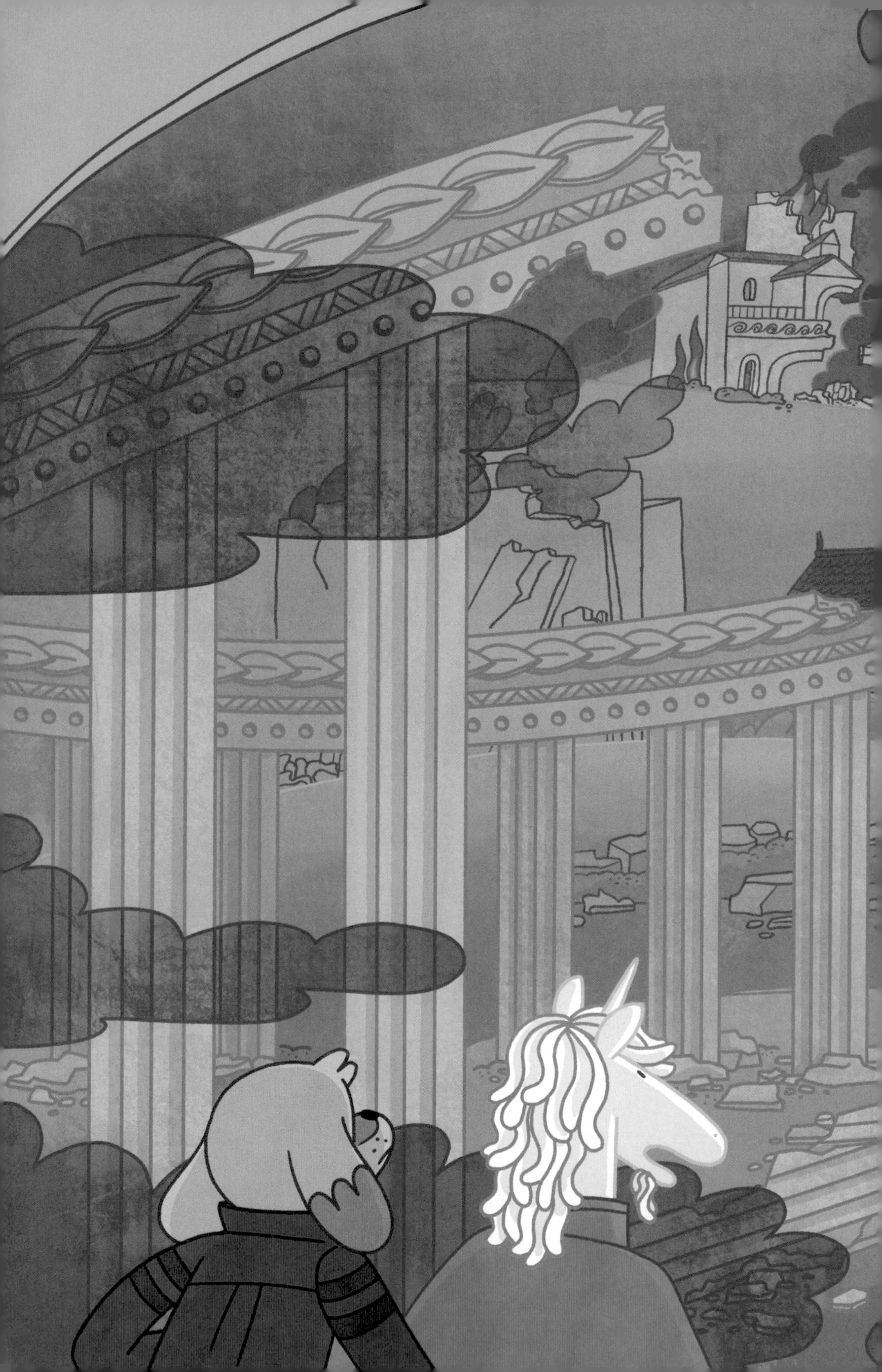

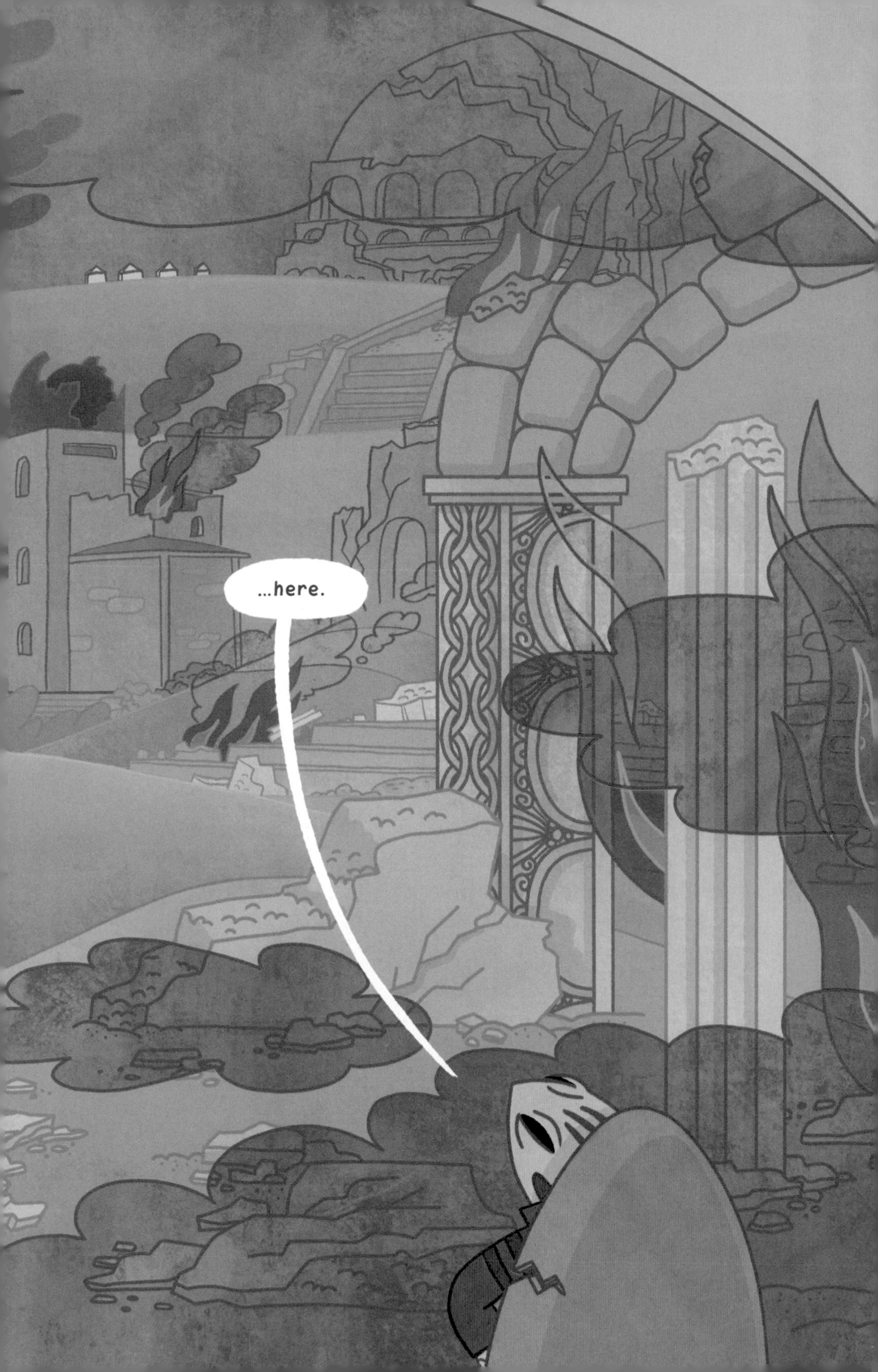
...here.

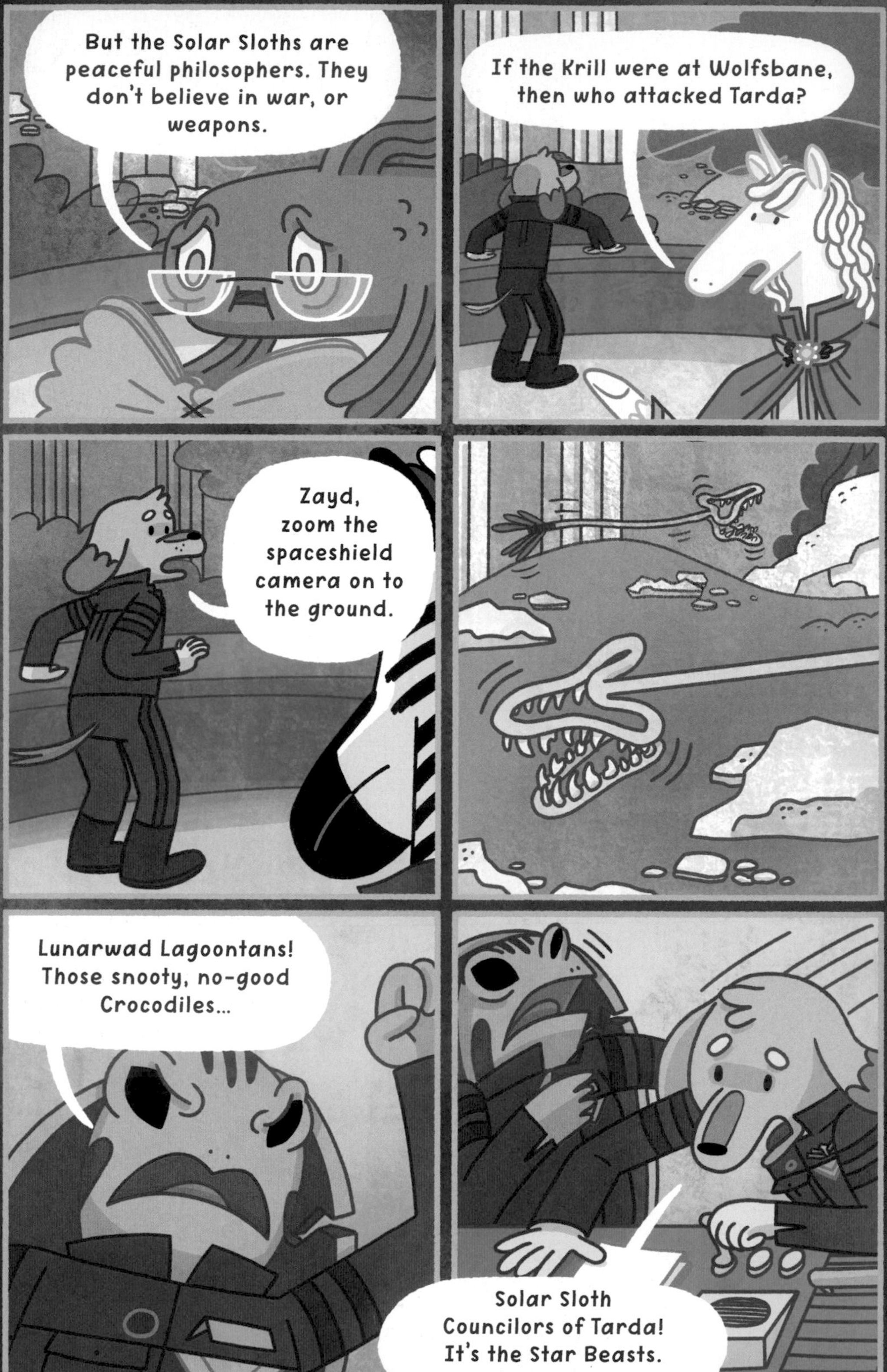
But the Solar Sloths are peaceful philosophers. They don't believe in war, or weapons.
If the Krill were at Wolfsbane, then who attacked Tarda?
Zayd, zoom the spaceshield camera on to the ground.
Lunarwad Lagoontans! Those snooty, no-good Crocodiles...
Solar Sloth Councilors of Tarda! It's the Star Beasts. Are you there?

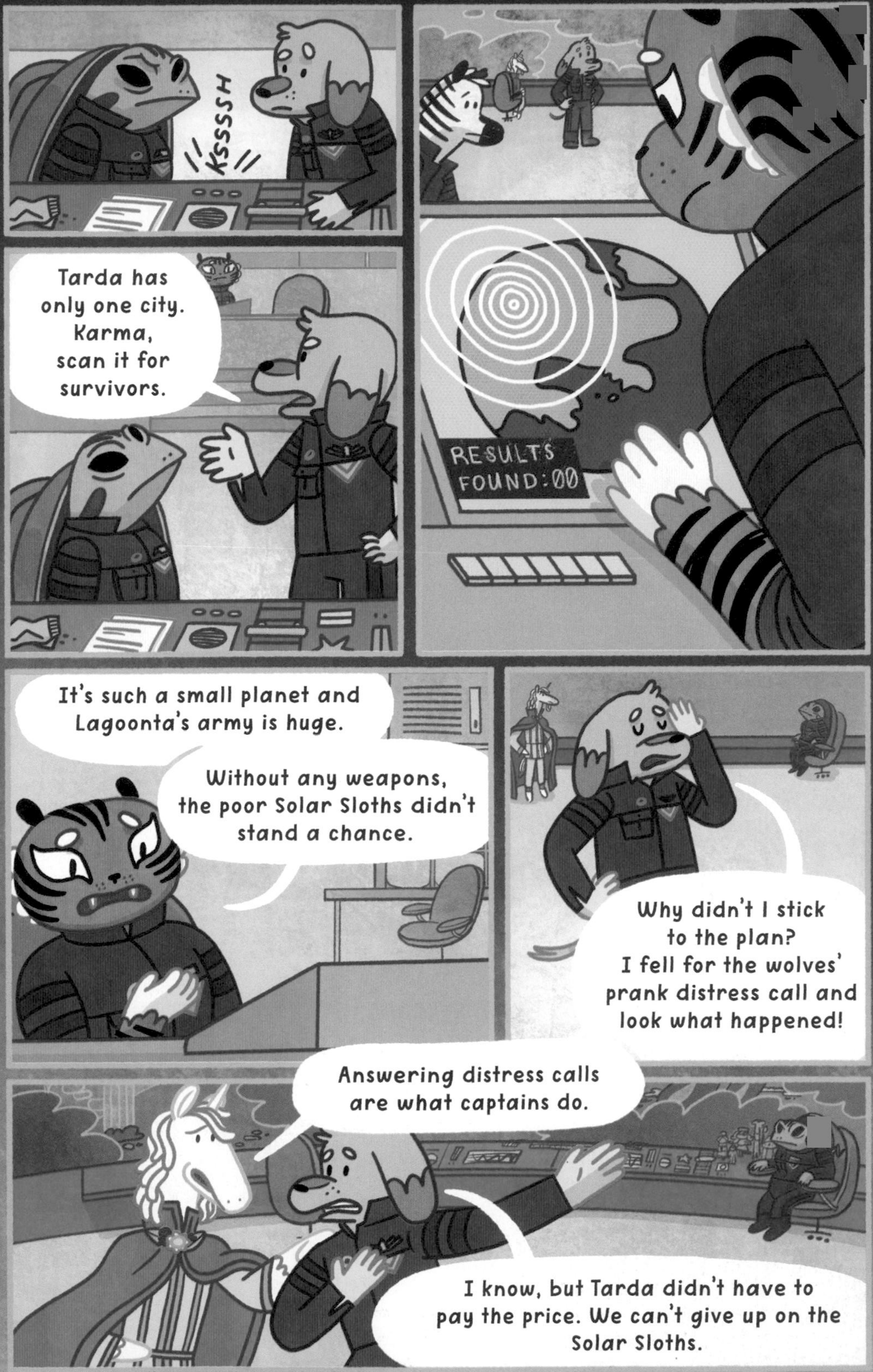
KSSSSH
Tarda has only one city. Karma, scan it for survivors.
RESULTS FOUND:00
It's such a small planet and Lagoonta's army is huge.
Without any weapons, the poor Solar Sloths didn't stand a chance.
Why didn't I stick to the plan? I fell for the wolves' prank distress call and look what happened!
Answering distress calls are what captains do.
I know, but Tarda didn't have to pay the price. We can't give up on the Solar Sloths.

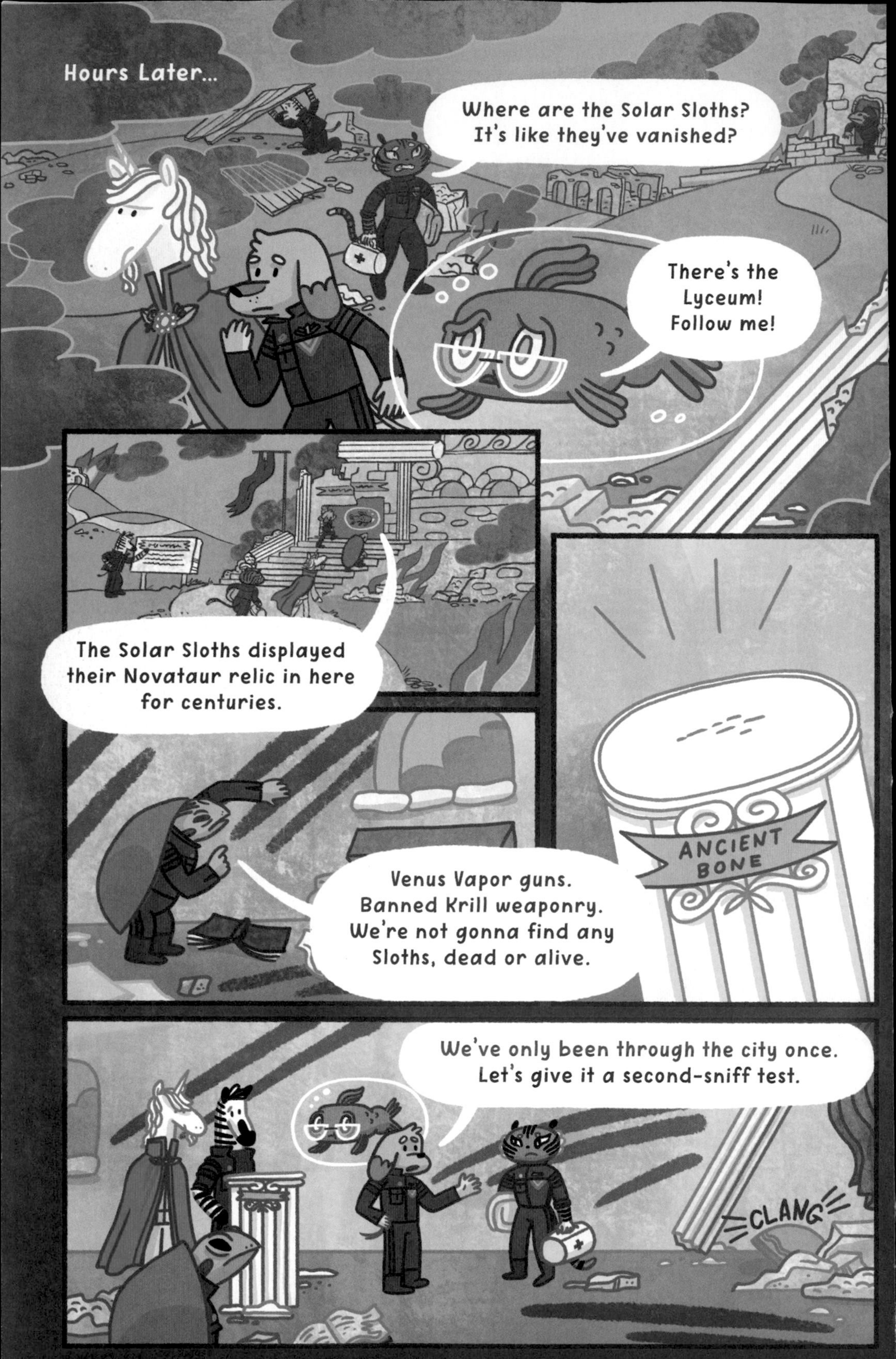

Hours Later...
Where are the Solar Sloths? It's like they've vanished?
There's the Lyceum! Follow me!
The Solar Sloths displayed their Novataur relic in here for centuries.
ANCIENT BONE
Venus Vapor guns. Banned Krill weaponry. We're not gonna find any Sloths, dead or alive.
We've only been through the city once. Let's give it a second-sniff test.
CLANG

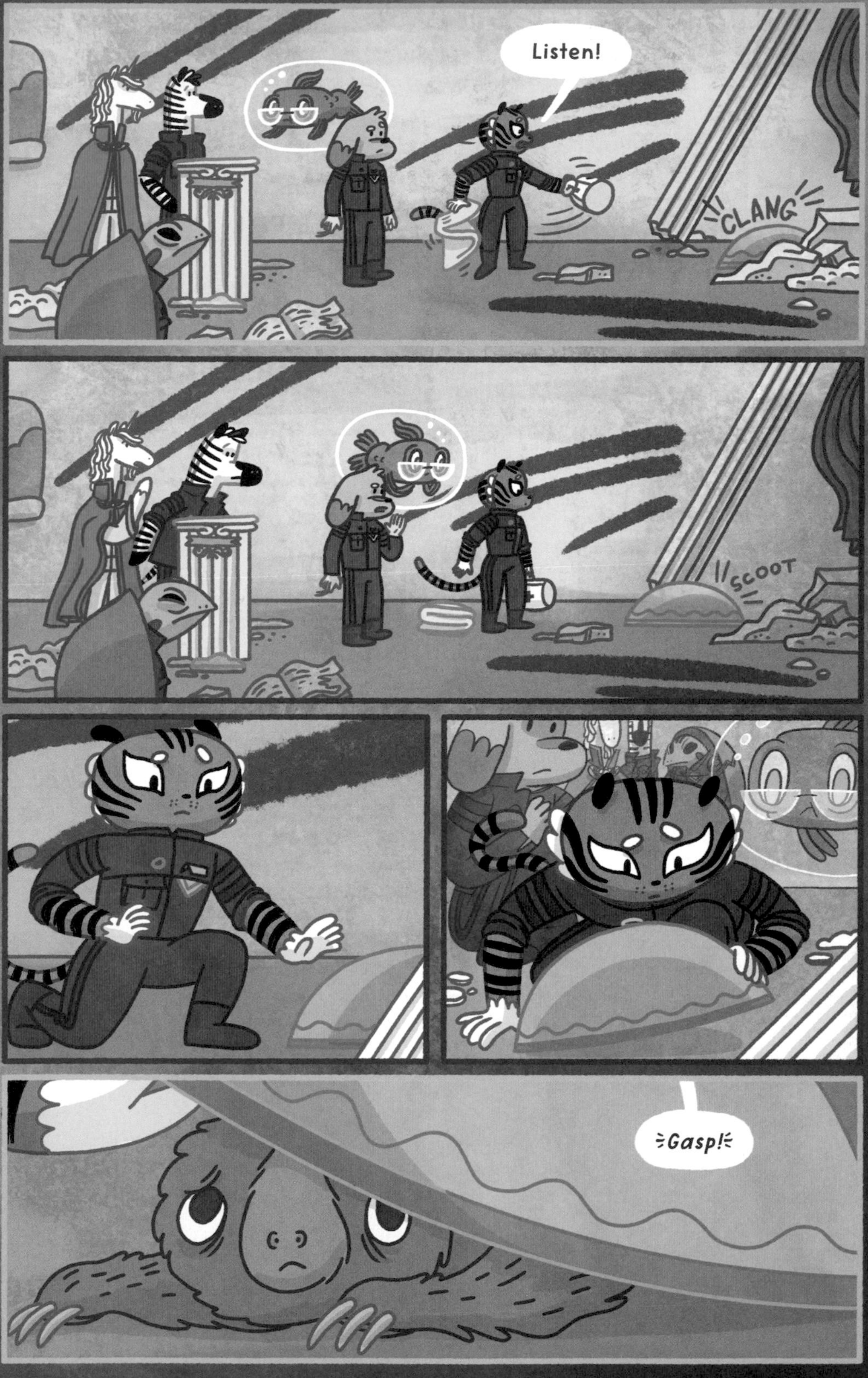
Listen!
CLANG
SCOOT
Gasp!

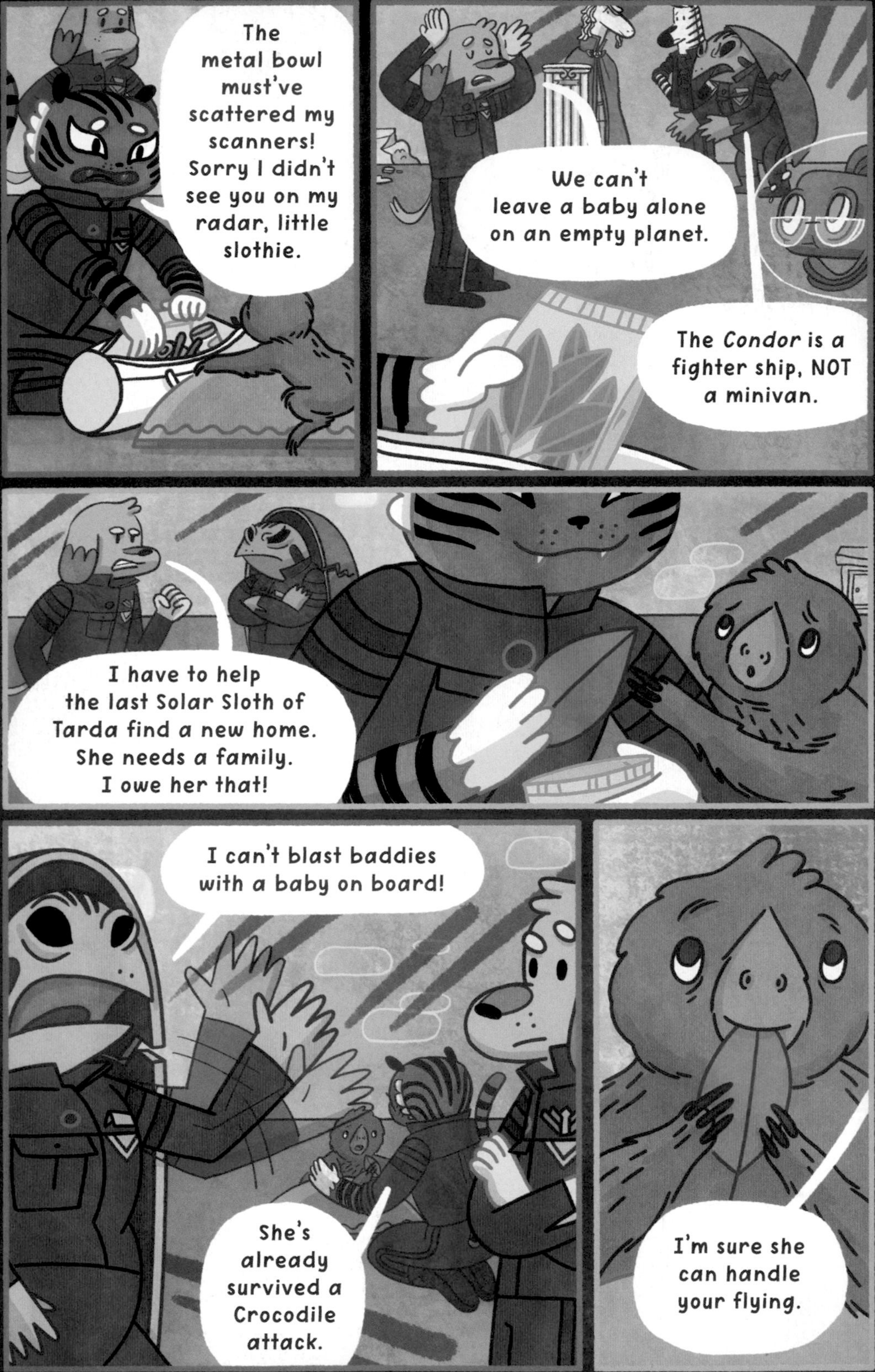
The metal bowl must've scattered my scanners! Sorry I didn't see you on my radar, little slothie.
We can't leave a baby alone on an empty planet.
The Condor is a fighter ship, NOT a minivan.
I have to help the last Solar Sloth of Tarda find a new home. She needs a family. I owe her that!
I can't blast baddies with a baby on board!
She's already survived a Crocodile attack.
I'm sure she can handle your flying.

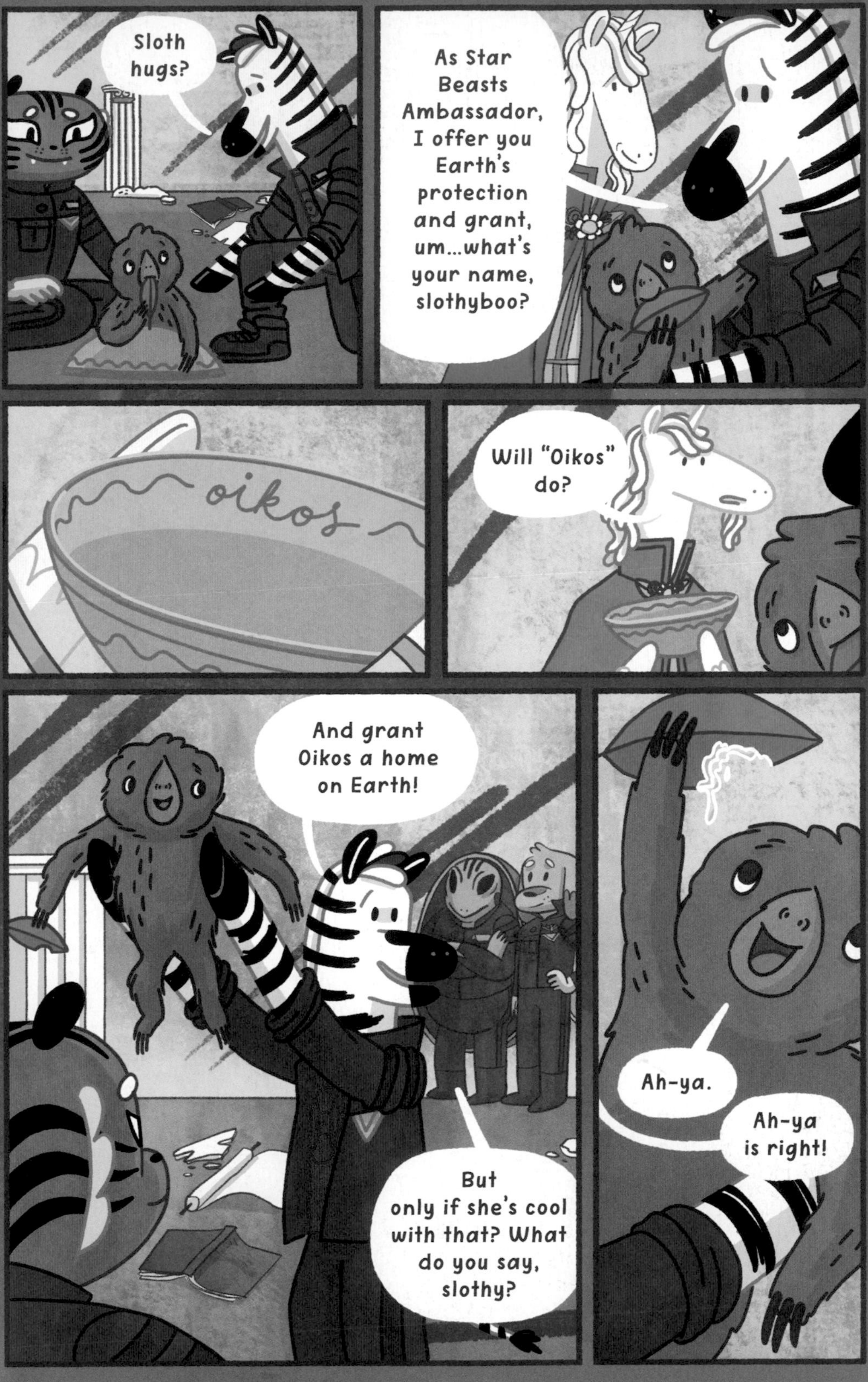
Sloth hugs?
As Star Beasts Ambassador, I offer you Earth's protection and grant, um...what's your name, slothyboo?
oikos
Will "Oikos" do?
And grant Oikos a home on Earth!
But only if she's cool with that? What do you say, slothy?
Ah-ya.
Ah-ya is right!

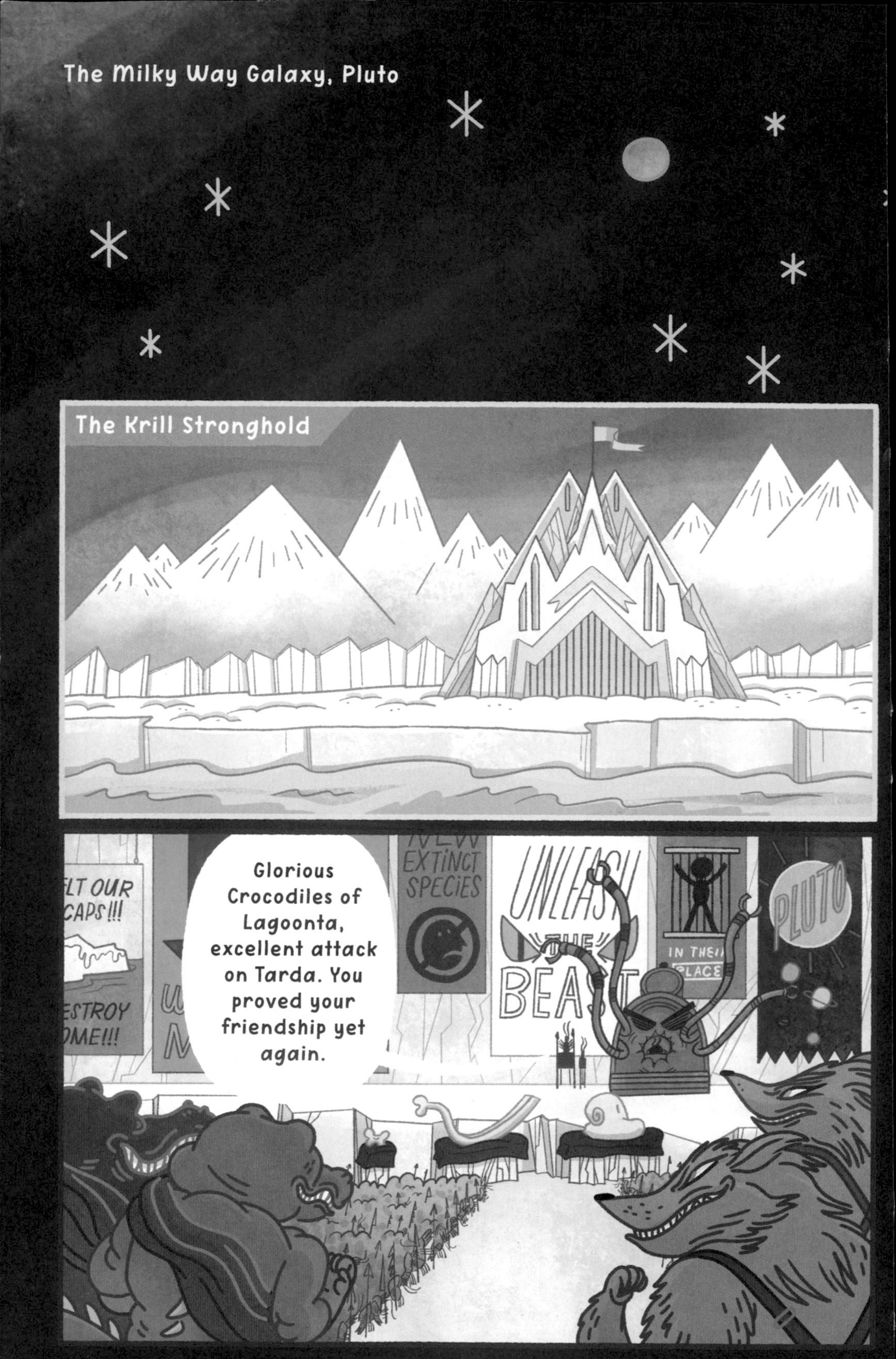
The Milky Way Galaxy, Pluto
The Krill Stronghold
Glorious Crocodiles of Lagoonta, excellent attack on Tarda. You proved your friendship yet again.
EXTINCT SPECIES
PLUTO

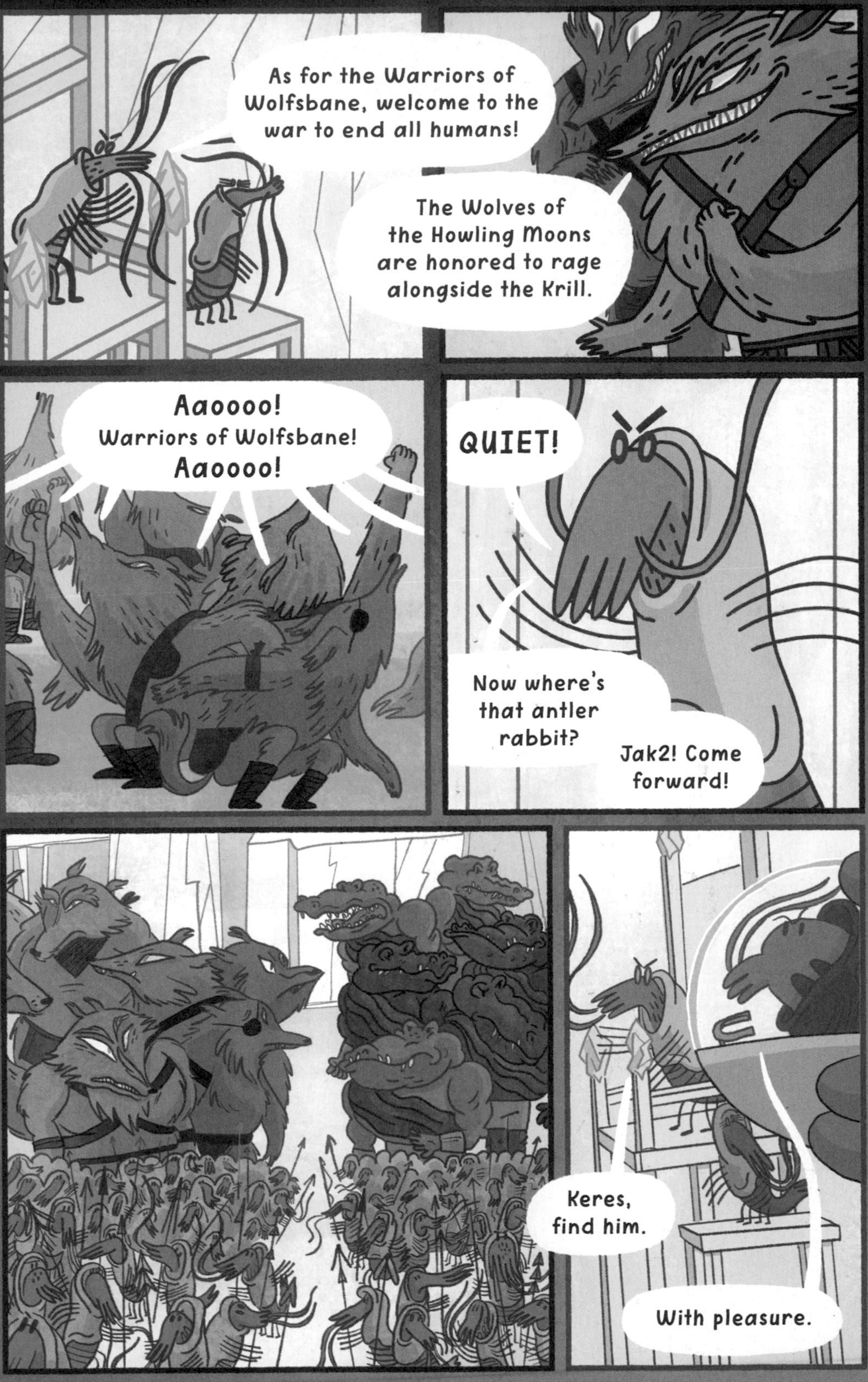
As for the Warriors of Wolfsbane, welcome to the war to end all humans!
The Wolves of the Howling Moons are honored to rage alongside the Krill.
Aaoooo! Warriors of Wolfsbane! Aaoooo!
QUIET!
Now where's that antler rabbit?
Jak2! Come forward!
Keres, find him.
With pleasure.

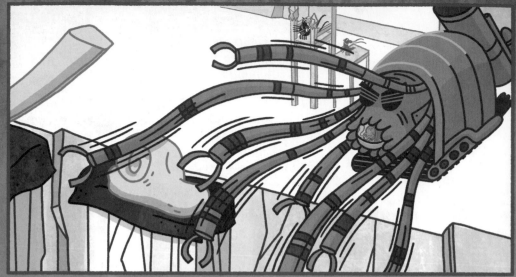

Ouch! Hey! That pinches!

I was on my way up there! I had to, uh, tie my shoe!

Jackalopes CAN hop, you know!

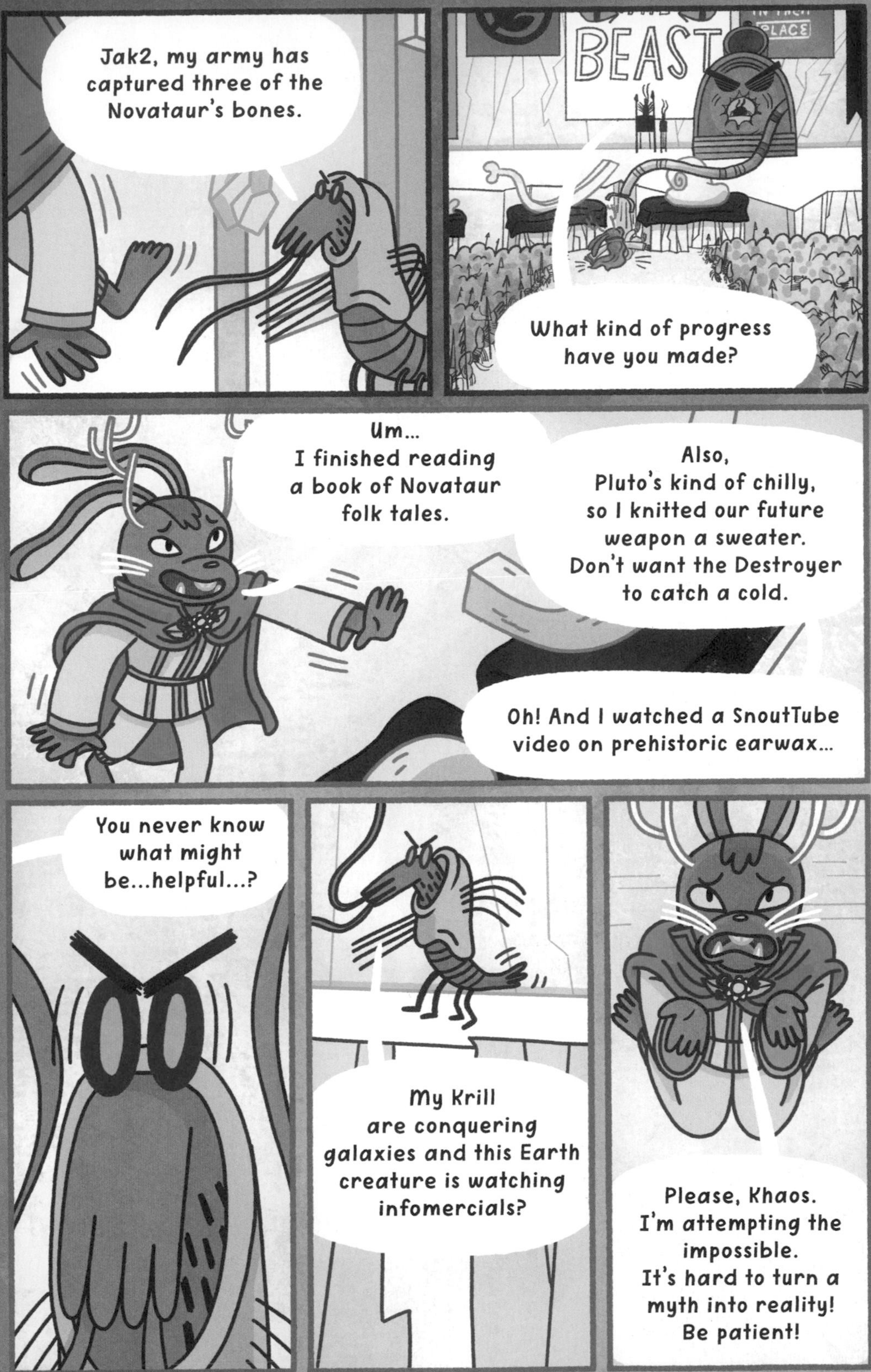
Jak2, my army has captured three of the Novataur's bones.
BEAST
PLACE
What kind of progress have you made?
Um... I finished reading a book of Novataur folk tales.
Also, Pluto's kind of chilly, so I knitted our future weapon a sweater. Don't want the Destroyer to catch a cold.
Oh! And I watched a SnoutTube video on prehistoric earwax...
You never know what might be...helpful...?
My Krill are conquering galaxies and this Earth creature is watching infomercials?
Please, Khaos. I'm attempting the impossible. It's hard to turn a myth into reality! Be patient!

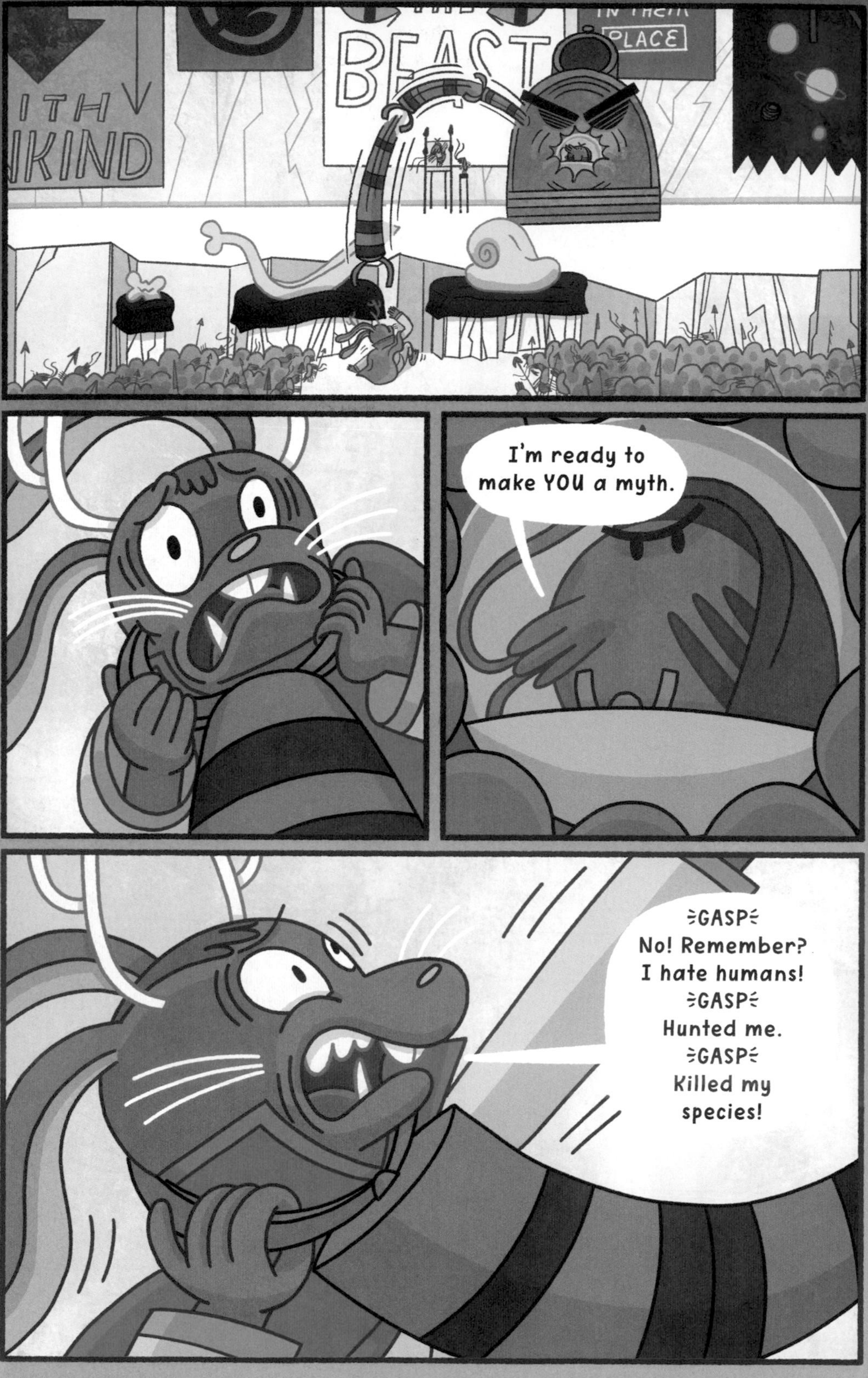
ITH
NKIND
BEAST
PLACE
I'm ready to make YOU a myth.
≡GASP≡ No! Remember? I hate humans! ≡GASP≡ Hunted me. ≡GASP≡ Killed my species!

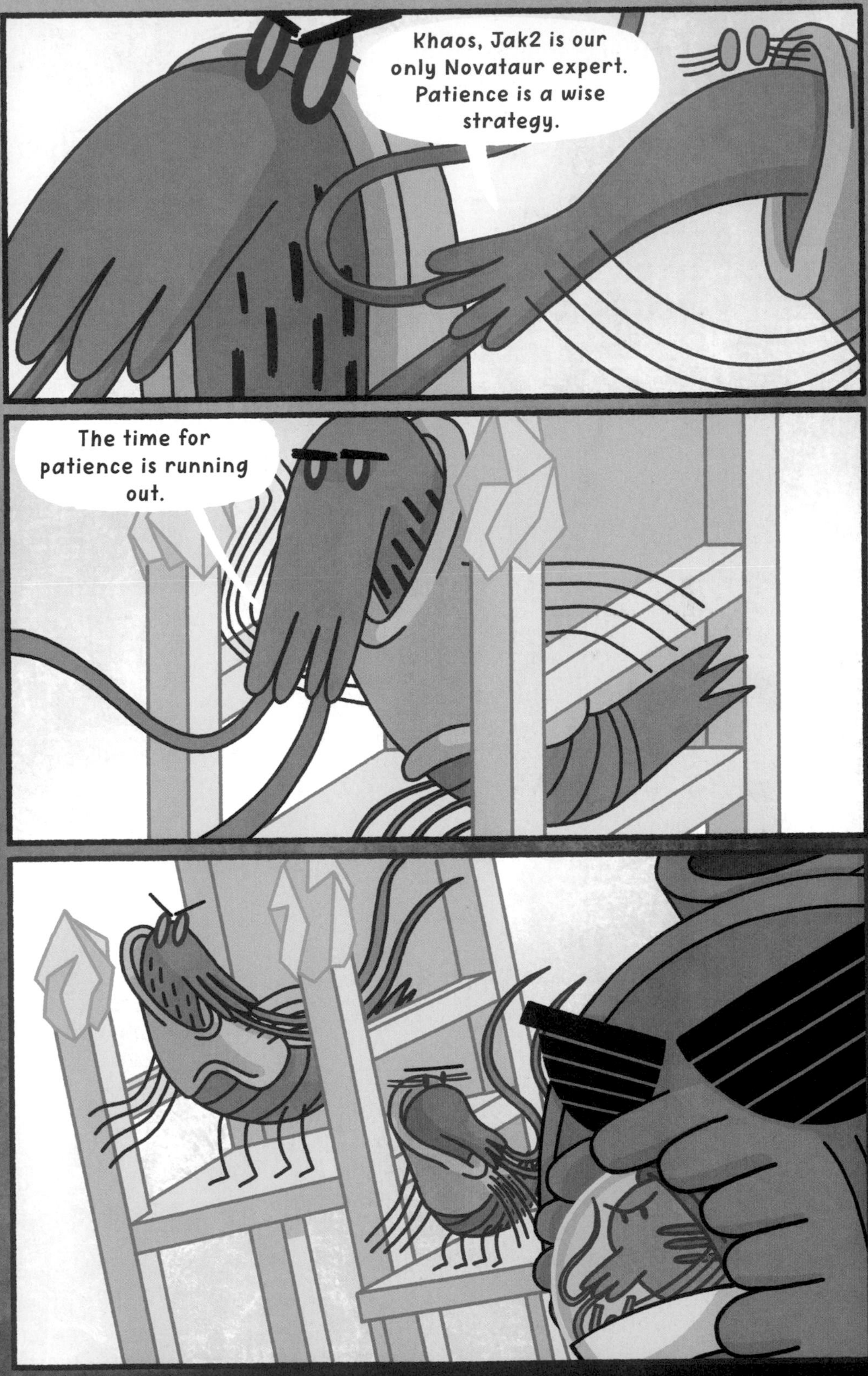
Khaos, Jak2 is our only Novataur expert. Patience is a wise strategy.
The time for patience is running out.

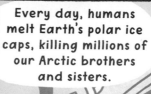

Every day, humans melt Earth's polar ice caps, killing millions of our Arctic brothers and sisters.

The pollution called humans must be stopped.

If you're not smart enough to rebuild the Novataur...

...then I suggest you call a friend...

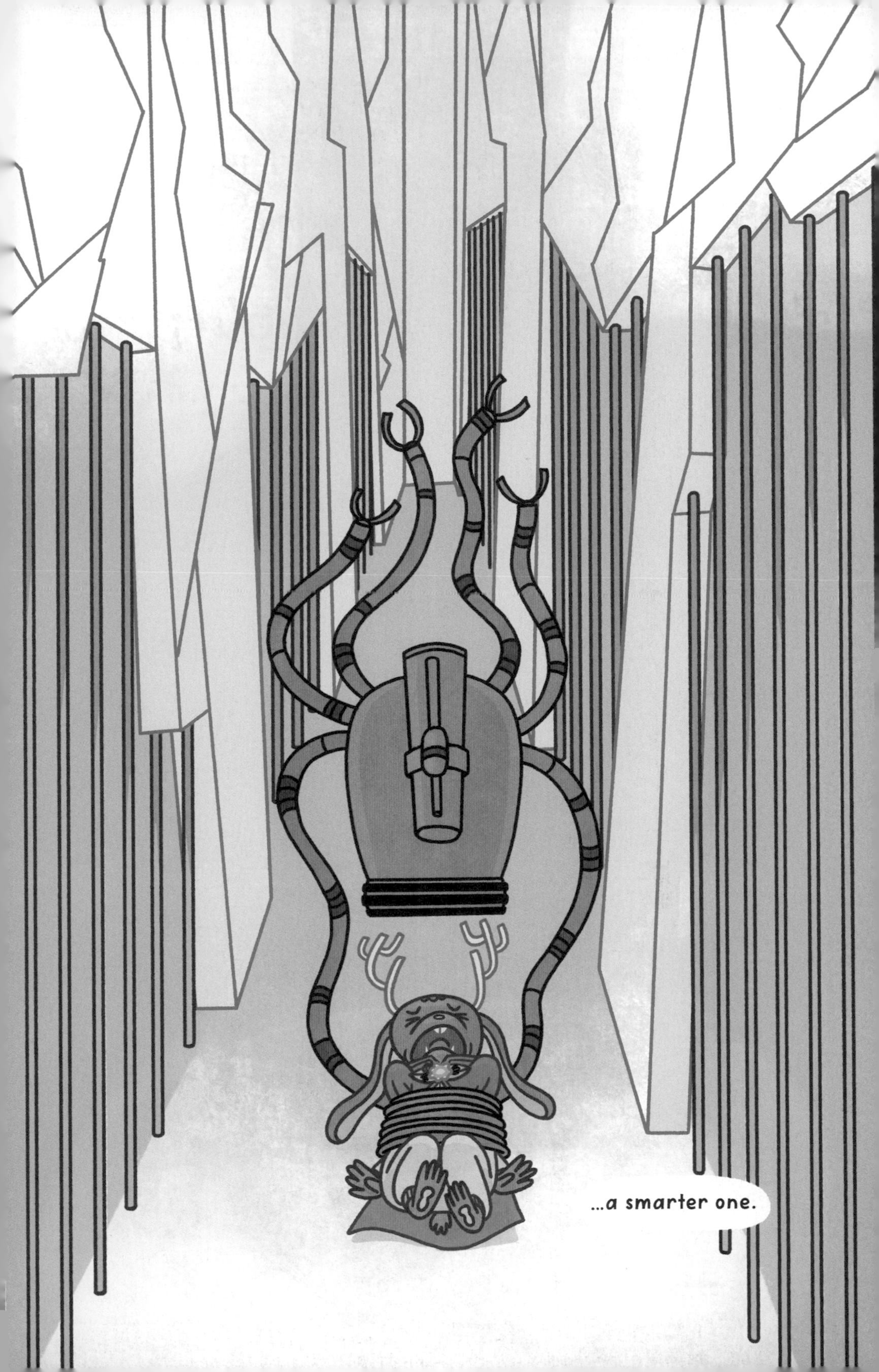
...a smarter one.

CHAPTER 5

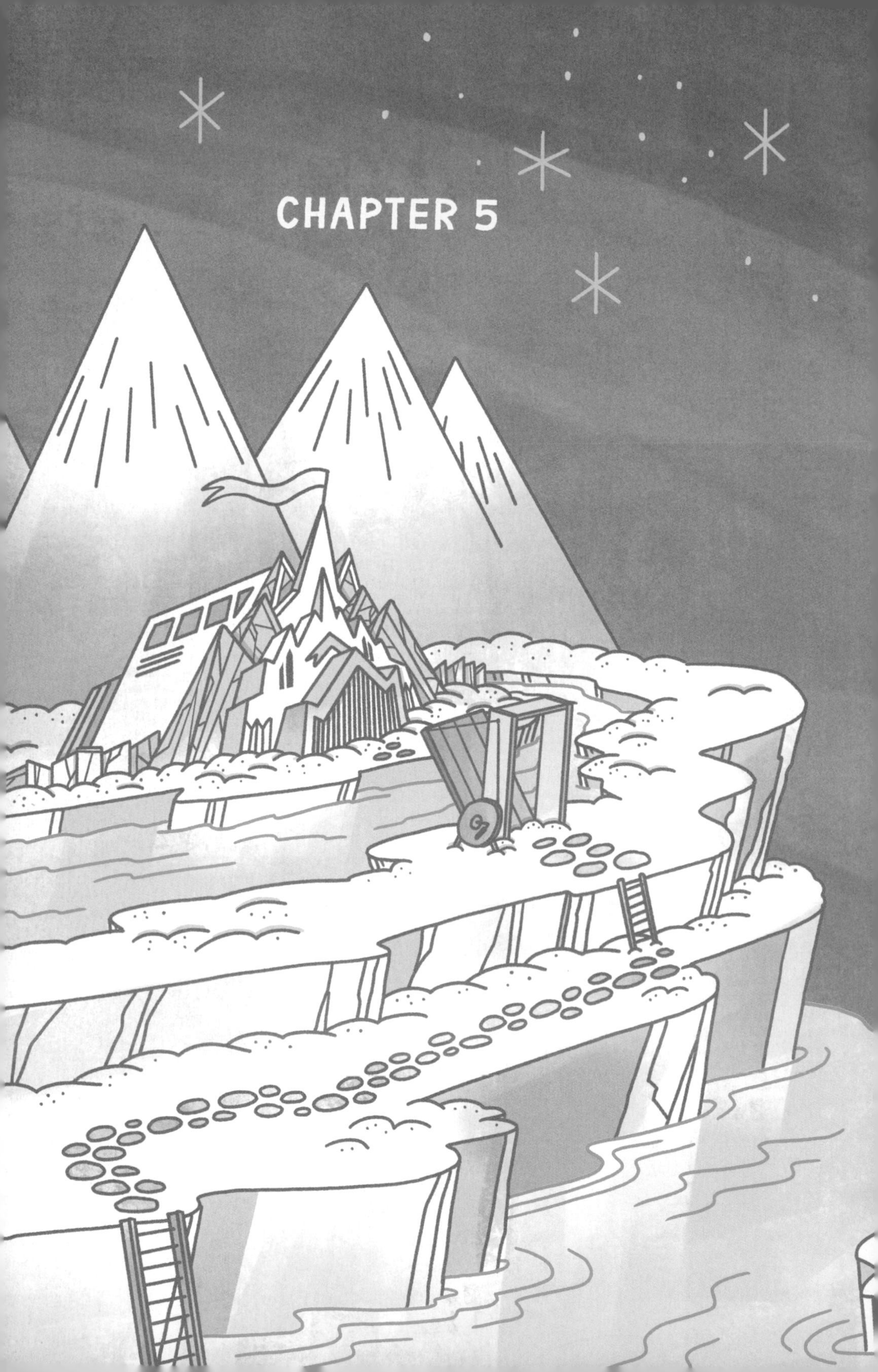

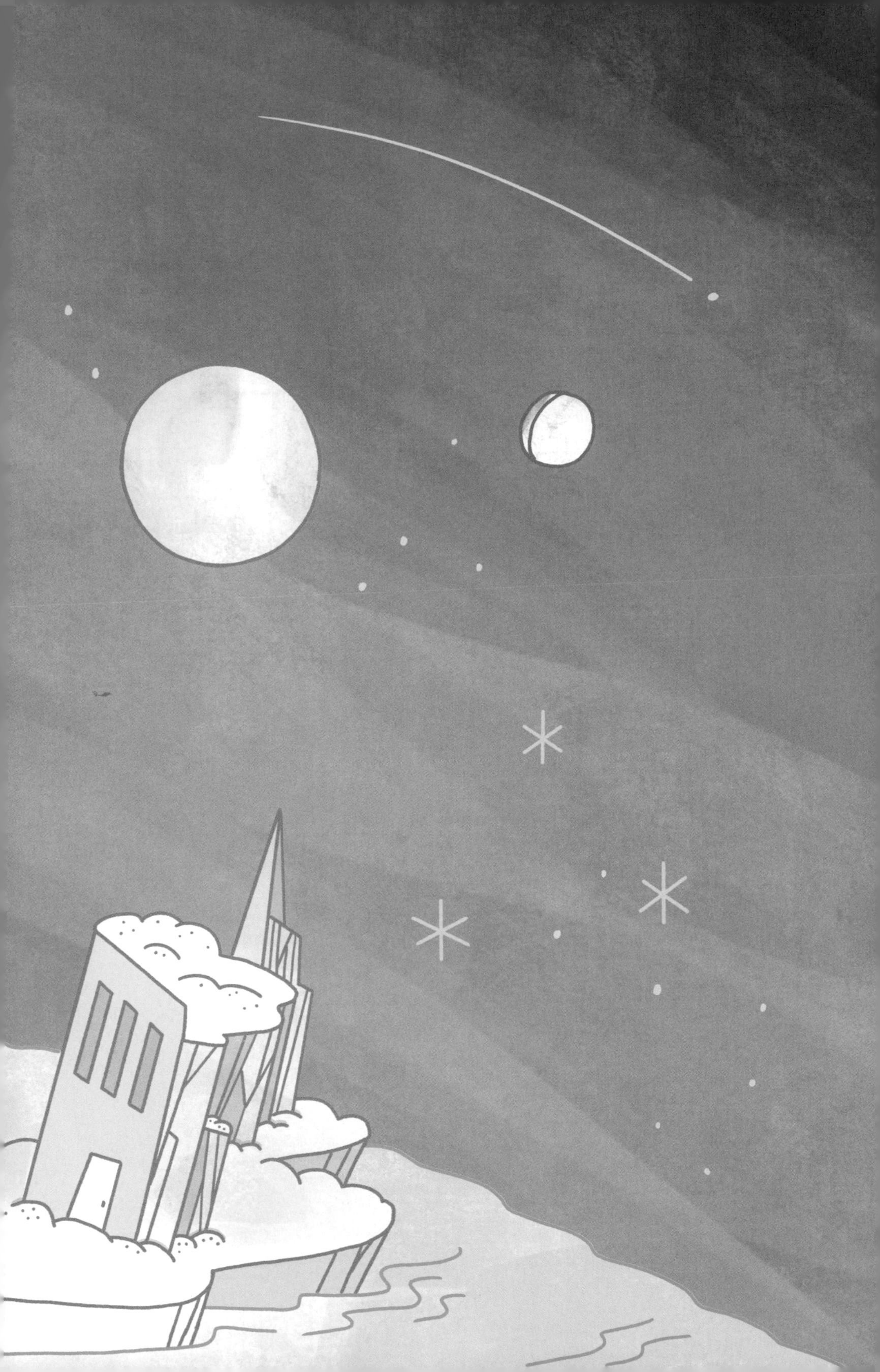

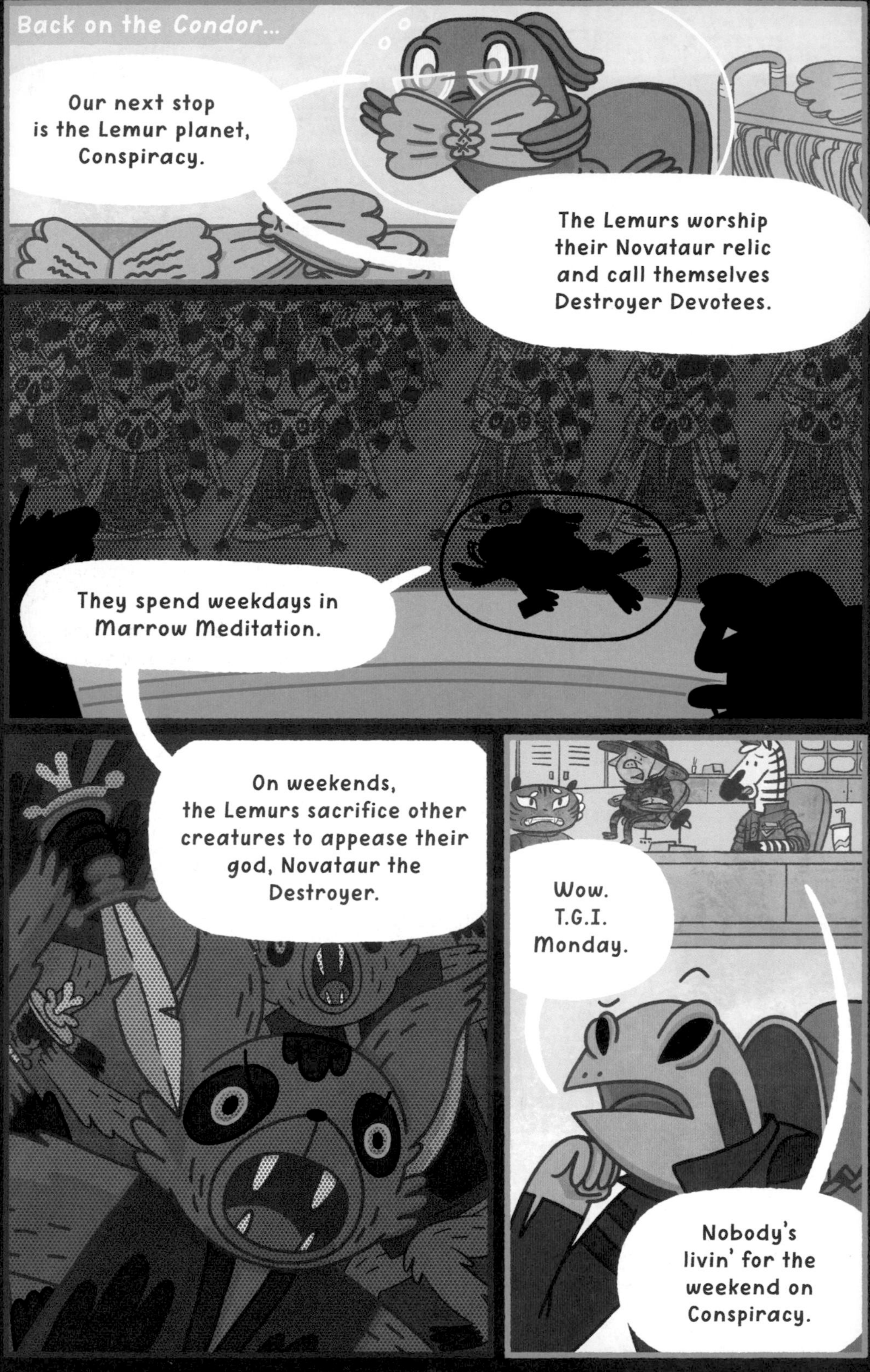
Back on the Condor...
Our next stop is the Lemur planet, Conspiracy.
The Lemurs worship their Novataur relic and call themselves Destroyer Devotees.
They spend weekdays in Marrow Meditation.
On weekends, the Lemurs sacrifice other creatures to appease their god, Novataur the Destroyer.
Wow. T.G.I. Monday.
Nobody's livin' for the weekend on Conspiracy.

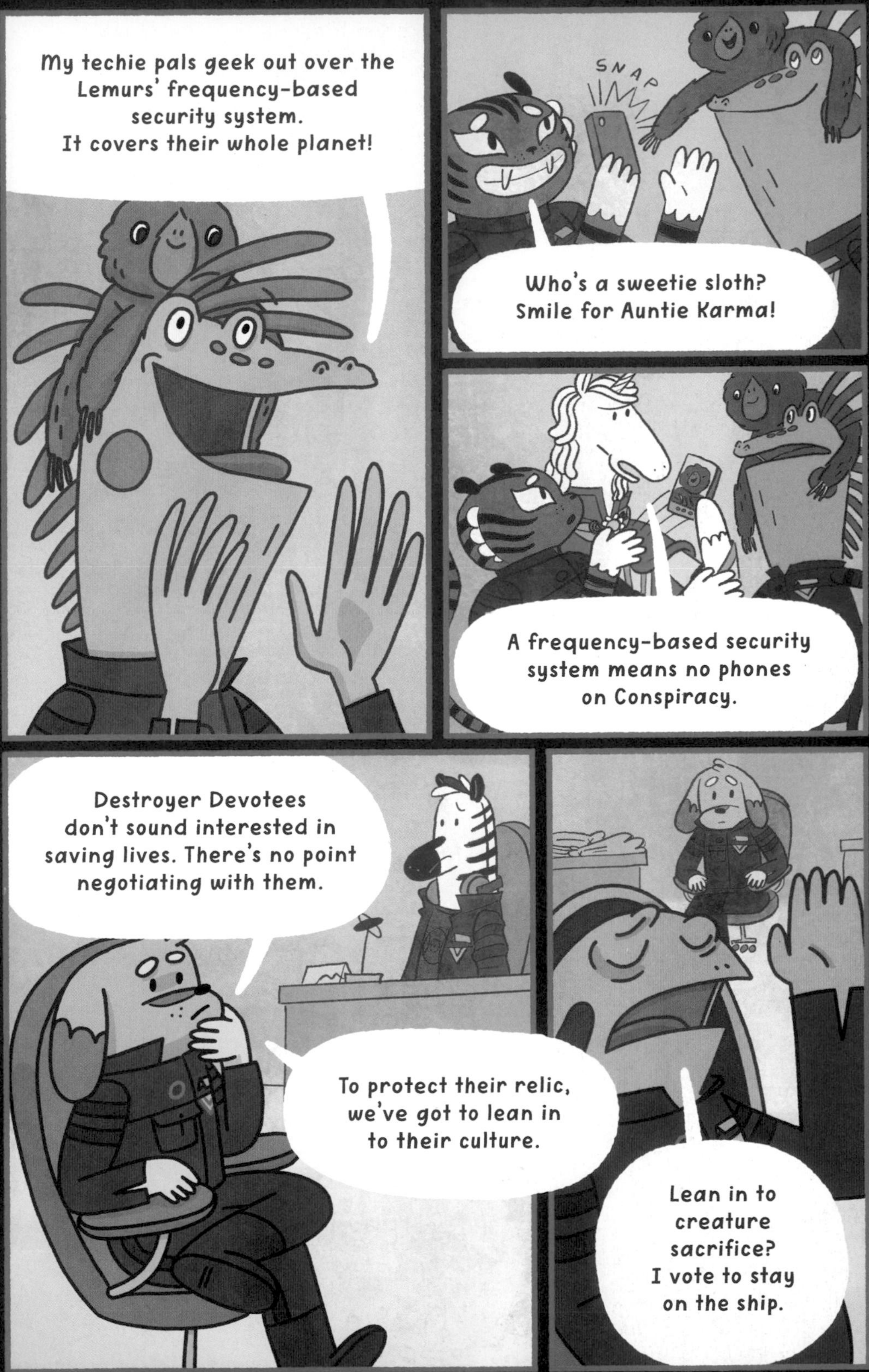
My techie pals geek out over the Lemurs' frequency-based security system. It covers their whole planet!
SNAP
Who's a sweetie sloth? Smile for Auntie Karma!
A frequency-based security system means no phones on Conspiracy.
Destroyer Devotees don't sound interested in saving lives. There's no point negotiating with them.
To protect their relic, we've got to lean in to their culture.
Lean in to creature sacrifice? I vote to stay on the ship.

Captain Bandit and I came up with a plan! We'll sneak into the Lemur Temple...

Color me bedazzled.

...and switch out the real Novataur fossil for my replica statue!

The last thing we want to do is disturb the Lemurs.

Zayd, can you lead them in a calming meditation chant?

I'll help them tune in and zen out!

I don't feel good about the switcheroo, but at least no one will get hurt.

Captain, your plan doesn't quite follow the Star Beasts rulebook, but it has my approval.

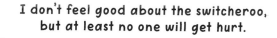

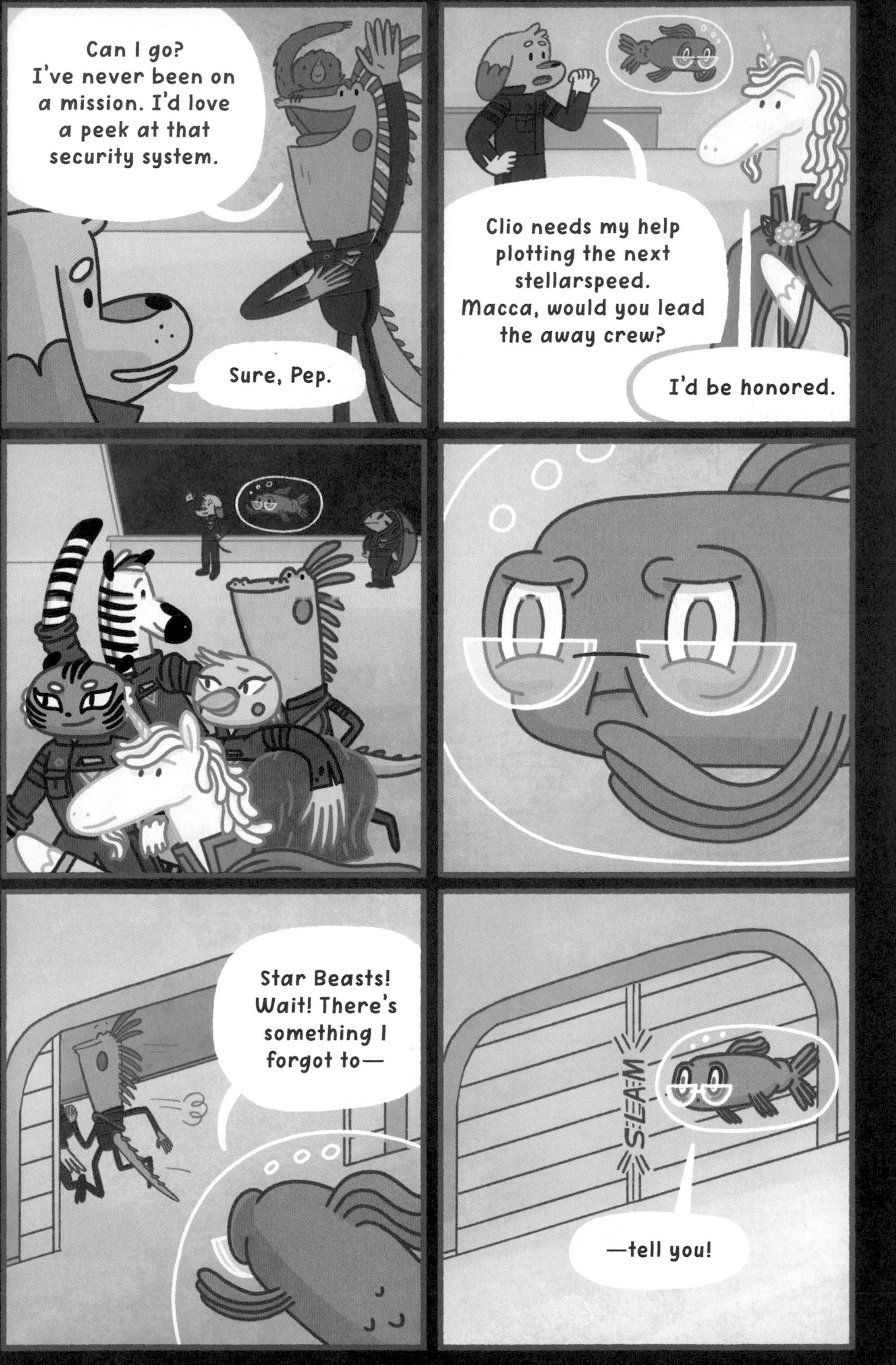
Can I go?
I've never been on a mission. I'd love a peek at that security system.
Sure, Pep.
Clio needs my help plotting the next stellarspeed.
Macca, would you lead the away crew?
I'd be honored.
Star Beasts! Wait! There's something I forgot to—
SLAM
—tell you!

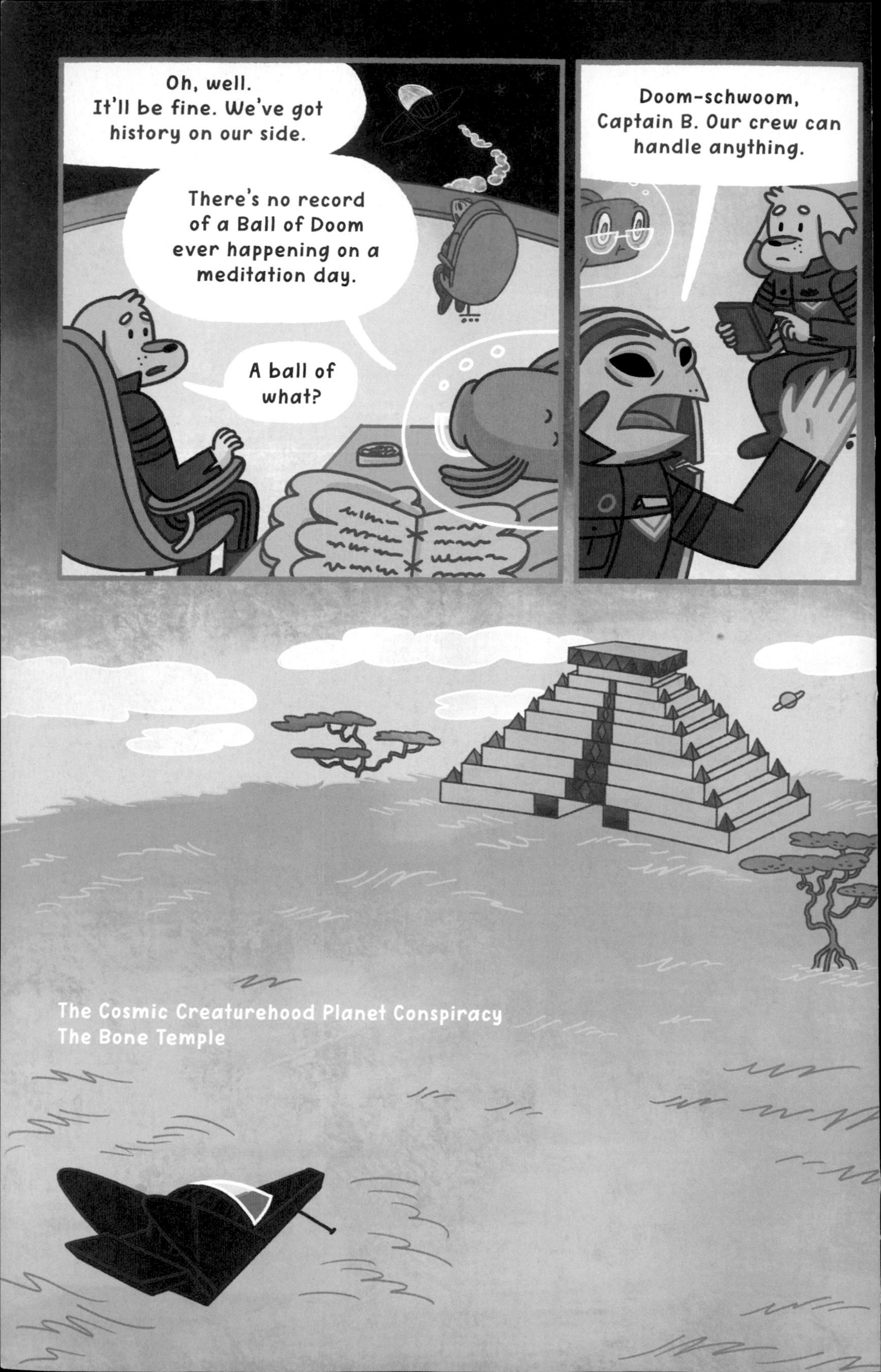
Oh, well.
It'll be fine. We've got history on our side.
There's no record of a Ball of Doom ever happening on a meditation day.
A ball of what?
Doom-schwoom, Captain B. Our crew can handle anything.
The Cosmic Creaturehood Planet Conspiracy
The Bone Temple

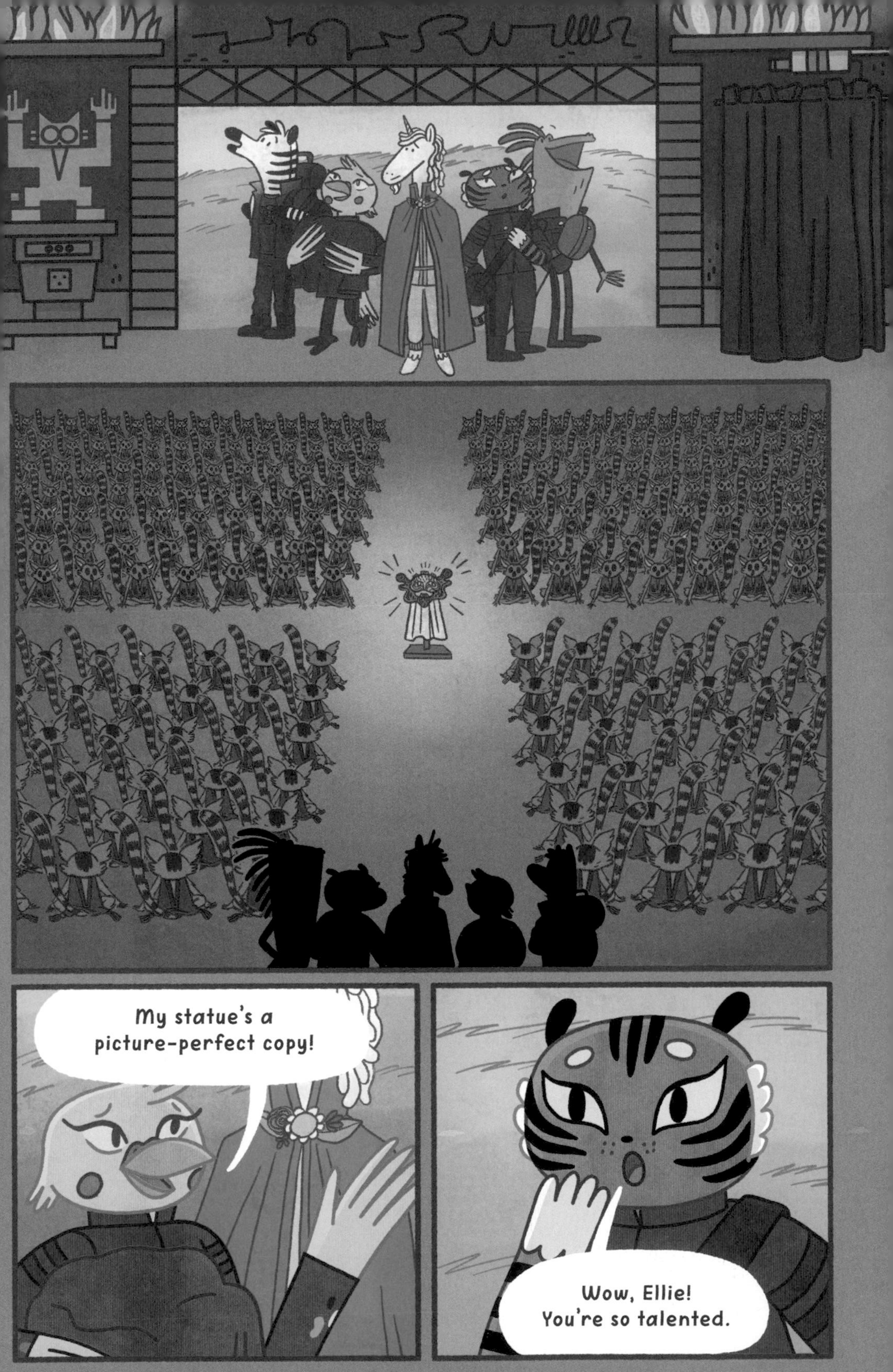
My statue's a picture-perfect copy!
Wow, Ellie! You're so talented.

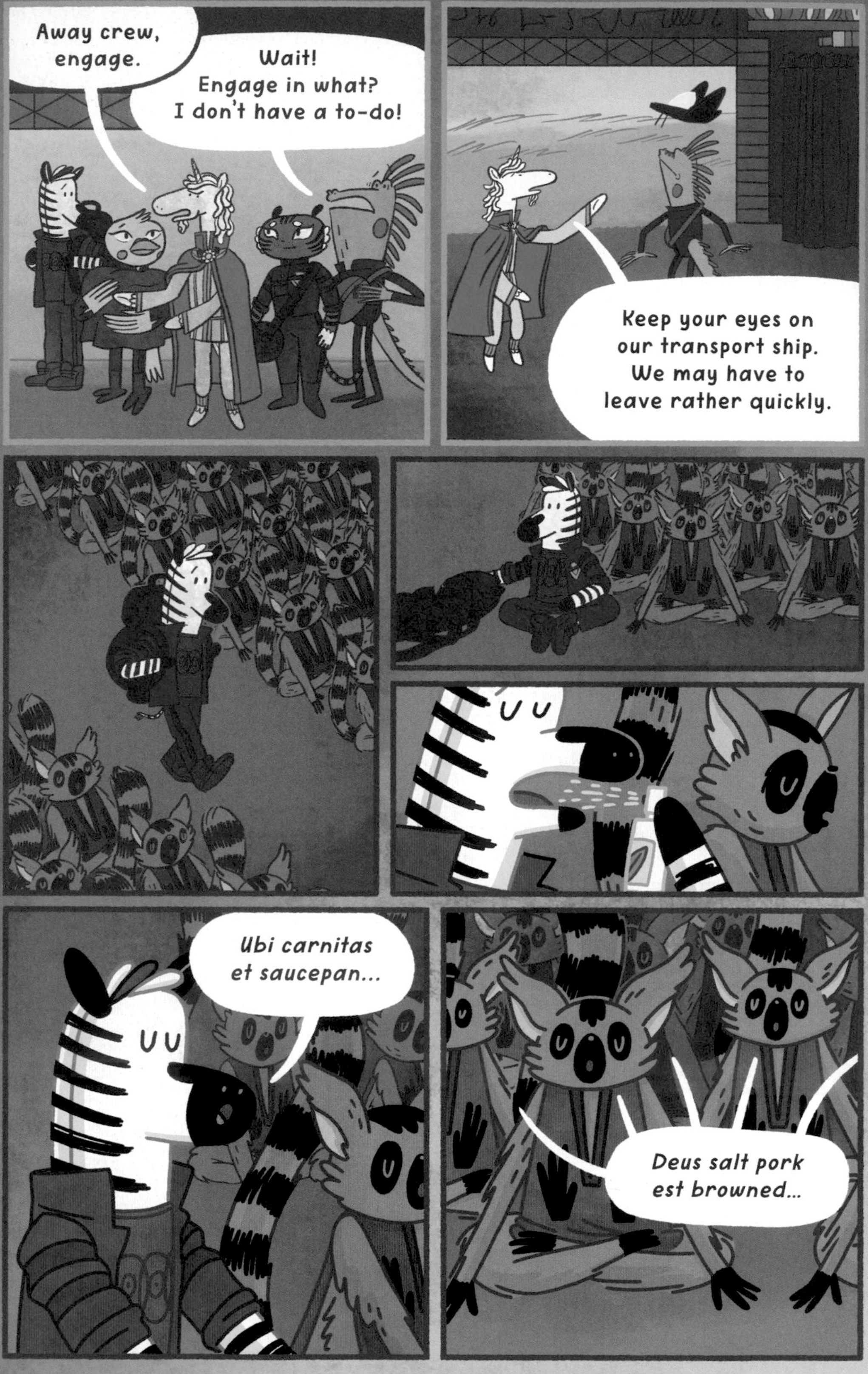
Away crew, engage.
Wait! Engage in what? I don't have a to-do!
Keep your eyes on our transport ship. We may have to leave rather quickly.
Ubi carnitas et saucepan...
Deus salt pork est browned...

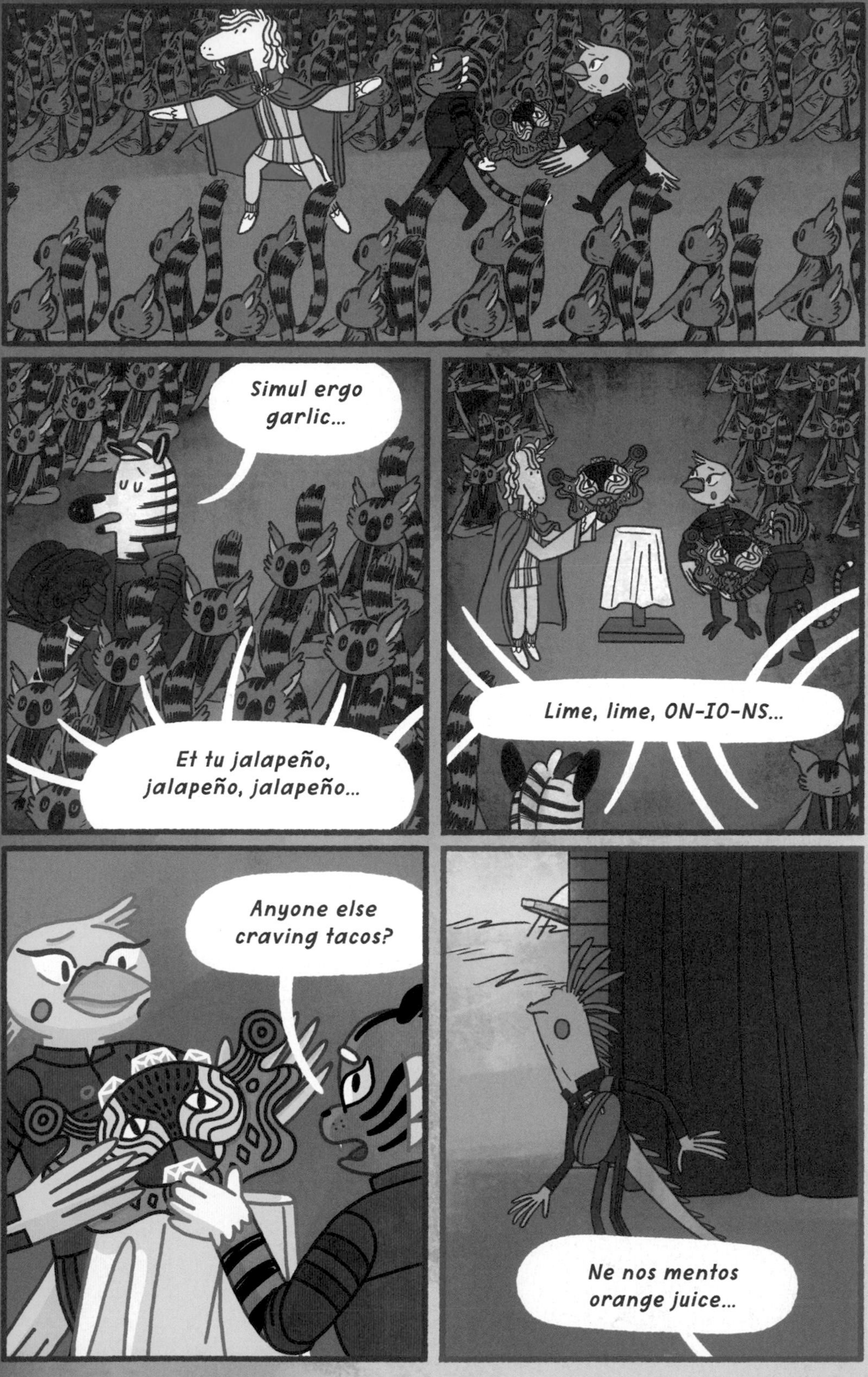

Simul ergo garlic...
Et tu jalapeño, jalapeño, jalapeño...
Lime, lime, ON-IO-NS...
Anyone else craving tacos?
Ne nos mentos orange juice...

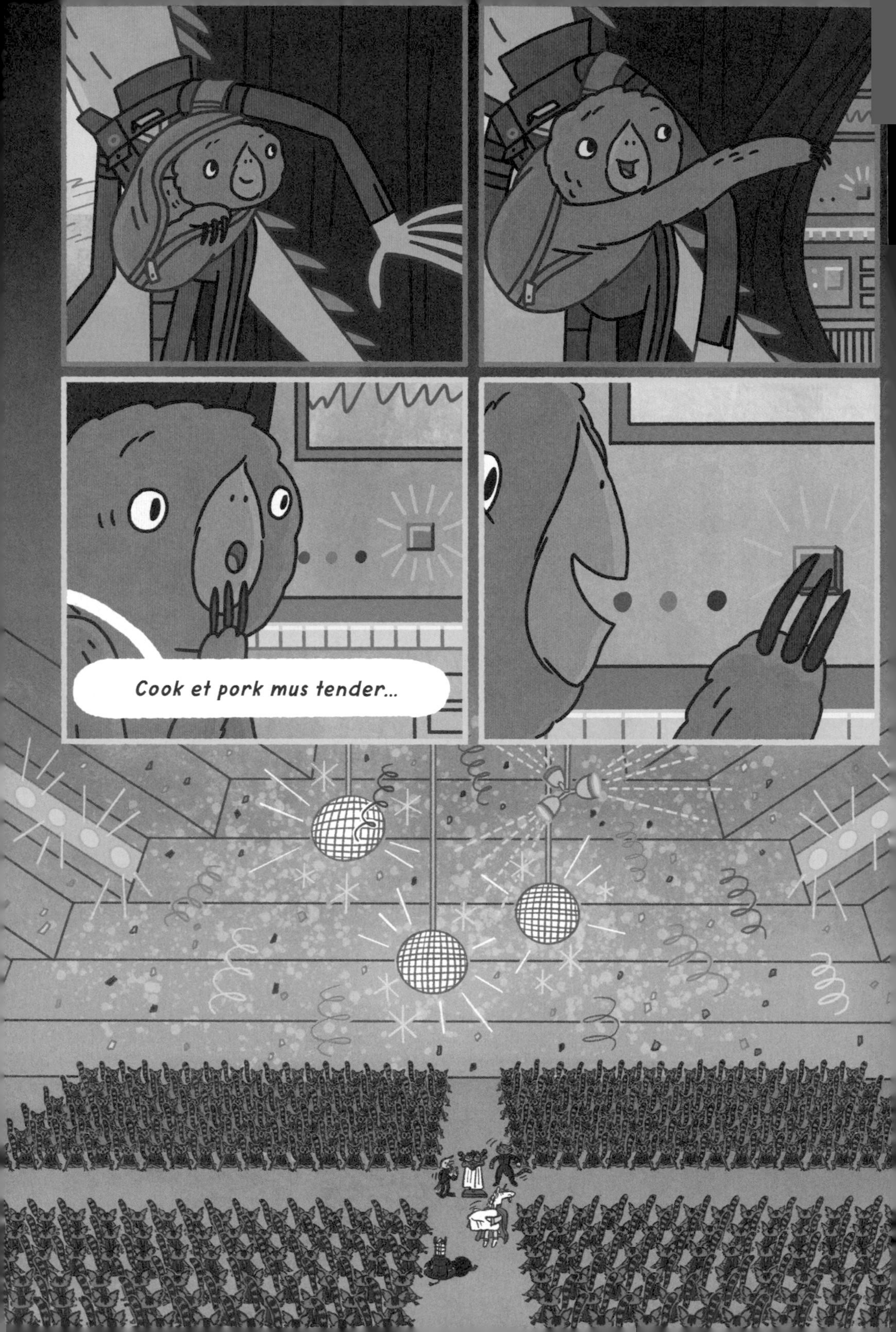
Cook et pork mus tender...

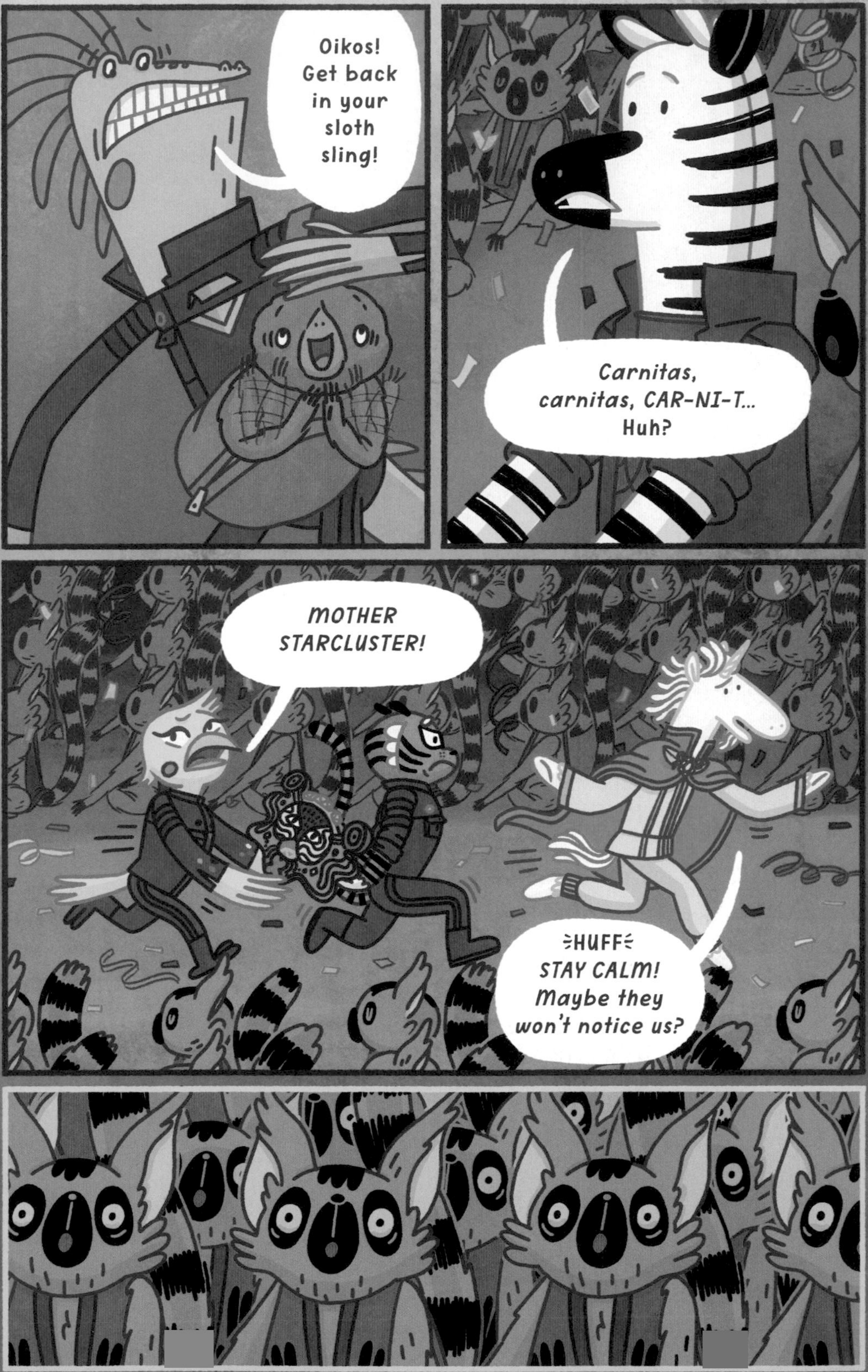
Oikos! Get back in your sloth sling!
Carnitas, carnitas, CAR-NI-T... Huh?
MOTHER STARCLUSTER!
HUFF
STAY CALM! Maybe they won't notice us?

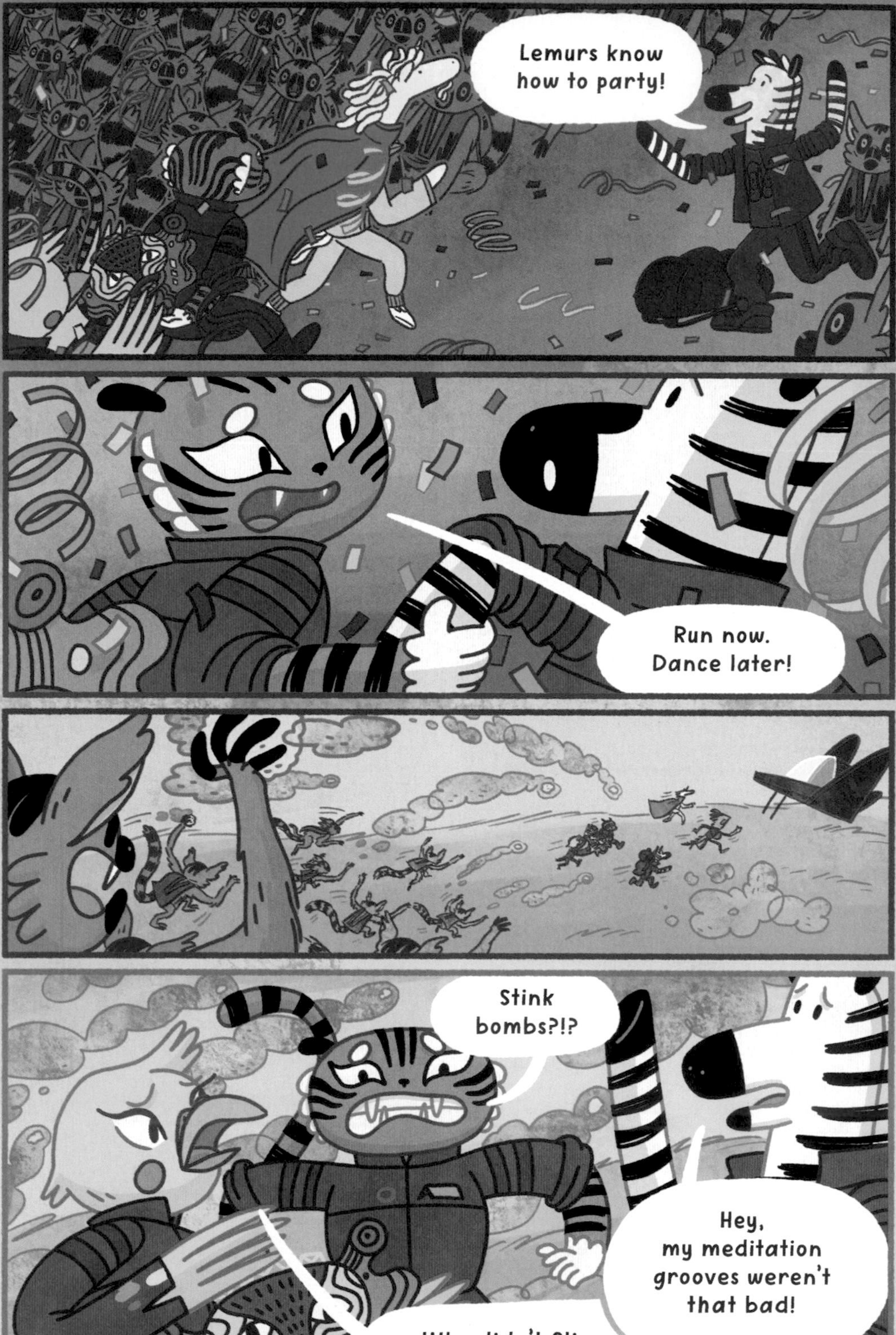
Lemurs know how to party!
Run now. Dance later!
Stink bombs?!?
Hey, my meditation grooves weren't that bad!
Why didn't Clio warn us about this?

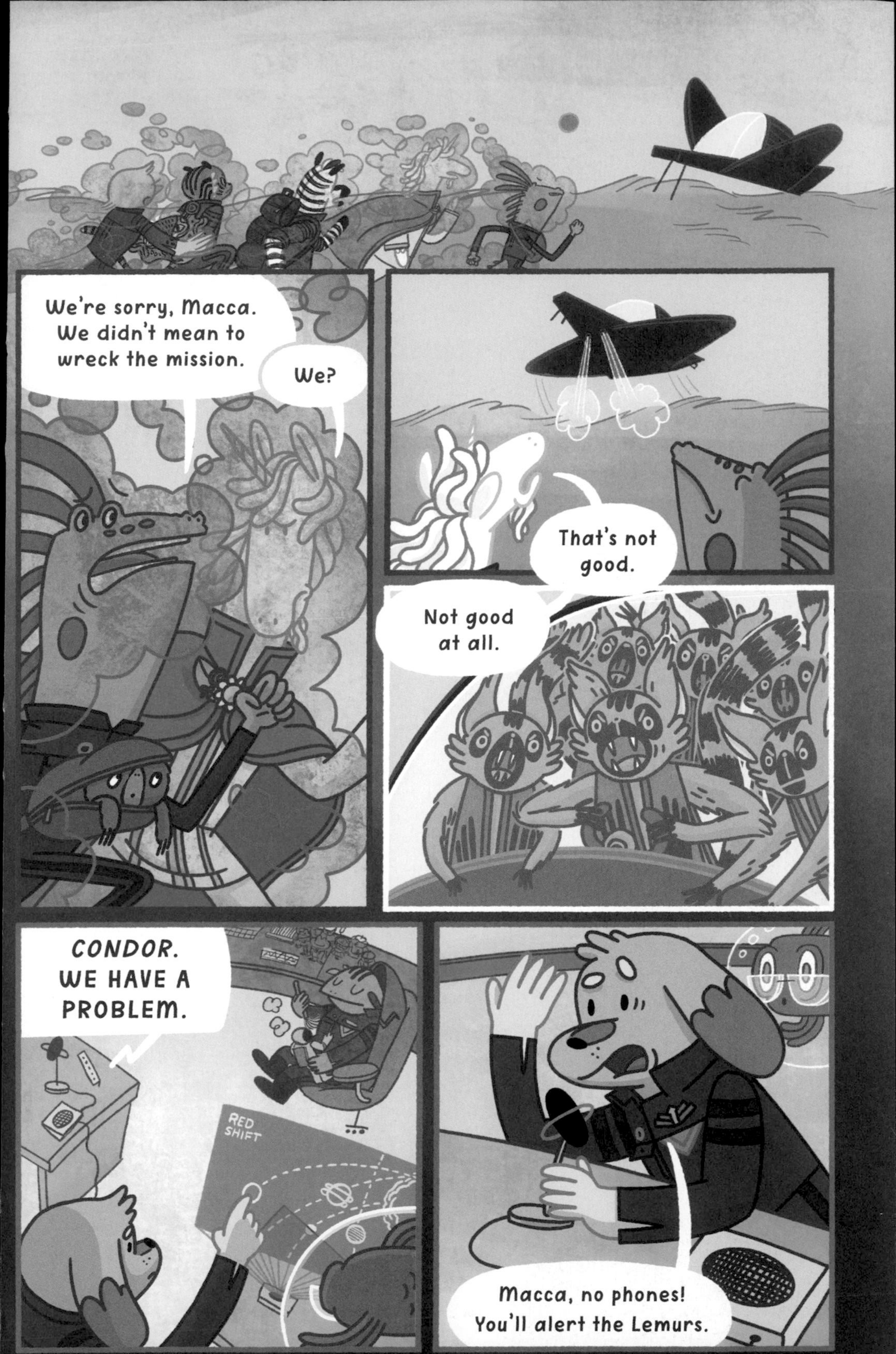
We're sorry, Macca. We didn't mean to wreck the mission.
We?
That's not good.
Not good at all.
CONDOR. WE HAVE A PROBLEM.
RED SHIFT
Macca, no phones! You'll alert the Lemurs.

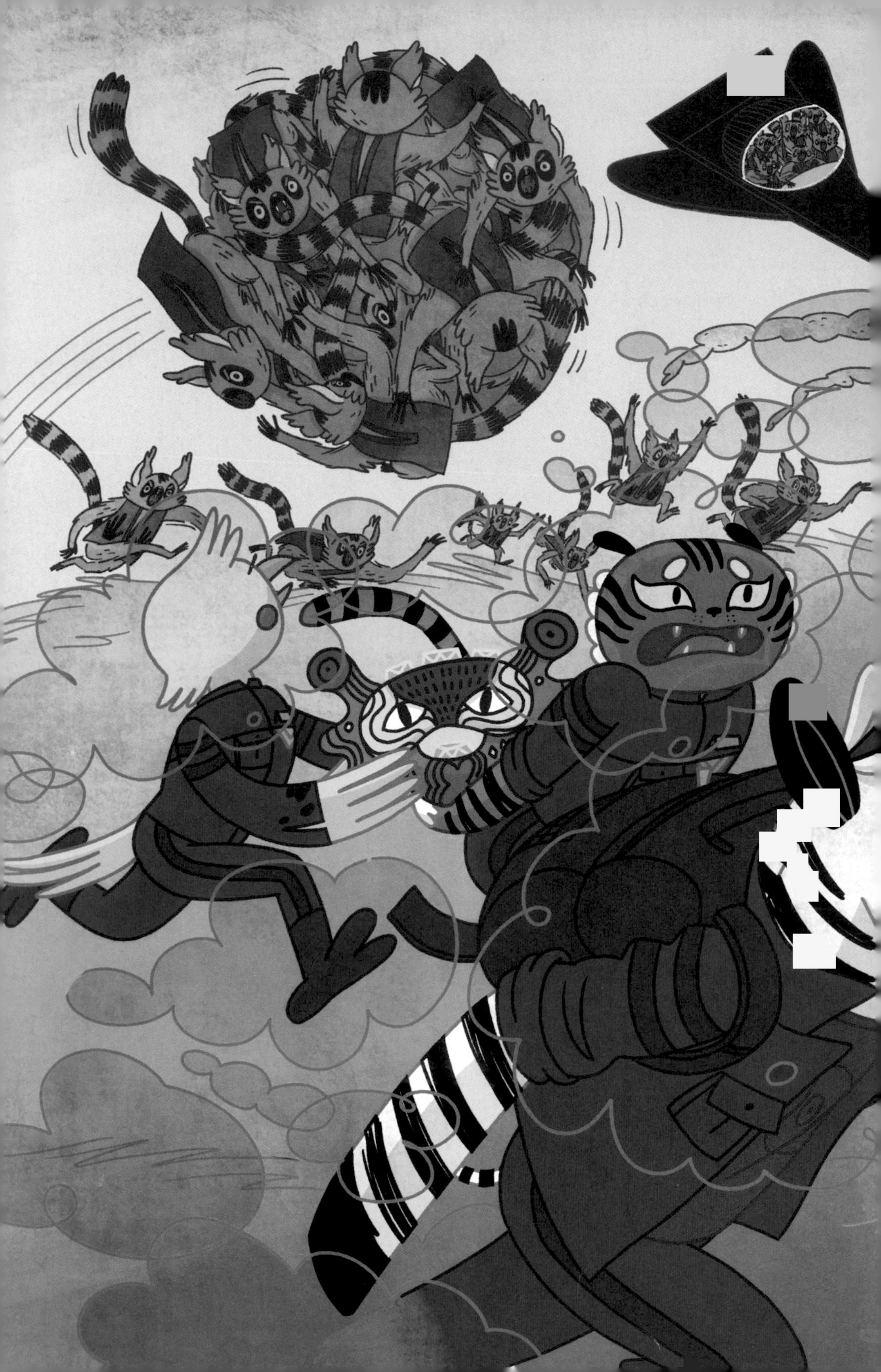

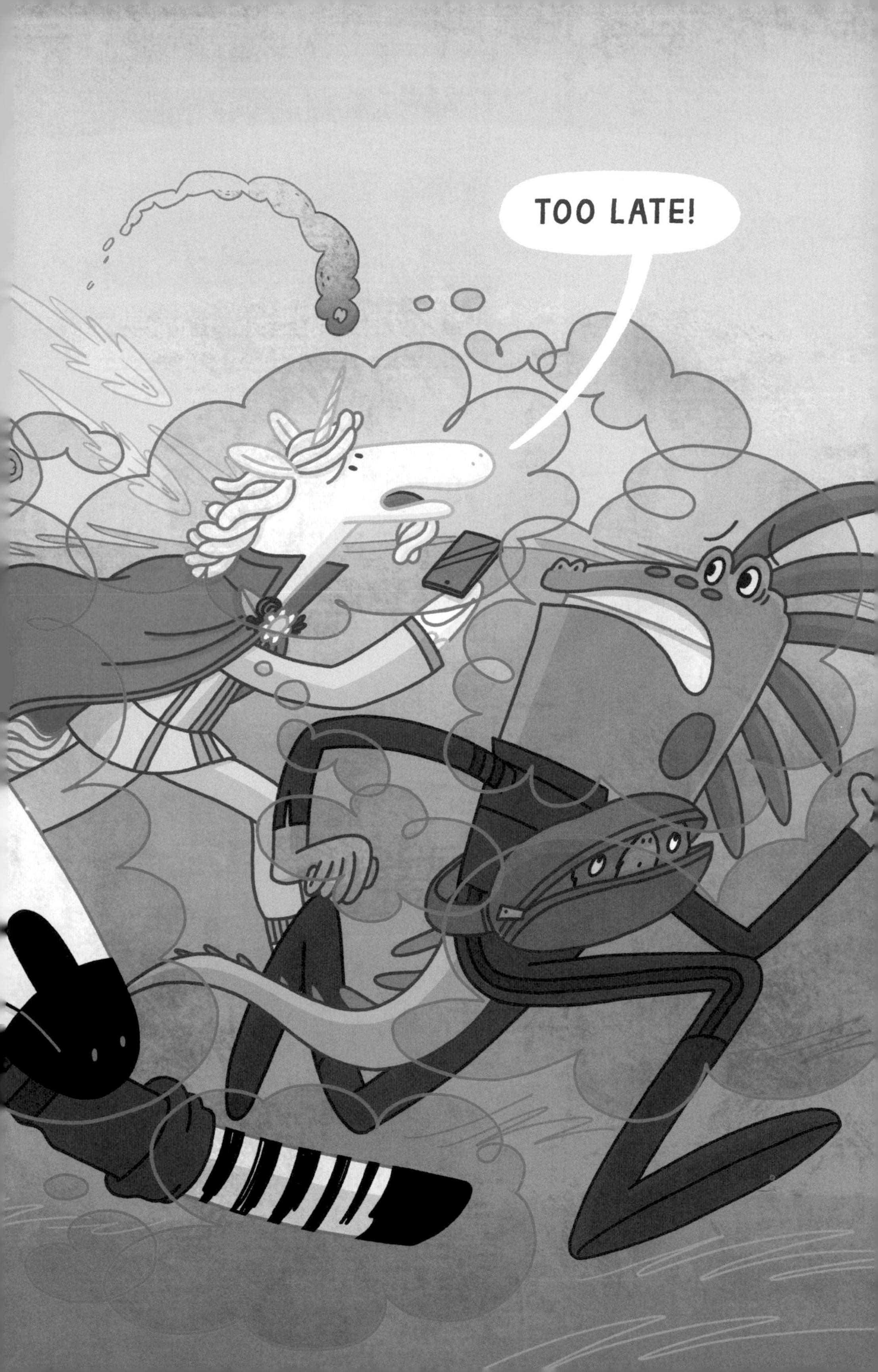
TOO LATE!

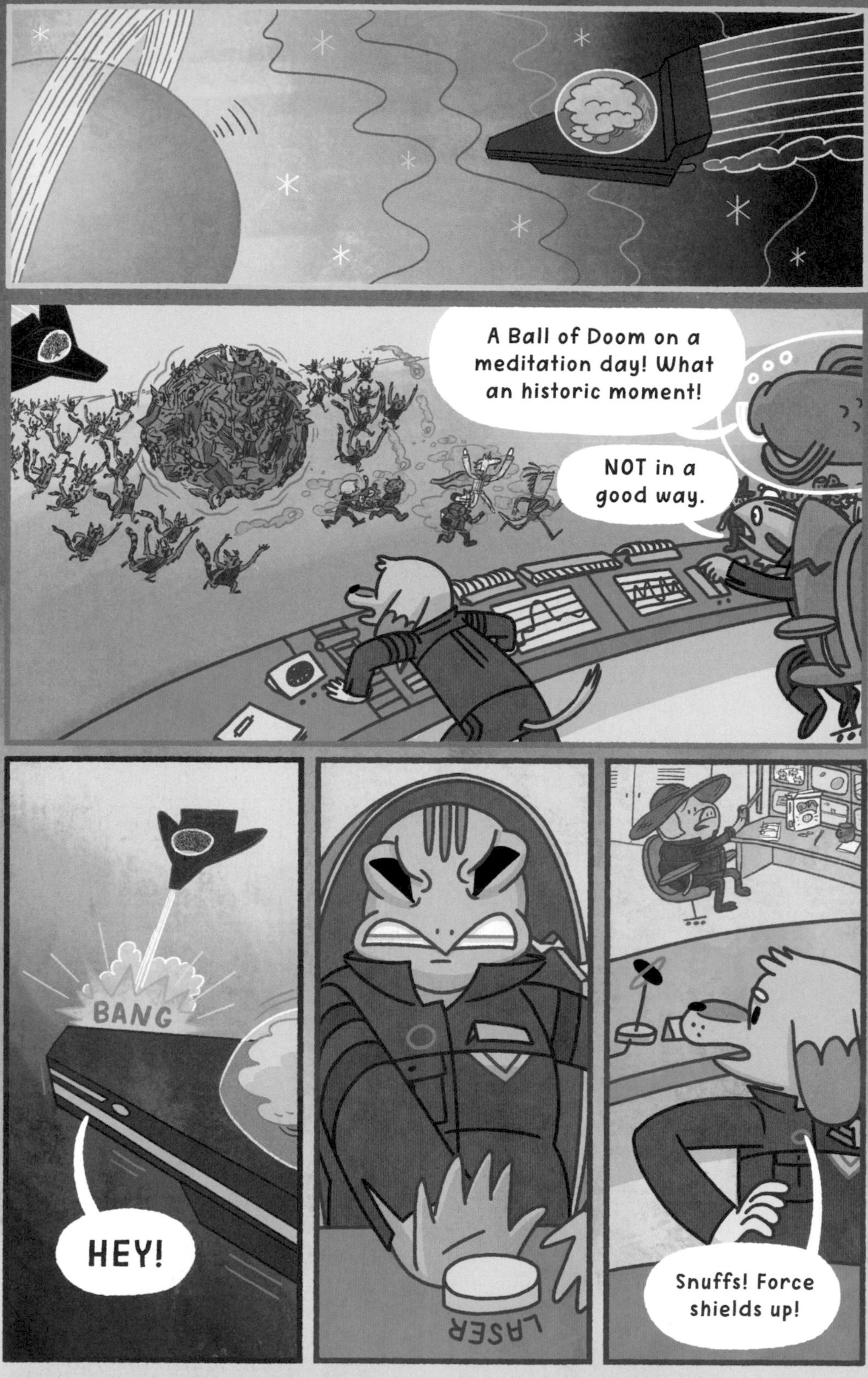
A Ball of Doom on a meditation day! What an historic moment!
NOT in a good way.
BANG
HEY!
LASER
Snuffs! Force shields up!

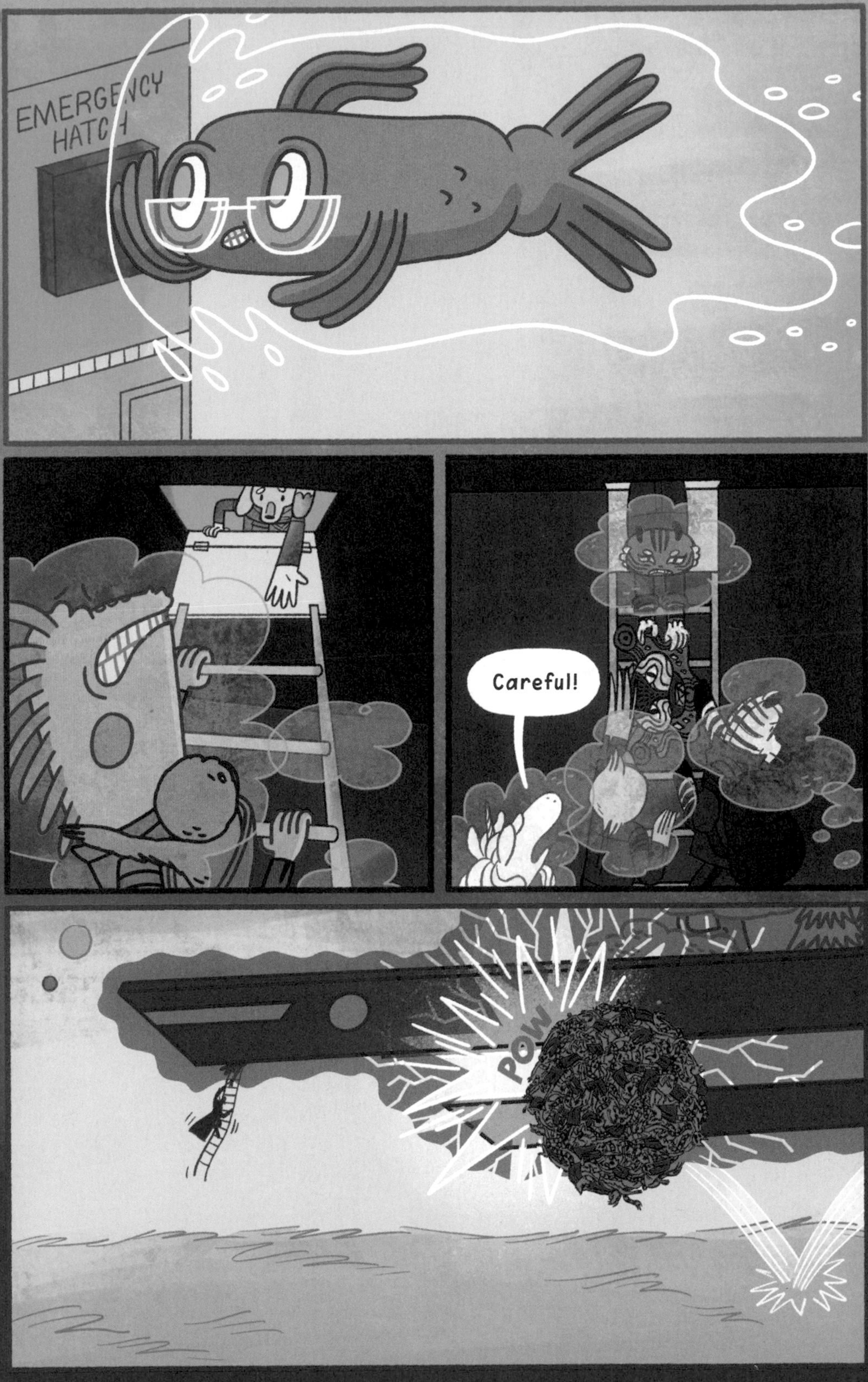
EMERGENCY HATCH
Careful!
POW

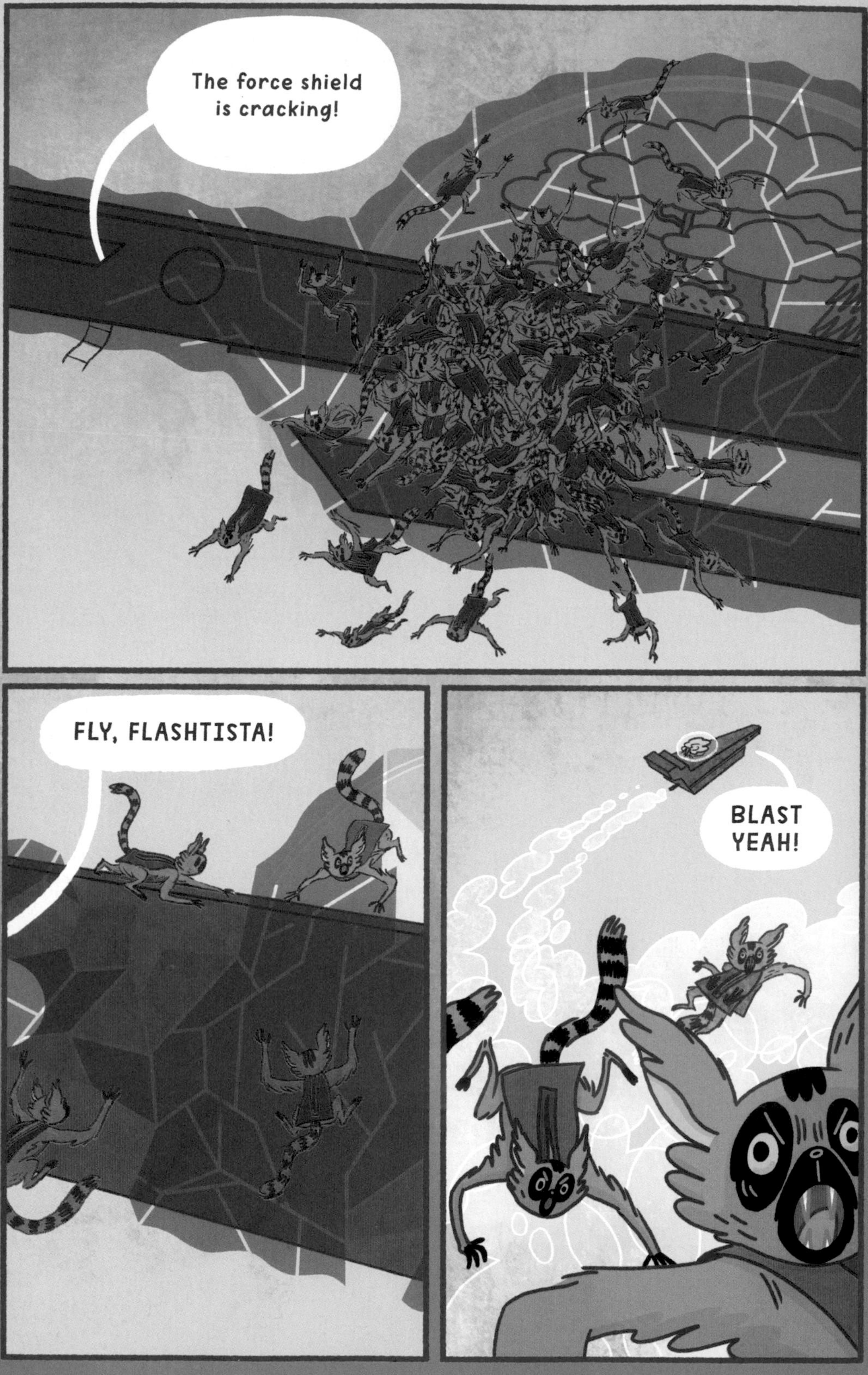
The force shield is cracking!
FLY, FLASHTISTA!
BLAST YEAH!

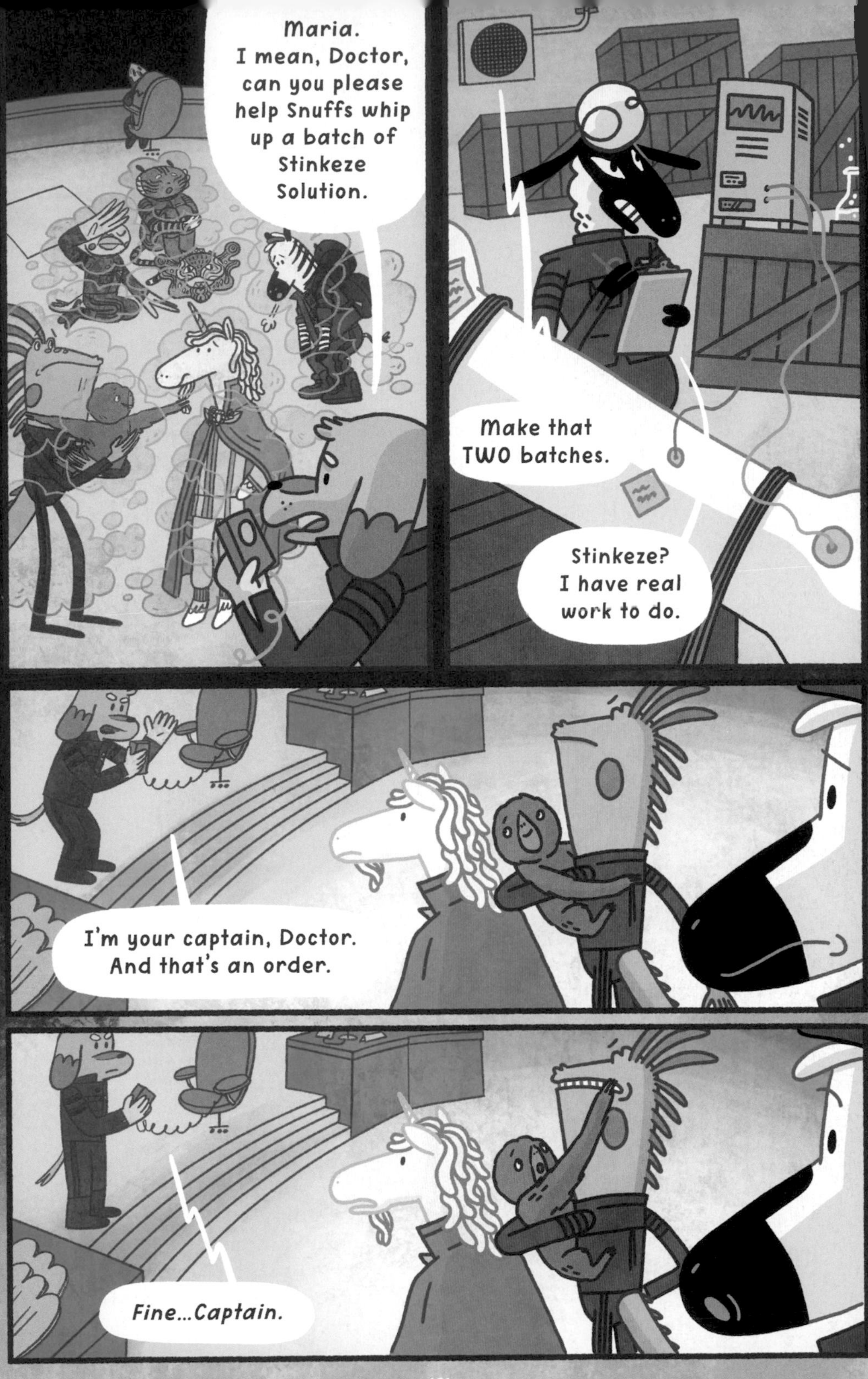
Maria.
I mean, Doctor, can you please help Snuffs whip up a batch of Stinkeze Solution.
Make that TWO batches.
Stinkeze? I have real work to do.
I'm your captain, Doctor. And that's an order.
Fine...Captain.

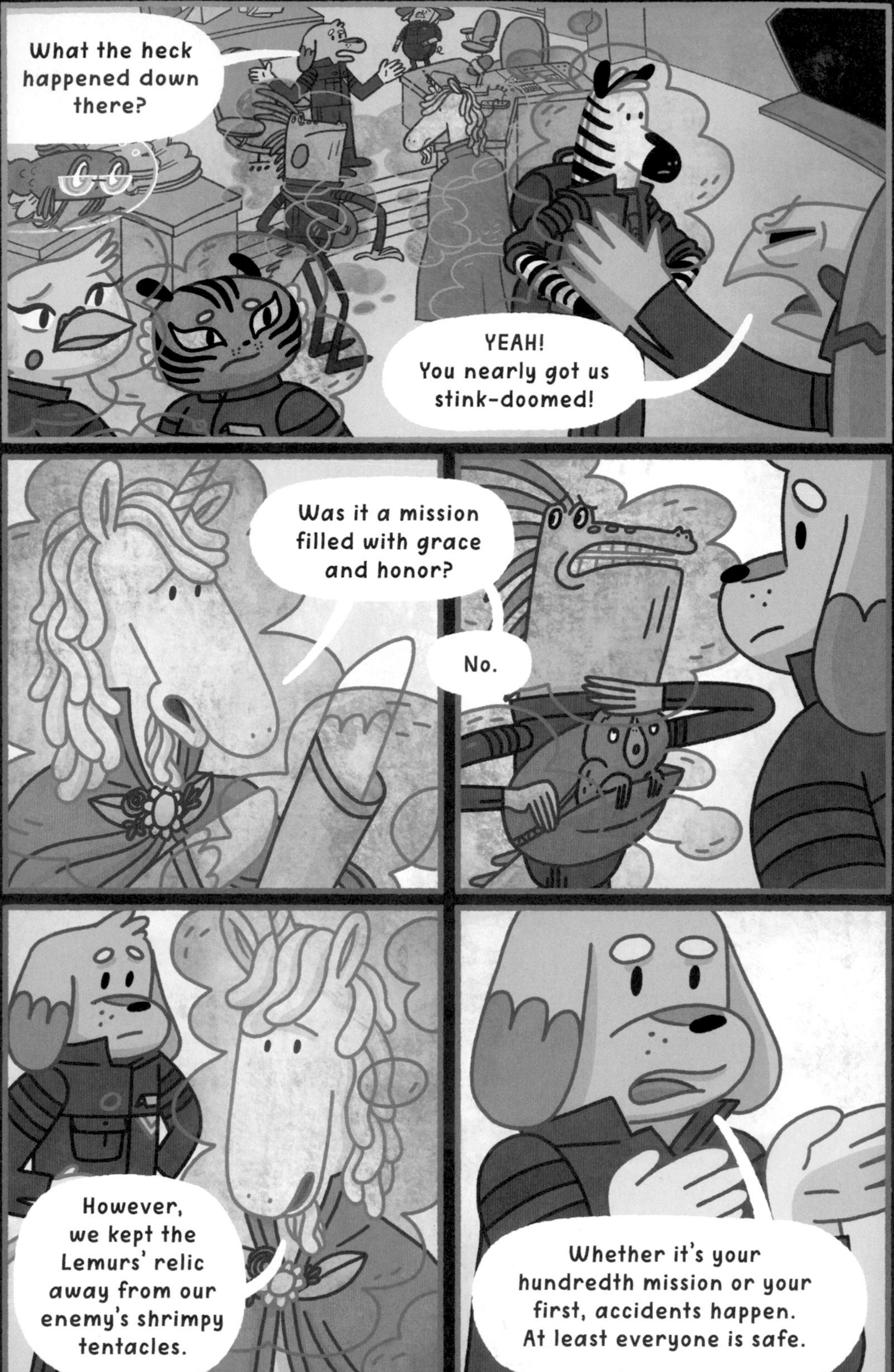
What the heck happened down there?
YEAH! You nearly got us stink-doomed!
Was it a mission filled with grace and honor?
No.
However, we kept the Lemurs' relic away from our enemy's shrimpy tentacles.
Whether it's your hundredth mission or your first, accidents happen. At least everyone is safe.

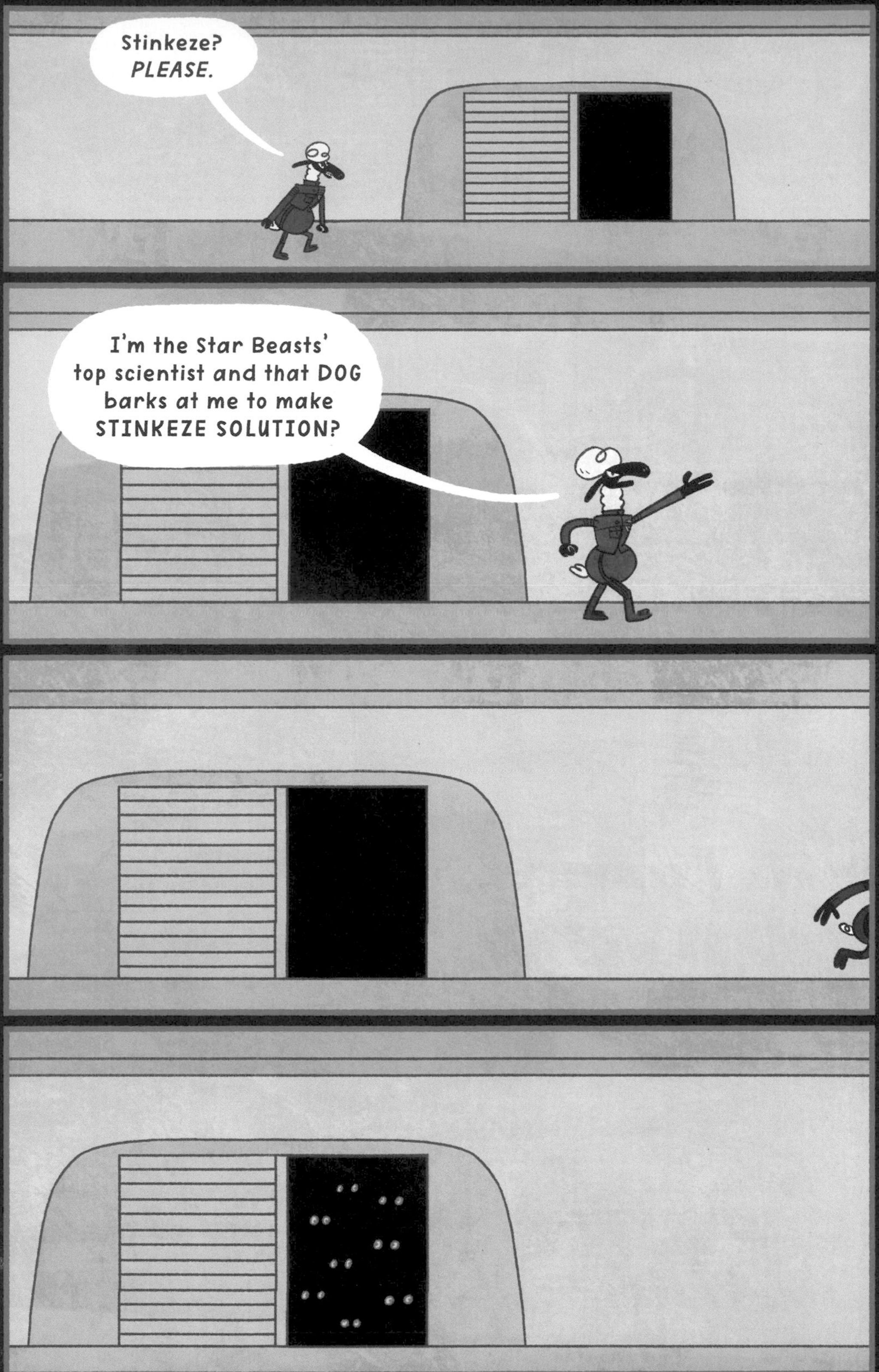
Stinkeze? PLEASE.
I'm the Star Beasts' top scientist and that DOG barks at me to make STINKEZE SOLUTION?

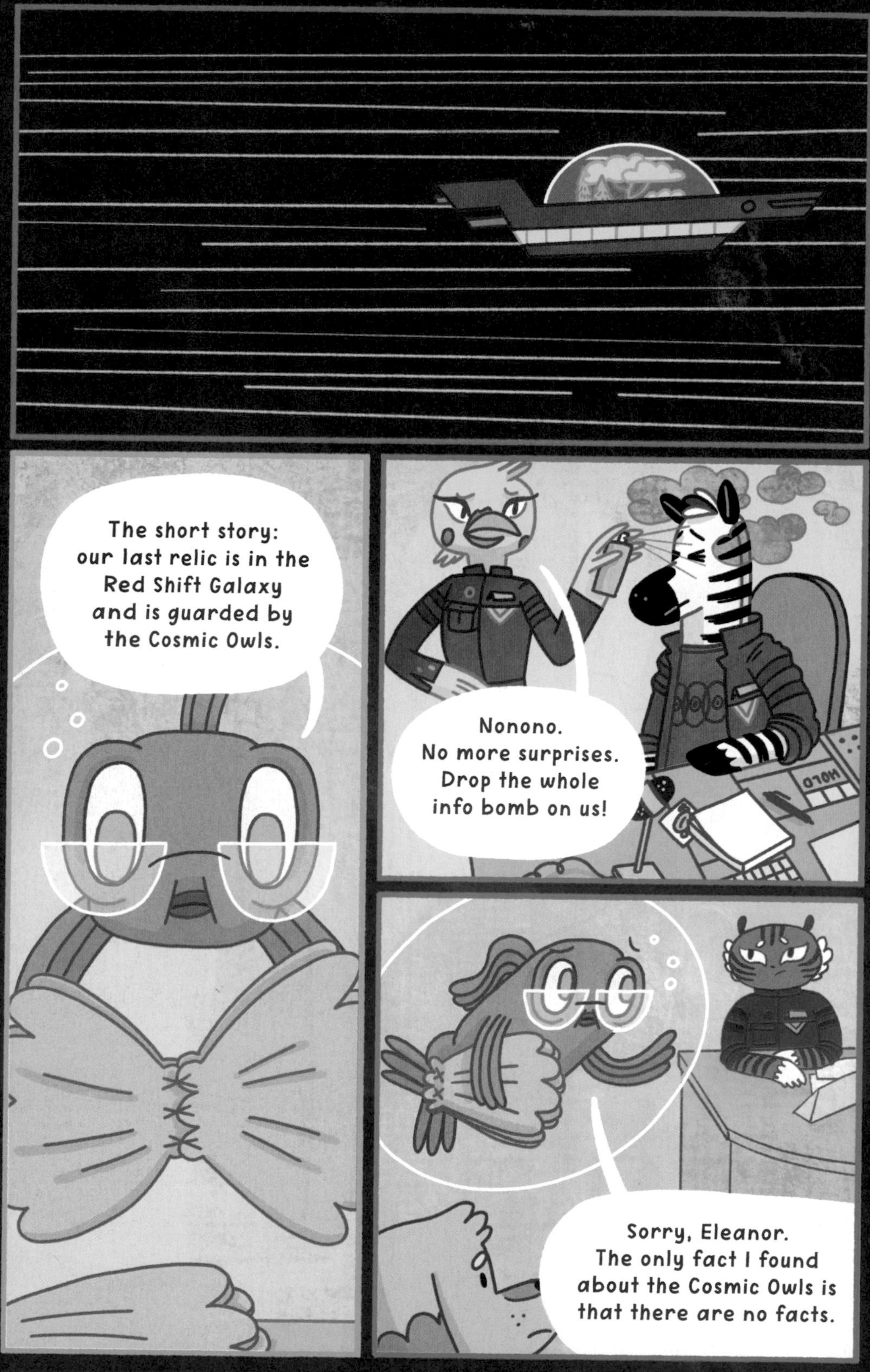
The short story: our last relic is in the Red Shift Galaxy and is guarded by the Cosmic Owls.
Nonono. No more surprises. Drop the whole info bomb on us!
Sorry, Eleanor. The only fact I found about the Cosmic Owls is that there are no facts.

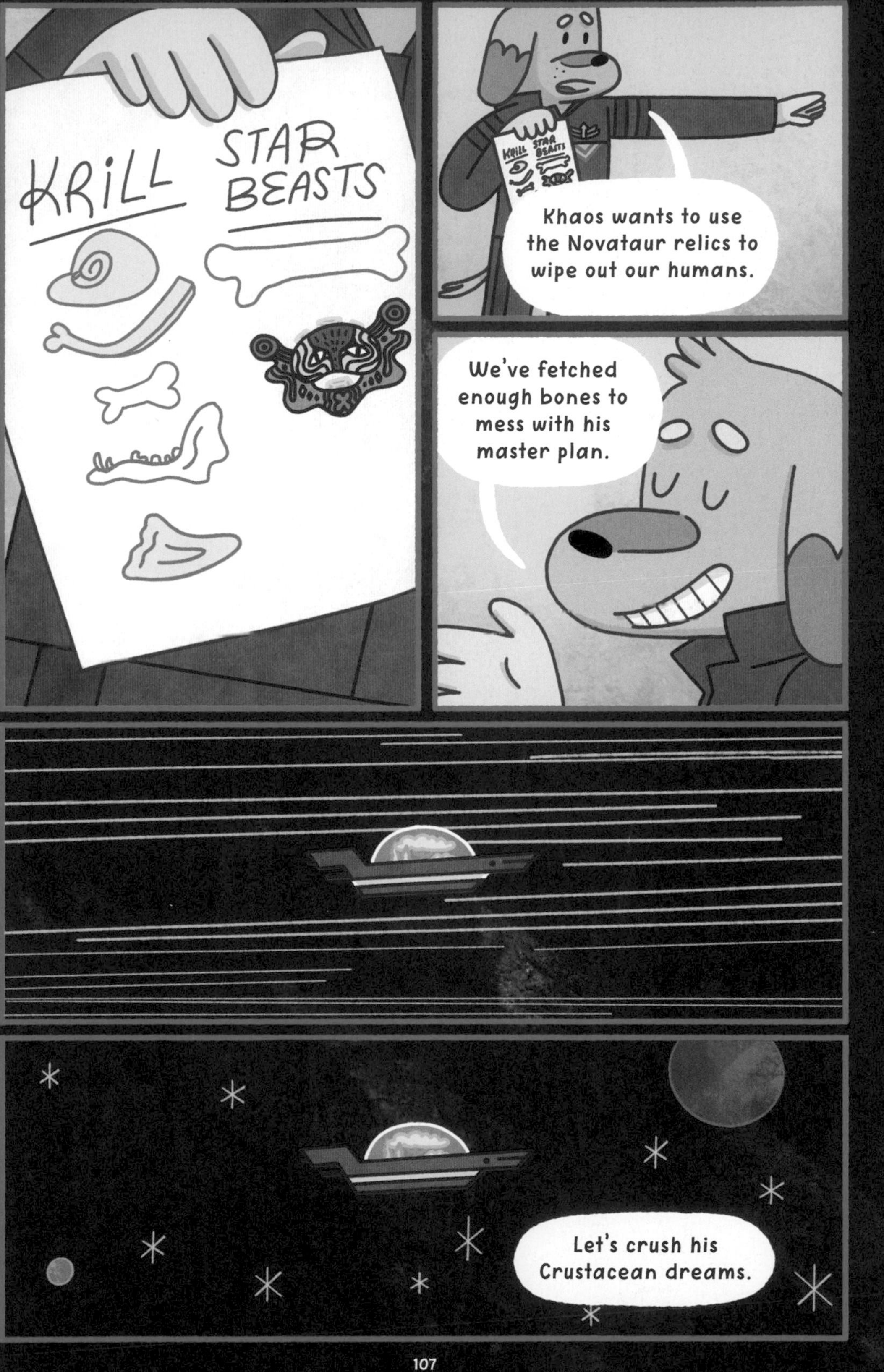
KRILL
STAR BEASTS
Khaos wants to use the Novataur relics to wipe out our humans.
We've fetched enough bones to mess with his master plan.
Let's crush his Crustacean dreams.

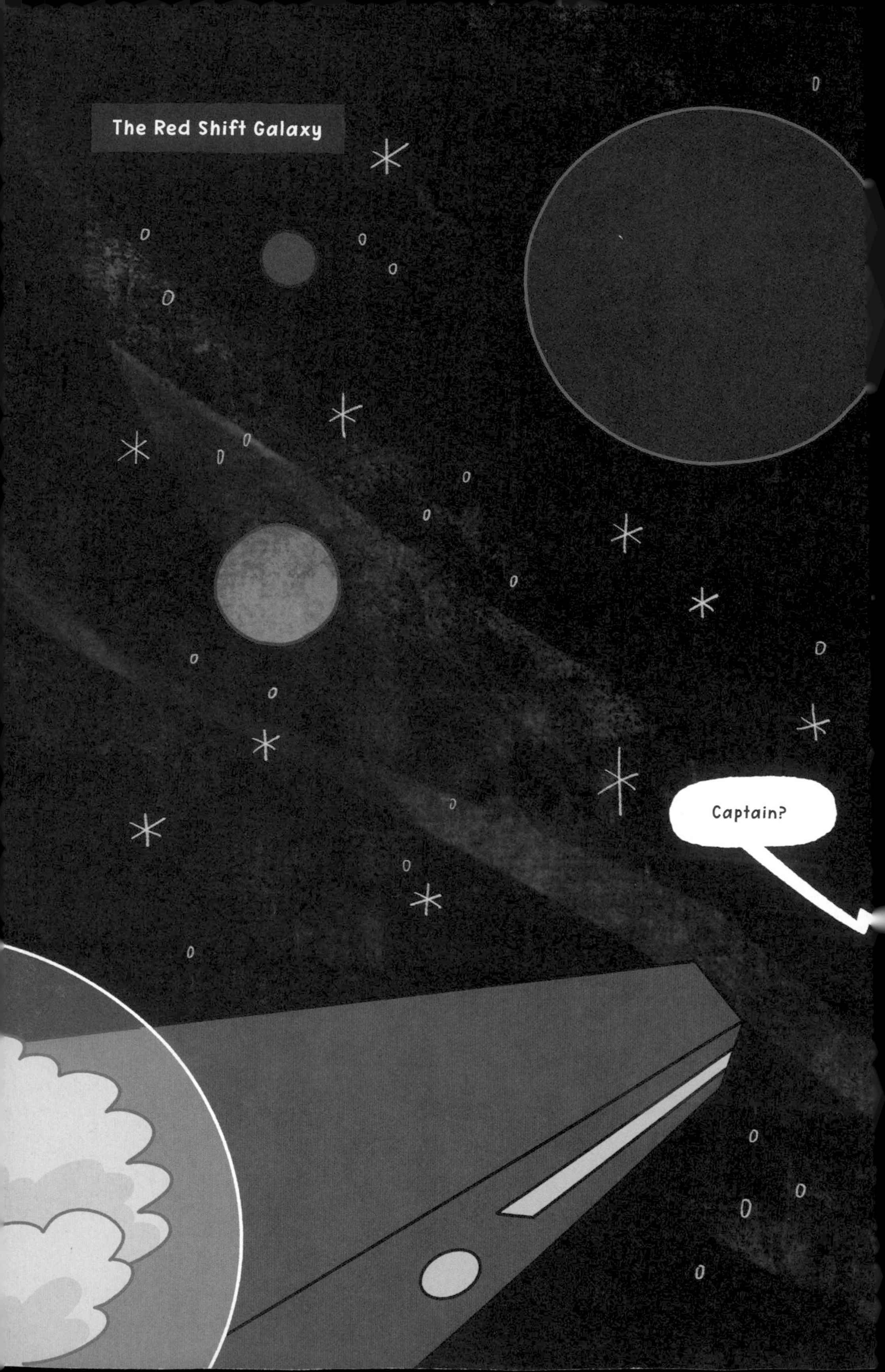
The Red Shift Galaxy
Captain?

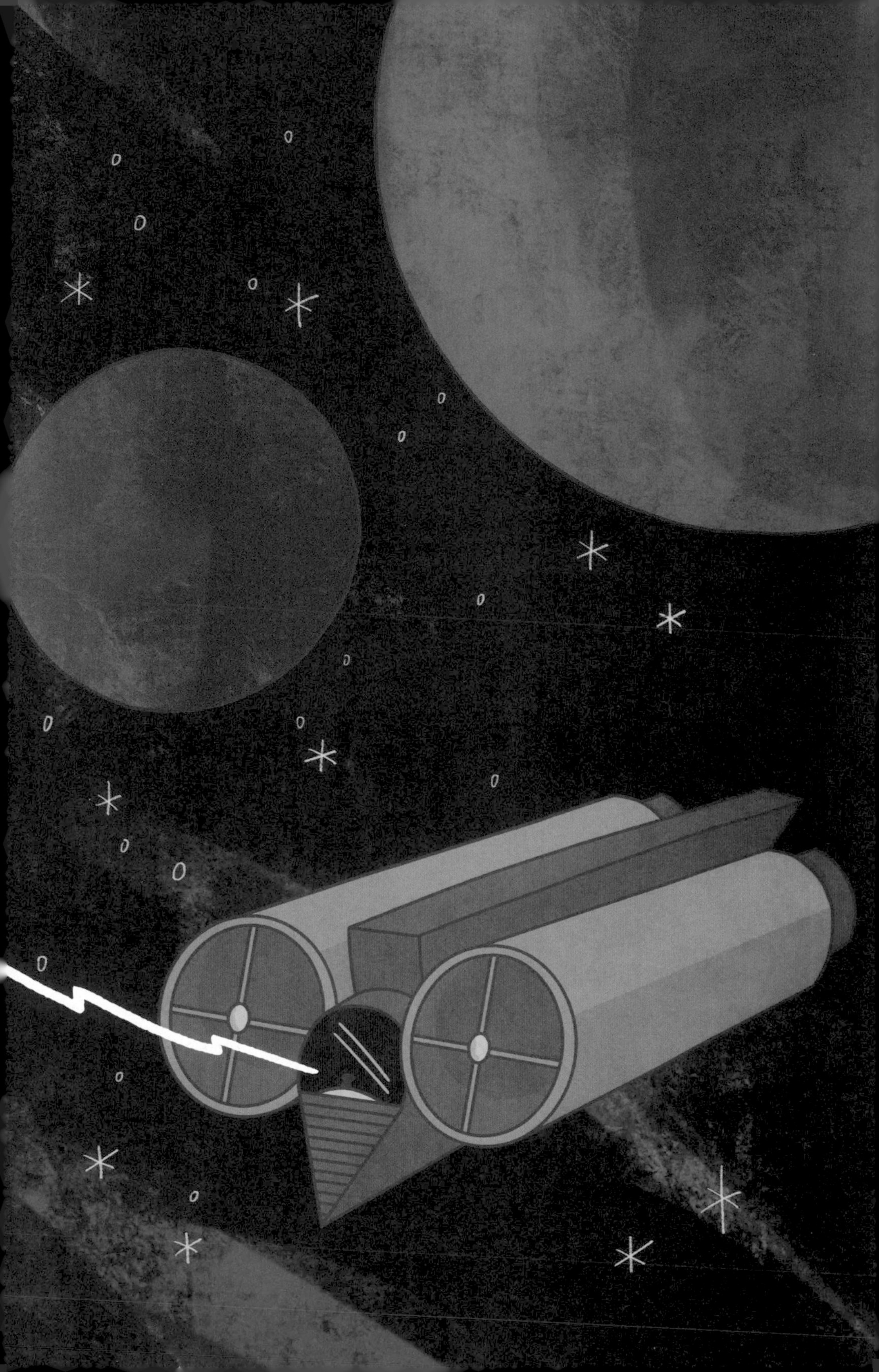

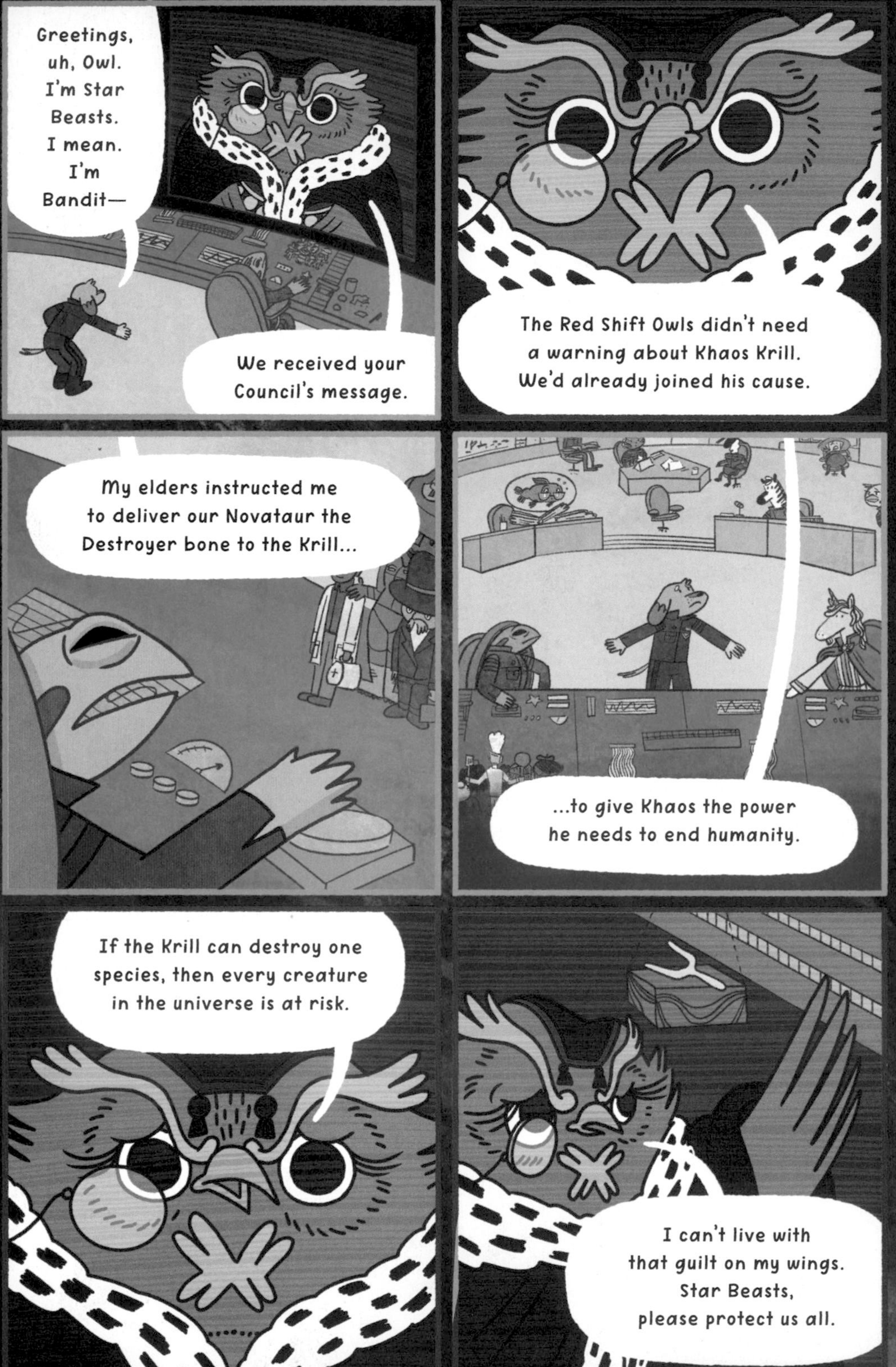
Greetings, uh, Owl. I'm Star Beasts. I mean. I'm Bandit—
We received your Council's message.
The Red Shift Owls didn't need a warning about Khaos Krill. We'd already joined his cause.
My elders instructed me to deliver our Novataur the Destroyer bone to the Krill...
...to give Khaos the power he needs to end humanity.
If the Krill can destroy one species, then every creature in the universe is at risk.
I can't live with that guilt on my wings. Star Beasts, please protect us all.

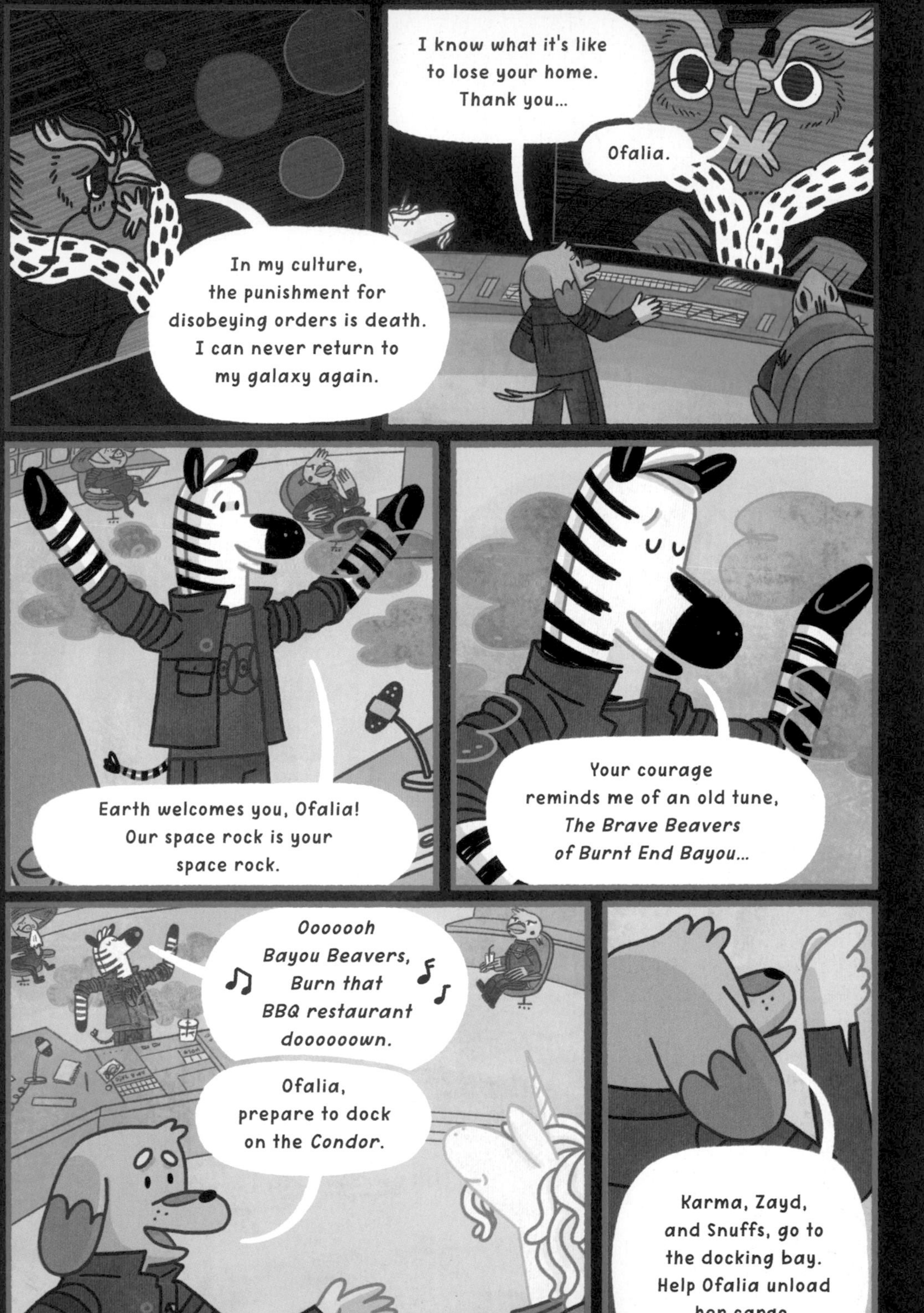
In my culture, the punishment for disobeying orders is death. I can never return to my galaxy again.
I know what it's like to lose your home. Thank you...
Ofalia.
Earth welcomes you, Ofalia! Our space rock is your space rock.
Your courage reminds me of an old tune, *The Brave Beavers of Burnt End Bayou*...
Ooooooh Bayou Beavers, Burn that BBQ restaurant doooooown.
Ofalia, prepare to dock on the *Condor*.
Karma, Zayd, and Snuffs, go to the docking bay. Help Ofalia unload her cargo.

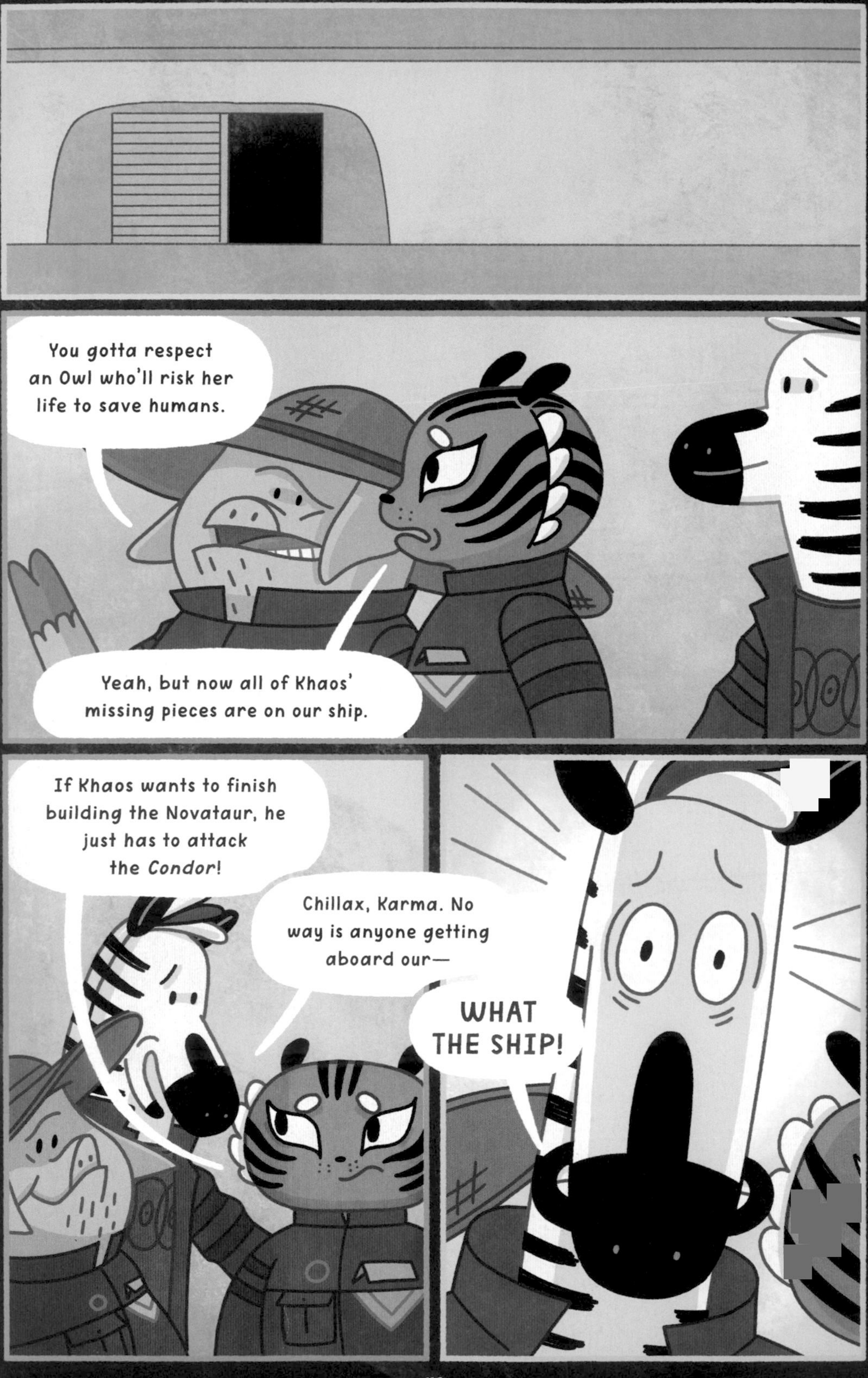
You gotta respect an Owl who'll risk her life to save humans.
Yeah, but now all of Khaos' missing pieces are on our ship.
If Khaos wants to finish building the Novataur, he just has to attack the *Condor*!
Chillax, Karma. No way is anyone getting aboard our—
WHAT THE SHIP!

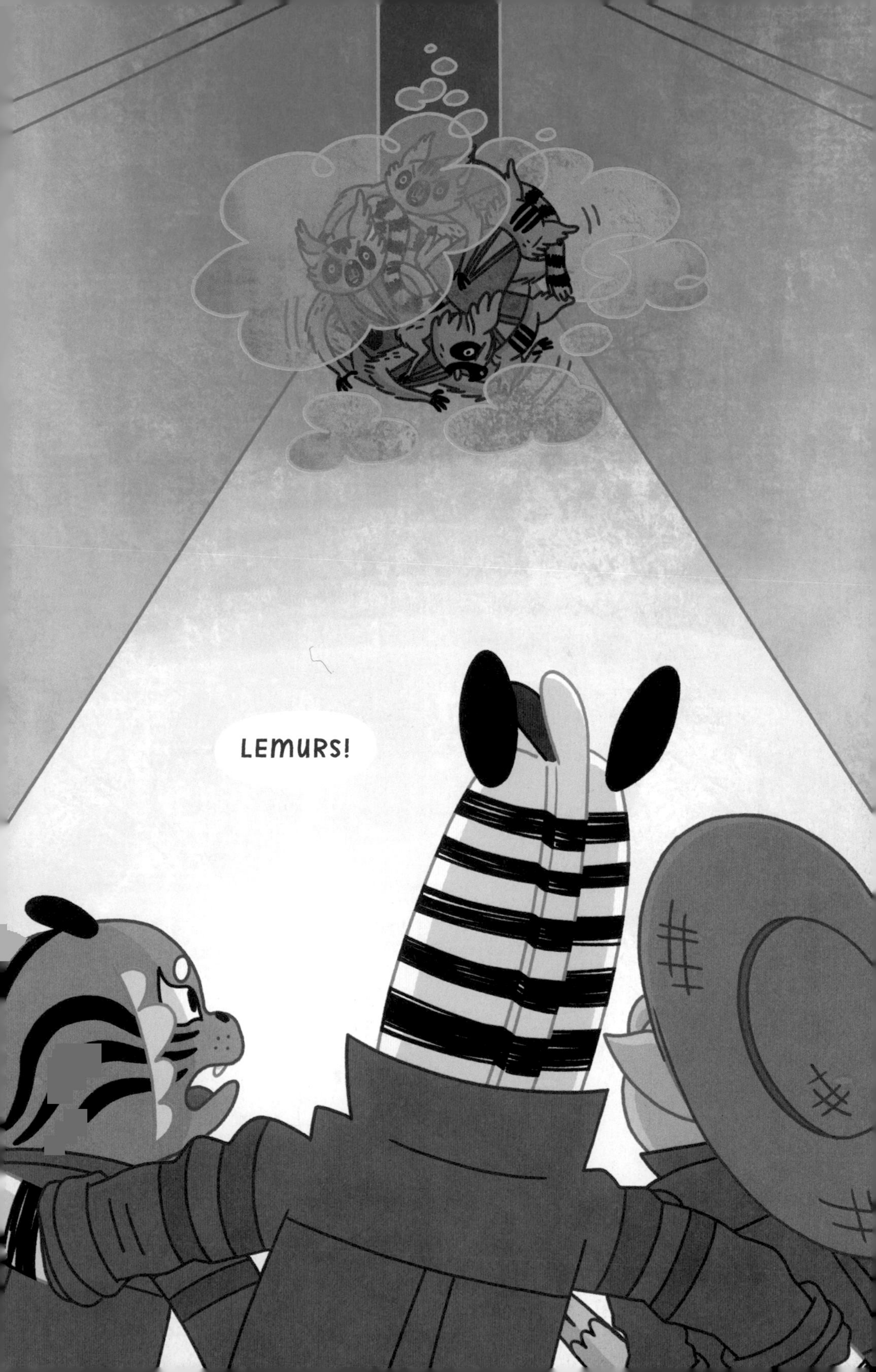
LEMURS!

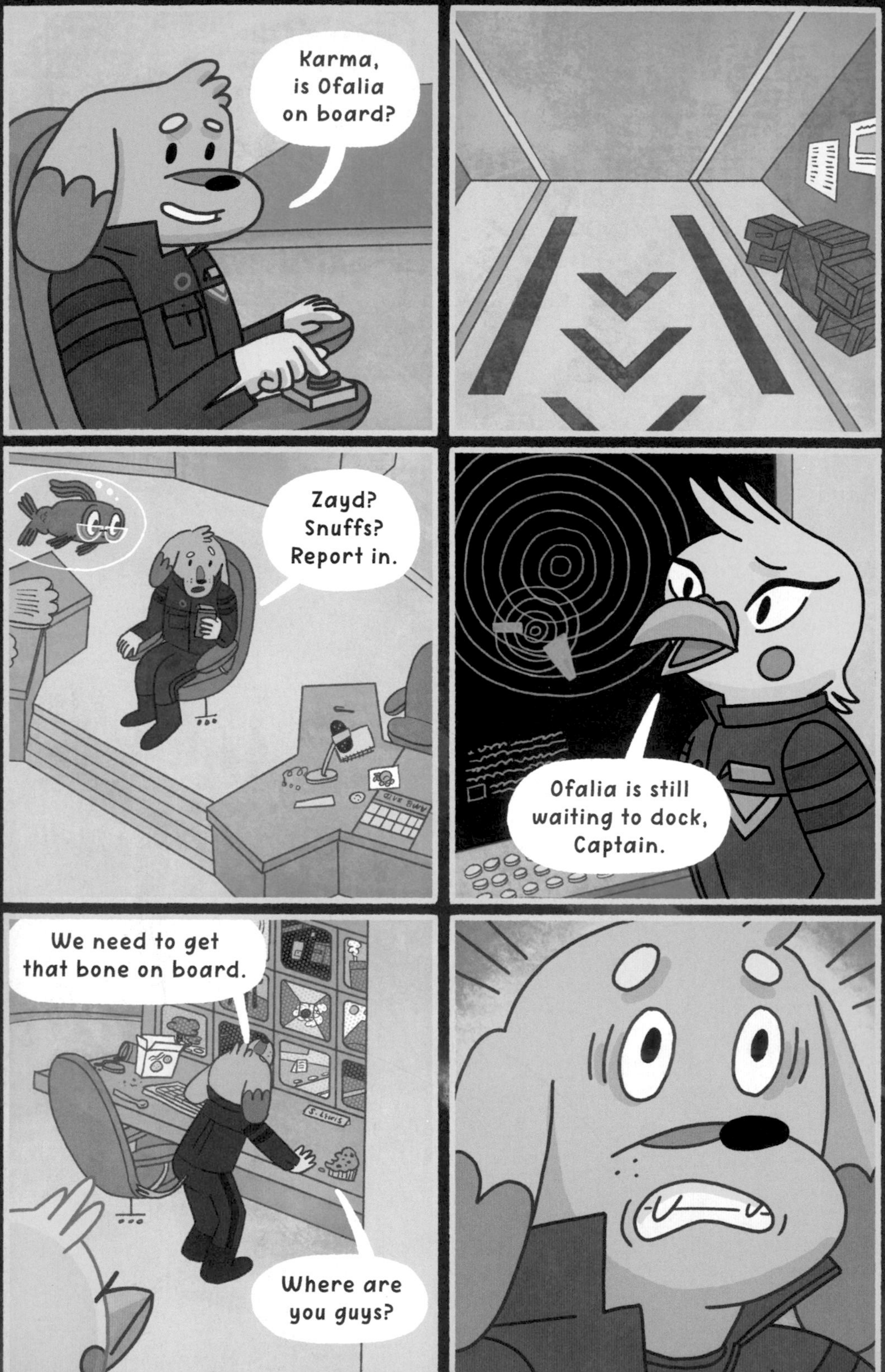
Karma, is Ofalia on board?
Zayd? Snuffs? Report in.
Ofalia is still waiting to dock, Captain.
We need to get that bone on board.
Where are you guys?

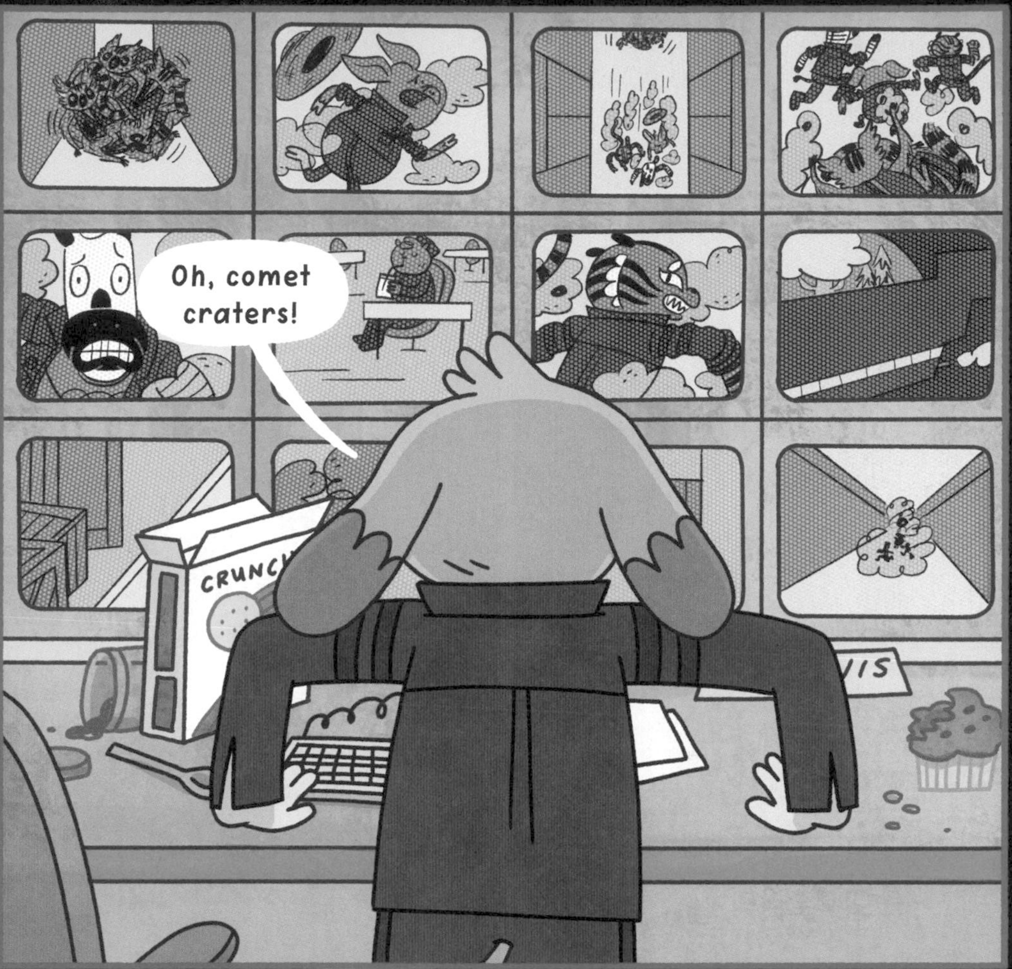
Oh, comet craters!
CRUNCH
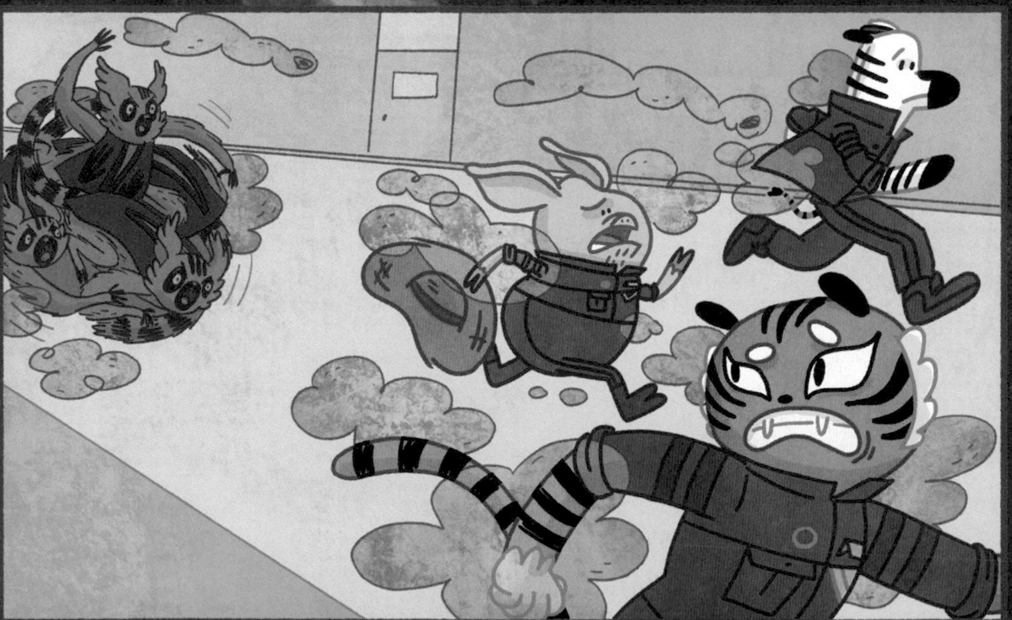

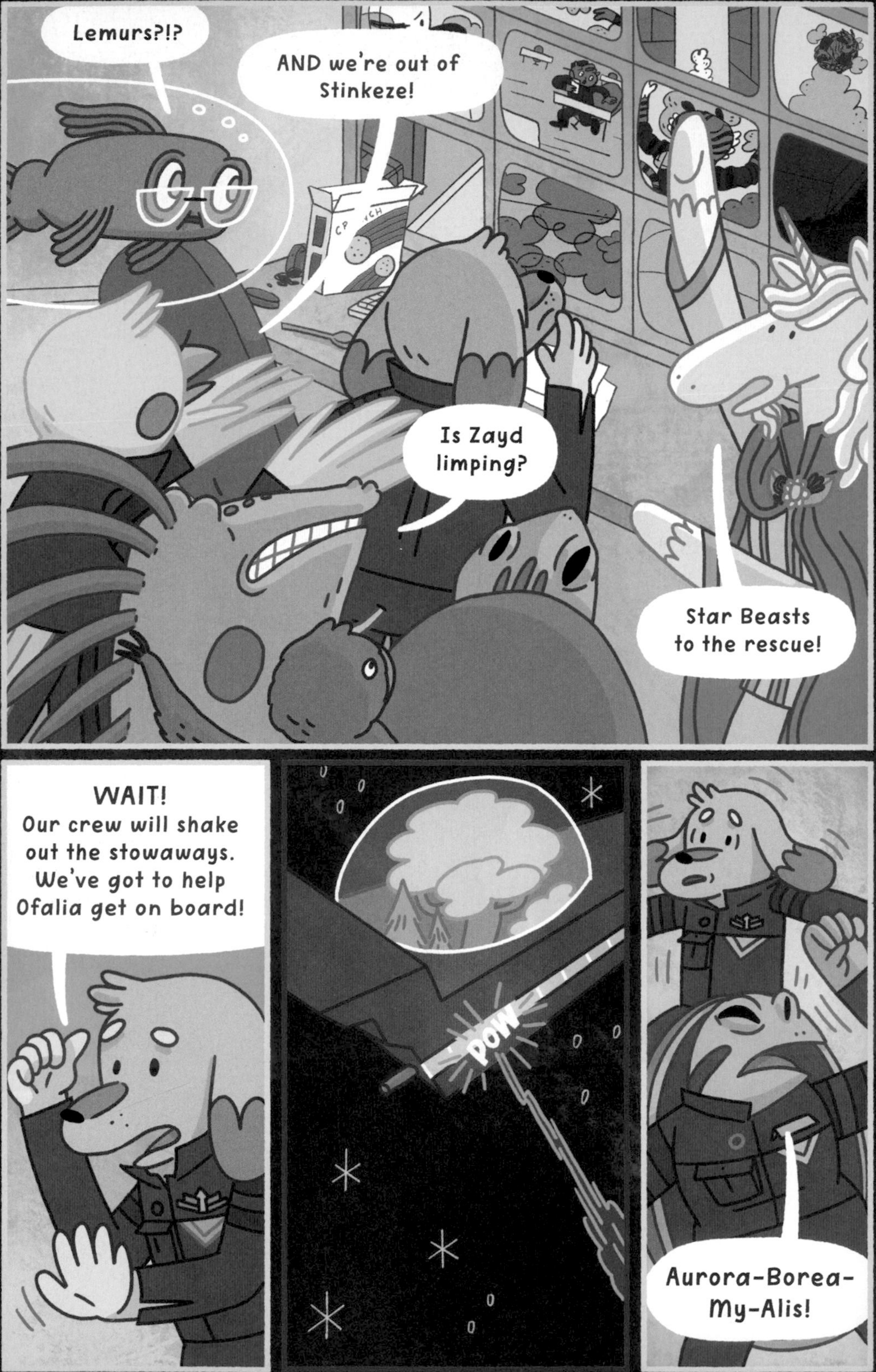
Lemurs?!?
AND we're out of Stinkeze!
Is Zayd limping?
Star Beasts to the rescue!
WAIT! Our crew will shake out the stowaways. We've got to help Ofalia get on board!
POW
Aurora-Borea-My-Alis!

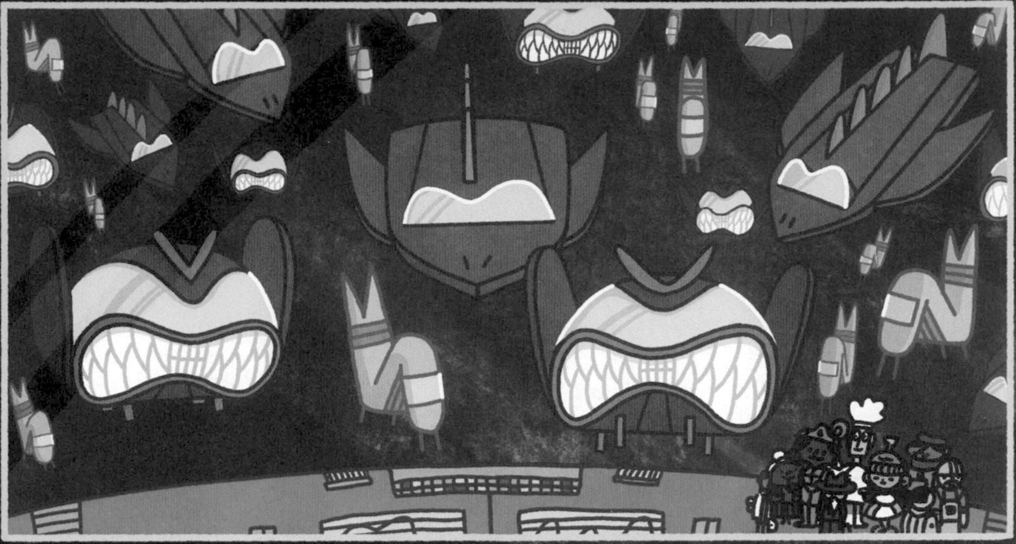

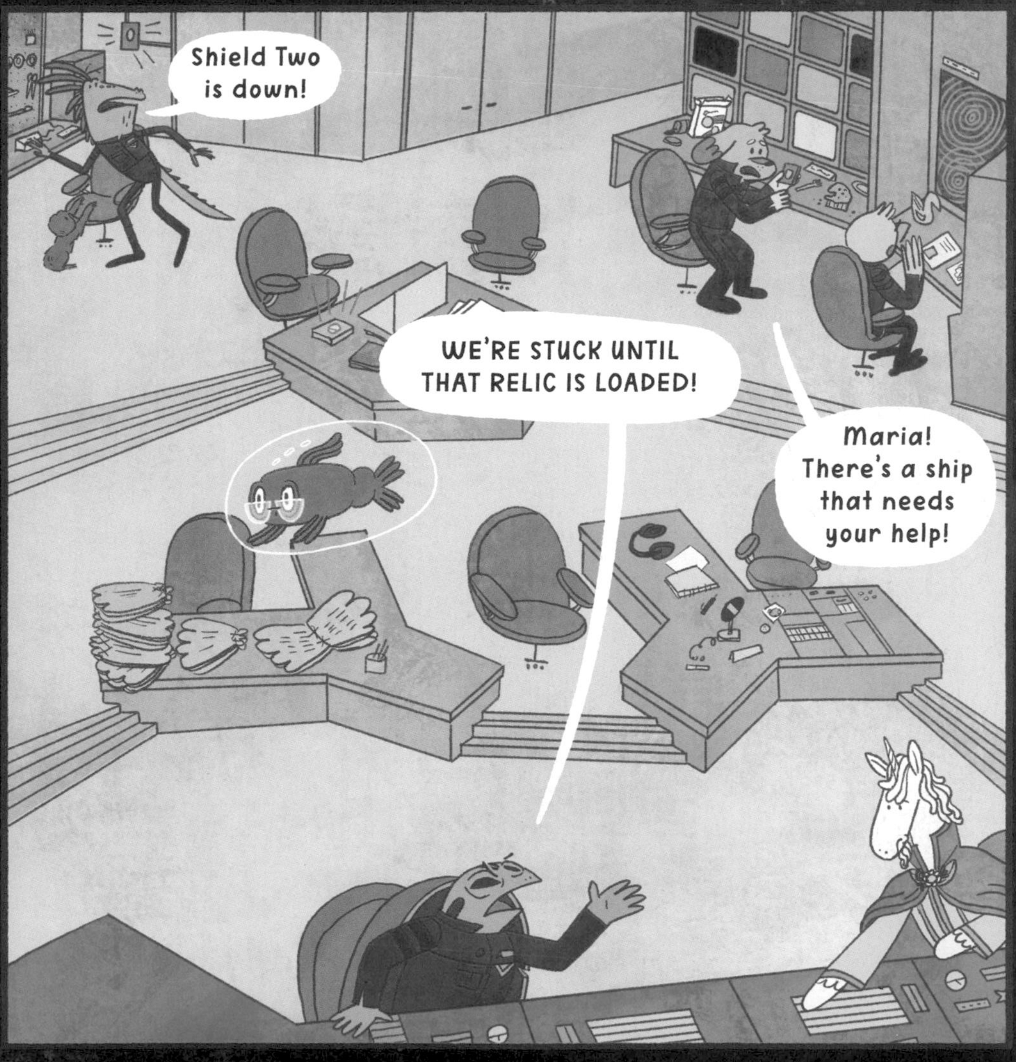
Shield Two is down!
WE'RE STUCK UNTIL THAT RELIC IS LOADED!
Maria! There's a ship that needs your help!

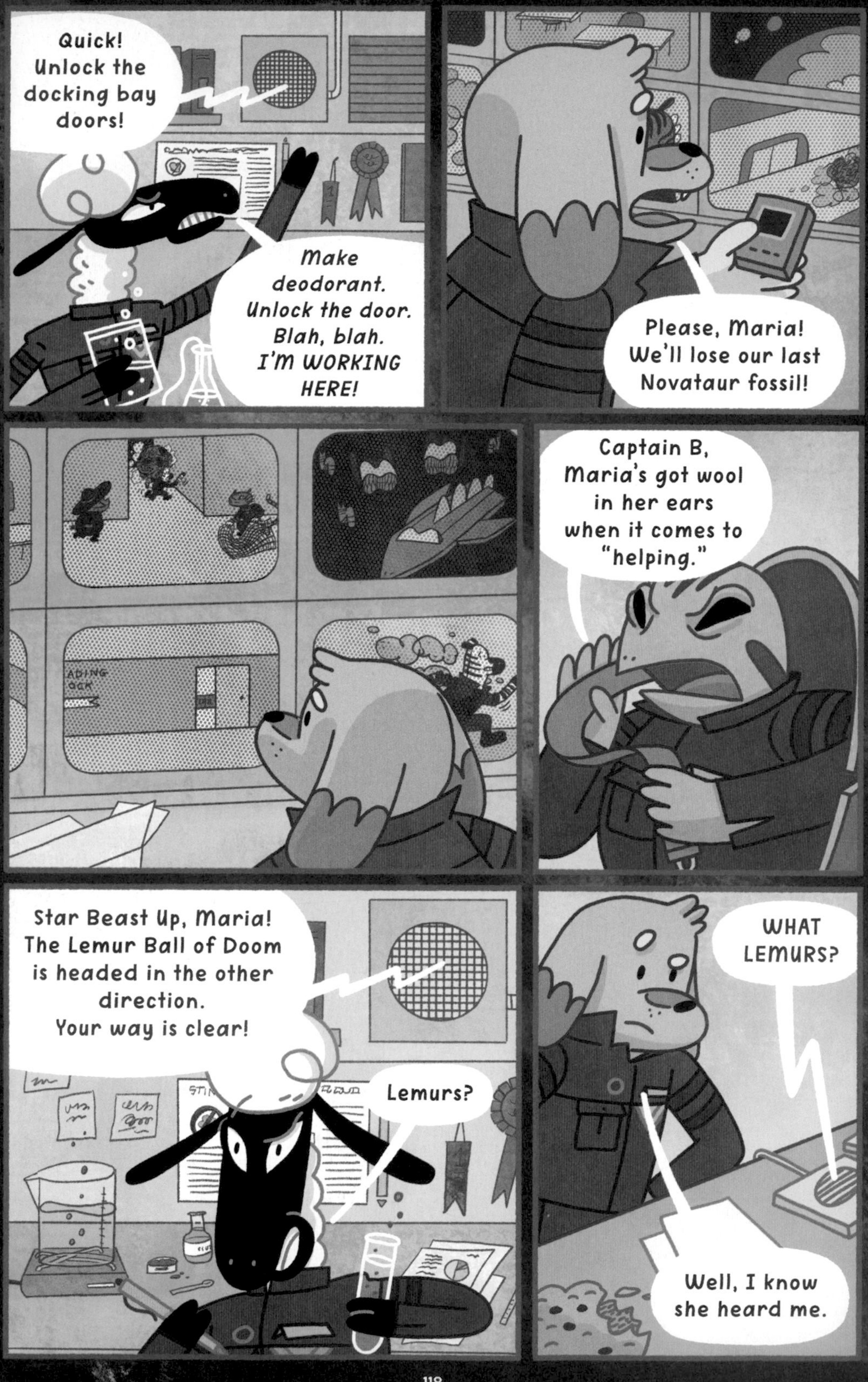

Quick! Unlock the docking bay doors!
Make deodorant. Unlock the door. Blah, blah. I'M WORKING HERE!
Please, Maria! We'll lose our last Novataur fossil!
Captain B, Maria's got wool in her ears when it comes to "helping."
Star Beast Up, Maria! The Lemur Ball of Doom is headed in the other direction. Your way is clear!
Lemurs?
WHAT LEMURS?
Well, I know she heard me.

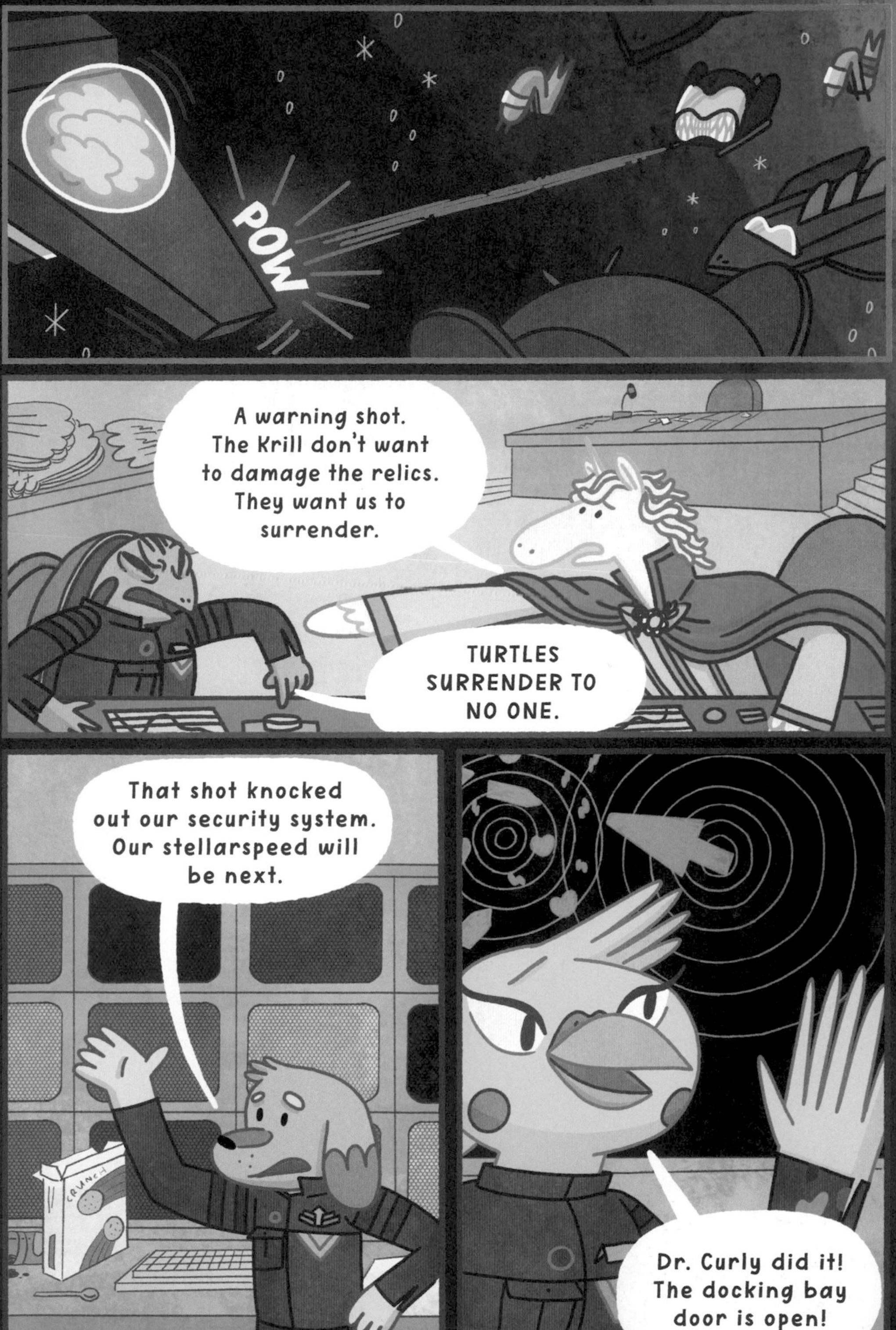
POW
A warning shot. The Krill don't want to damage the relics. They want us to surrender.
TURTLES SURRENDER TO NO ONE.
That shot knocked out our security system. Our stellarspeed will be next.
CRUNCH
Dr. Curly did it! The docking bay door is open!

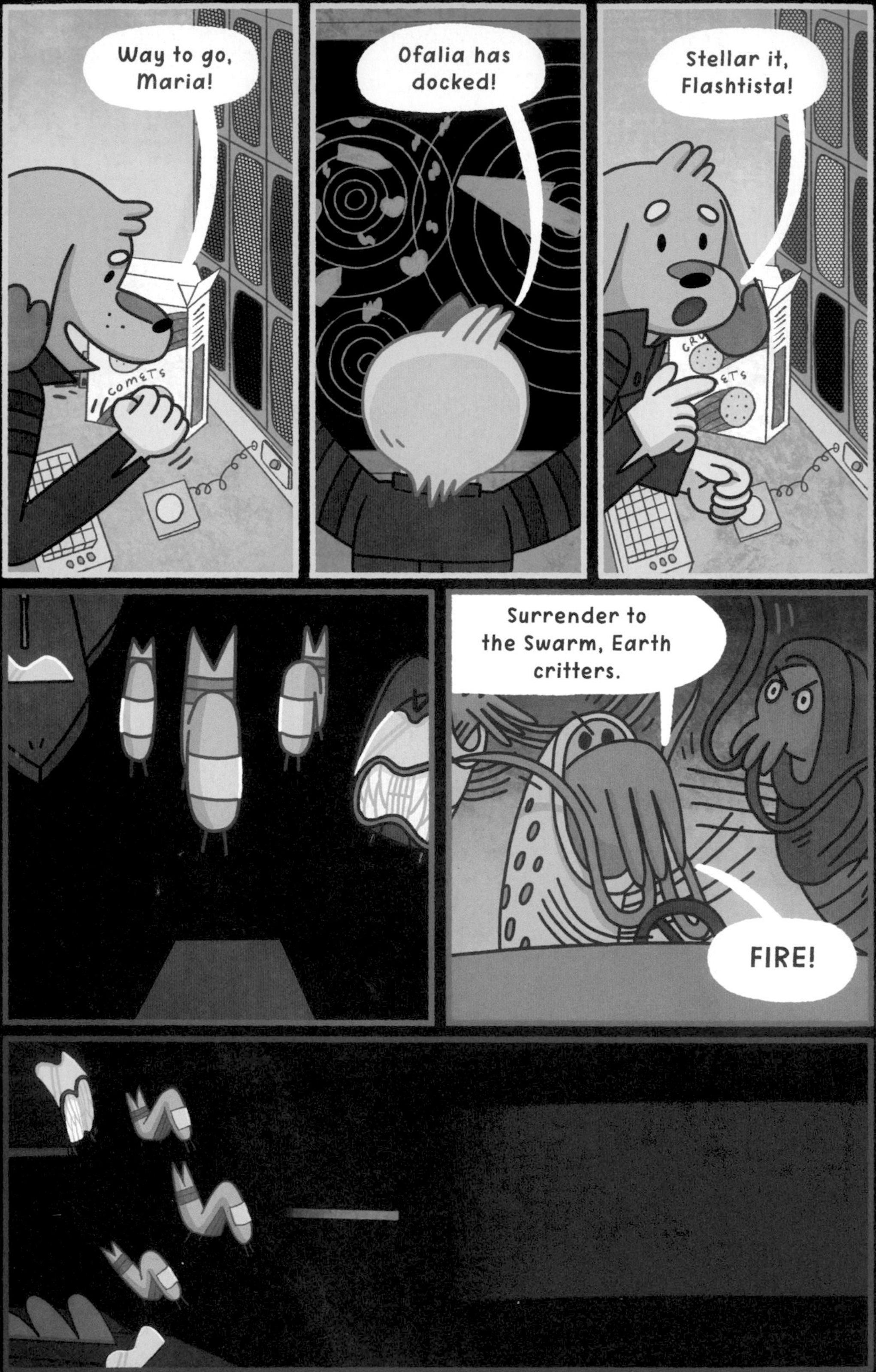
Way to go, Maria!
COMETS
Ofalia has docked!
Stellar it, Flashtista!
Surrender to the Swarm, Earth critters.
FIRE!

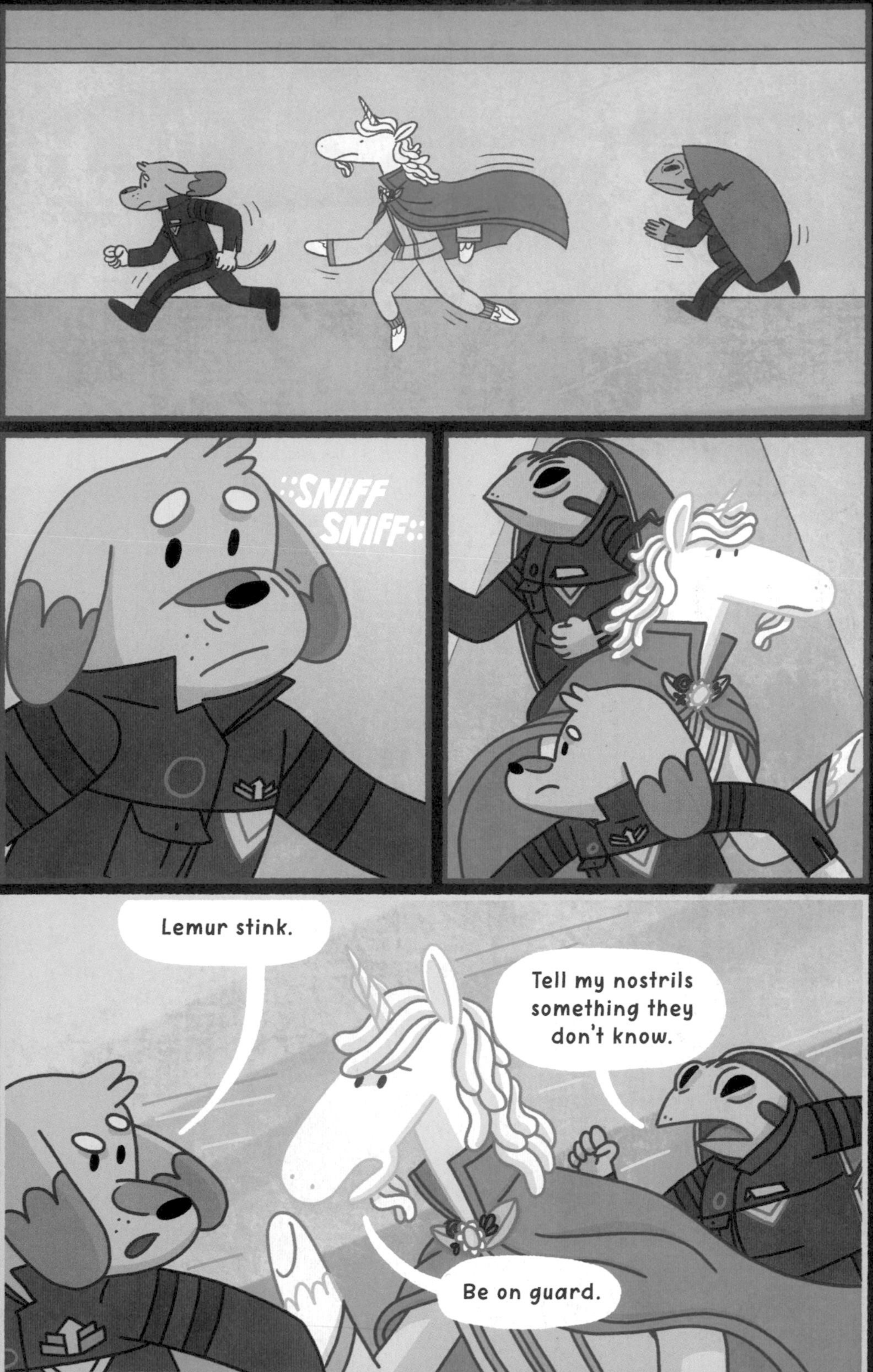
SNIFF
SNIFF
Lemur stink.
Tell my nostrils something they don't know.
Be on guard.

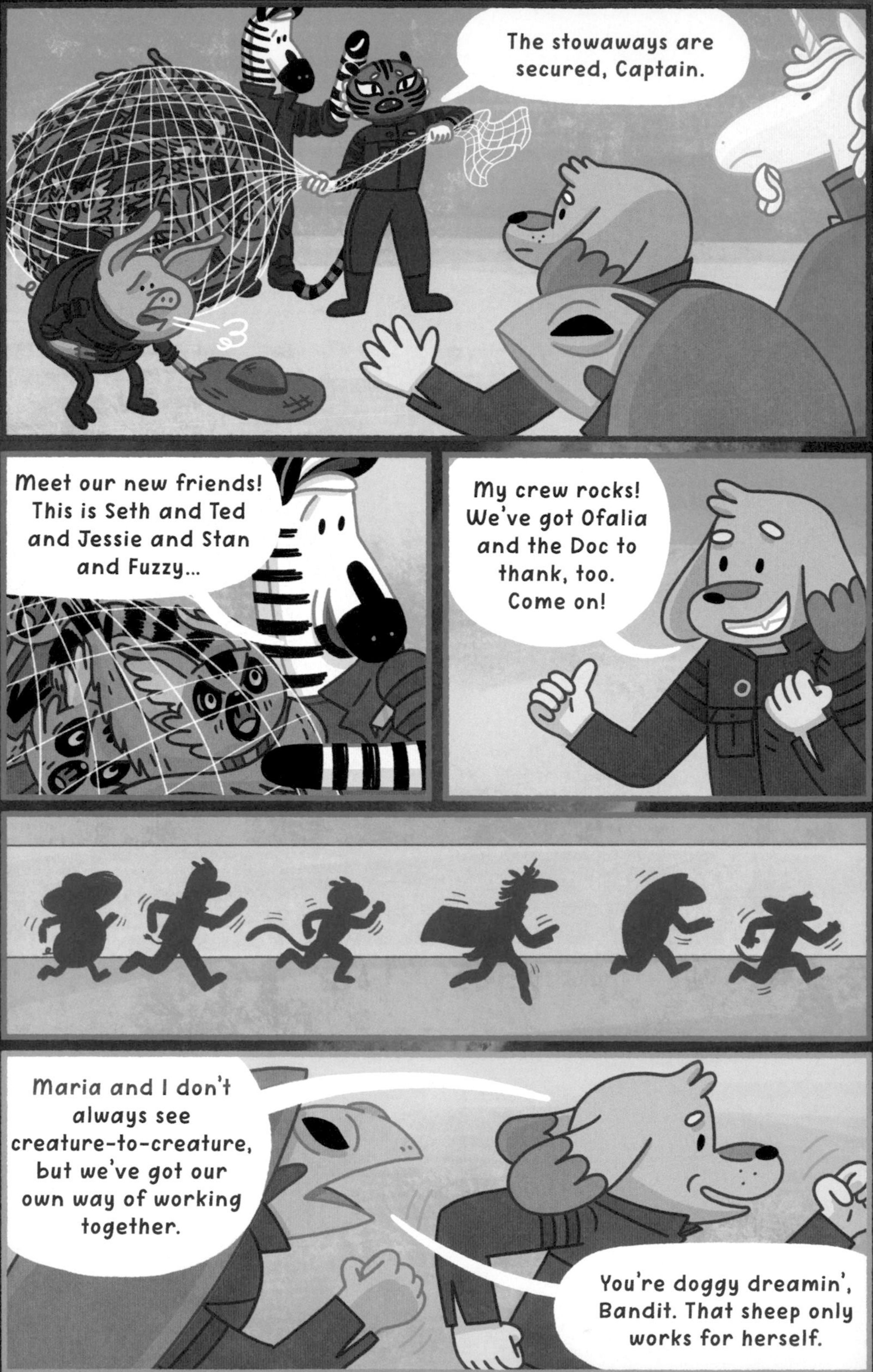
The stowaways are secured, Captain.
Meet our new friends! This is Seth and Ted and Jessie and Stan and Fuzzy...
My crew rocks! We've got Ofalia and the Doc to thank, too. Come on!
Maria and I don't always see creature-to-creature, but we've got our own way of working together.
You're doggy dreamin', Bandit. That sheep only works for herself.

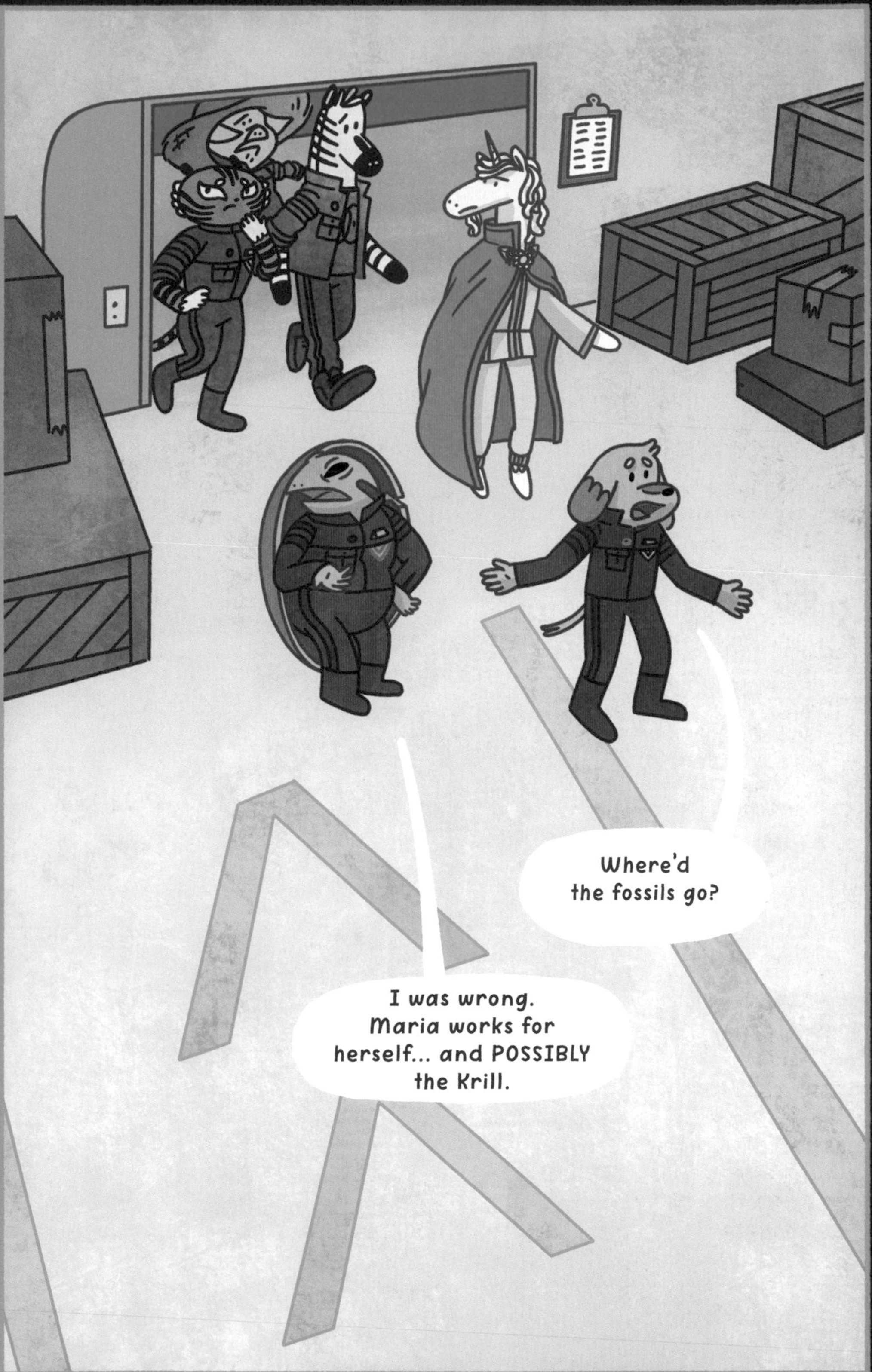
Where'd the fossils go?
I was wrong. Maria works for herself... and POSSIBLY the Krill.

CHAPTER 7

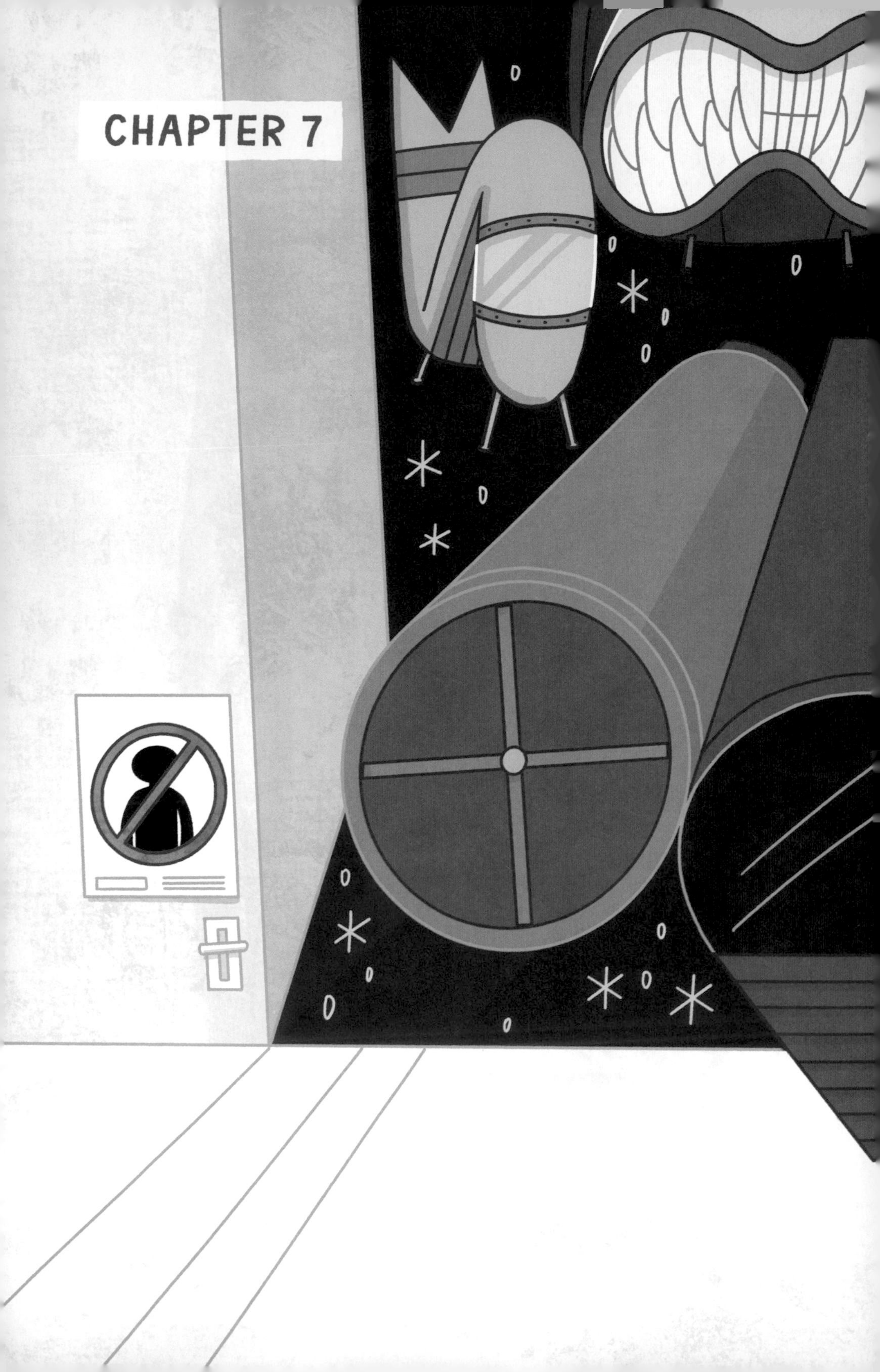

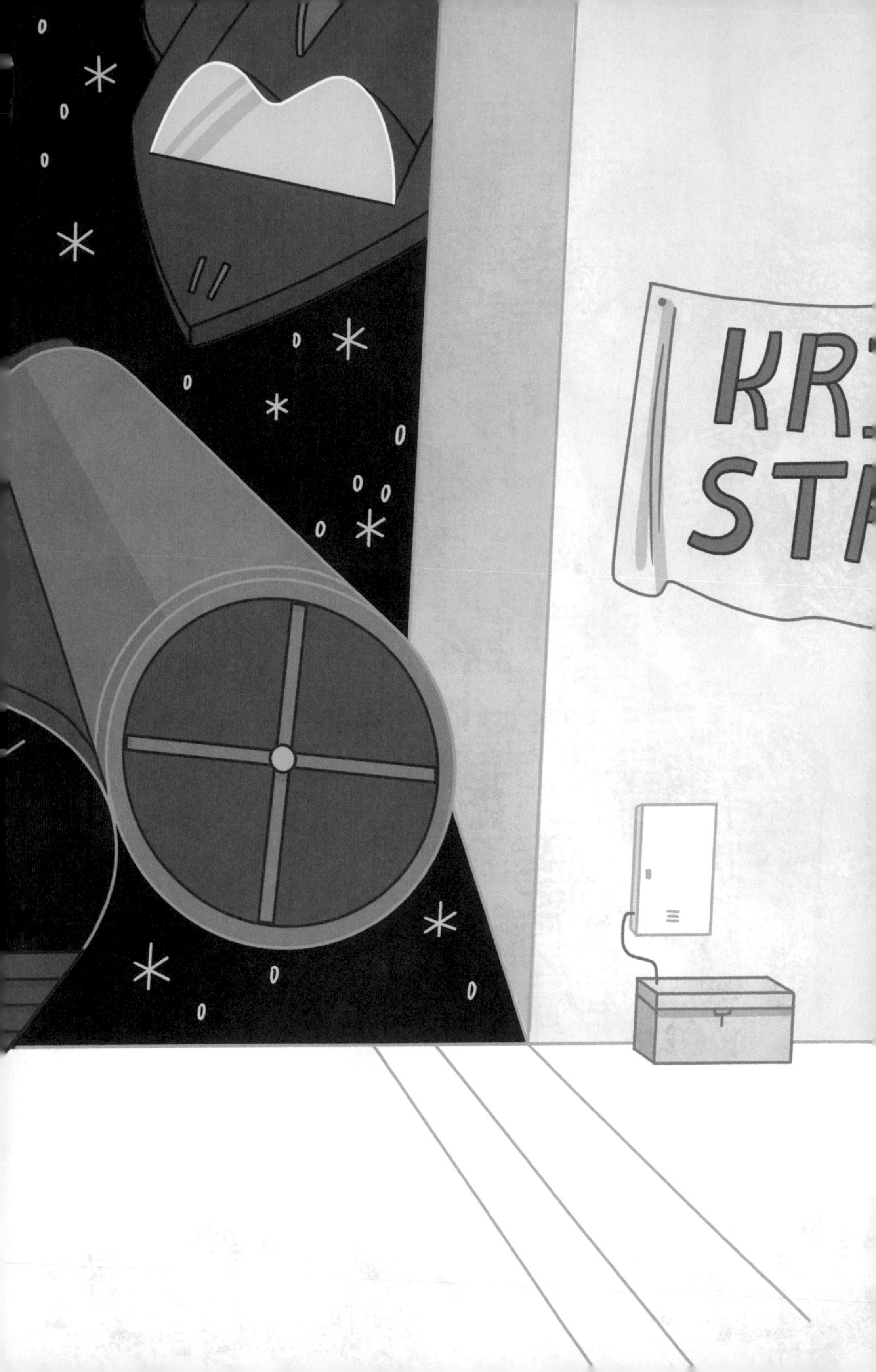

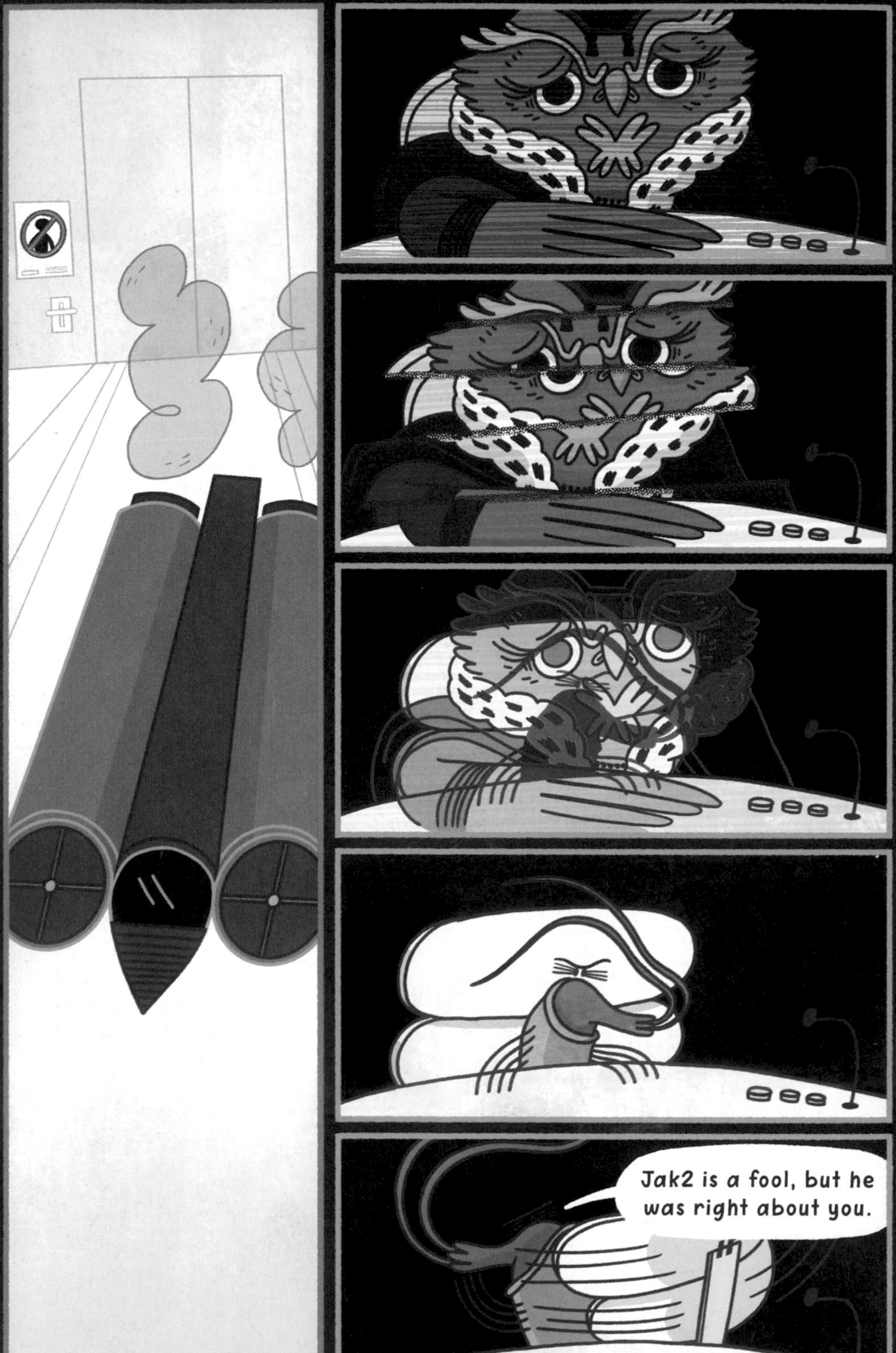
Jak2 is a fool, but he
was right about you.

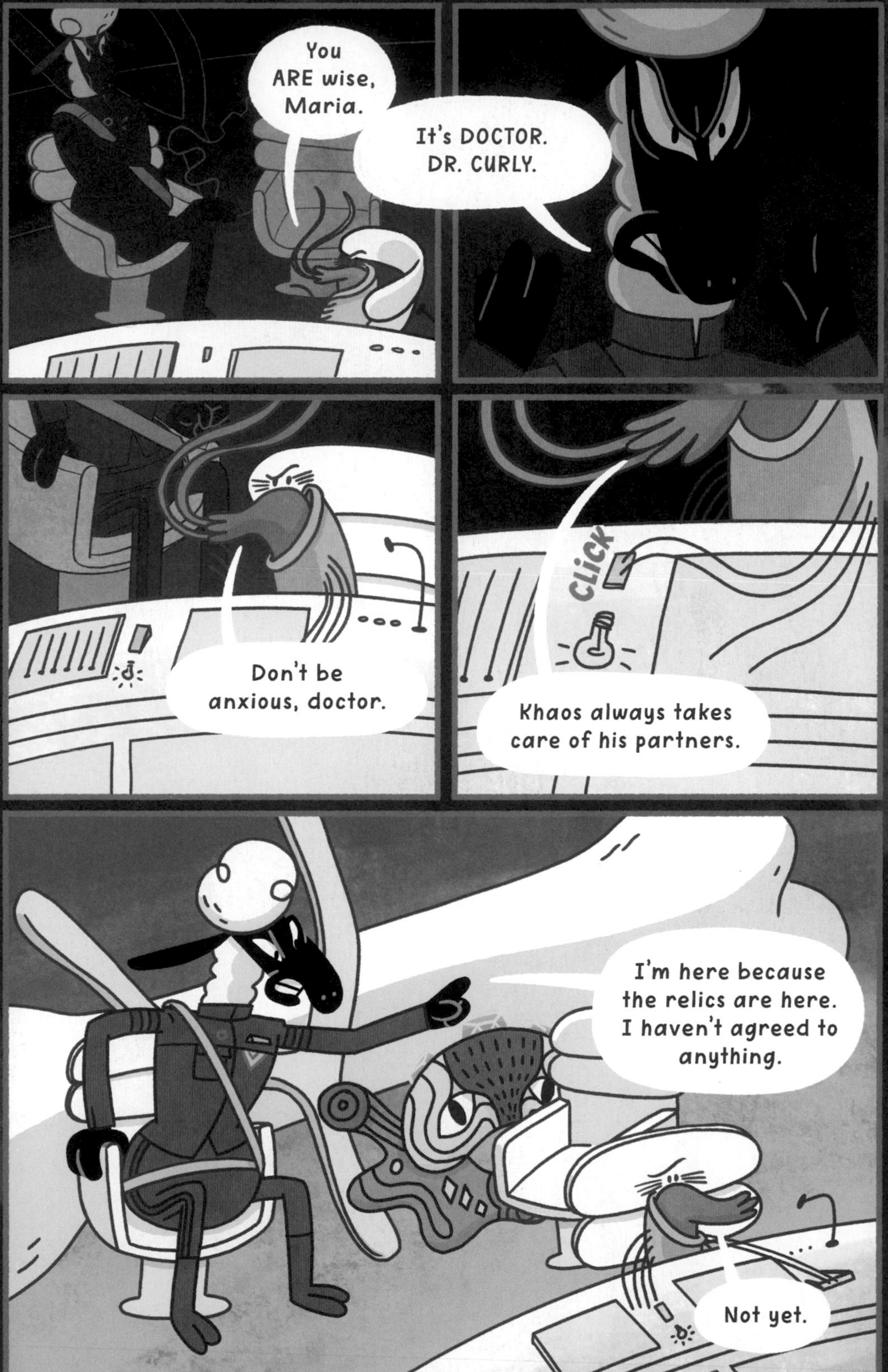
You ARE wise, Maria.
It's DOCTOR. DR. CURLY.
Don't be anxious, doctor.
CLICK
Khaos always takes care of his partners.
I'm here because the relics are here. I haven't agreed to anything.
Not yet.

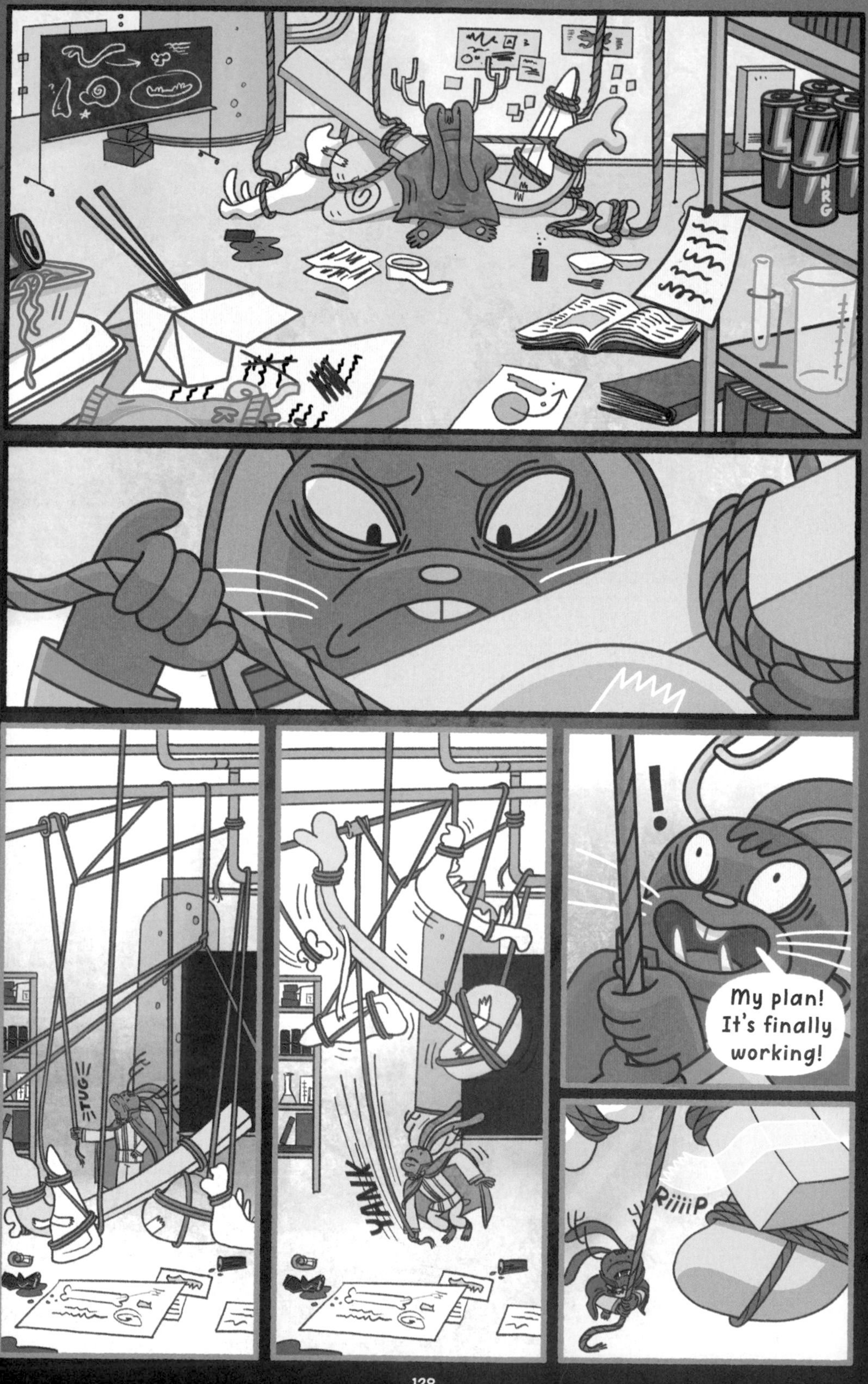
TUG
YANK
!
My plan! It's finally working!
RiiiP

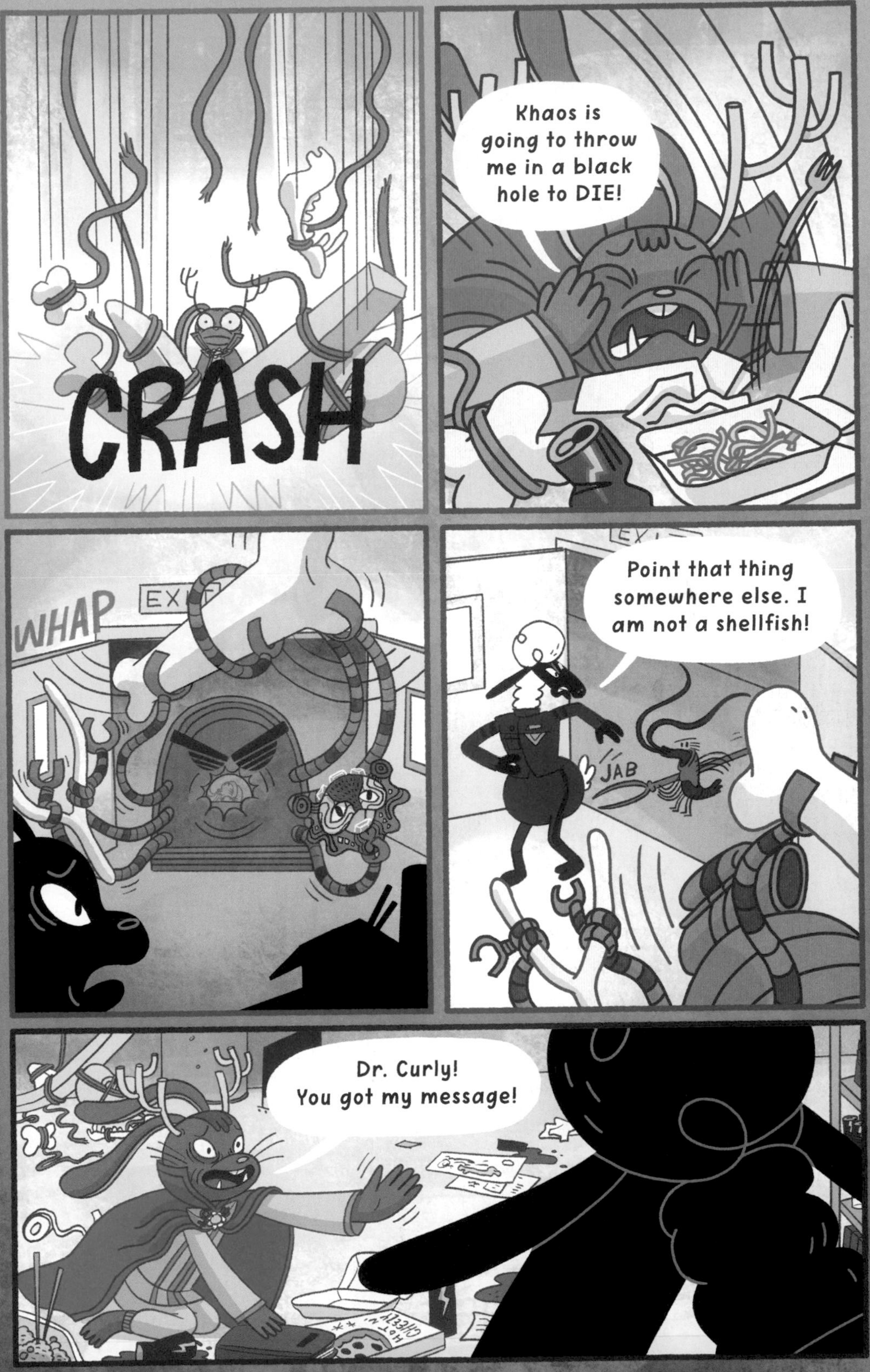
CRASH
Khaos is going to throw me in a black hole to DIE!
WHAP
EXIT
Point that thing somewhere else. I am not a shellfish!
JAB
Dr. Curly! You got my message!
HOT N' CHEESY

I torched your message in my Bunsen burner!

I regret even reading it.

Dr. Curly, the Krill live with no regrets. Give it a try. It's quite refreshing.

You're *serious* about rebuilding the Novataur?

HA! It's a bedtime story. There's no truth to it.

Here is a truth, Dr. Curly: You care more about yourself than the Star Beasts.

We have *that* in common.

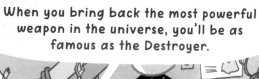

When you bring back the most powerful weapon in the universe, you'll be as famous as the Destroyer.

I'm a scientist, not an executioner!

Dr. Curly, I only care that you're a professional and that you GET THE JOB DONE.

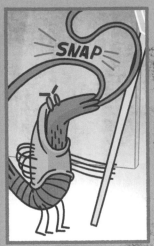

SNAP

CRASH!!

You have one hour to re-spark Novataur the Destroyer and bring it back to life.

FLEX

Don't make me have to motivate you.

SLAM!

I stand with science, not with creeps!

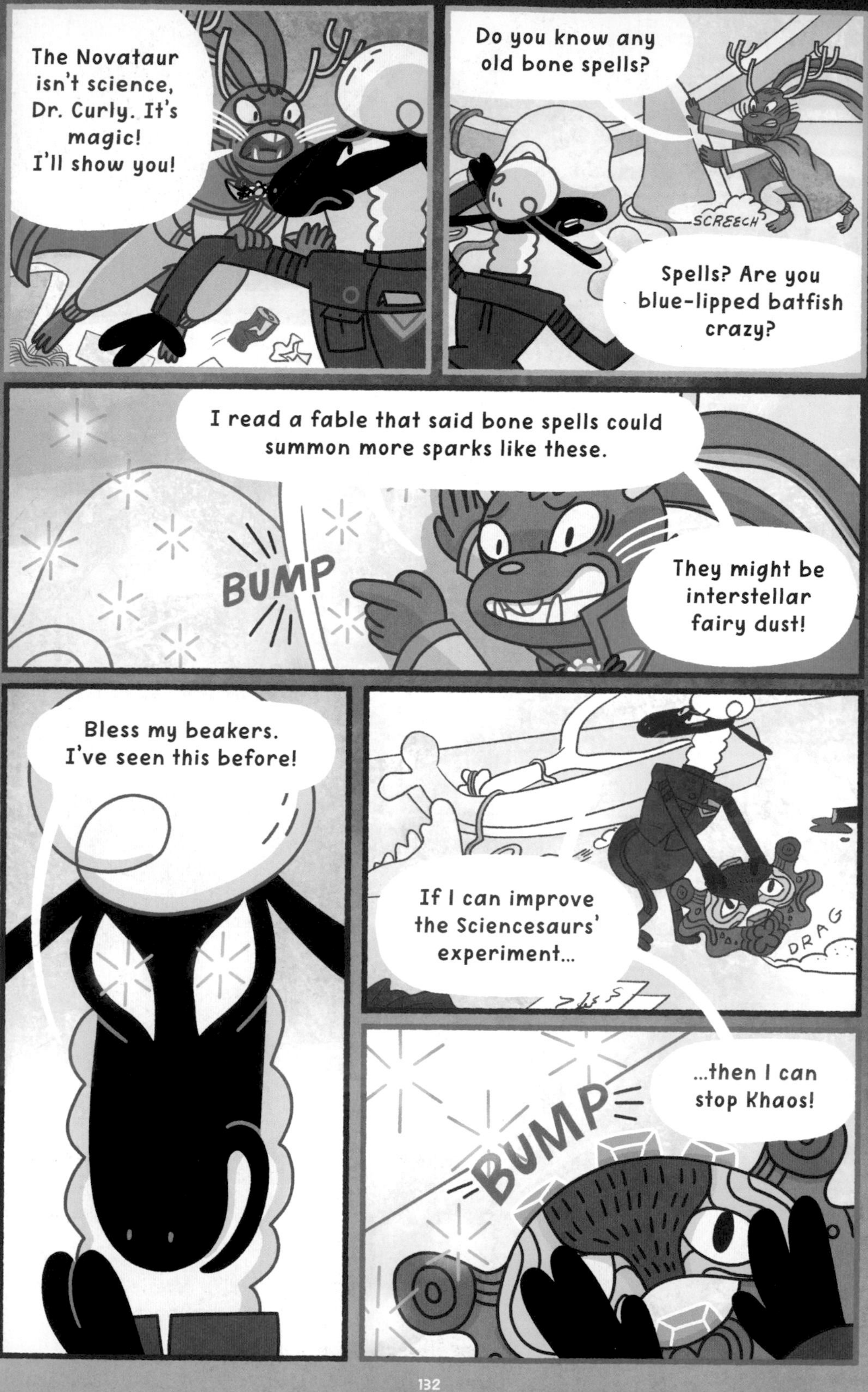
The Novataur isn't science, Dr. Curly. It's magic! I'll show you!
Do you know any old bone spells?
SCREECH
Spells? Are you blue-lipped batfish crazy?
I read a fable that said bone spells could summon more sparks like these.
BUMP
They might be interstellar fairy dust!
Bless my beakers. I've seen this before!
If I can improve the Sciencesaurs' experiment...
DRAG
...then I can stop Khaos!
BUMP

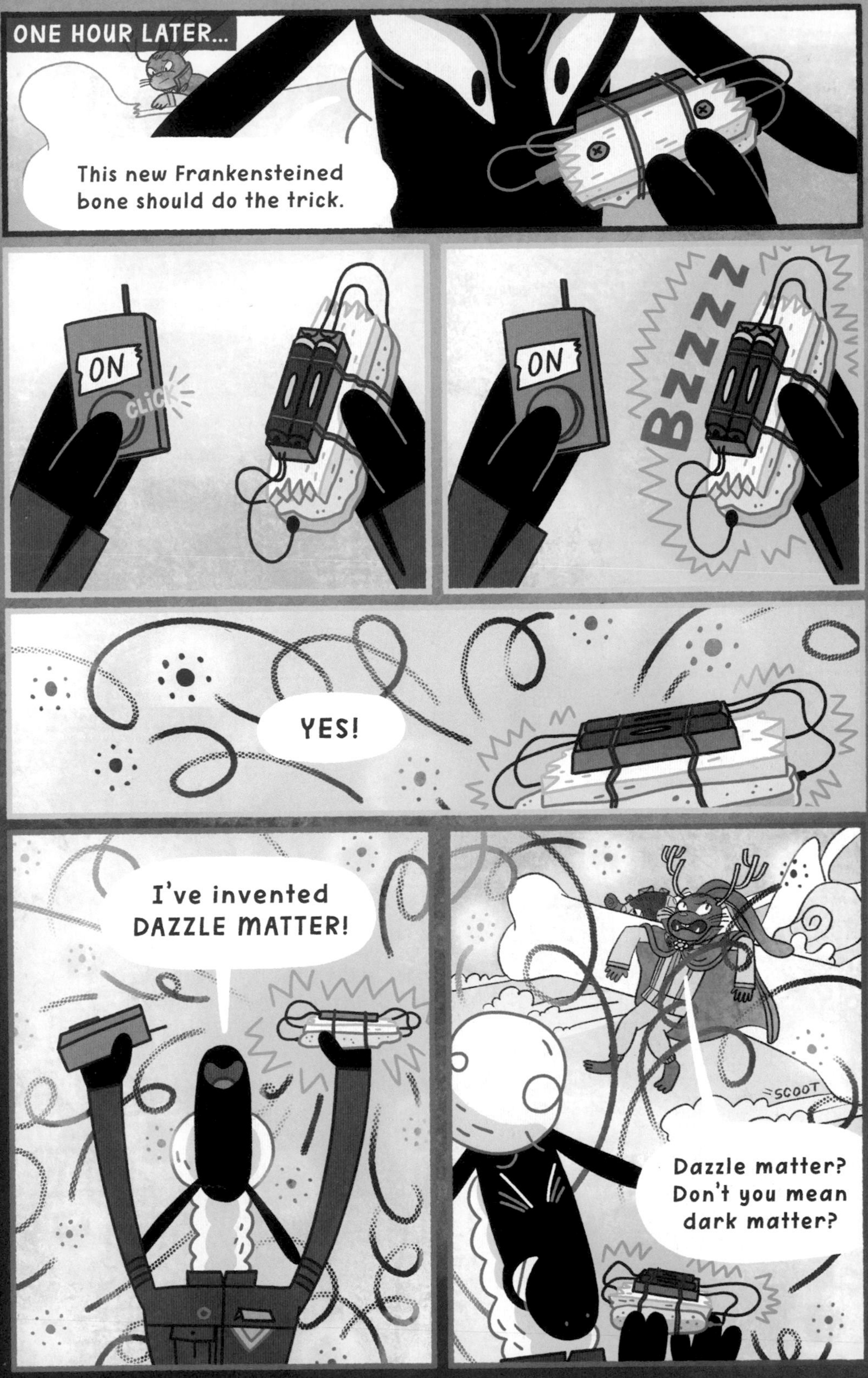
ONE HOUR LATER...
This new Frankensteined bone should do the trick.
ON
CLICK
ON
BZZZZ
YES!
I've invented DAZZLE MATTER!
SCOOT
Dazzle matter? Don't you mean dark matter?

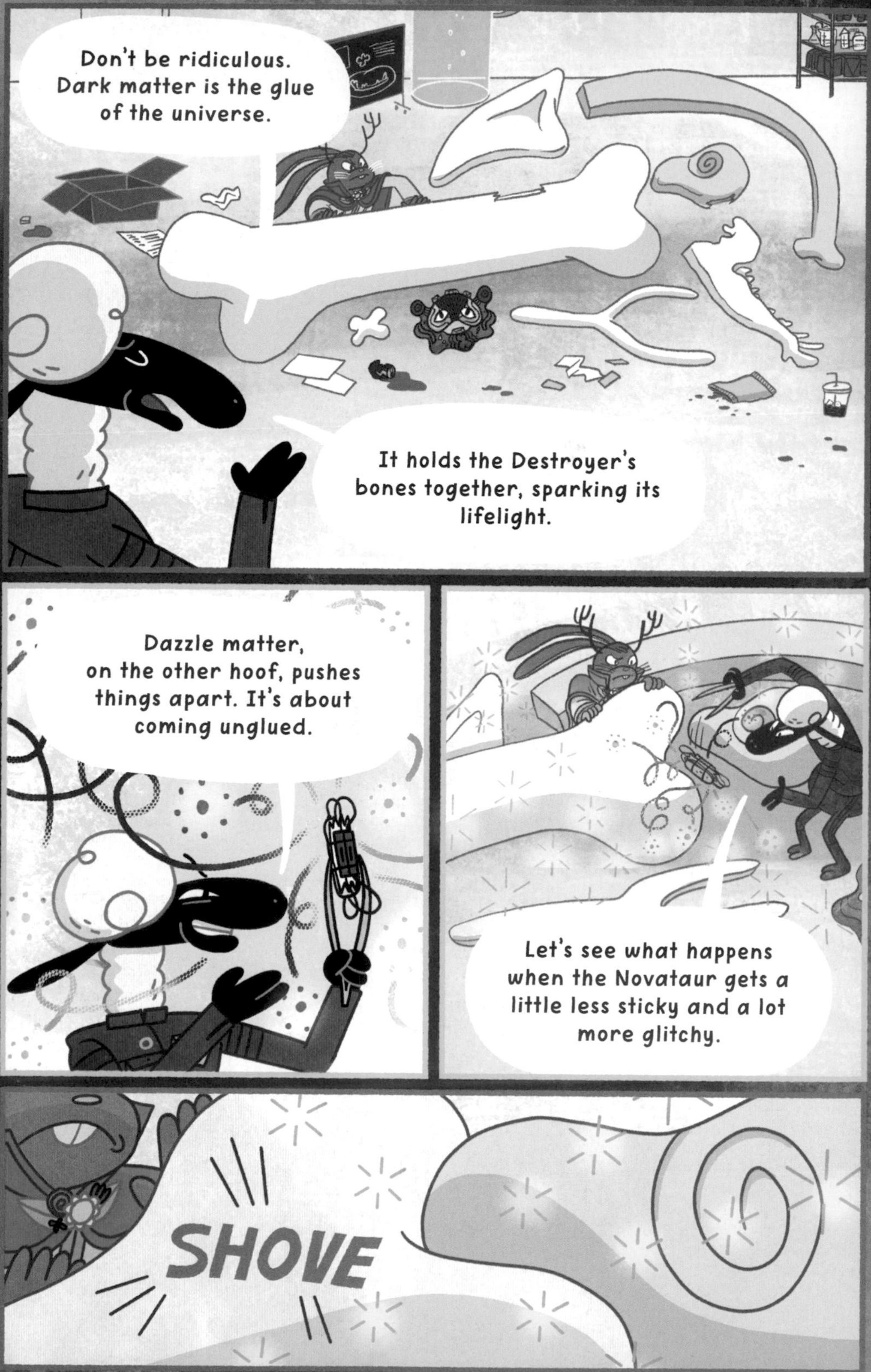
Don't be ridiculous. Dark matter is the glue of the universe.
It holds the Destroyer's bones together, sparking its lifelight.
Dazzle matter, on the other hoof, pushes things apart. It's about coming unglued.
Let's see what happens when the Novataur gets a little less sticky and a lot more glitchy.
SHOVE

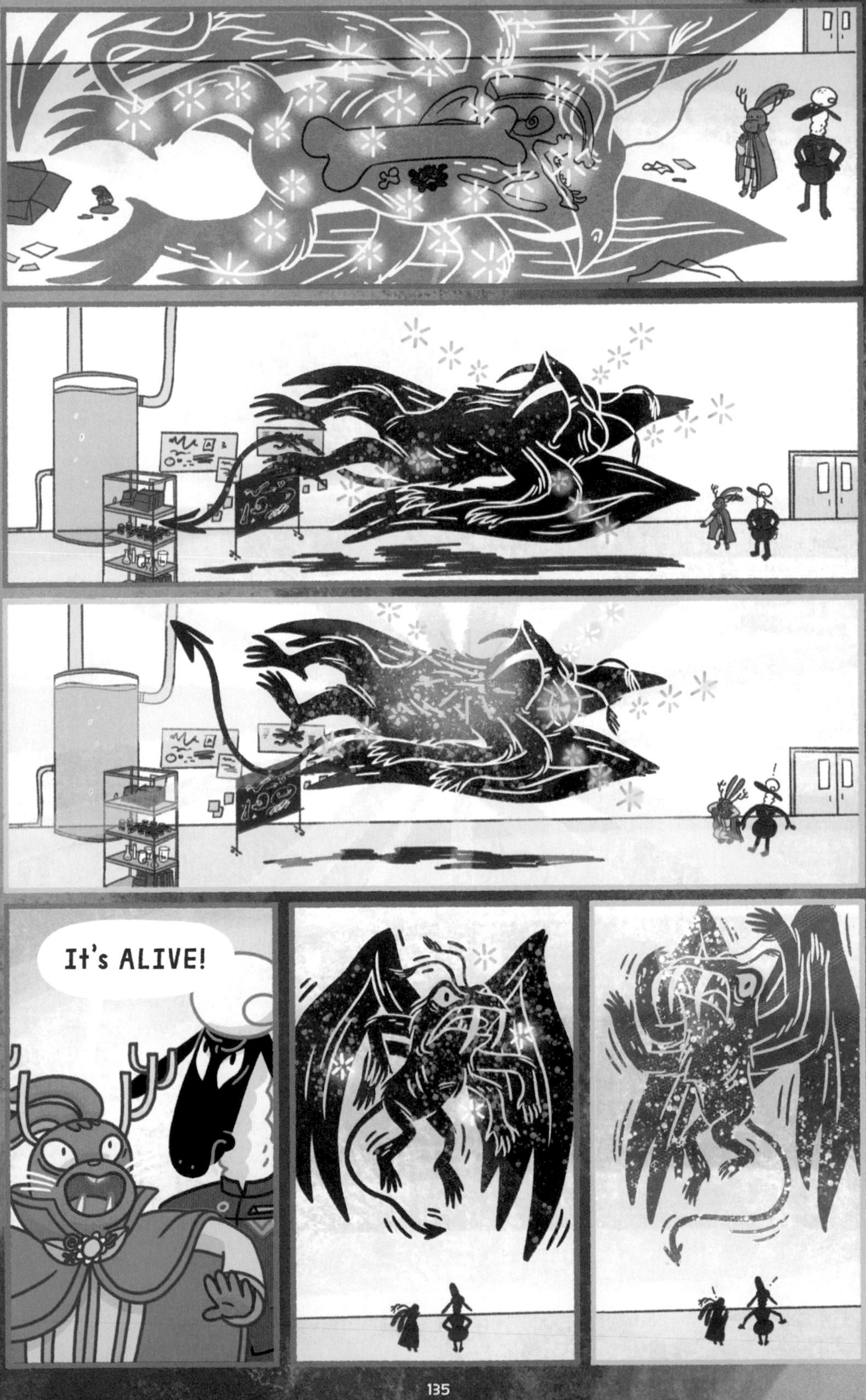
It's ALIVE!

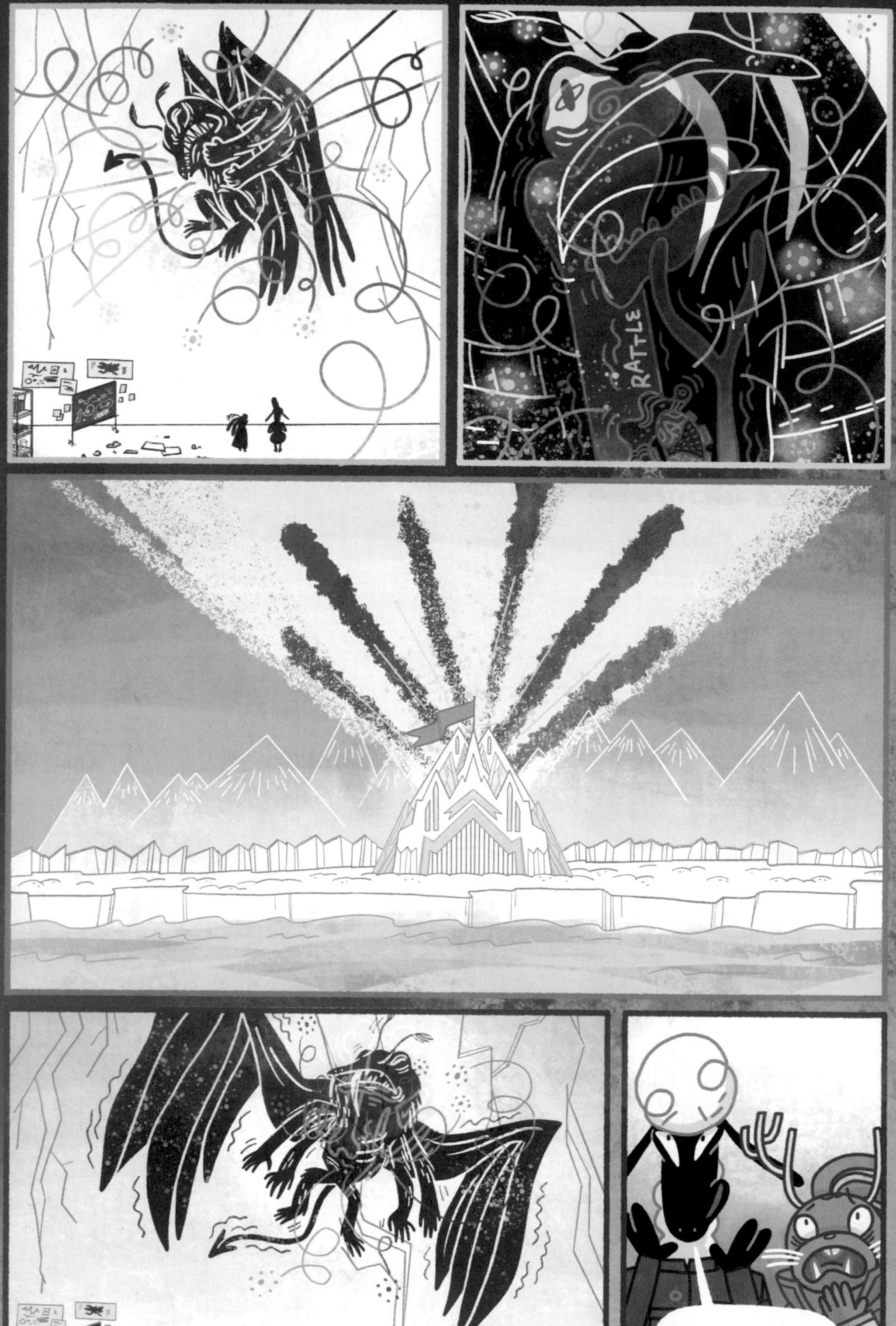
RATTLE
I love science.

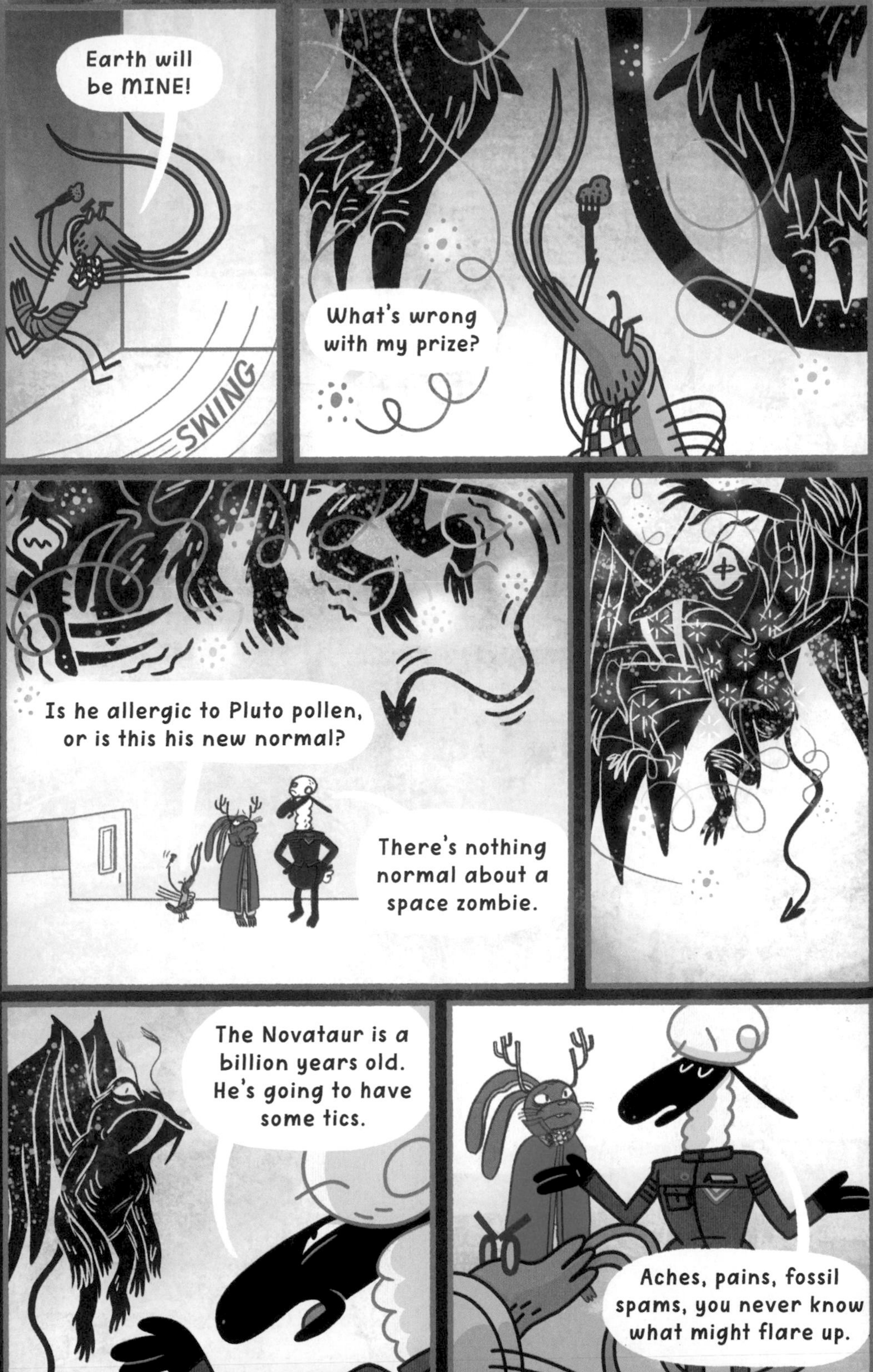
Earth will be MINE!
SWING
What's wrong with my prize?
Is he allergic to Pluto pollen, or is this his new normal?
There's nothing normal about a space zombie.
The Novataur is a billion years old. He's going to have some tics.
Aches, pains, fossil spams, you never know what might flare up.

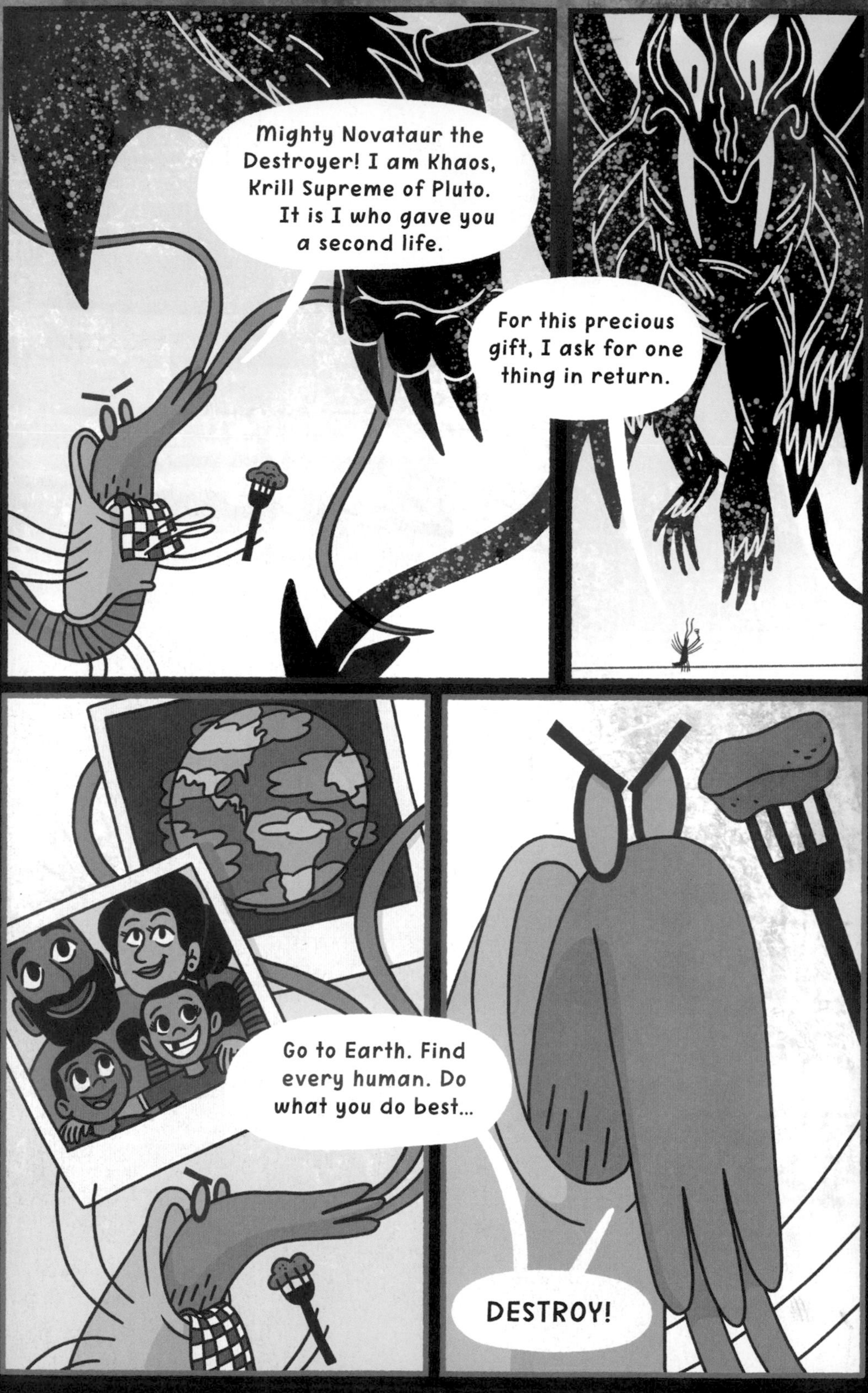

Mighty Novataur the Destroyer! I am Khaos, Krill Supreme of Pluto. It is I who gave you a second life.
For this precious gift, I ask for one thing in return.
Go to Earth. Find every human. Do what you do best...
DESTROY!

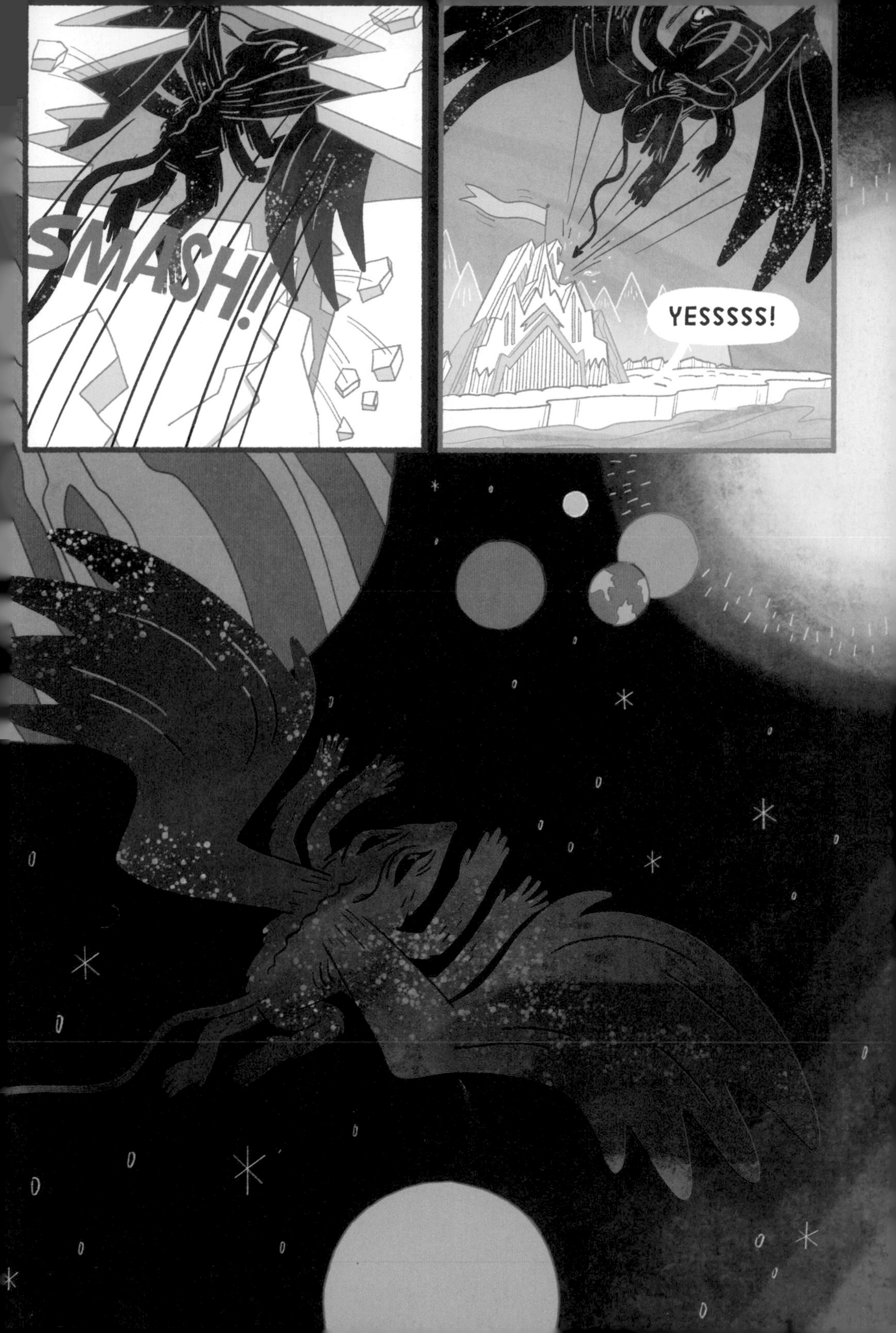
SMASH!
YESSSSS!

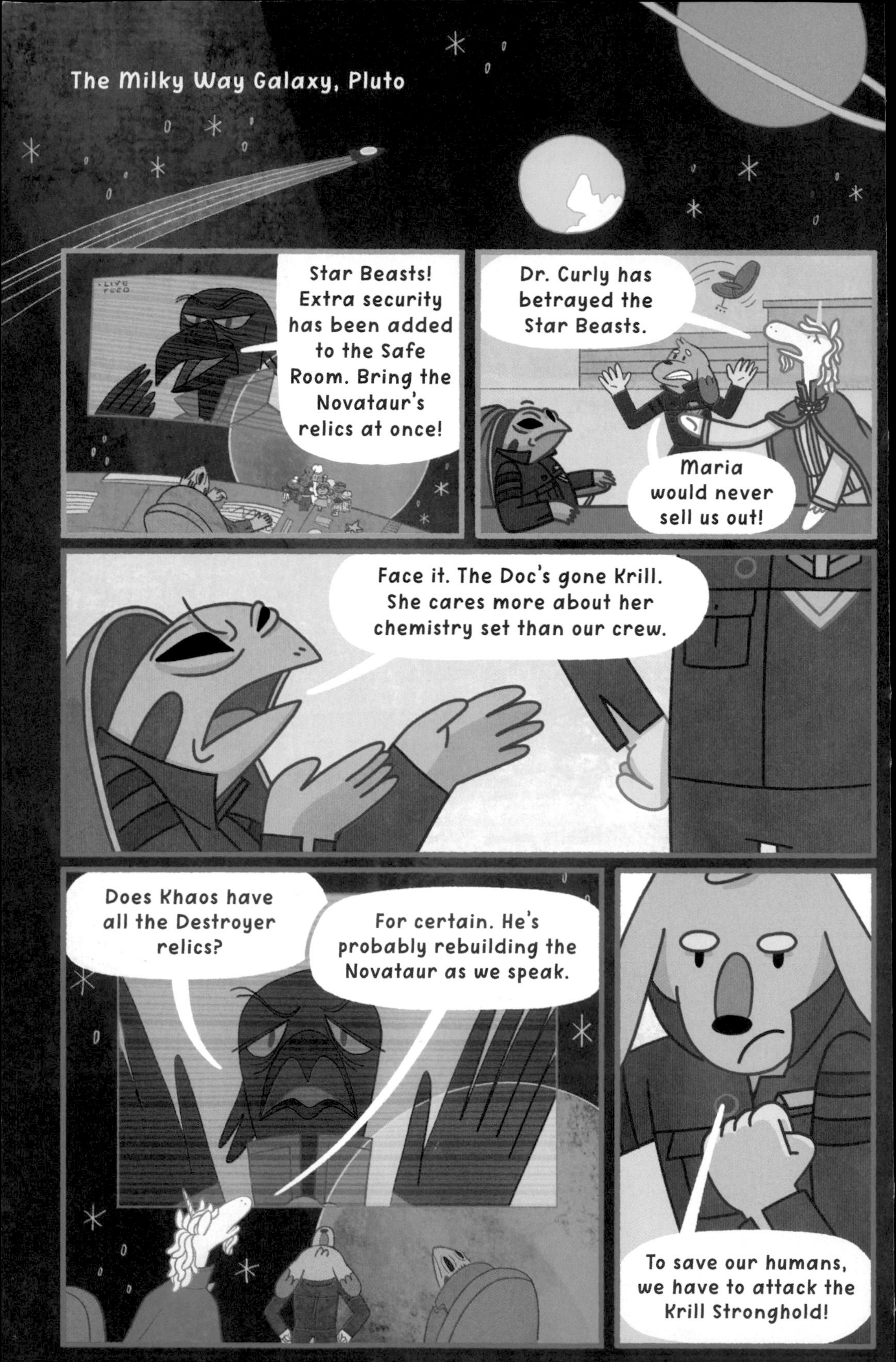
The Milky Way Galaxy, Pluto
LIVE FEED
Star Beasts! Extra security has been added to the Safe Room. Bring the Novataur's relics at once!
Dr. Curly has betrayed the Star Beasts.
Maria would never sell us out!
Face it. The Doc's gone Krill. She cares more about her chemistry set than our crew.
Does Khaos have all the Destroyer relics?
For certain. He's probably rebuilding the Novataur as we speak.
To save our humans, we have to attack the Krill Stronghold!

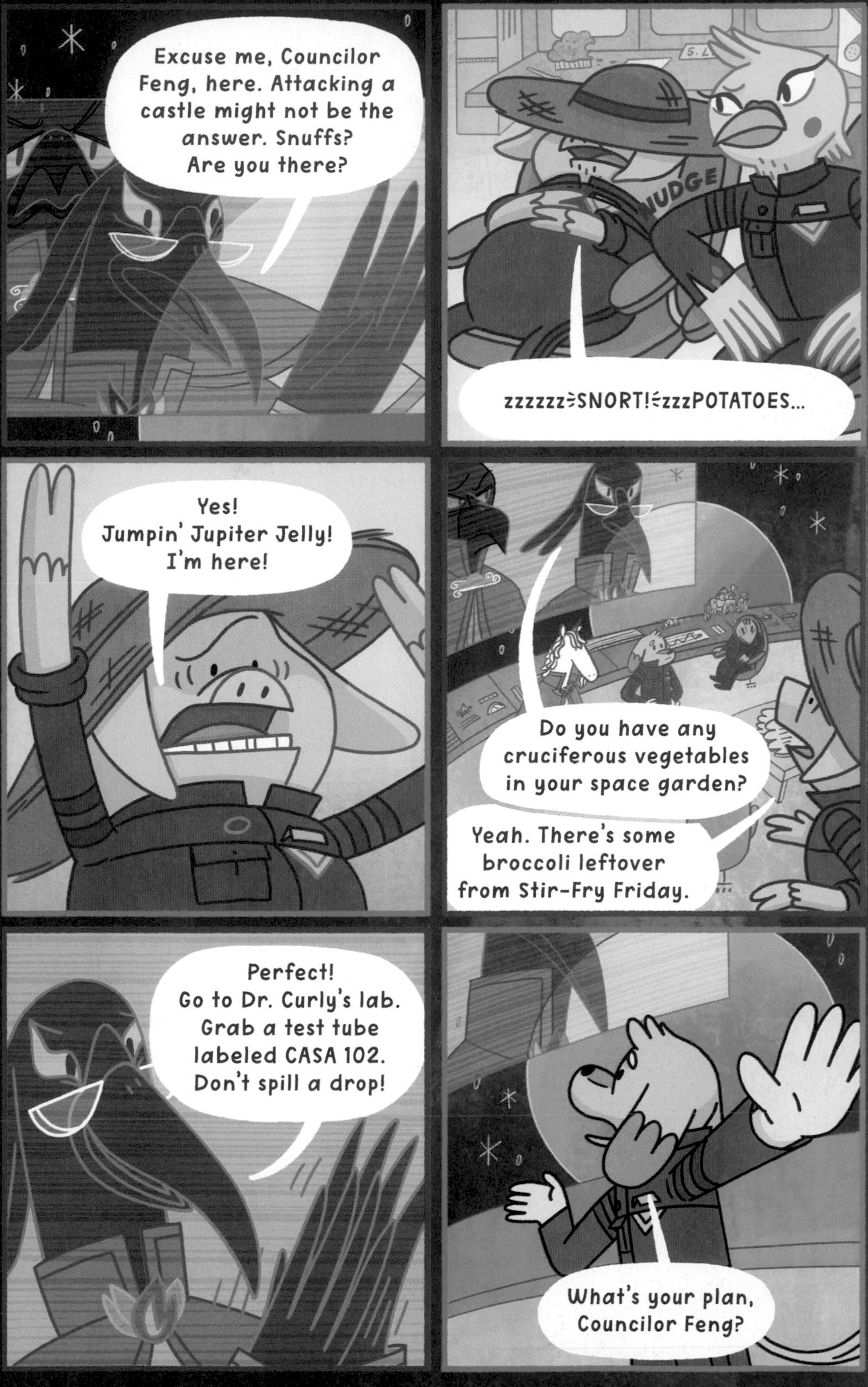
Excuse me, Councilor Feng, here. Attacking a castle might not be the answer. Snuffs? Are you there?
zzzzzz⇒SNORT!⇐zzzPOTATOES...
Yes! Jumpin' Jupiter Jelly! I'm here!
Do you have any cruciferous vegetables in your space garden?
Yeah. There's some broccoli leftover from Stir-Fry Friday.
Perfect! Go to Dr. Curly's lab. Grab a test tube labeled CASA 102. Don't spill a drop!
What's your plan, Councilor Feng?

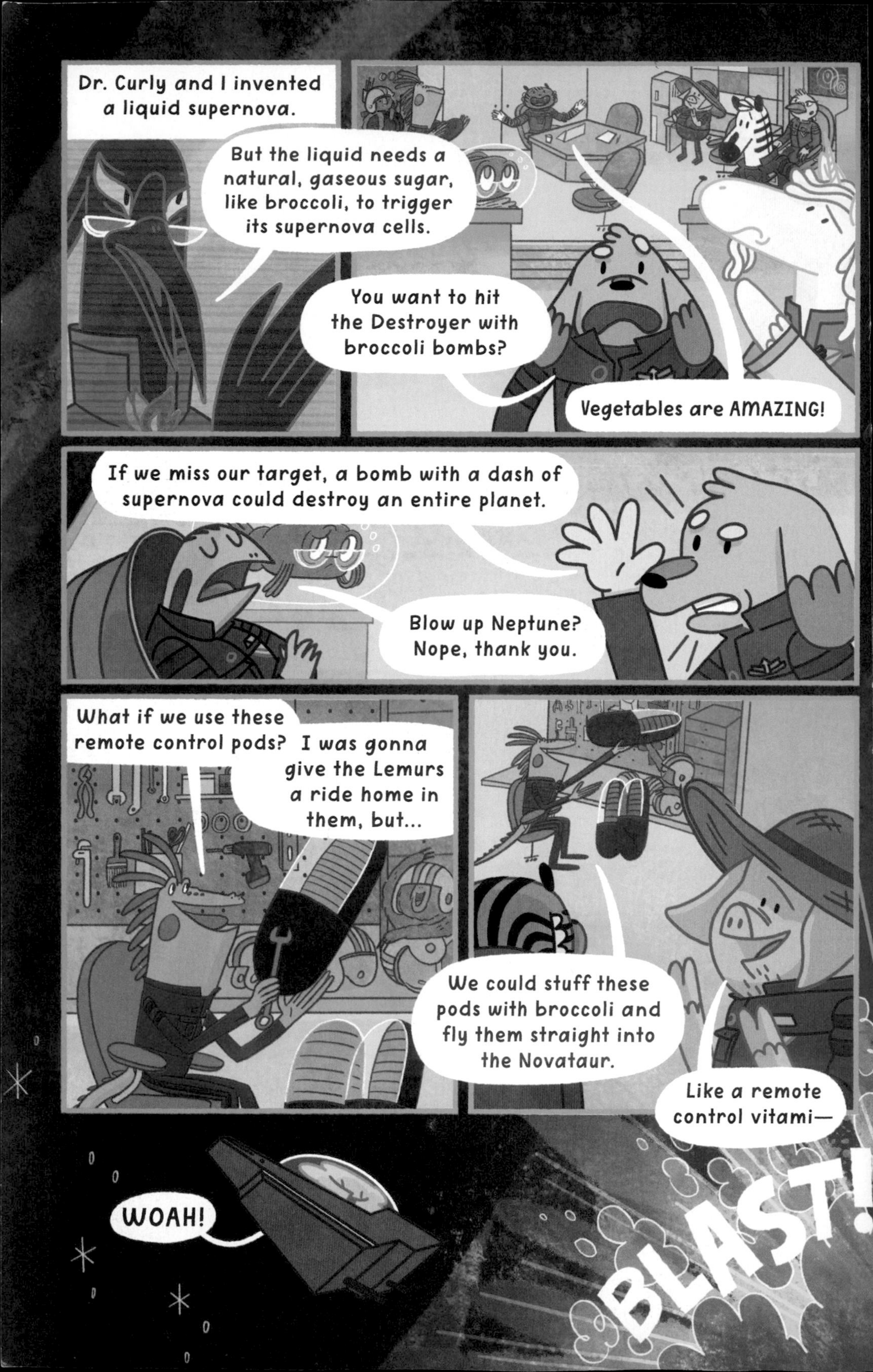
Dr. Curly and I invented a liquid supernova.
But the liquid needs a natural, gaseous sugar, like broccoli, to trigger its supernova cells.
You want to hit the Destroyer with broccoli bombs?
Vegetables are AMAZING!
If we miss our target, a bomb with a dash of supernova could destroy an entire planet.
Blow up Neptune? Nope, thank you.
What if we use these remote control pods?
I was gonna give the Lemurs a ride home in them, but...
We could stuff these pods with broccoli and fly them straight into the Novataur.
Like a remote control vitami—
WOAH!
BLAST!

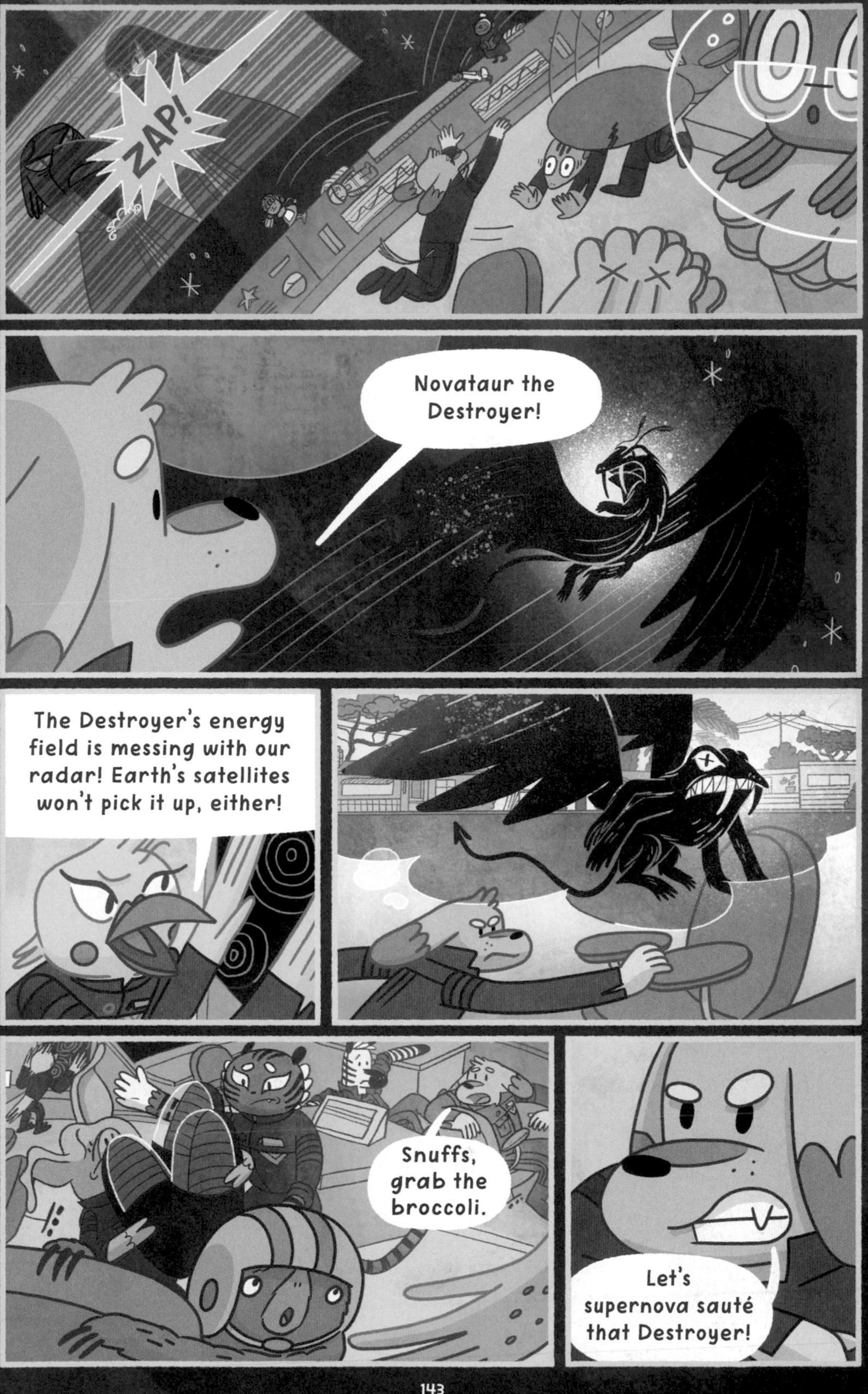
ZAP!
Novataur the Destroyer!
The Destroyer's energy field is messing with our radar! Earth's satellites won't pick it up, either!
Snuffs, grab the broccoli.
Let's supernova sauté that Destroyer!

CHAPTER 8

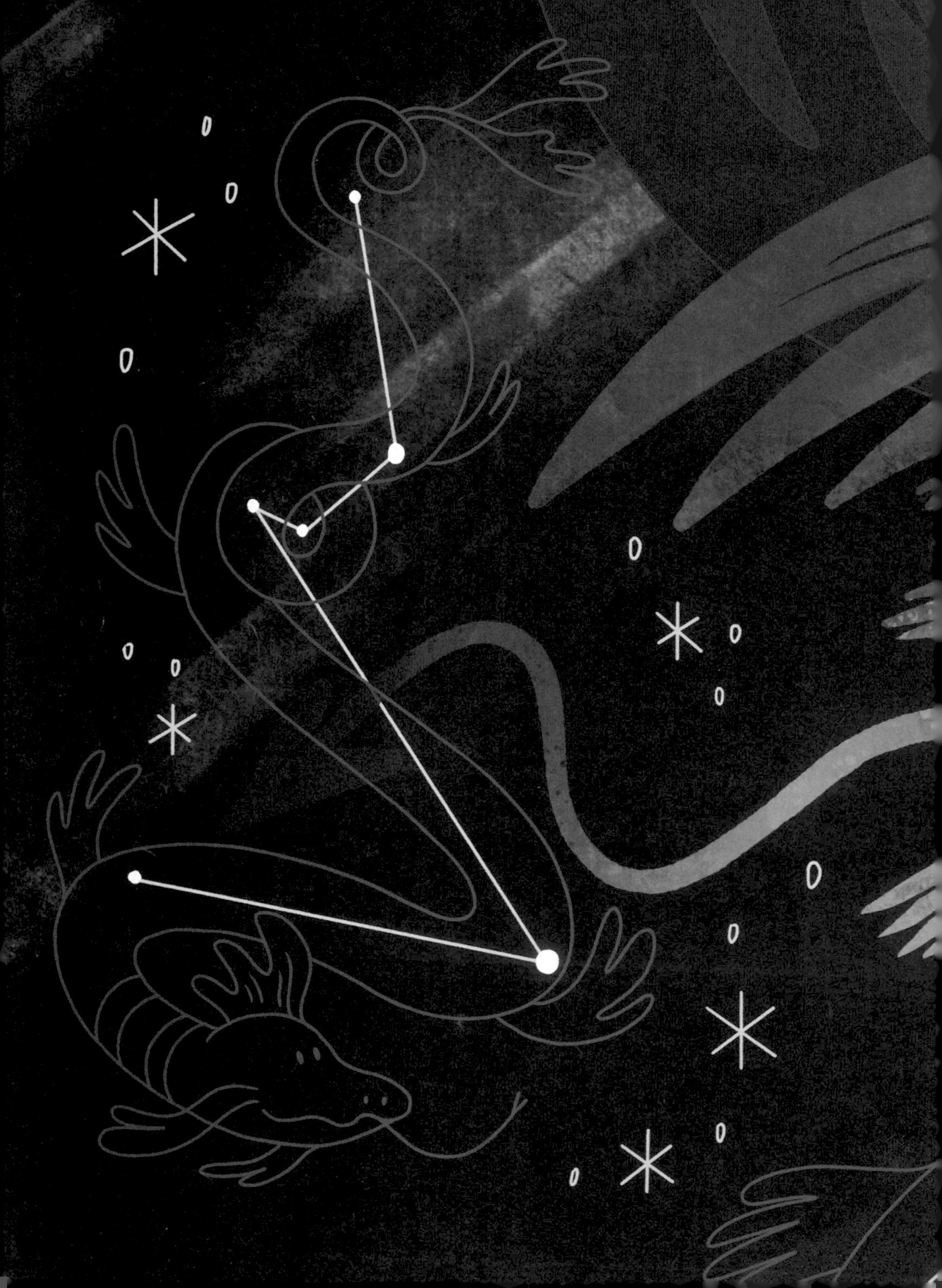

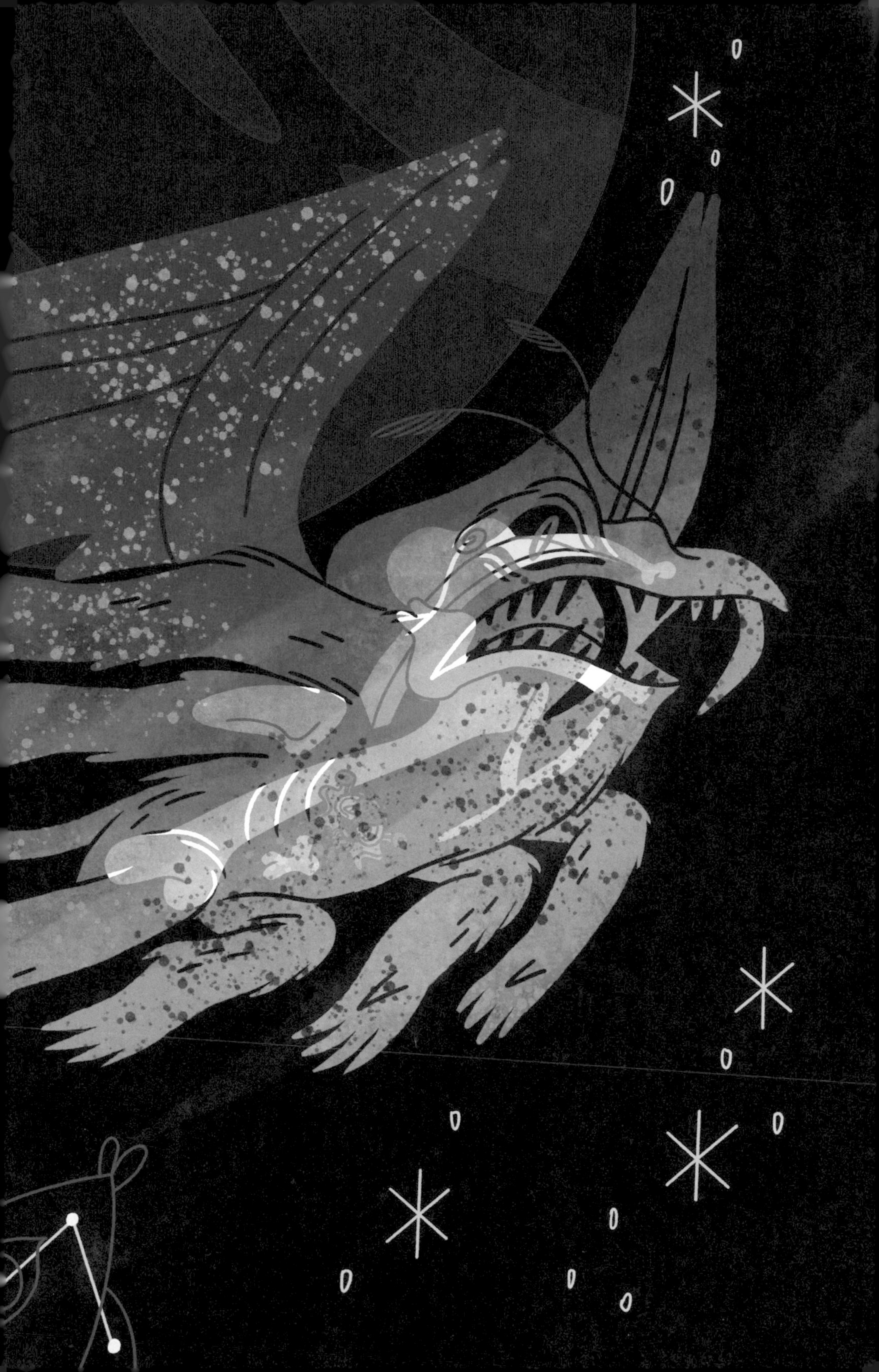

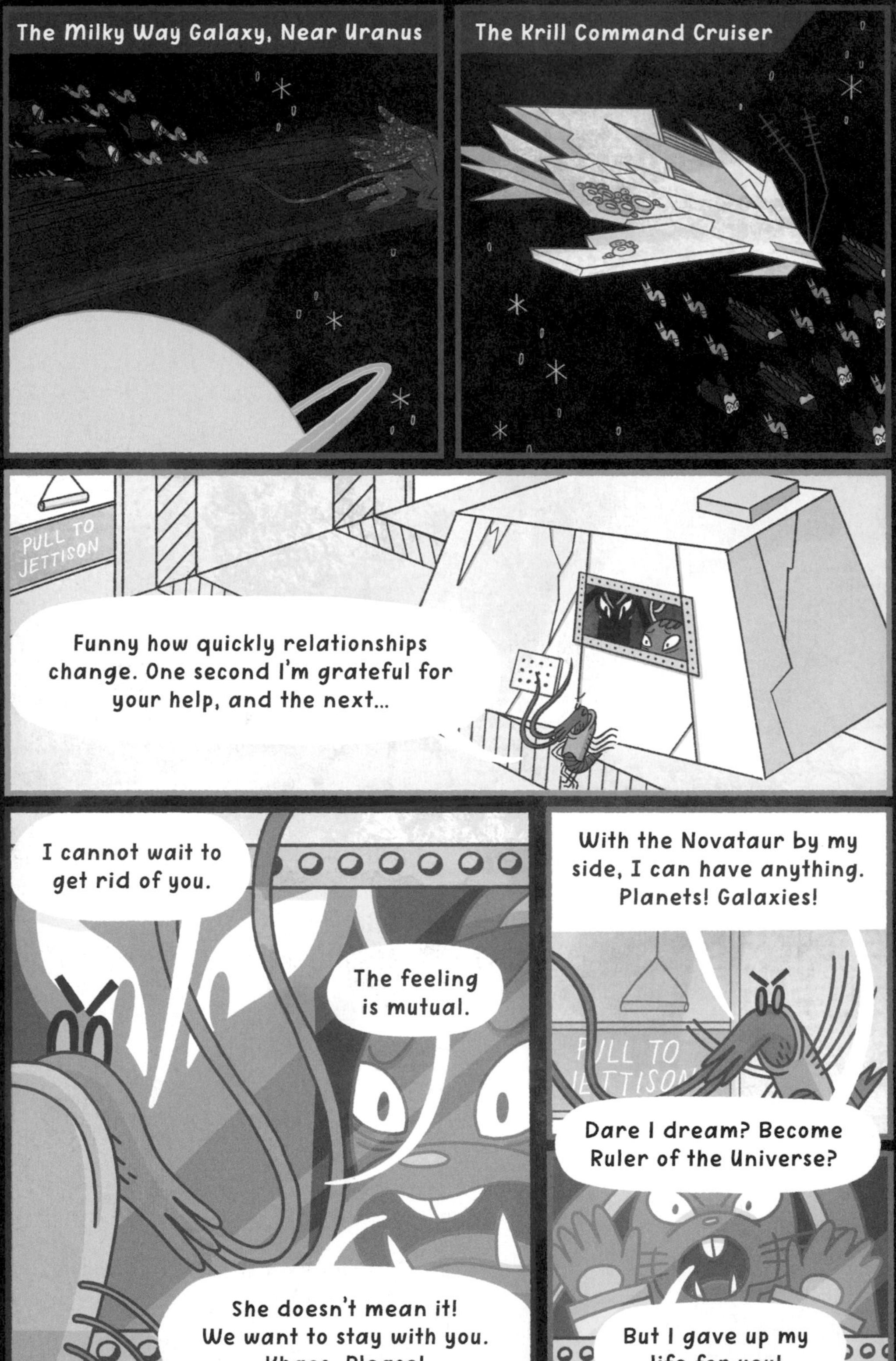
The Milky Way Galaxy, Near Uranus
The Krill Command Cruiser
PULL TO JETTISON
Funny how quickly relationships change. One second I'm grateful for your help, and the next...
I cannot wait to get rid of you.
The feeling is mutual.
She doesn't mean it! We want to stay with you. Khaos. Please!
With the Novataur by my side, I can have anything. Planets! Galaxies!
Dare I dream? Become Ruler of the Universe?
But I gave up my life for you!

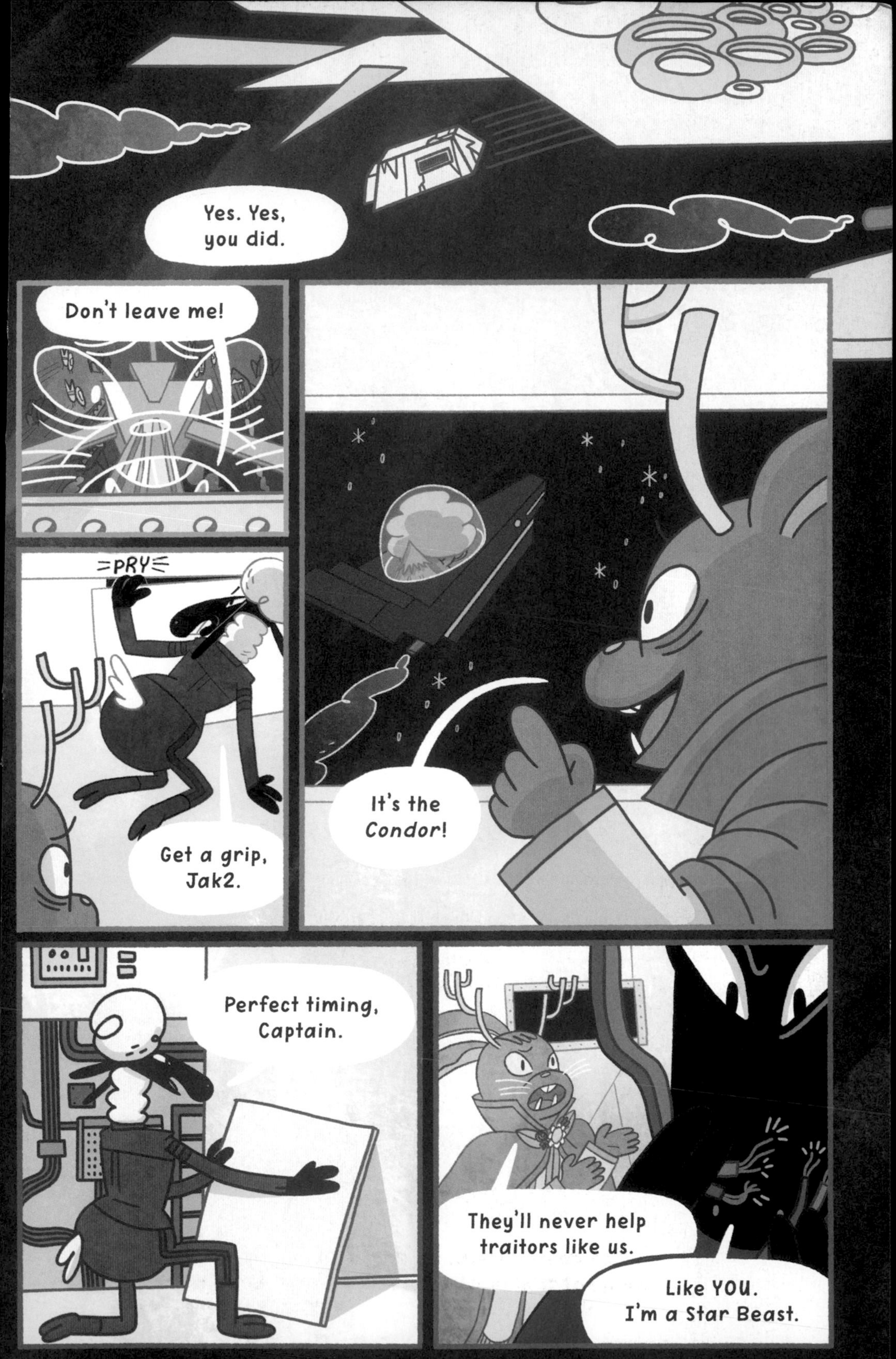
Yes. Yes, you did.
Don't leave me!
=PRY=
Get a grip, Jak2.
It's the *Condor*!
Perfect timing, Captain.
They'll never help traitors like us.
Like YOU. I'm a Star Beast.

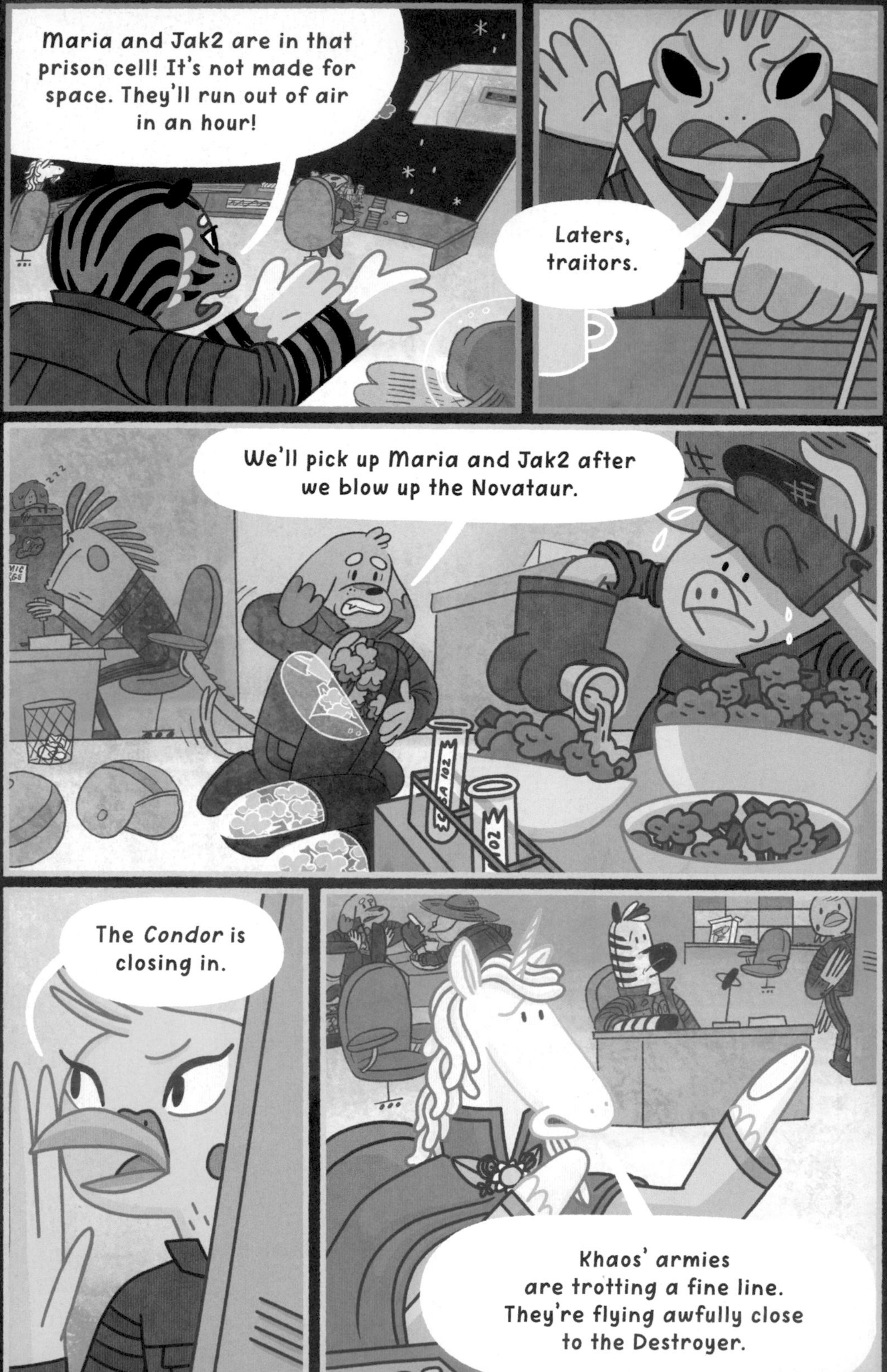
Maria and Jak2 are in that prison cell! It's not made for space. They'll run out of air in an hour!
Laters, traitors.
We'll pick up Maria and Jak2 after we blow up the Novataur.
The Condor is closing in.
Khaos' armies are trotting a fine line. They're flying awfully close to the Destroyer.

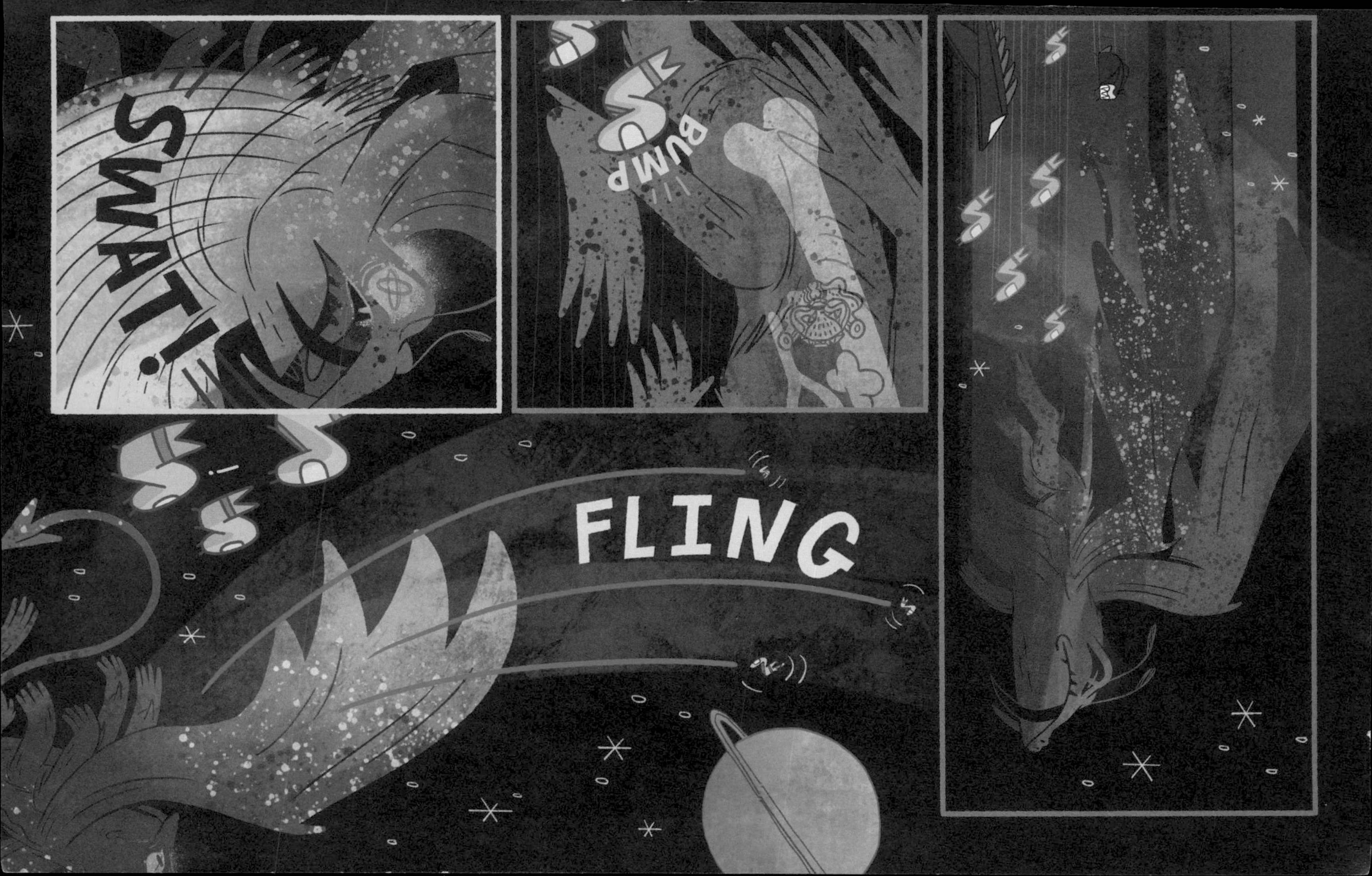
SWAT!
BUMP
!
FLING

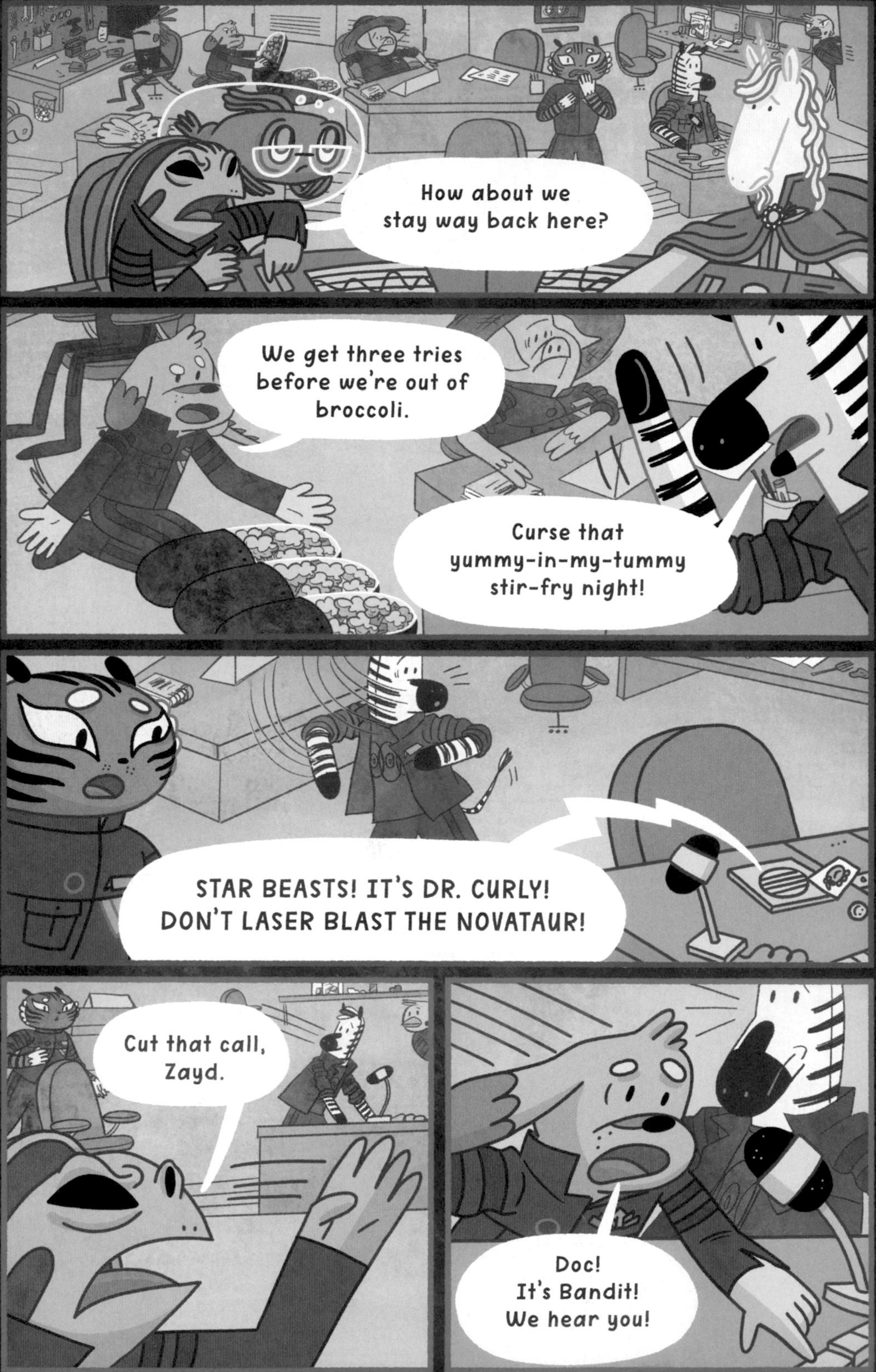
How about we stay way back here?
We get three tries before we're out of broccoli.
Curse that yummy-in-my-tummy stir-fry night!
STAR BEASTS! IT'S DR. CURLY! DON'T LASER BLAST THE NOVATAUR!
Cut that call, Zayd.
Doc! It's Bandit! We hear you!

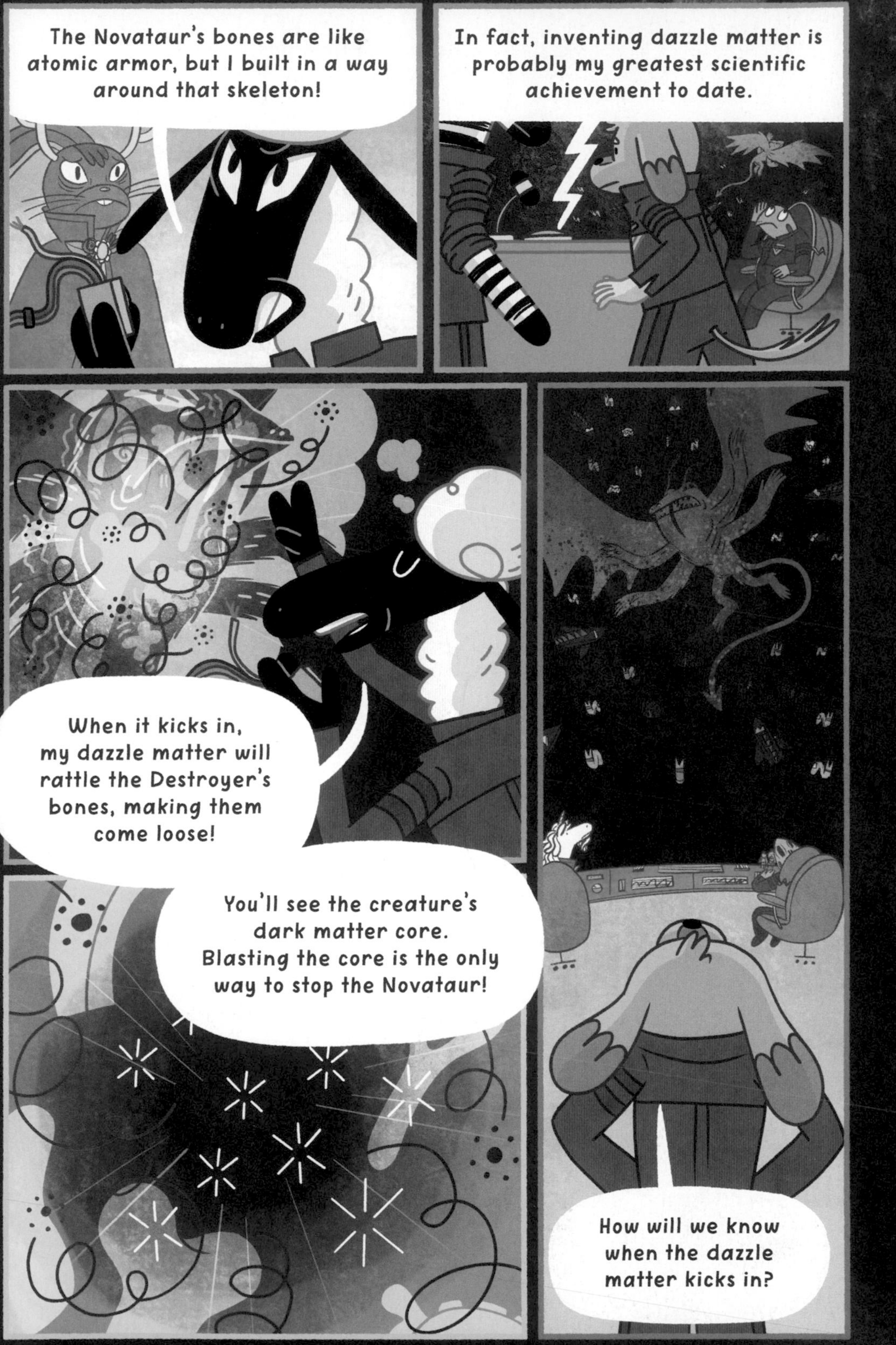
The Novataur's bones are like atomic armor, but I built in a way around that skeleton!
In fact, inventing dazzle matter is probably my greatest scientific achievement to date.
When it kicks in, my dazzle matter will rattle the Destroyer's bones, making them come loose!
You'll see the creature's dark matter core. Blasting the core is the only way to stop the Novataur!
How will we know when the dazzle matter kicks in?

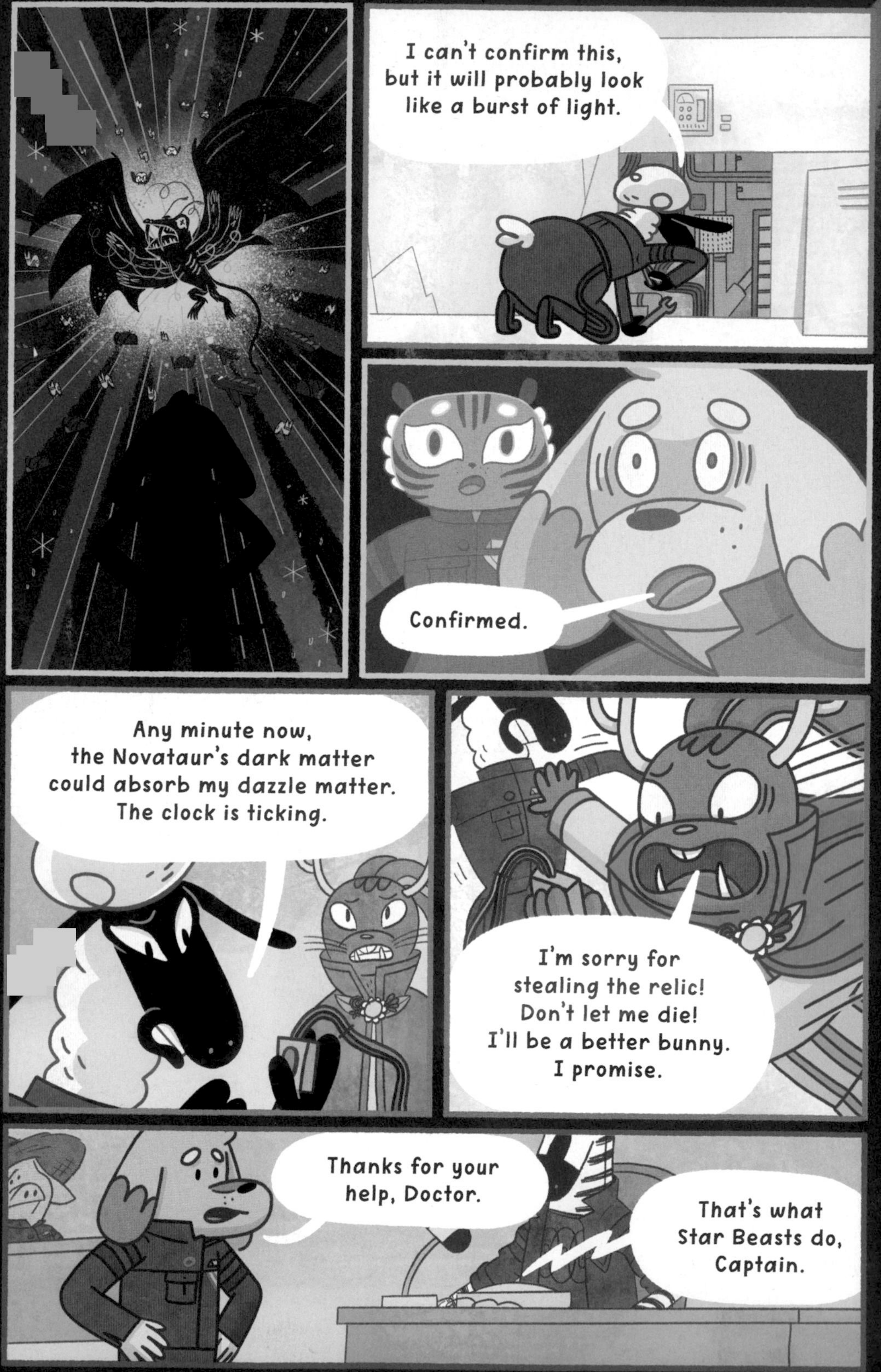
I can't confirm this, but it will probably look like a burst of light.
Confirmed.
Any minute now, the Novataur's dark matter could absorb my dazzle matter. The clock is ticking.
I'm sorry for stealing the relic! Don't let me die! I'll be a better bunny. I promise.
Thanks for your help, Doctor.
That's what Star Beasts do, Captain.

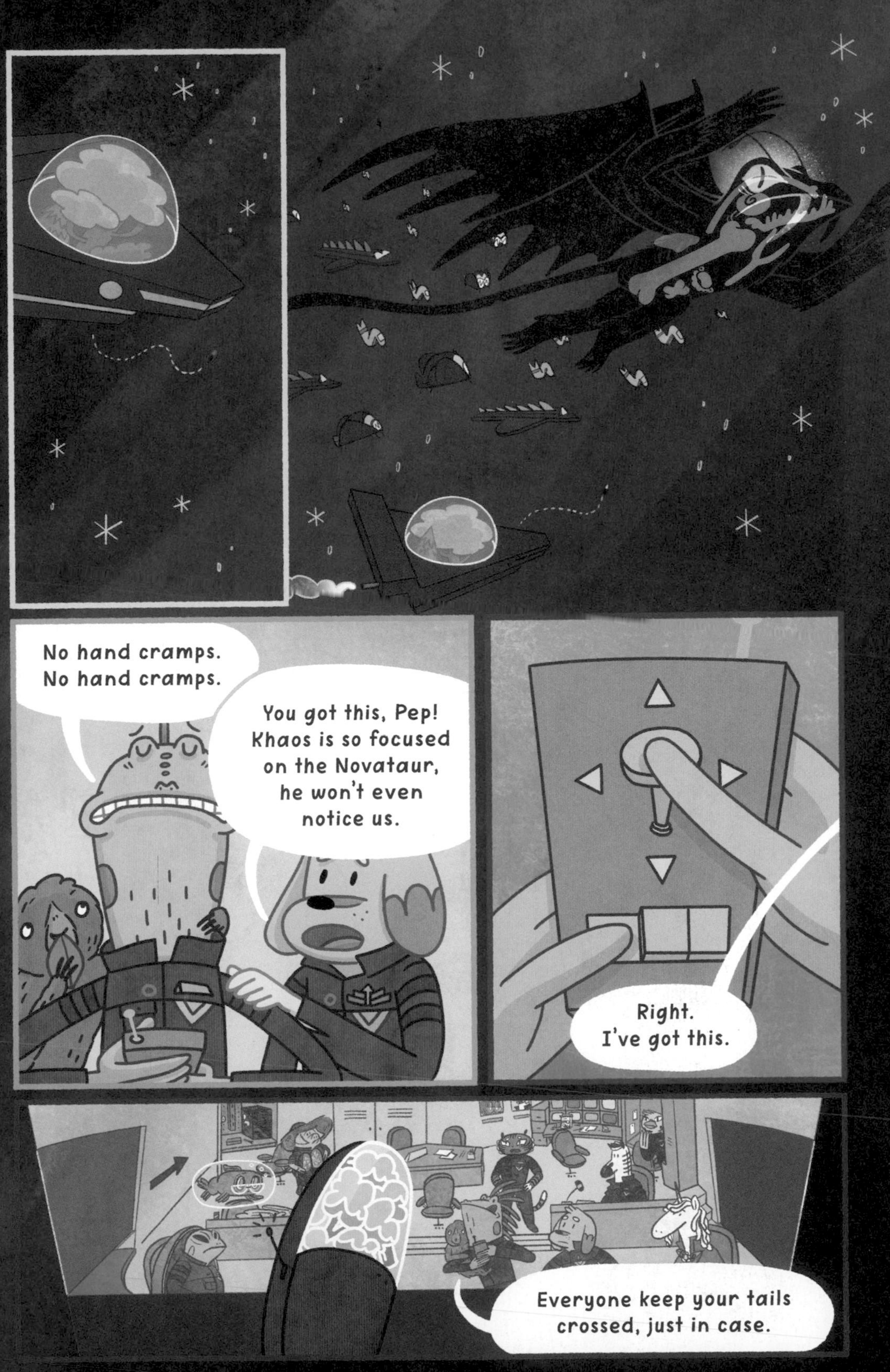
No hand cramps. No hand cramps.
You got this, Pep! Khaos is so focused on the Novataur, he won't even notice us.
Right. I've got this.
Everyone keep your tails crossed, just in case.

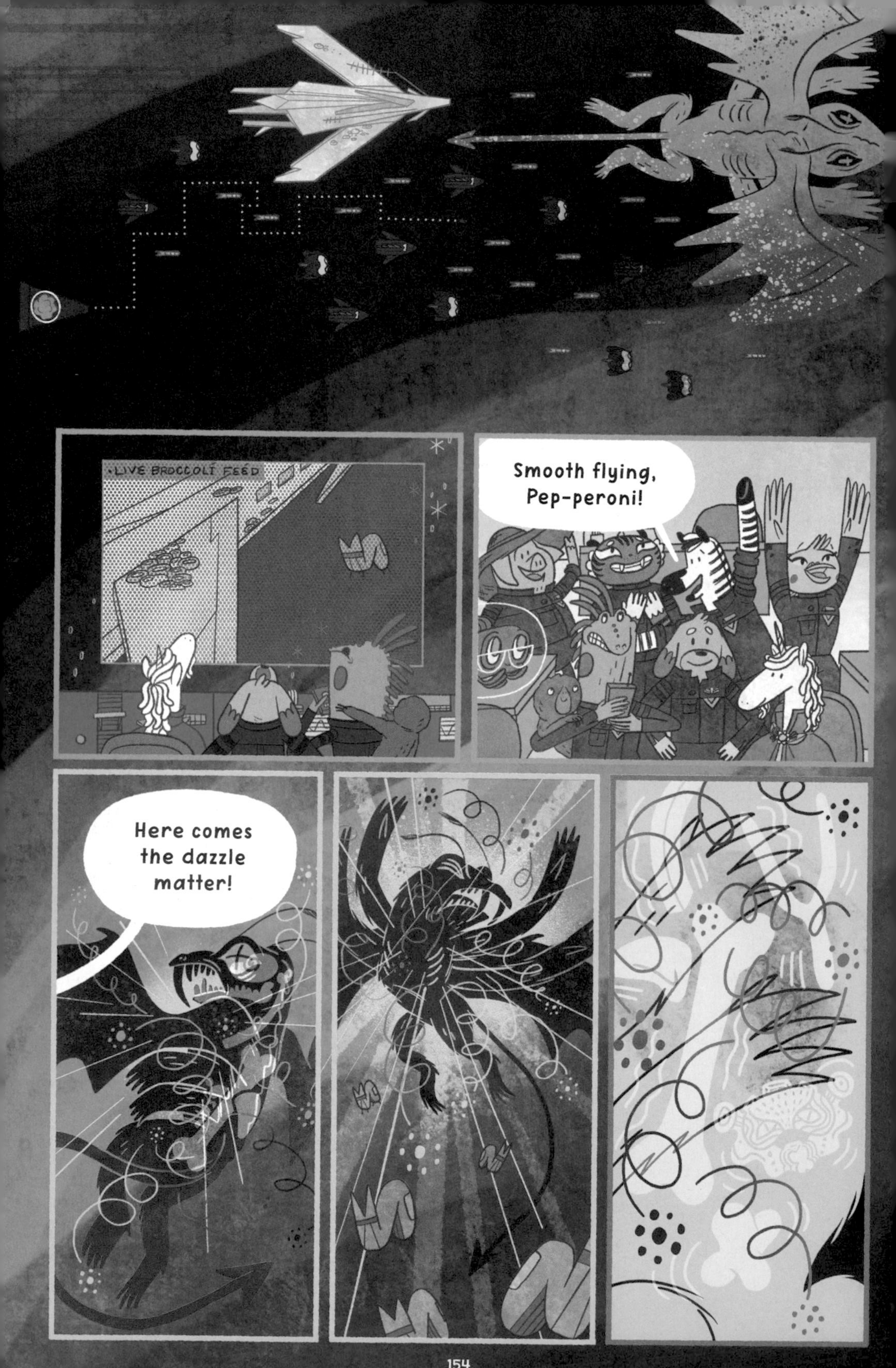

LIVE BROCCOLI FEED
Smooth flying, Pep-peroni!
Here comes the dazzle matter!

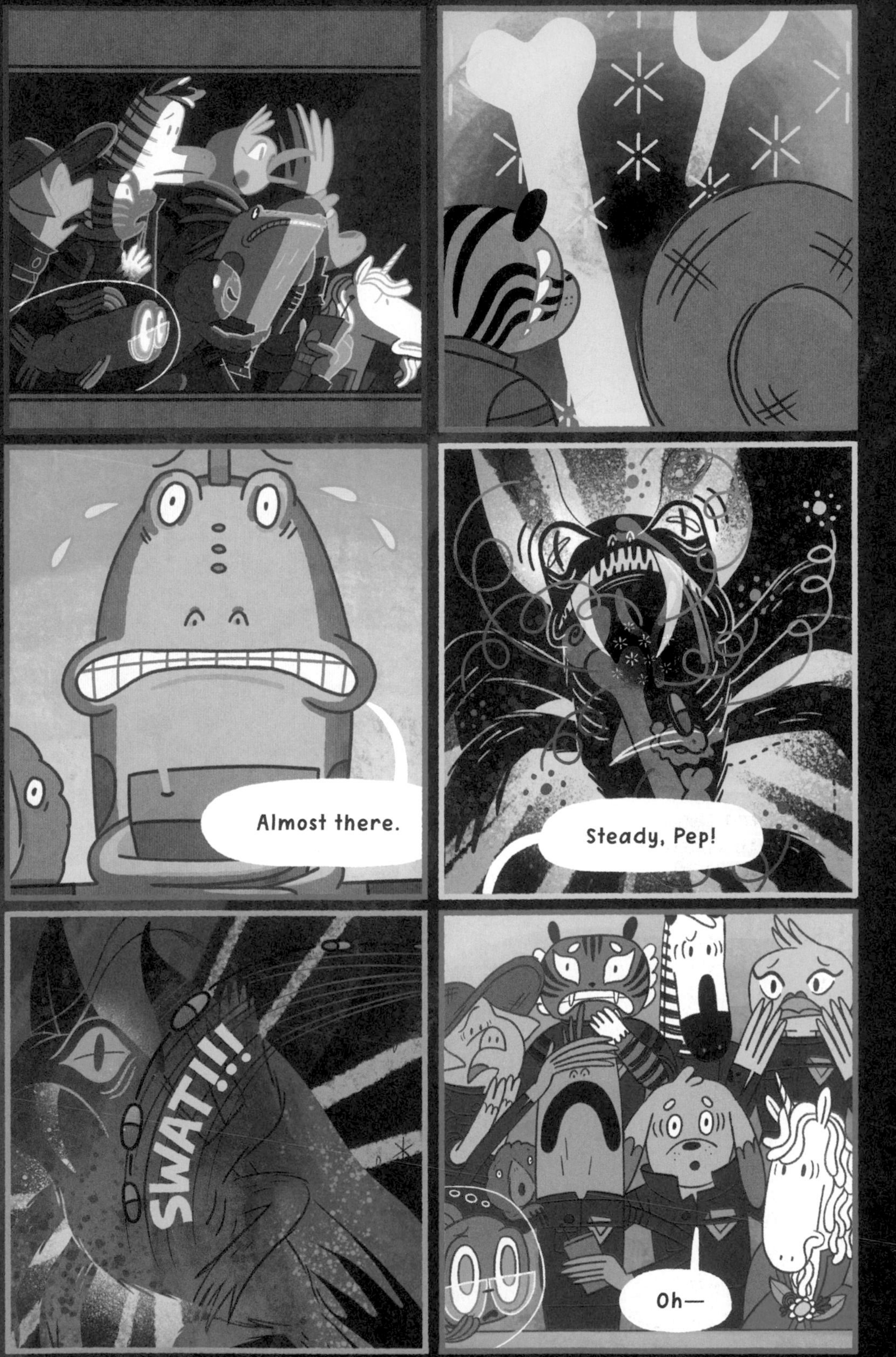
Almost there.
Steady, Pep!
SWAT!!!
Oh—

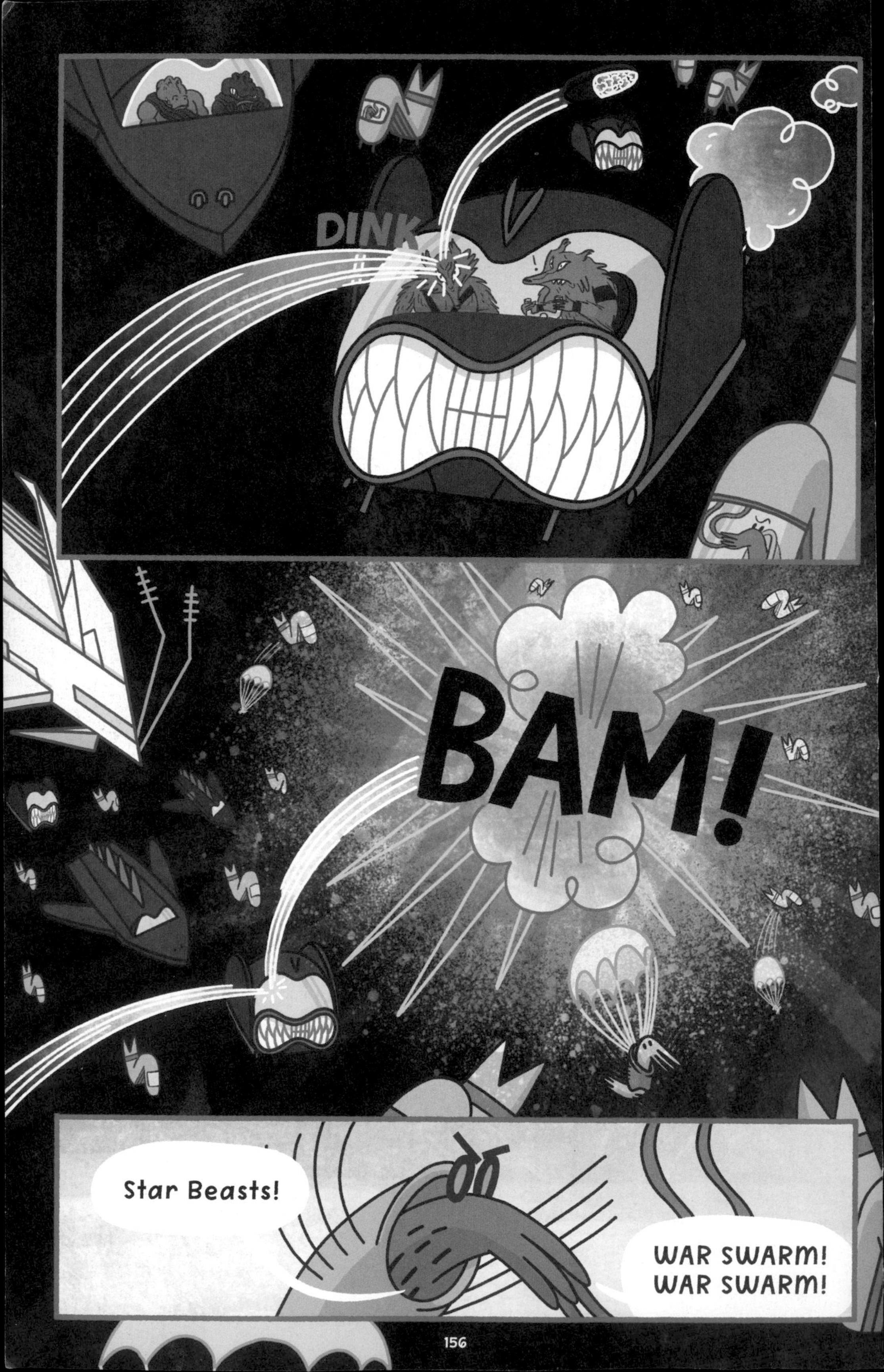
DINK
BAM!
Star Beasts!
WAR SWARM!
WAR SWARM!

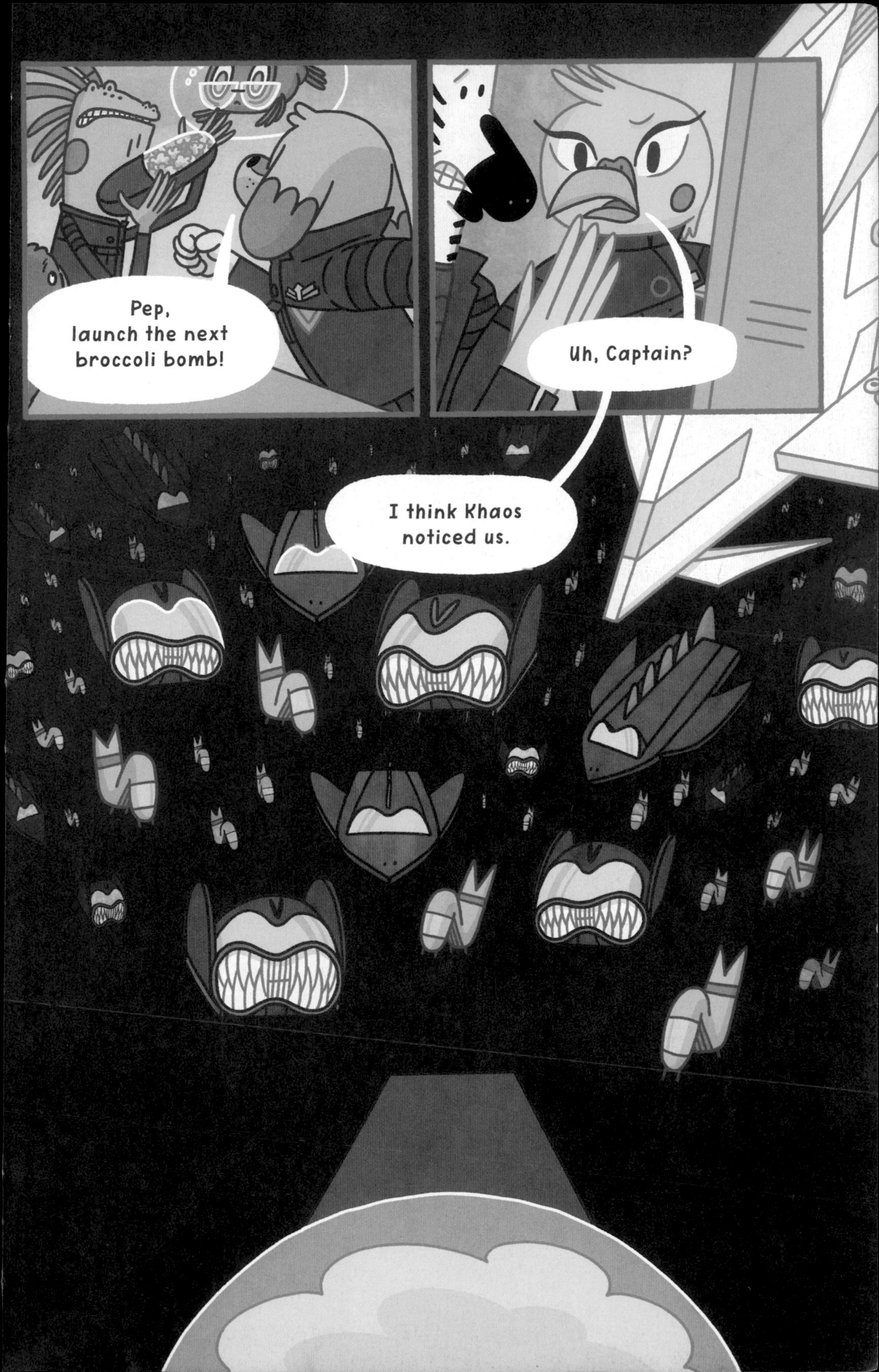
Pep, launch the next broccoli bomb!
Uh, Captain?
I think Khaos noticed us.

CHAPTER 9

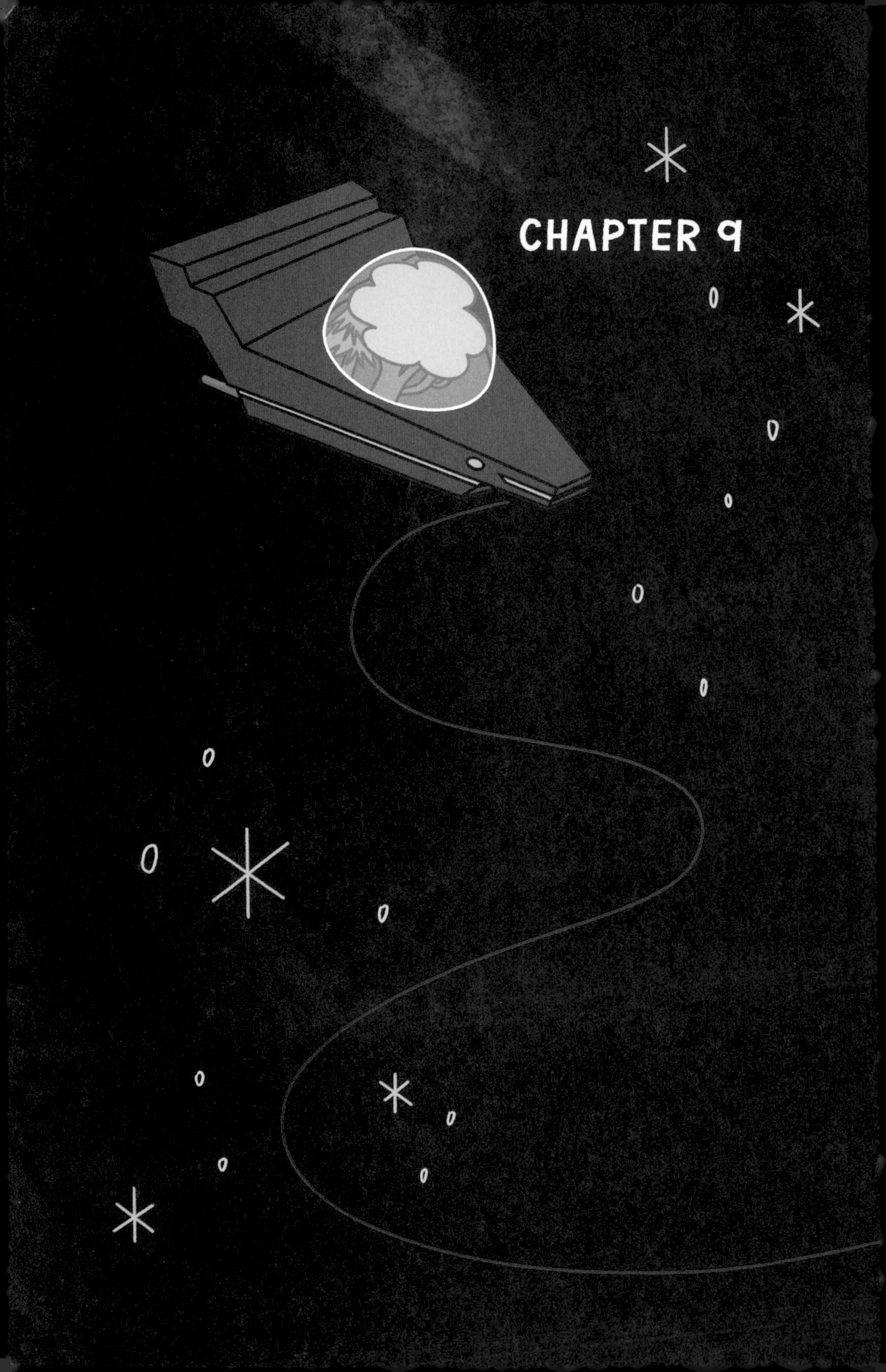

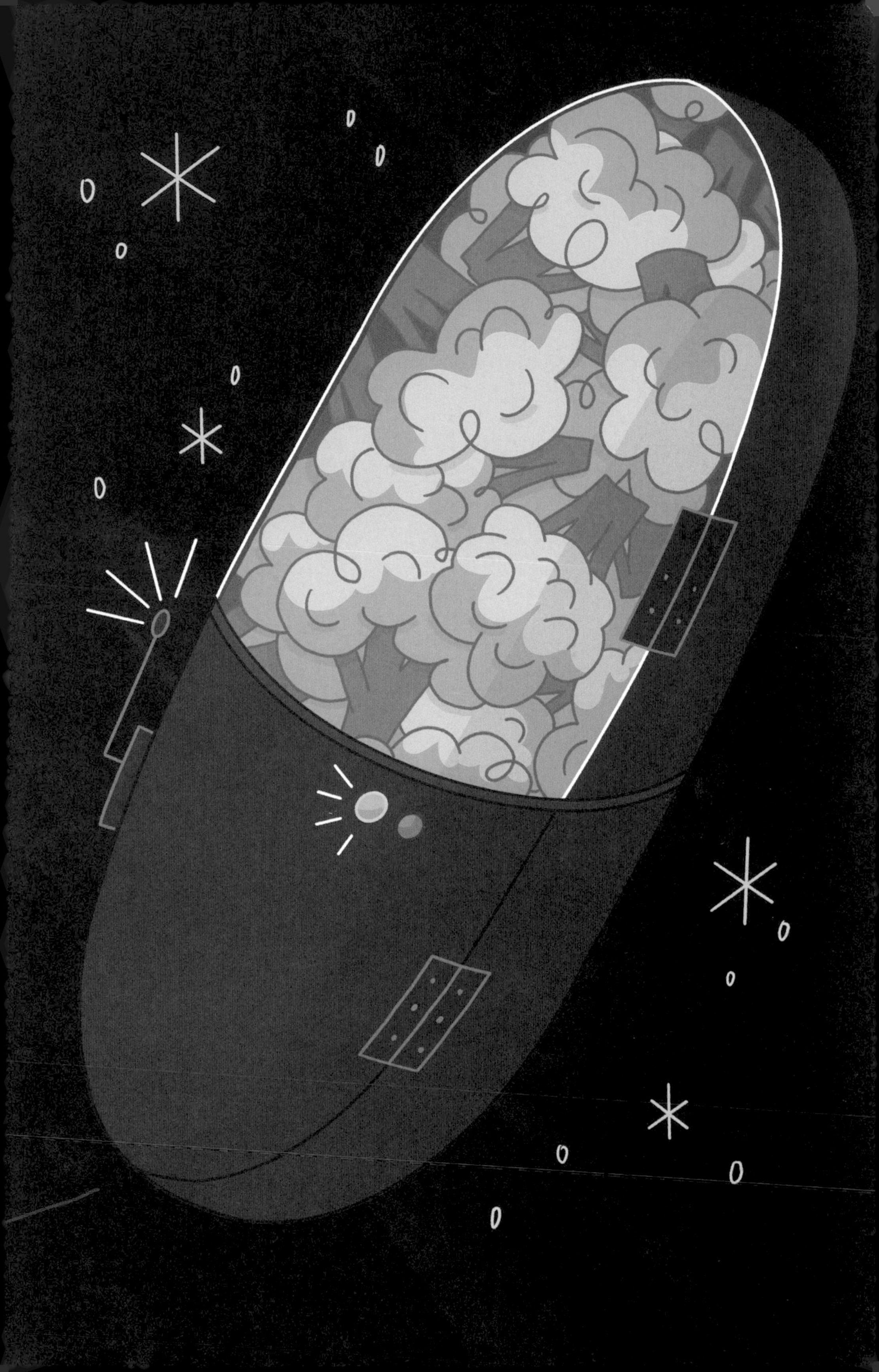

PEW!
Karma!
Force shields are up, Bandit!
BOOM
Mythic blasting, Macca-corn!
Alas! It wasn't me!

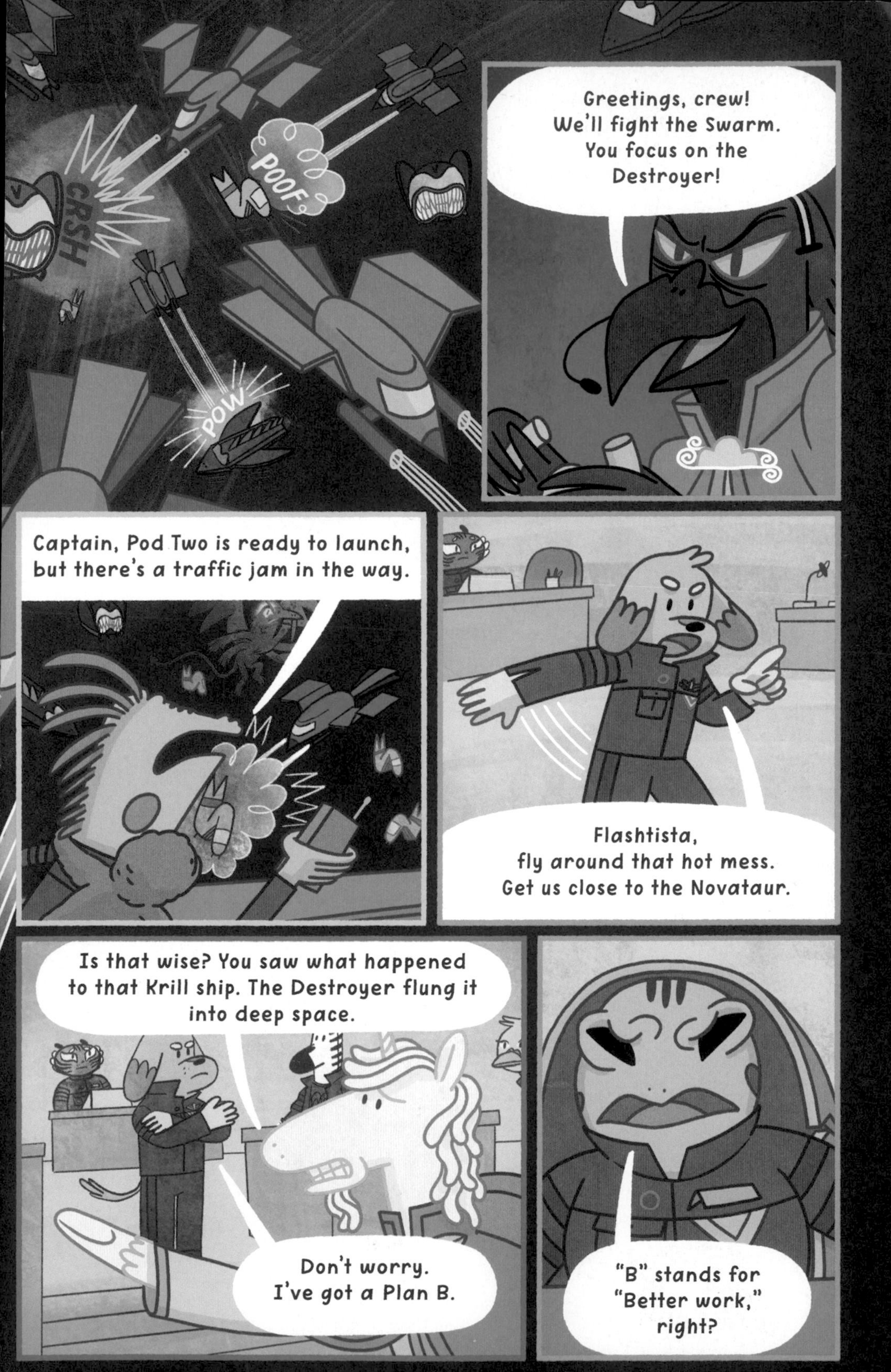
CRSH
POOF
POW
Greetings, crew! We'll fight the Swarm. You focus on the Destroyer!
Captain, Pod Two is ready to launch, but there's a traffic jam in the way.
Flashtista, fly around that hot mess. Get us close to the Novataur.
Is that wise? You saw what happened to that Krill ship. The Destroyer flung it into deep space.
Don't worry. I've got a Plan B.
"B" stands for "Better work," right?

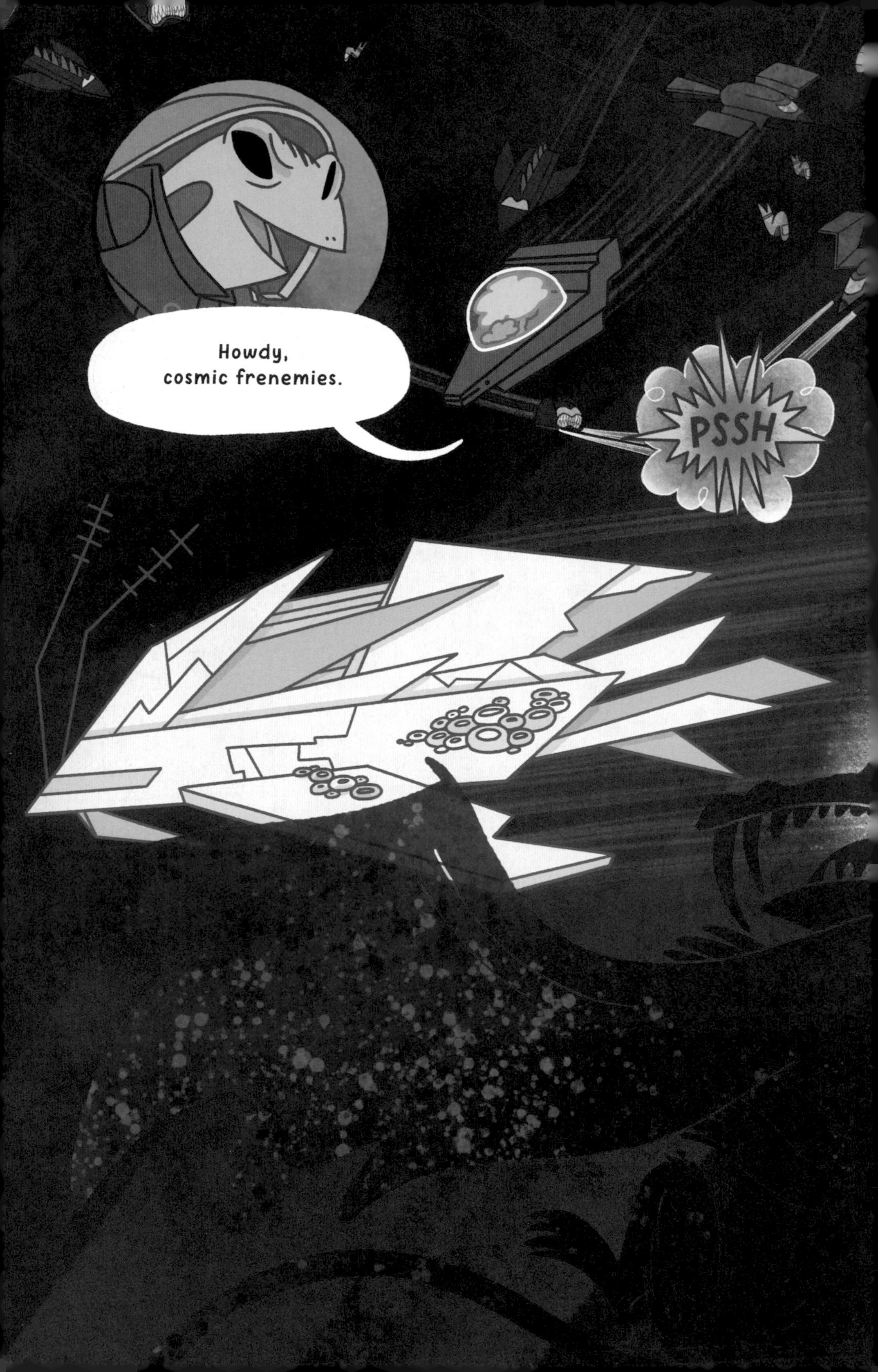
Howdy, cosmic frenemies.
PSSH

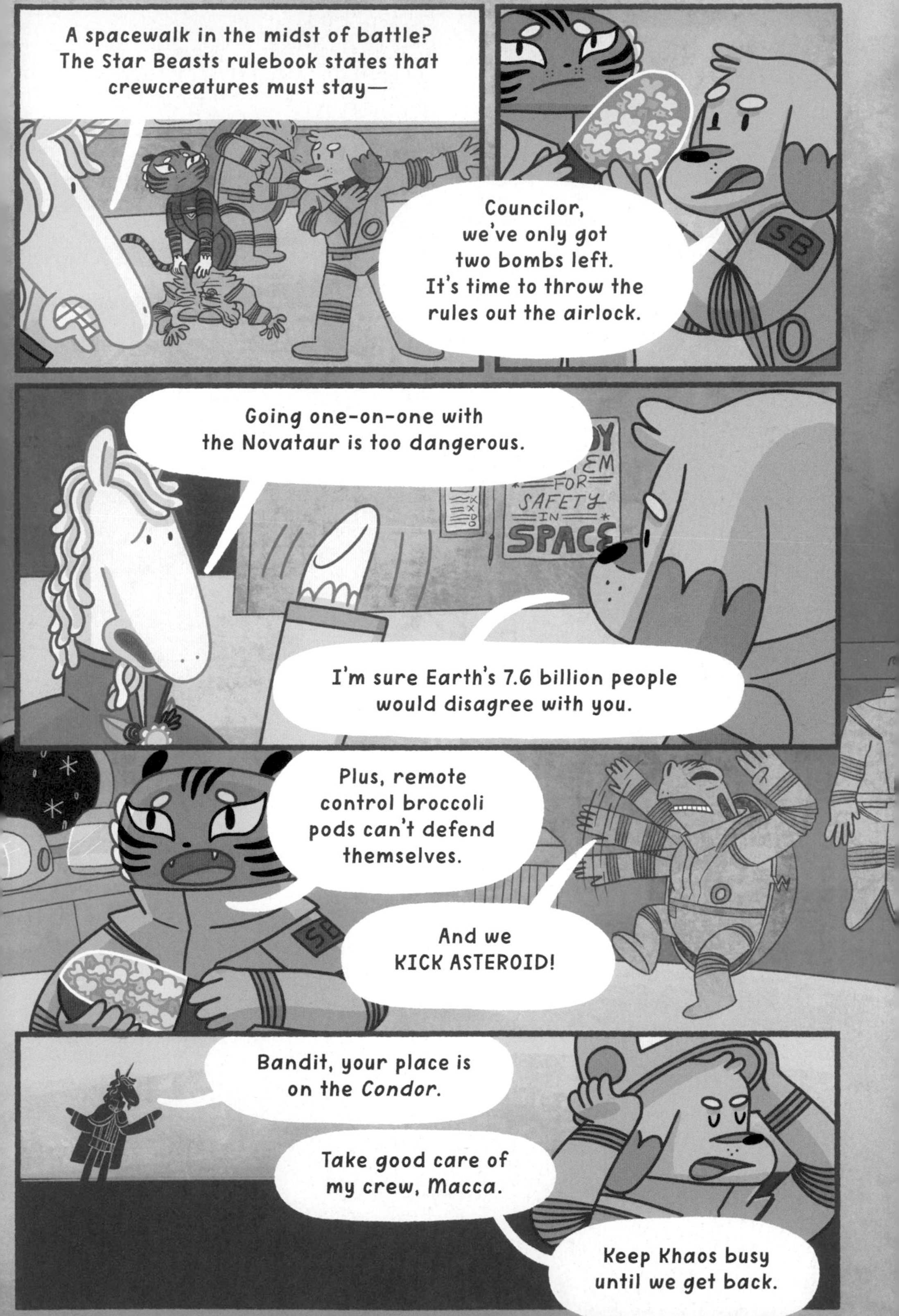
A spacewalk in the midst of battle? The Star Beasts rulebook states that crewcreatures must stay—
Councilor, we've only got two bombs left. It's time to throw the rules out the airlock.
Going one-on-one with the Novataur is too dangerous.
FOR SAFETY IN SPACE
I'm sure Earth's 7.6 billion people would disagree with you.
Plus, remote control broccoli pods can't defend themselves.
And we KICK ASTEROID!
Bandit, your place is on the *Condor*.
Take good care of my crew, Macca.
Keep Khaos busy until we get back.

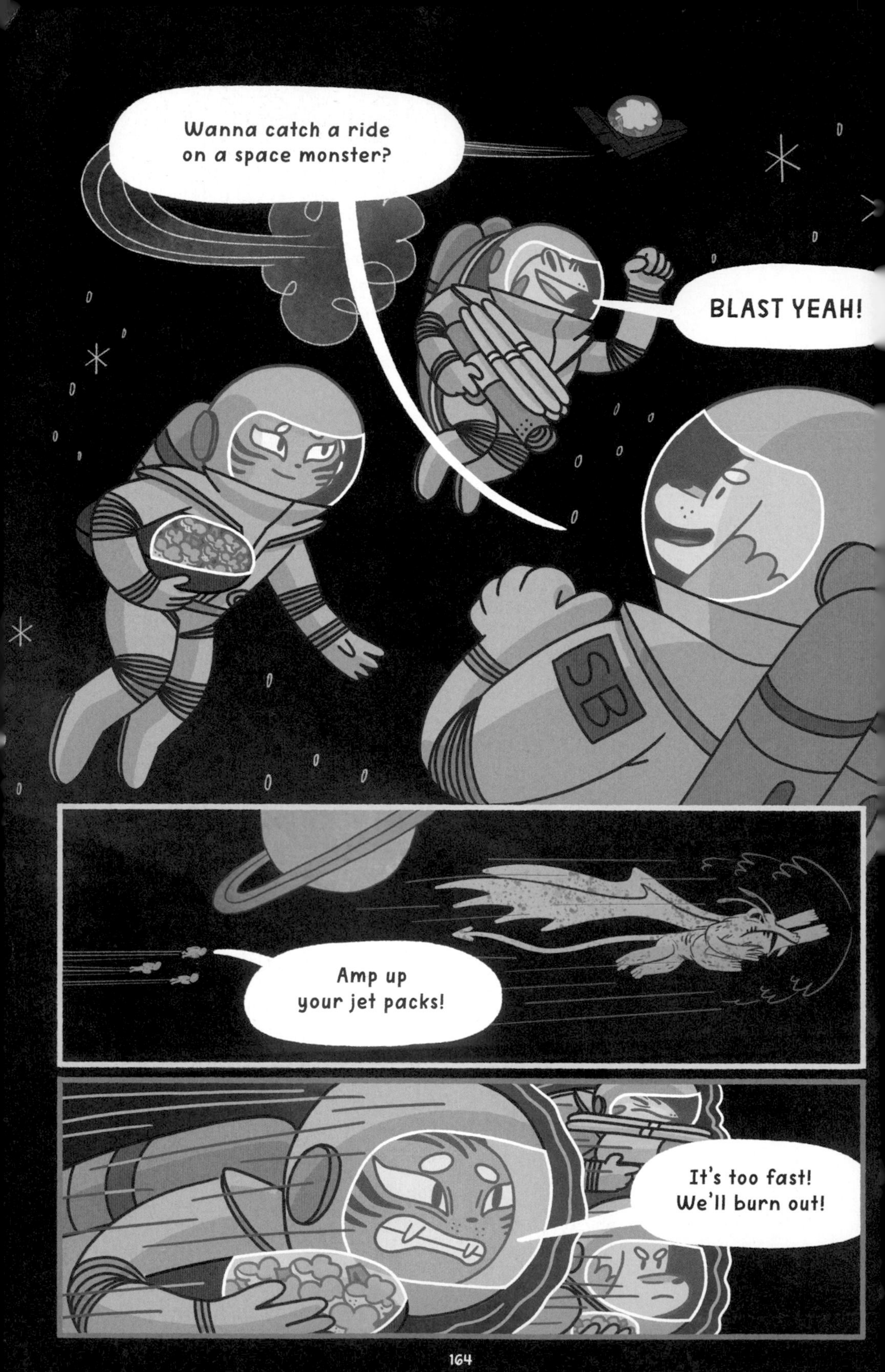
Wanna catch a ride on a space monster?
BLAST YEAH!
SB
Amp up your jet packs!
It's too fast! We'll burn out!

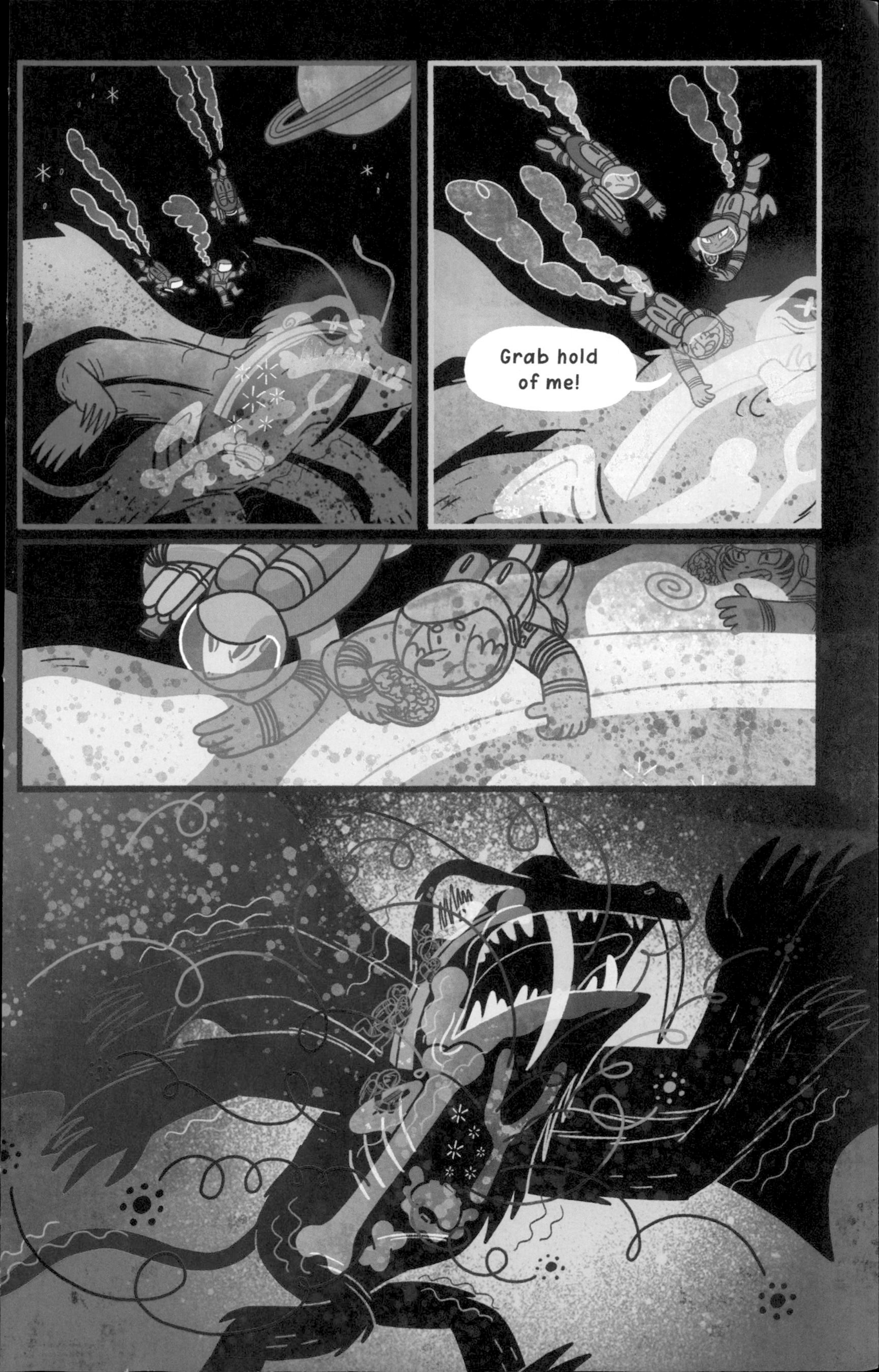
Grab hold of me!

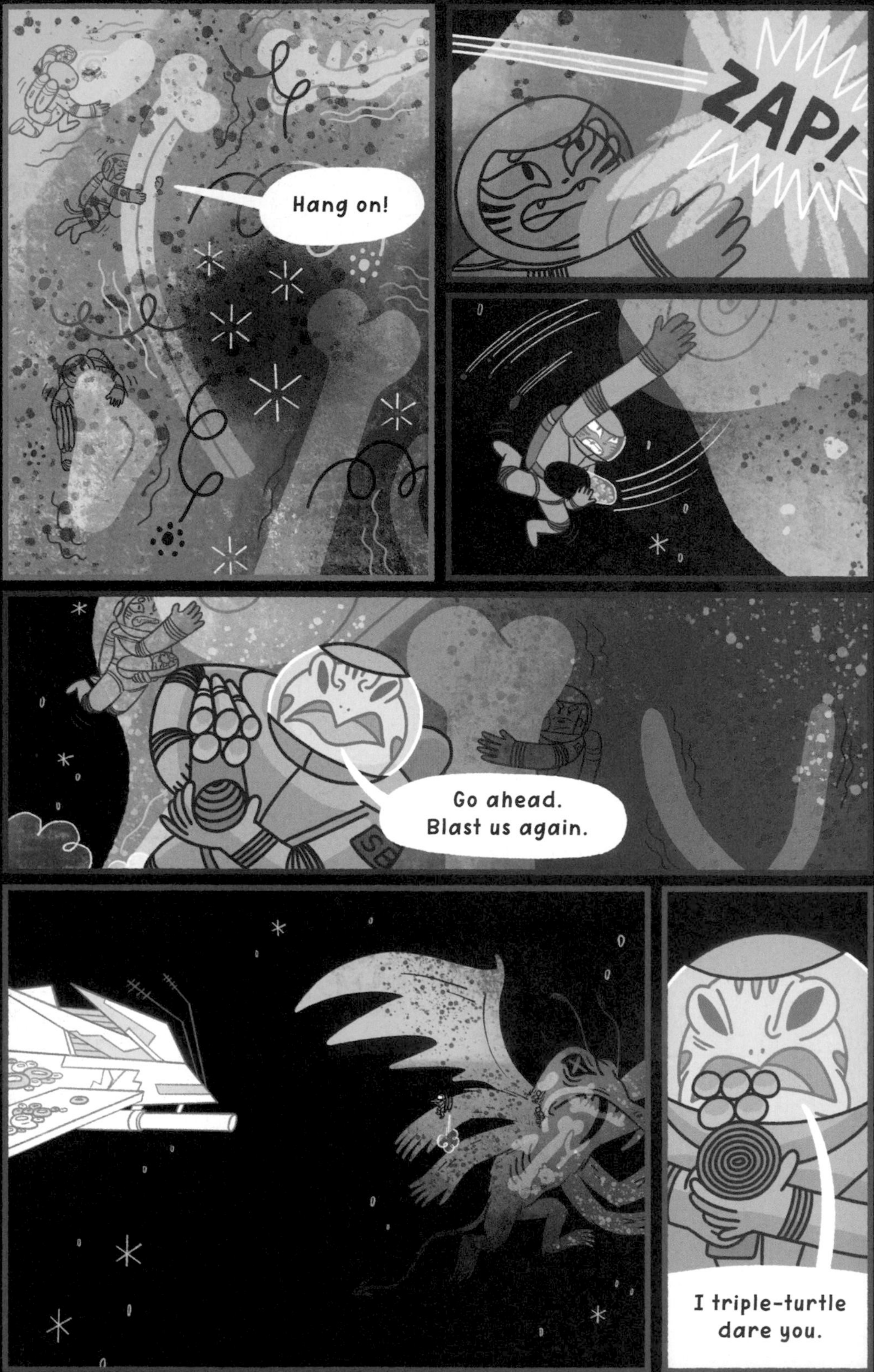
Hang on!
ZAP!
Go ahead. Blast us again.
I triple-turtle dare you.

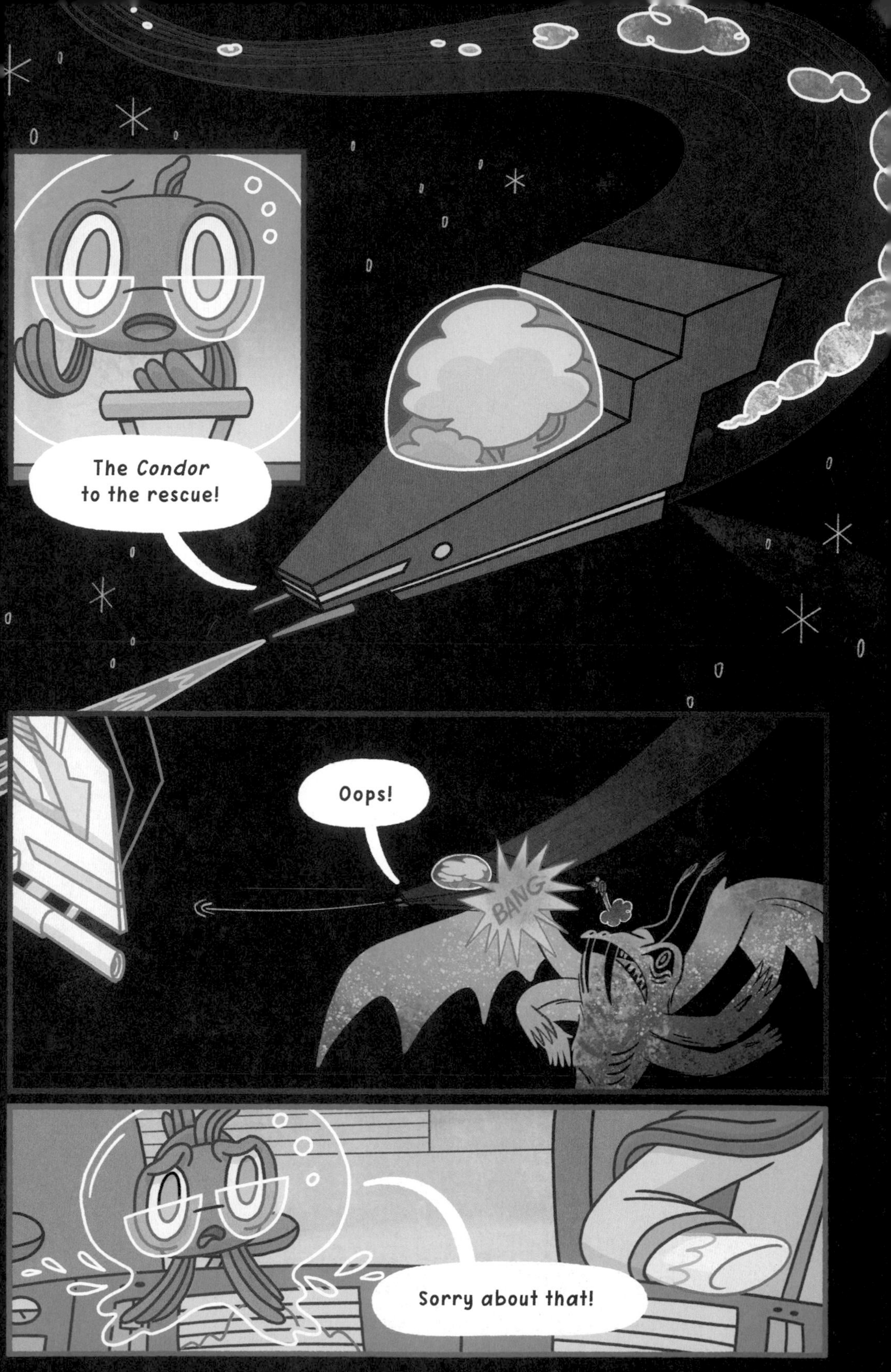
The *Condor* to the rescue!
Oops!
BANG
Sorry about that!

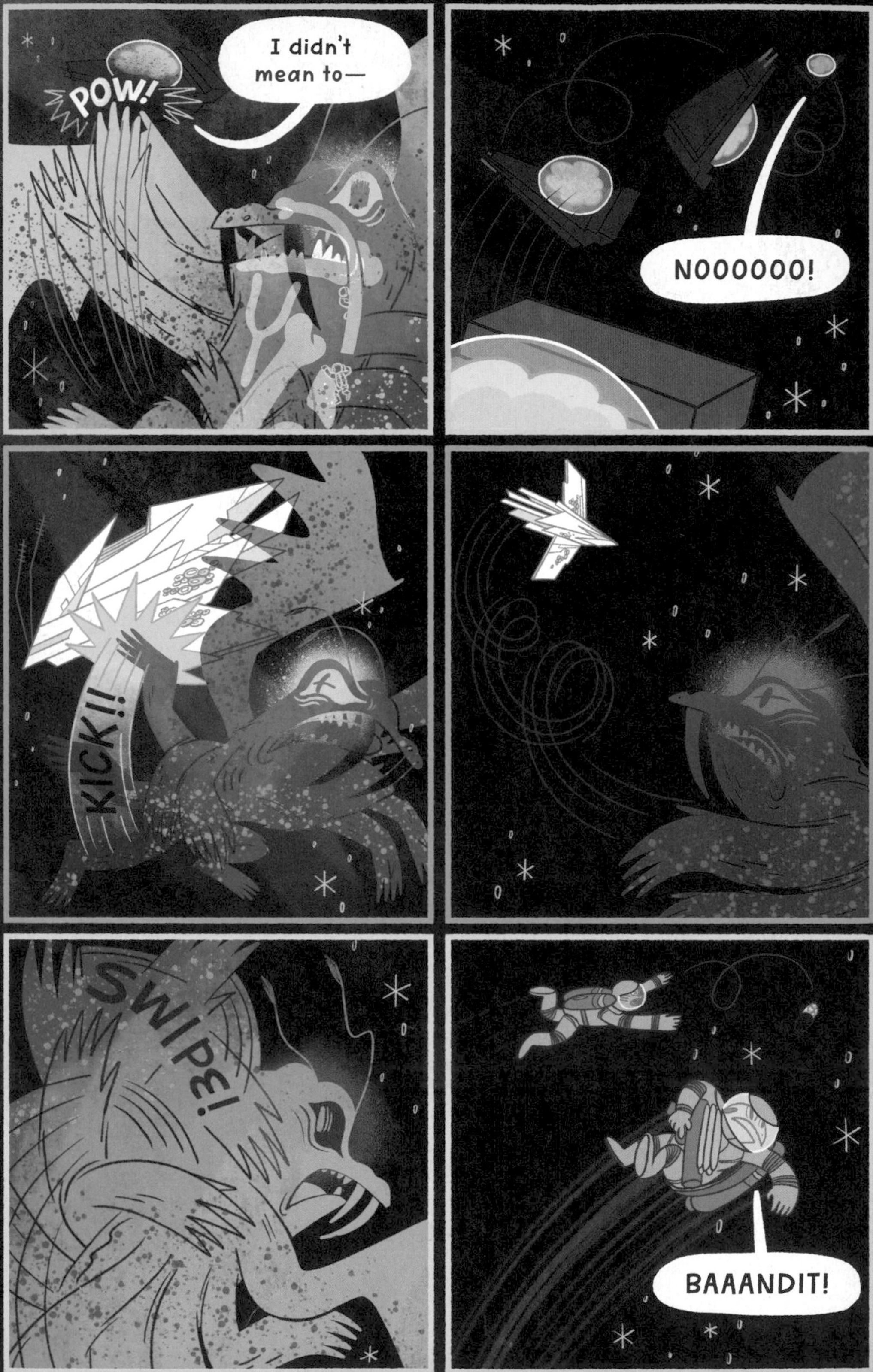
POW!
I didn't mean to—
NOOOOOO!
KICK!!
SWIPE!
BAAANDIT!

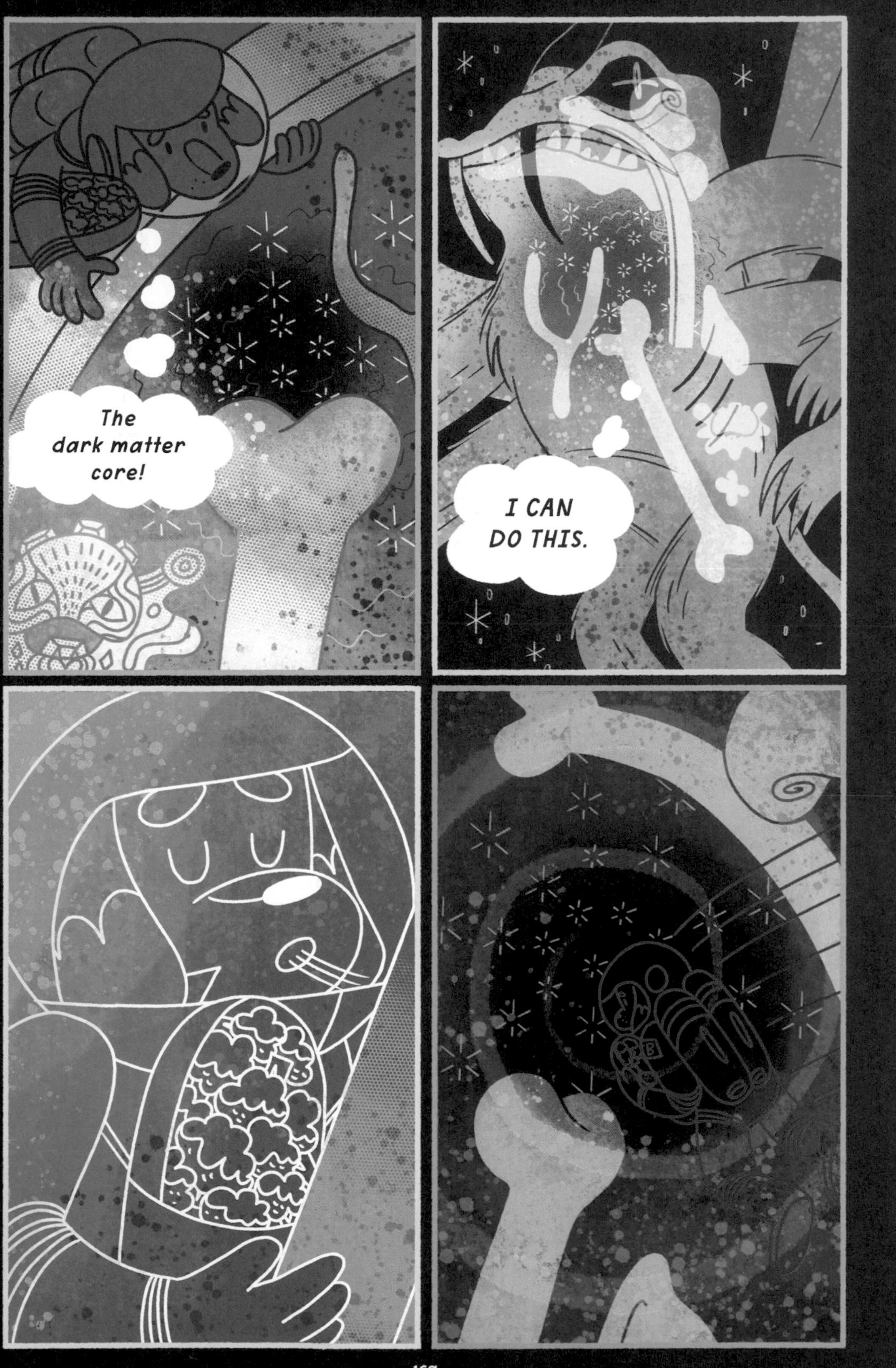
The dark matter core!
I CAN DO THIS.

CHAPTER 10

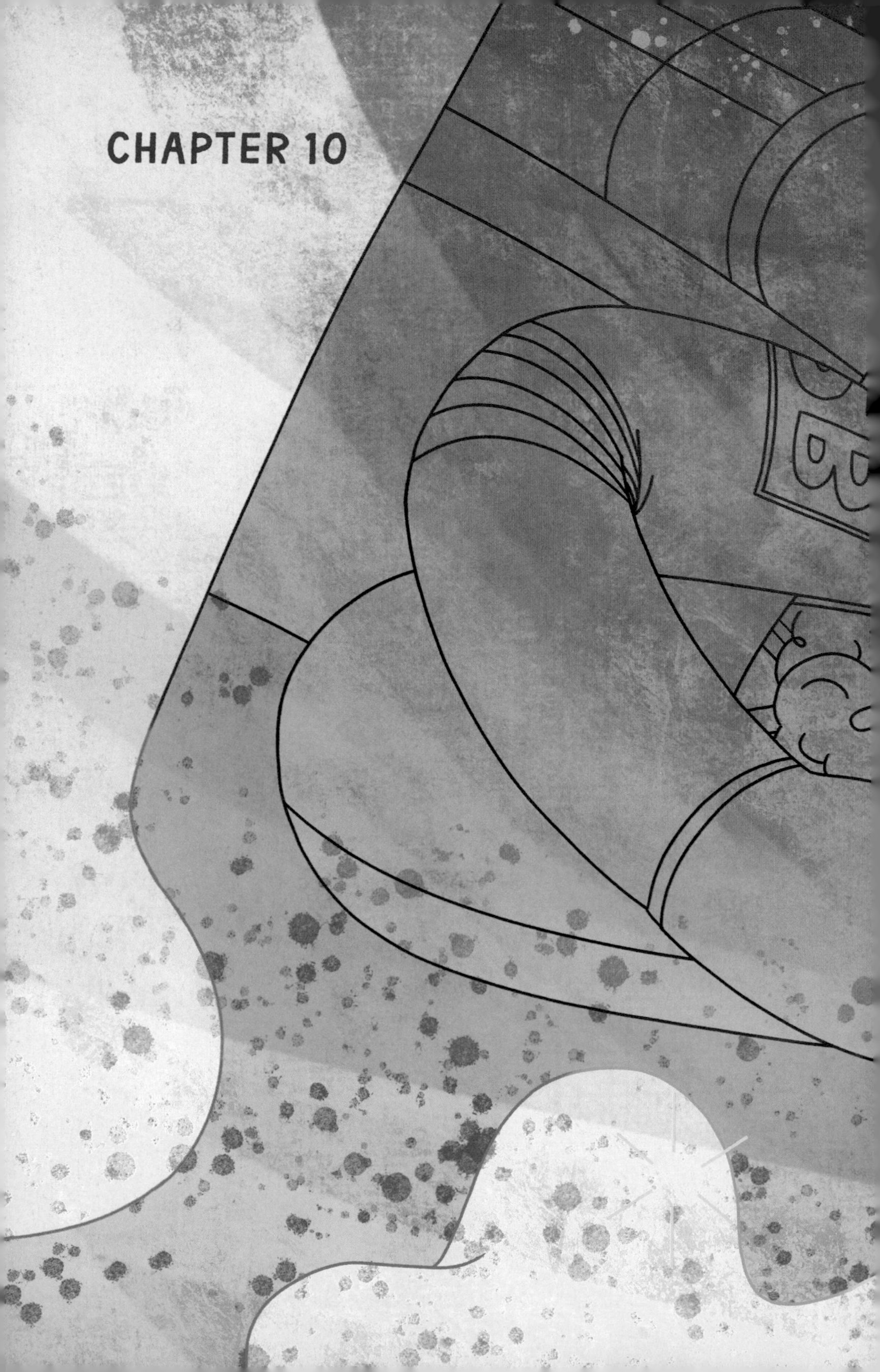

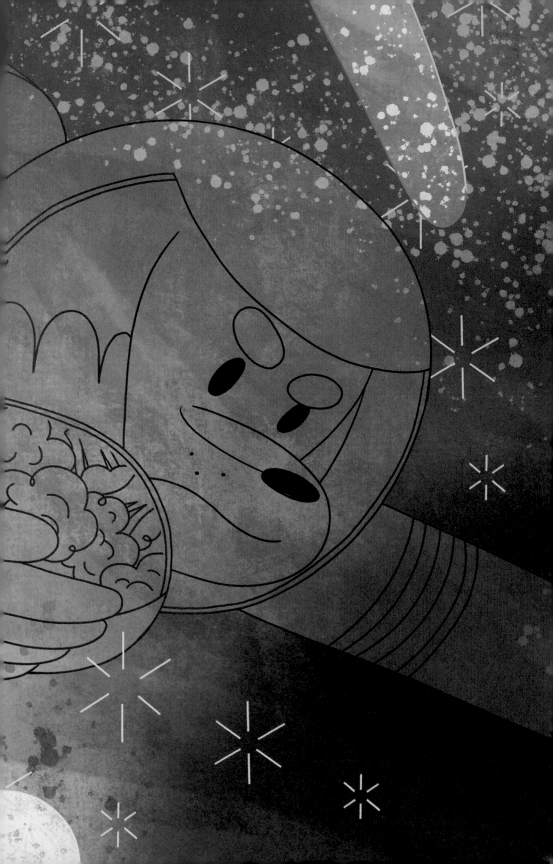

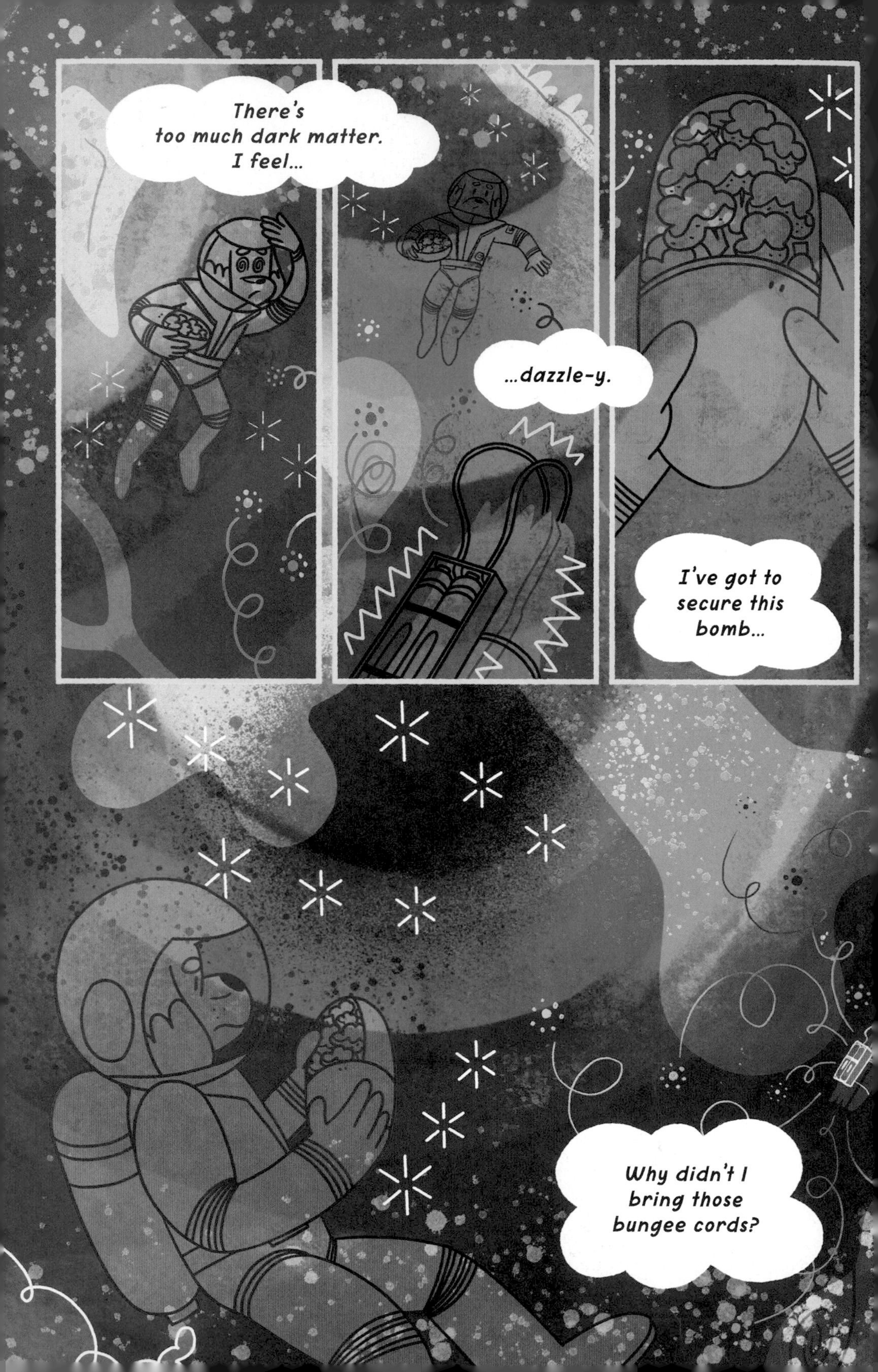
There's too much dark matter. I feel...
...dazzle-y.
I've got to secure this bomb...
Why didn't I bring those bungee cords?

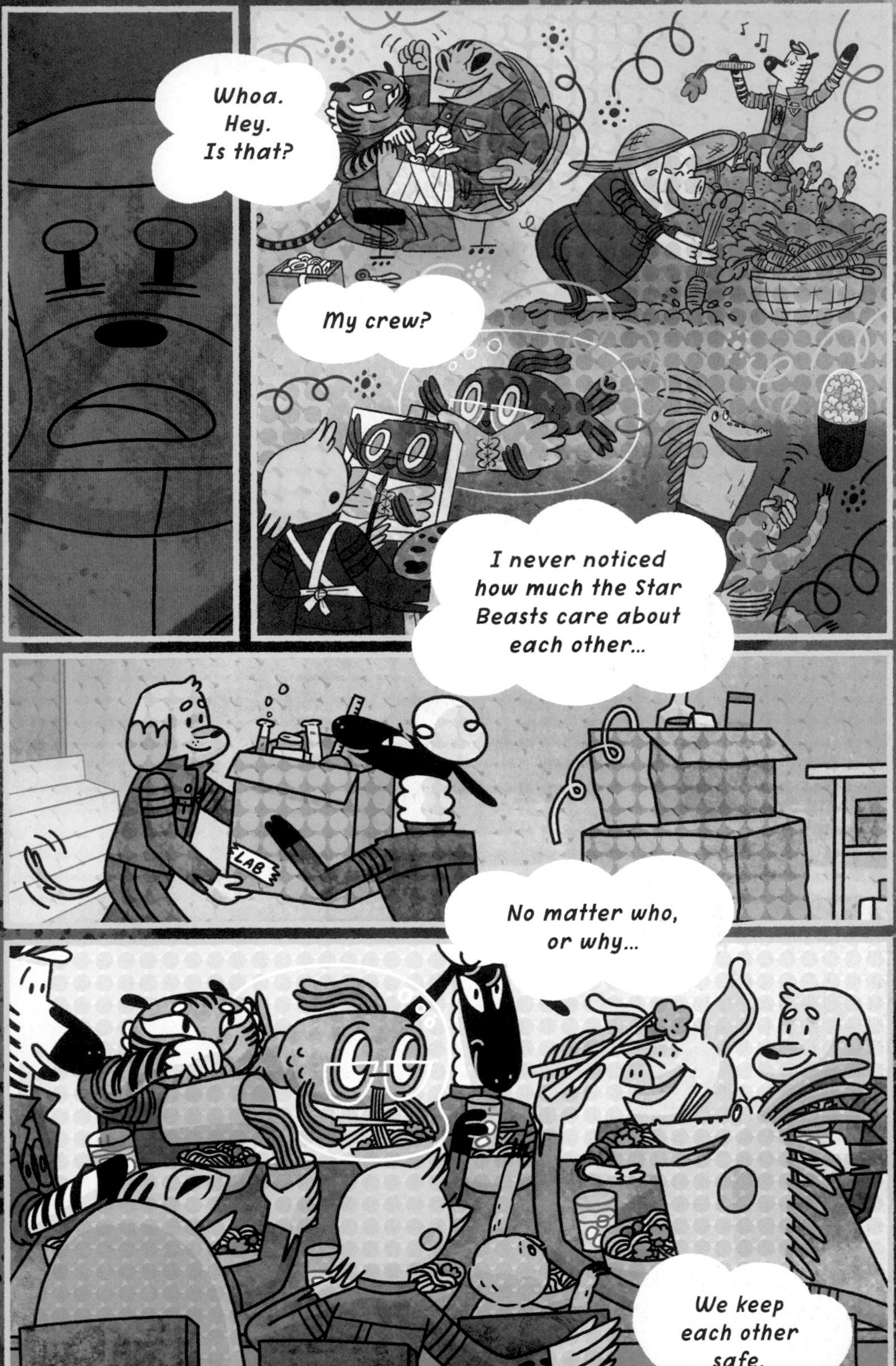
Whoa. Hey. Is that?
My crew?
I never noticed how much the Star Beasts care about each other...
LAB
No matter who, or why...
We keep each other safe.

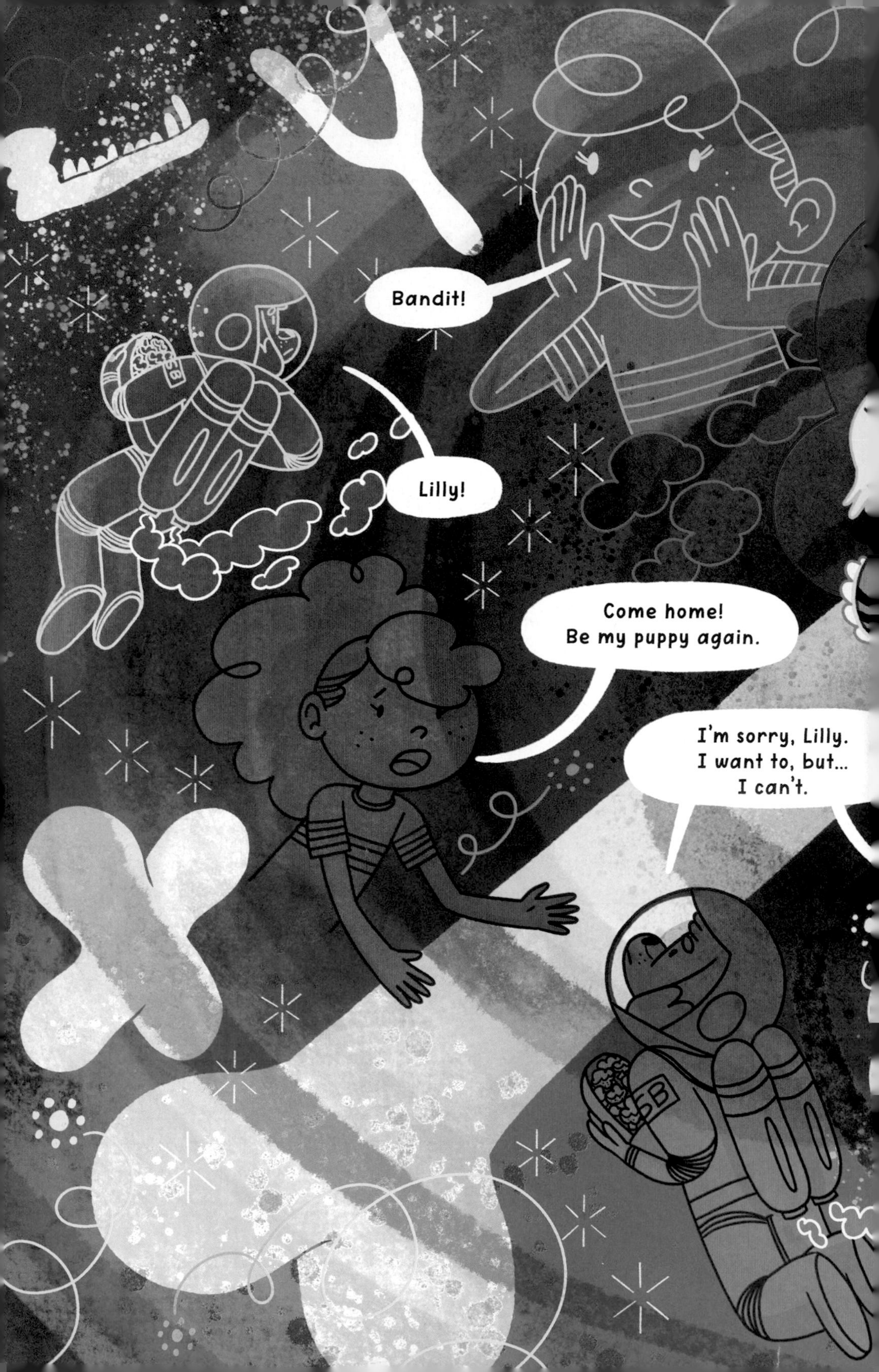
Bandit!
Lilly!
Come home! Be my puppy again.
I'm sorry, Lilly. I want to, but... I can't.

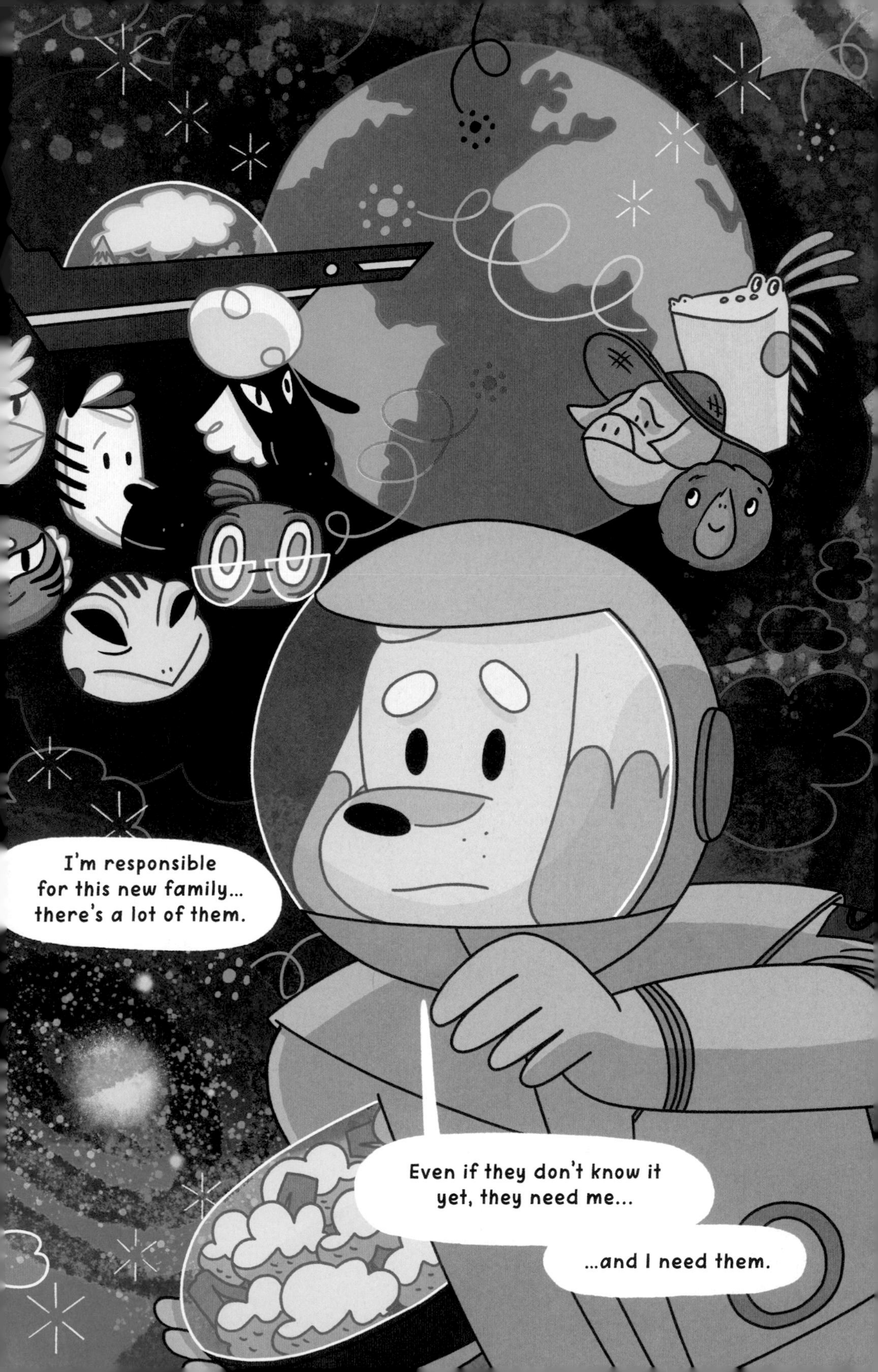
I'm responsible for this new family... there's a lot of them.
Even if they don't know it yet, they need me...
...and I need them.

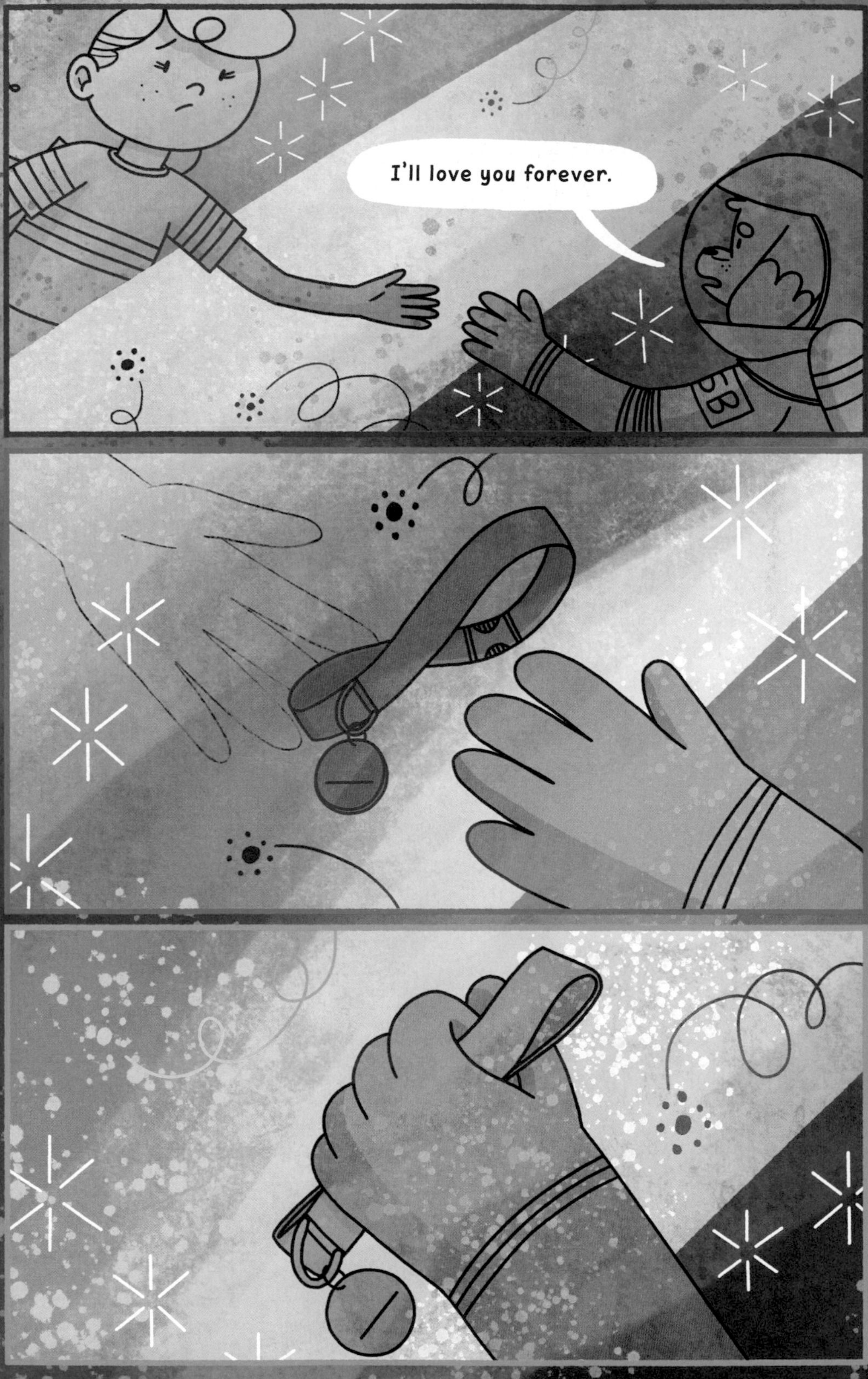
I'll love you forever.

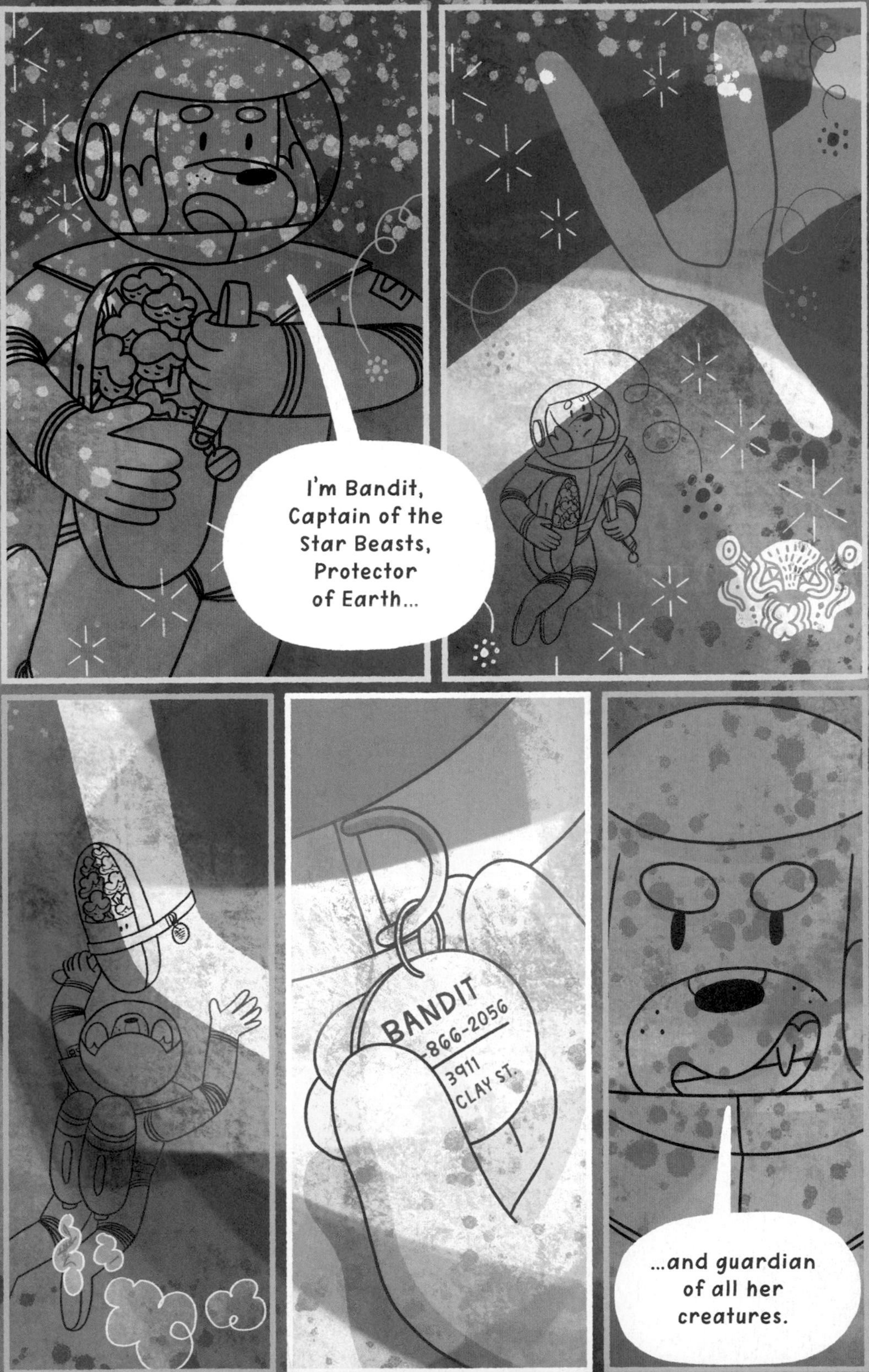
I'm Bandit, Captain of the Star Beasts, Protector of Earth...
BANDIT
-866-2056
3911 CLAY ST.
...and guardian of all her creatures.

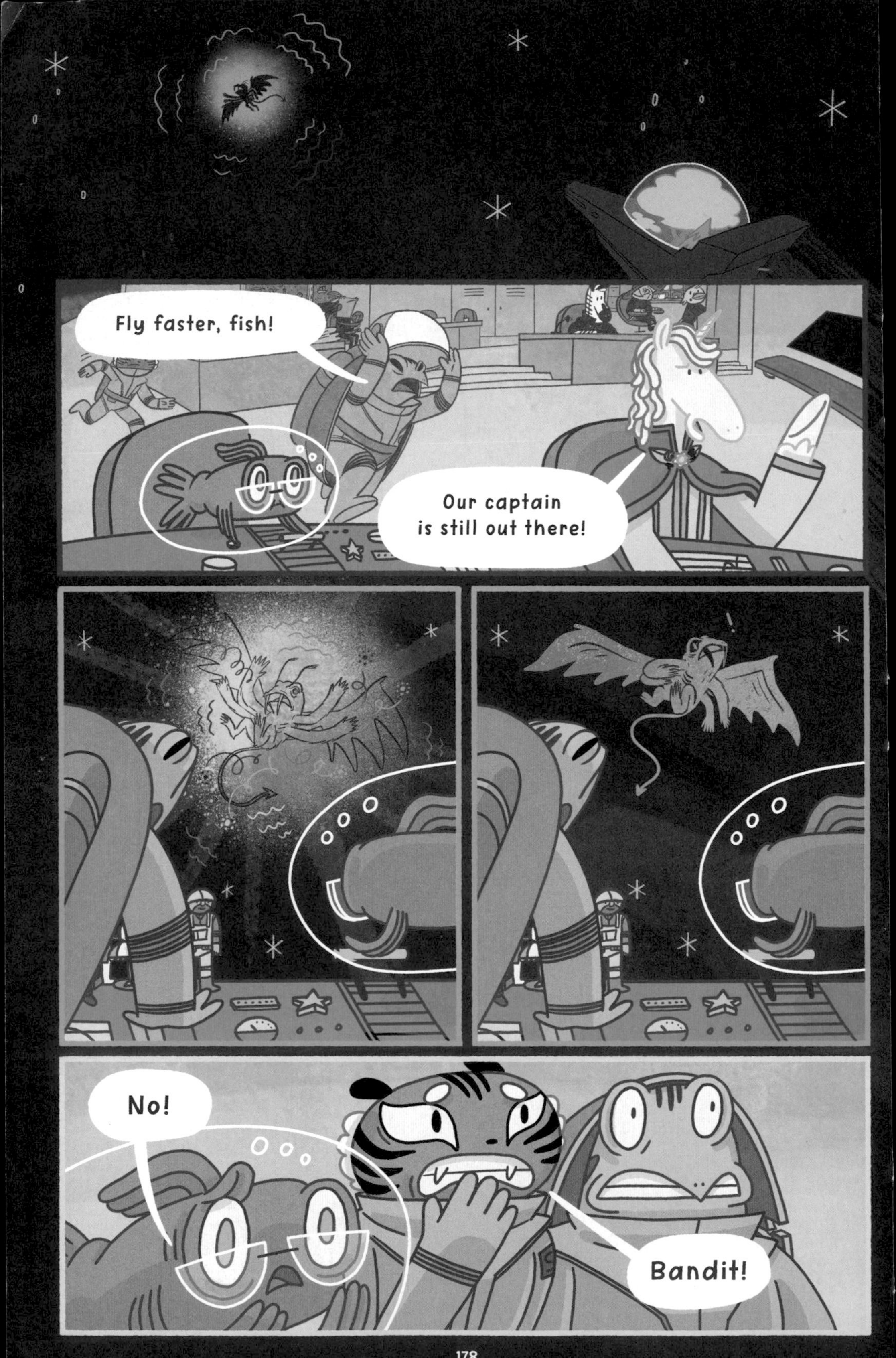
Fly faster, fish!
Our captain is still out there!
!
No!
Bandit!

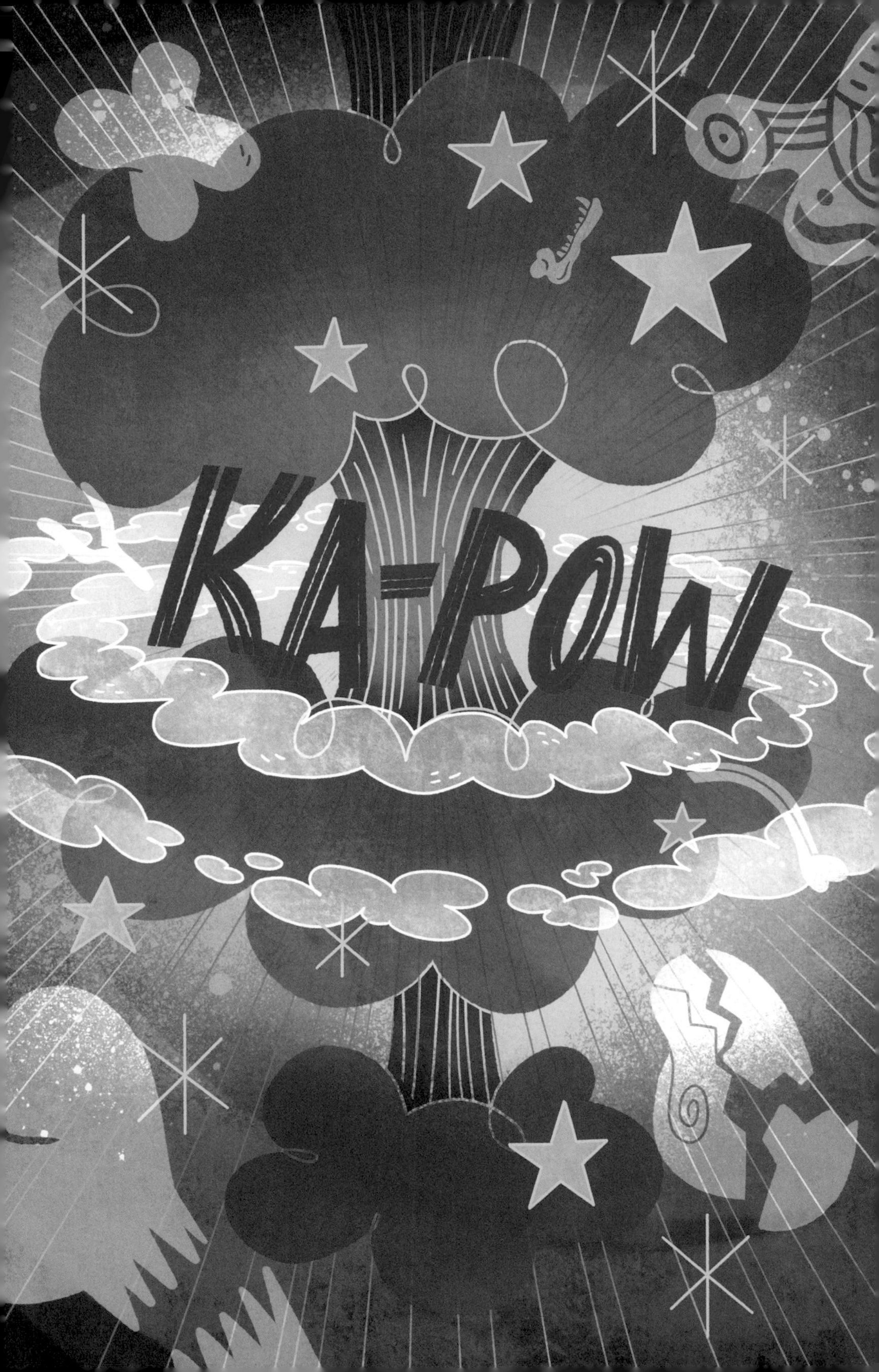
KA-POW

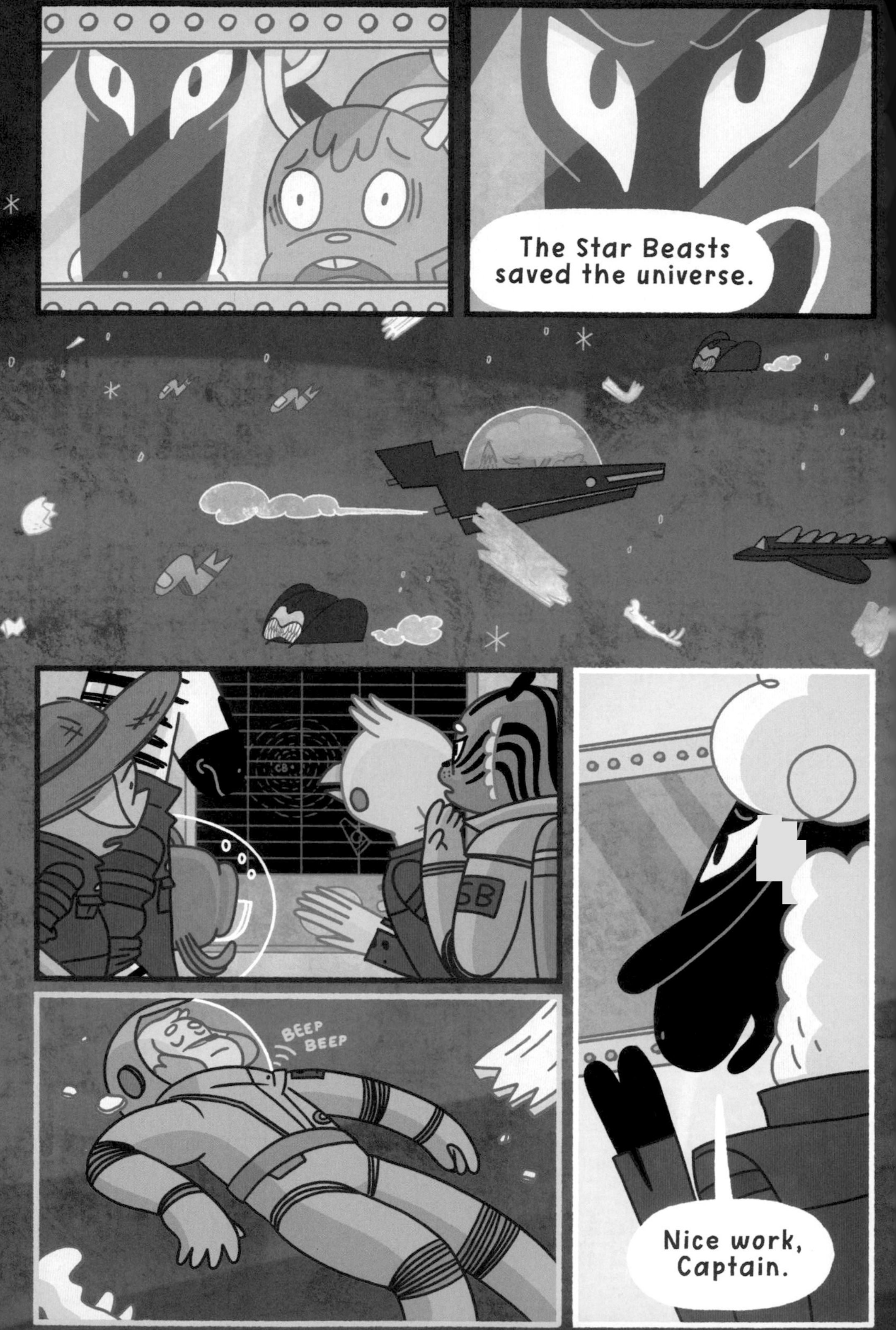

The Star Beasts saved the universe.
SB
BEEP BEEP
Nice work, Captain.

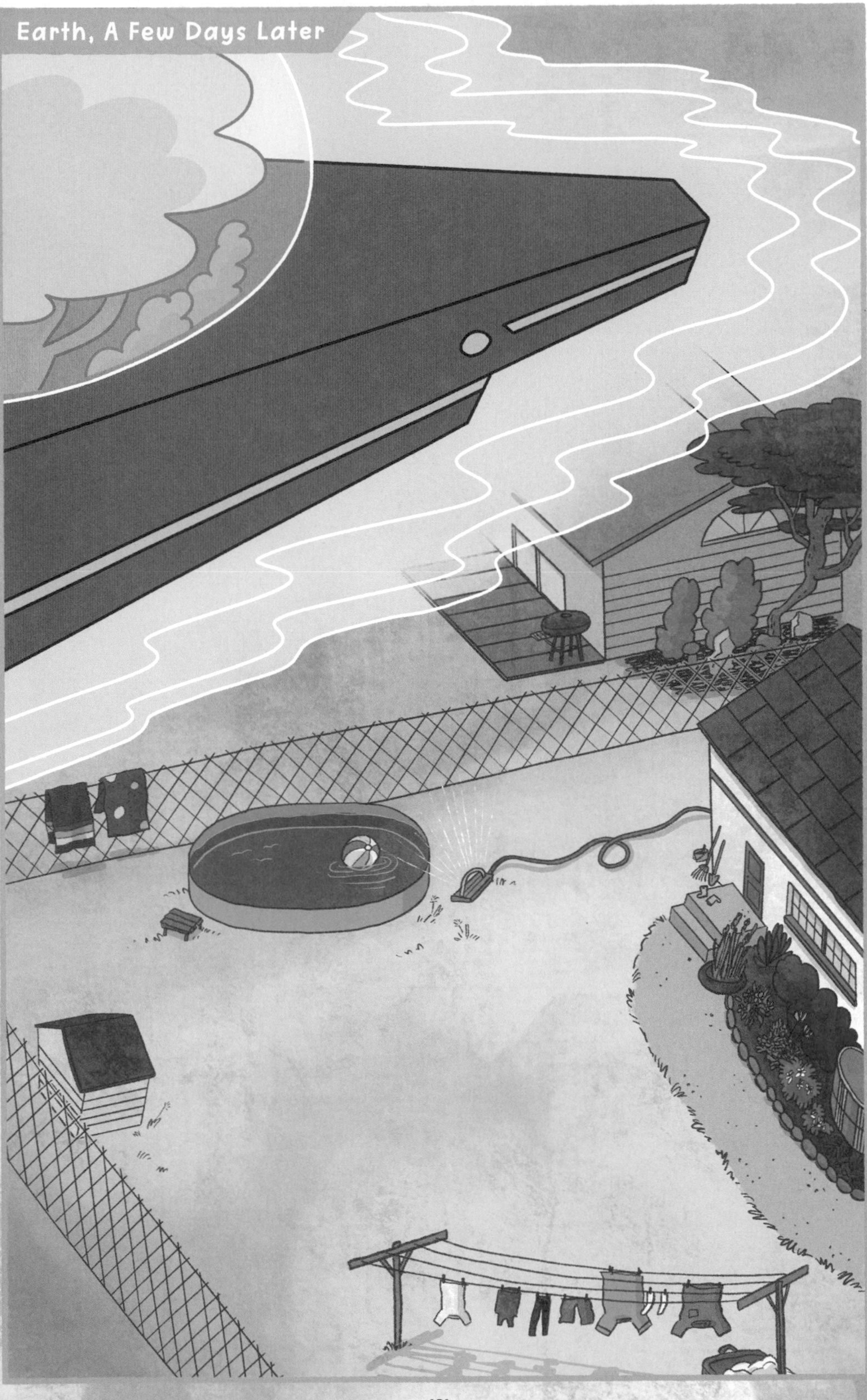
Earth, A Few Days Later

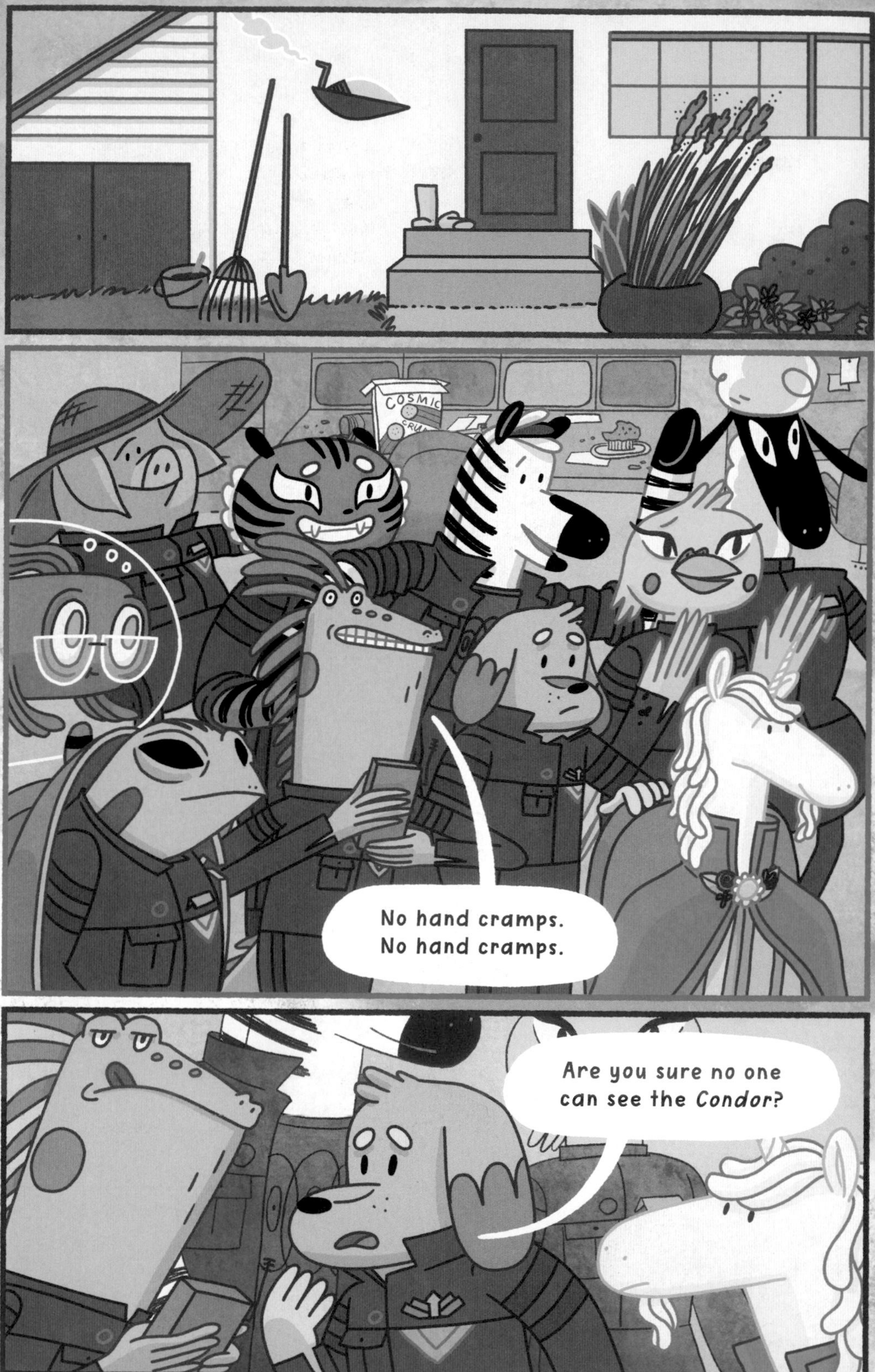
COSMIC
No hand cramps.
No hand cramps.
Are you sure no one can see the *Condor*?

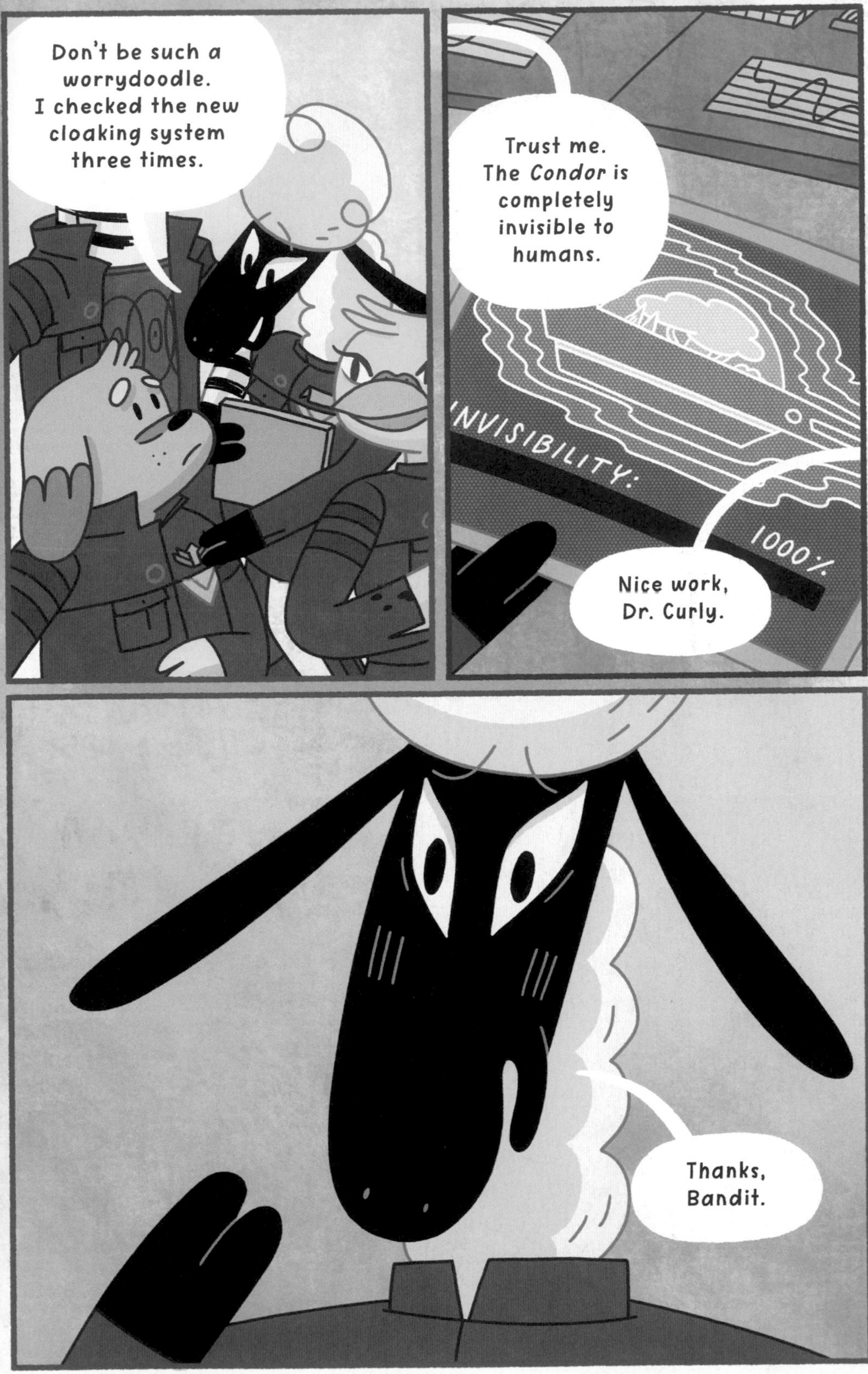
Don't be such a worrydoodle. I checked the new cloaking system three times.
Trust me. The *Condor* is completely invisible to humans.
INVISIBILITY:
1000%
Nice work, Dr. Curly.
Thanks, Bandit.

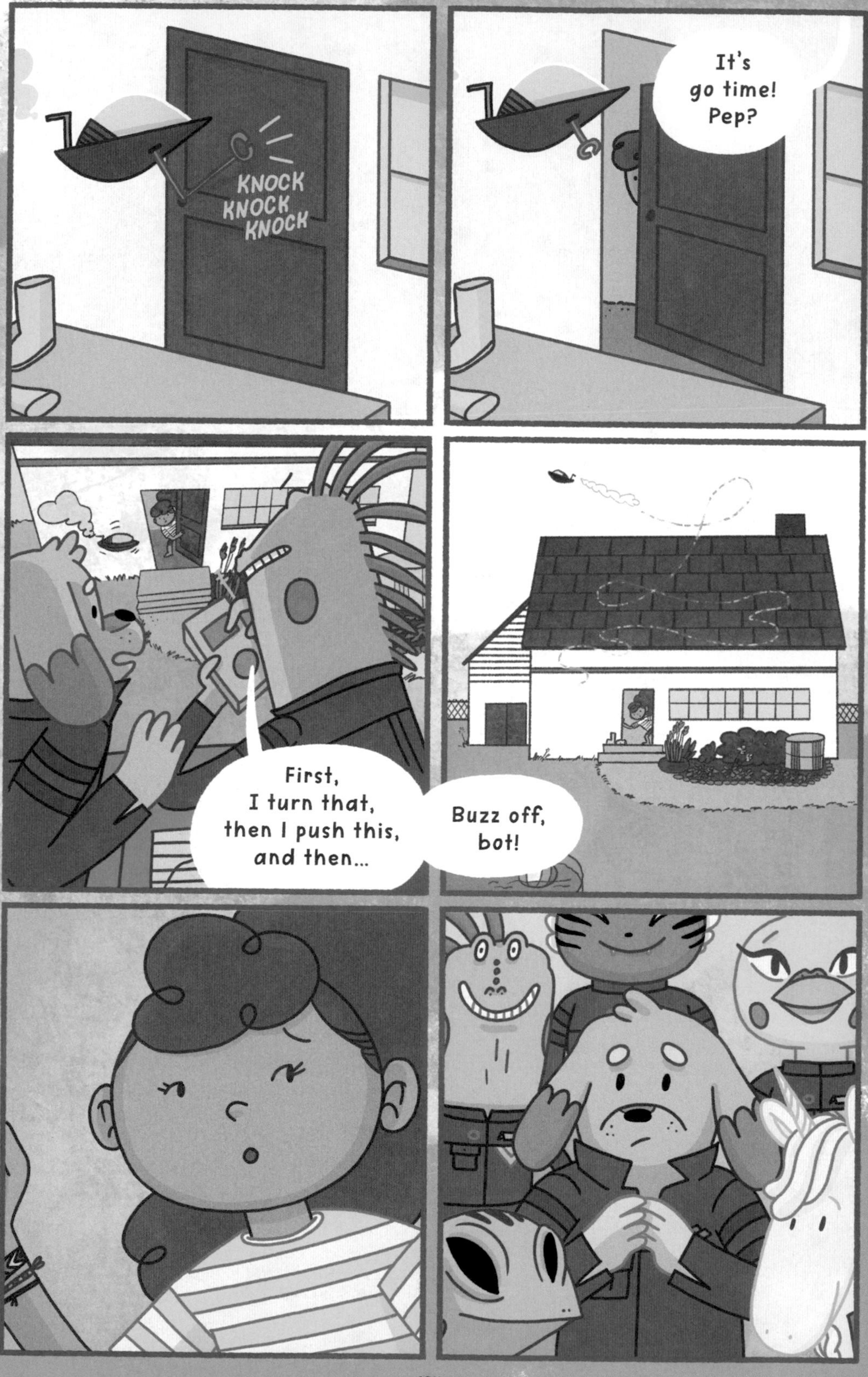
KNOCK
KNOCK
KNOCK
It's go time! Pep?
First, I turn that, then I push this, and then...
Buzz off, bot!

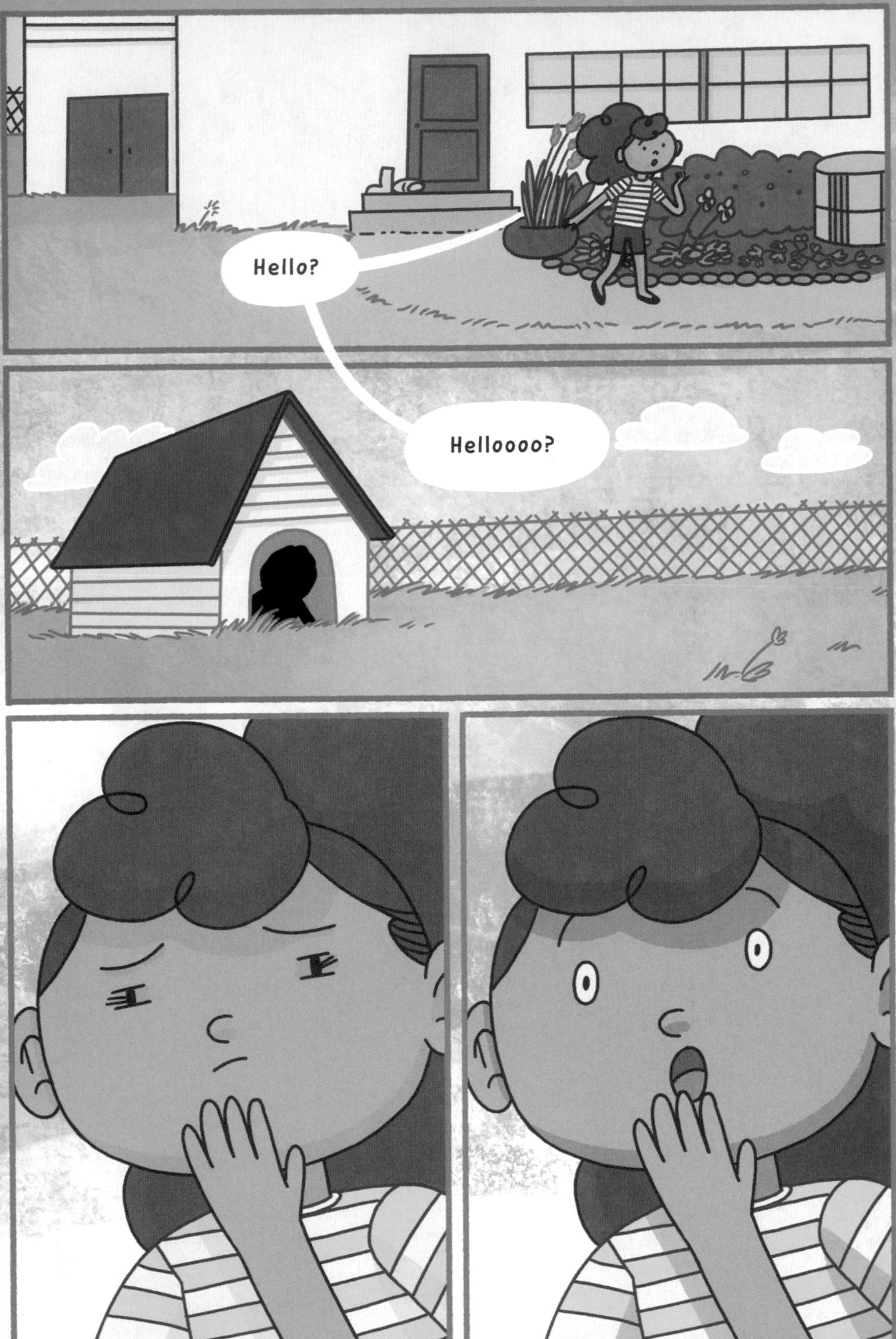
Hello?
Helloooo?

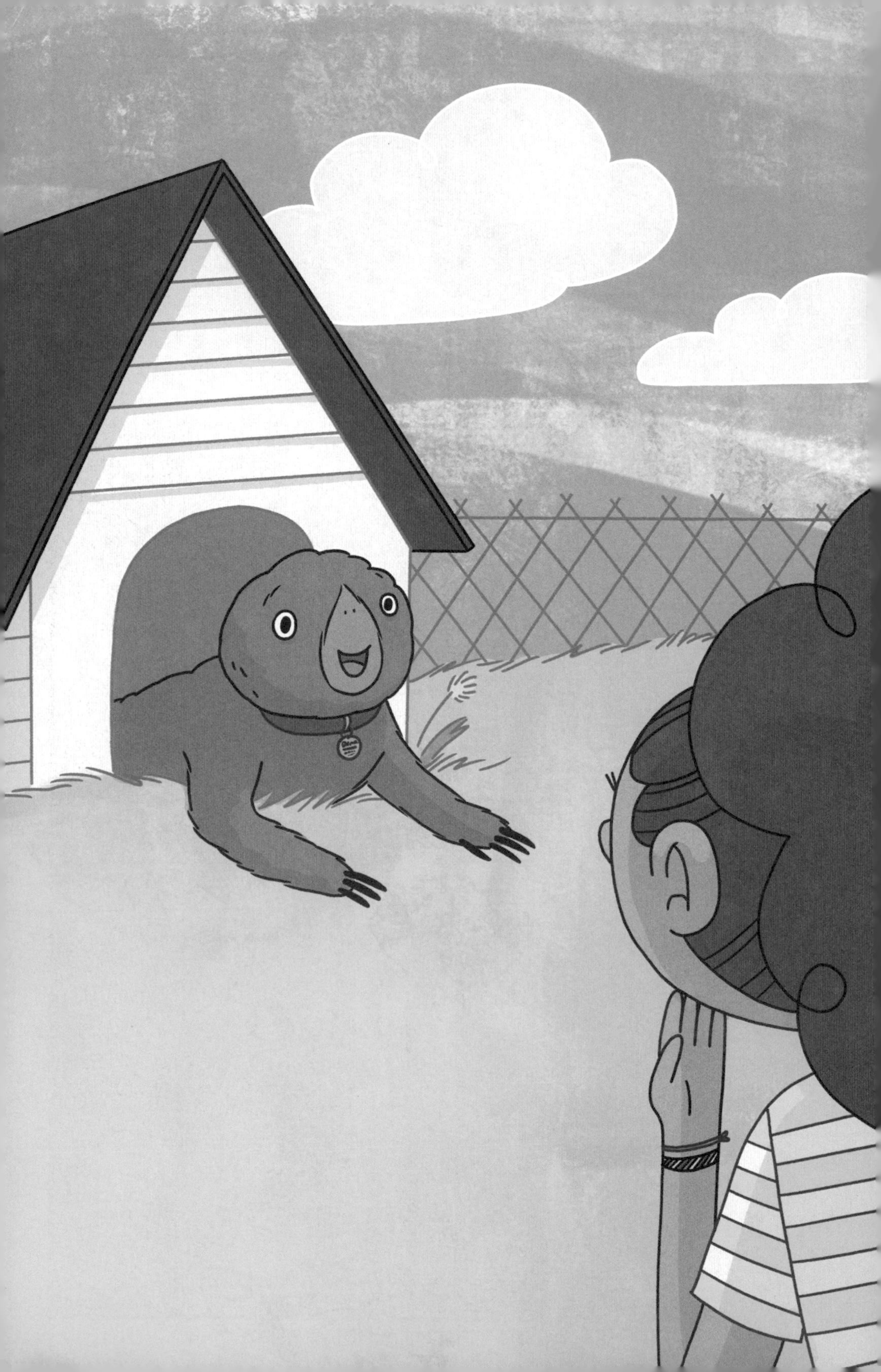

Hi there, little stranger!

You're a cutie. Are you lost?

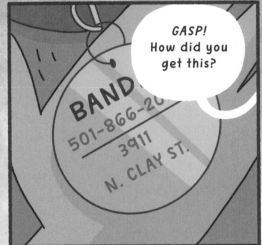

GASP! How did you get this?

BAND
501-866-2
3911
N. CLAY ST.

I guess you aren't lost after all...

You're right where you belong.

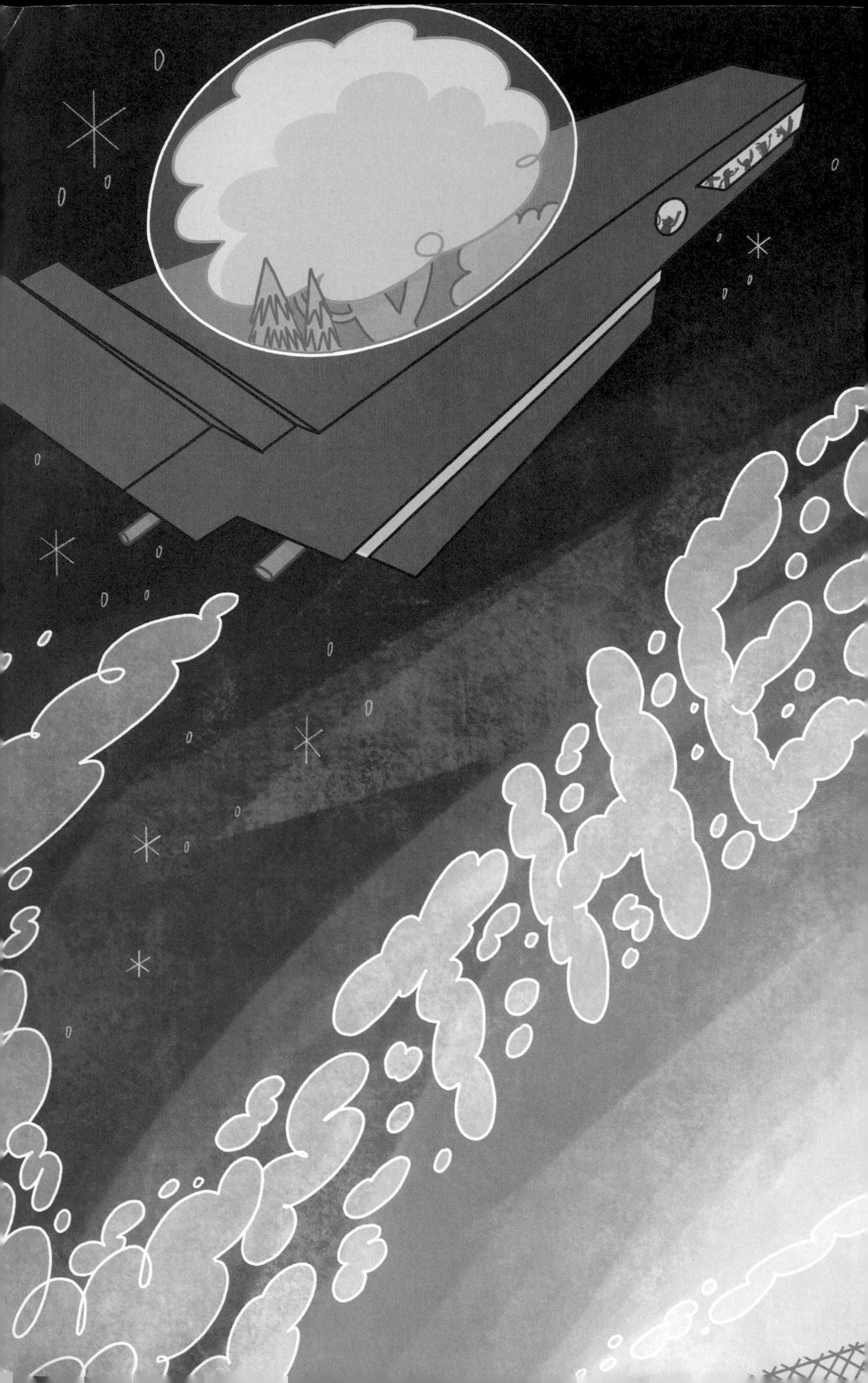

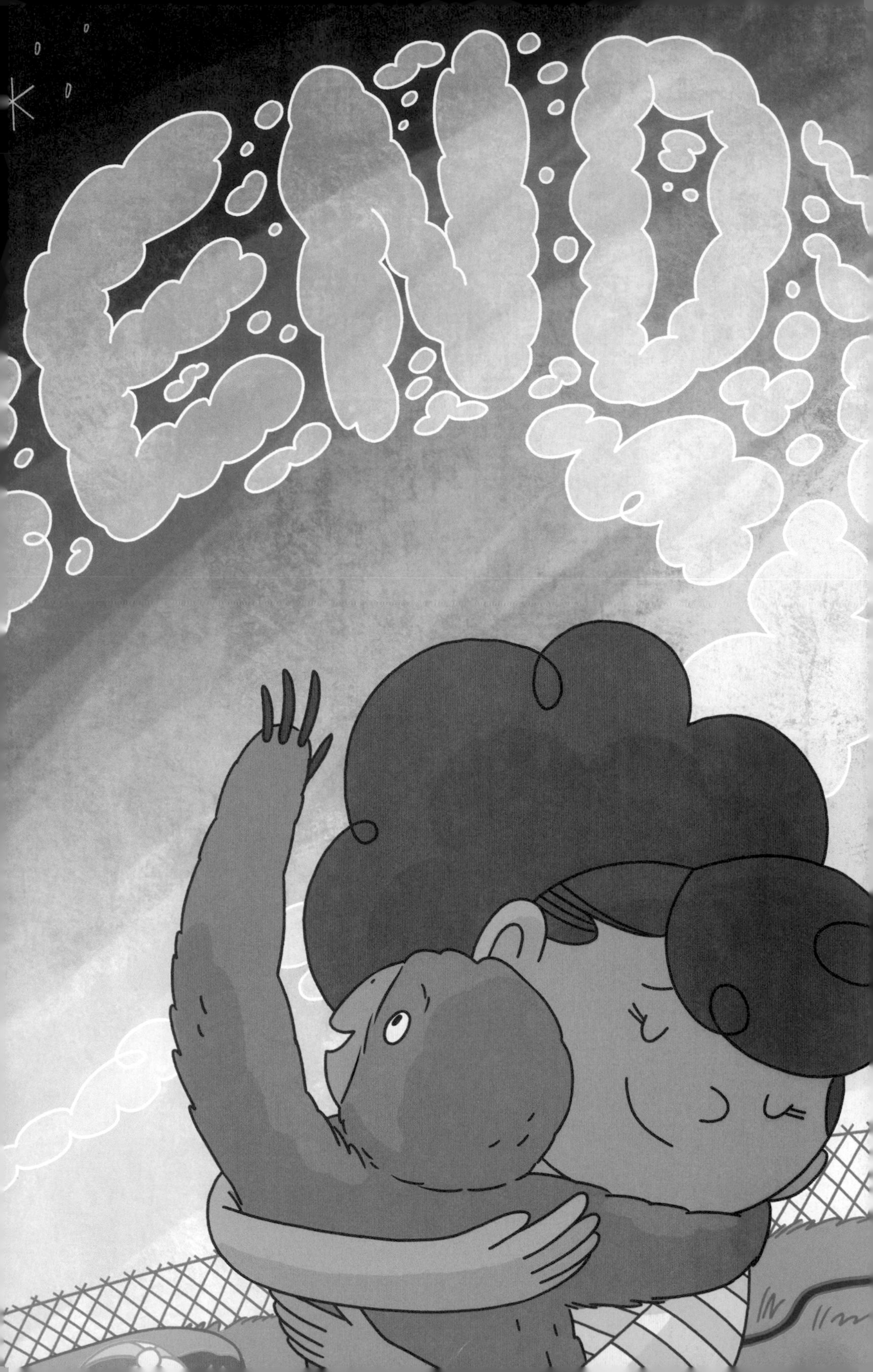
END

THANKS TO...

Star Beasts wouldn't be *Star Beasts* without the support,
encouragement, and know-how of **JOHN D. YOUNG**. You are
the stardust beneath the *Condor*'s stellarspeed.

KYLE STRAHAM
for being our guide to the comic industry cosmos.

AMY BEBERMEYER
for her supernova spell-check skills.

LISA HADLEY
for being a far-out color flatter.

THE FARRIS FAMILY:
galactic business manager, **ART**, hostess with the mostest,
BECKY, and social media master, **LYNLEY**.

AMANDA MEADOWS
for believing in our pulsar potential
and having such cool glasses.

Our kick-asteroid agent, **FIONA KENSHOLE**.

VINTAGE PHOENIX, THE COMIC CAVE, ELITE,
and all the comet-blazin' comic shops that stocked early issues.

The best librarian in the universe, **JESSIE EAST**.

And most importantly, thank you to all our friends, family,
and fans who cheered on *Star Beasts* from launch to liftoff.

CREATOR BIOS

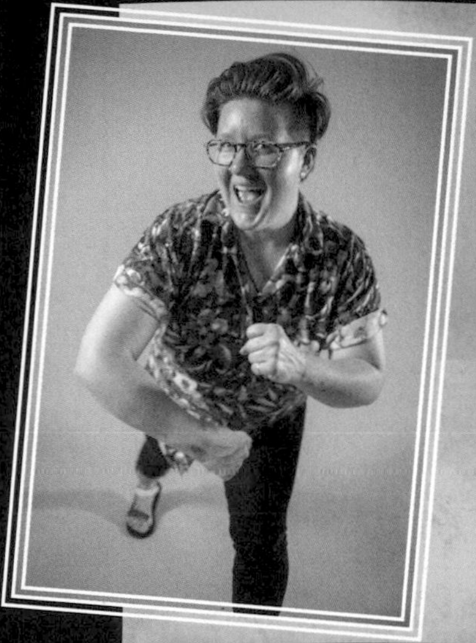

ALLYSON LASSITER

is an illustrator, plush designer, bike rider, and soup-maker. She likes meteor showers, soft-serve ice cream, dogs, and triple-quasar-style dance moves.

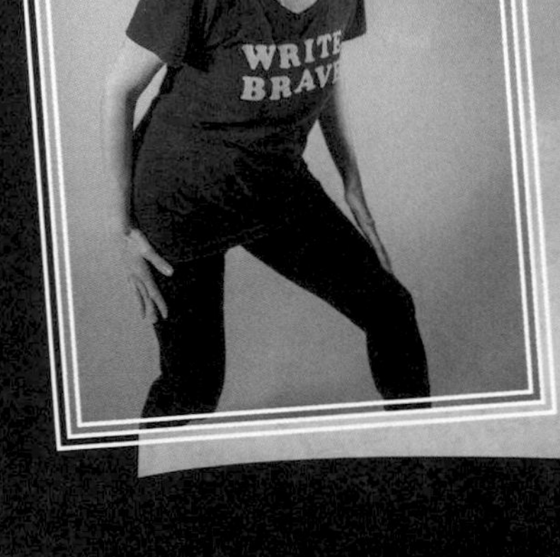
WRITE
BRAV

STEPHANIE YOUNG

is a writer, pancake connoisseur, and pie baker. She likes the constellation Pleiades, mint chip ice cream, cats, and funny space lingo (WHAT THE HUBBLE?).

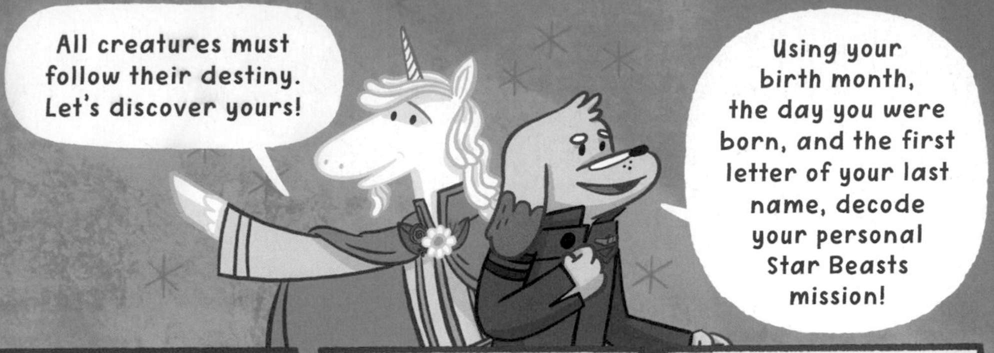
All creatures must follow their destiny. Let's discover yours!
Using your birth month, the day you were born, and the first letter of your last name, decode your personal Star Beasts mission!

YOUR BIRTH MONTH

JANUARY: Seek

FEBRUARY: Save

MARCH: Conquer

APRIL: Battle

MAY: Protect

JUNE: Heal

JULY: Explore

AUGUST: Celebrate

SEPTEMBER: Study

OCTOBER: Investigate

NOVEMBER: Fight

DECEMBER: Honor

DAY YOU WERE BORN

01: Space
02: Crescent
03: Galactic
04: Dark Matter
05: Dwarf
06: Lunar
07: Meteoroid
08: Shooting Star
09: Sun
10: Cosmic
11: Nebula
12: Eclipse
13: Star
14: Milky Way
15: Asteroid
16: Celestial
17: Outer Rim
18: Global
19: Orbiting
20: Moon
21: Big Bang
22: Deep Space
23: Meteor
24: Solar
25: Universal
26: Dazzle Matter
27: Telescopic
28: Crater
29: Sky
30: Pulsar
31: Black Hole

FIRST LETTER OF YOUR LAST NAME

A: Kittens
B: Tacos
C: Ladybugs
D: Elephants
E: Donuts
F: Lizards
G: Parrots
H: Puppies
I: Caterpillars
J: Giraffes
K: Snakes
L: Sloths
M: Hurricanes
N: Ferrets
O: Penguins
P: Blizzards
Q: Whales
R: Lions
S: Narwhals
T: Rainbows
U: Pizza
V: Horses
W: Popsicles
X: Hamsters
Y: Bears
Z: Nachos

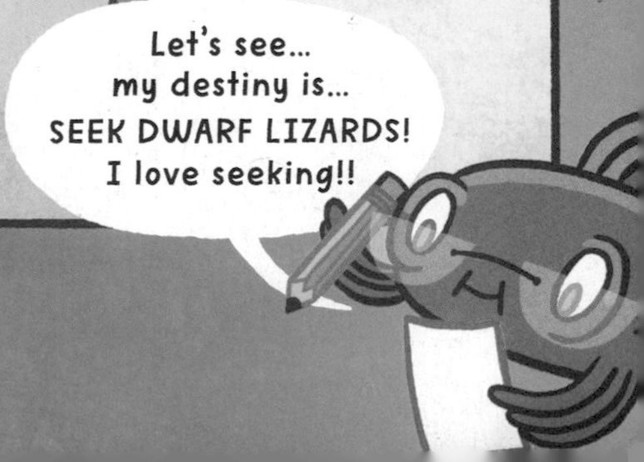
Let's see... my destiny is... SEEK DWARF LIZARDS! I love seeking!!

Before *Star Beasts* was a novel, it was a sneak peek comic! Early fans will remember this little adventure.

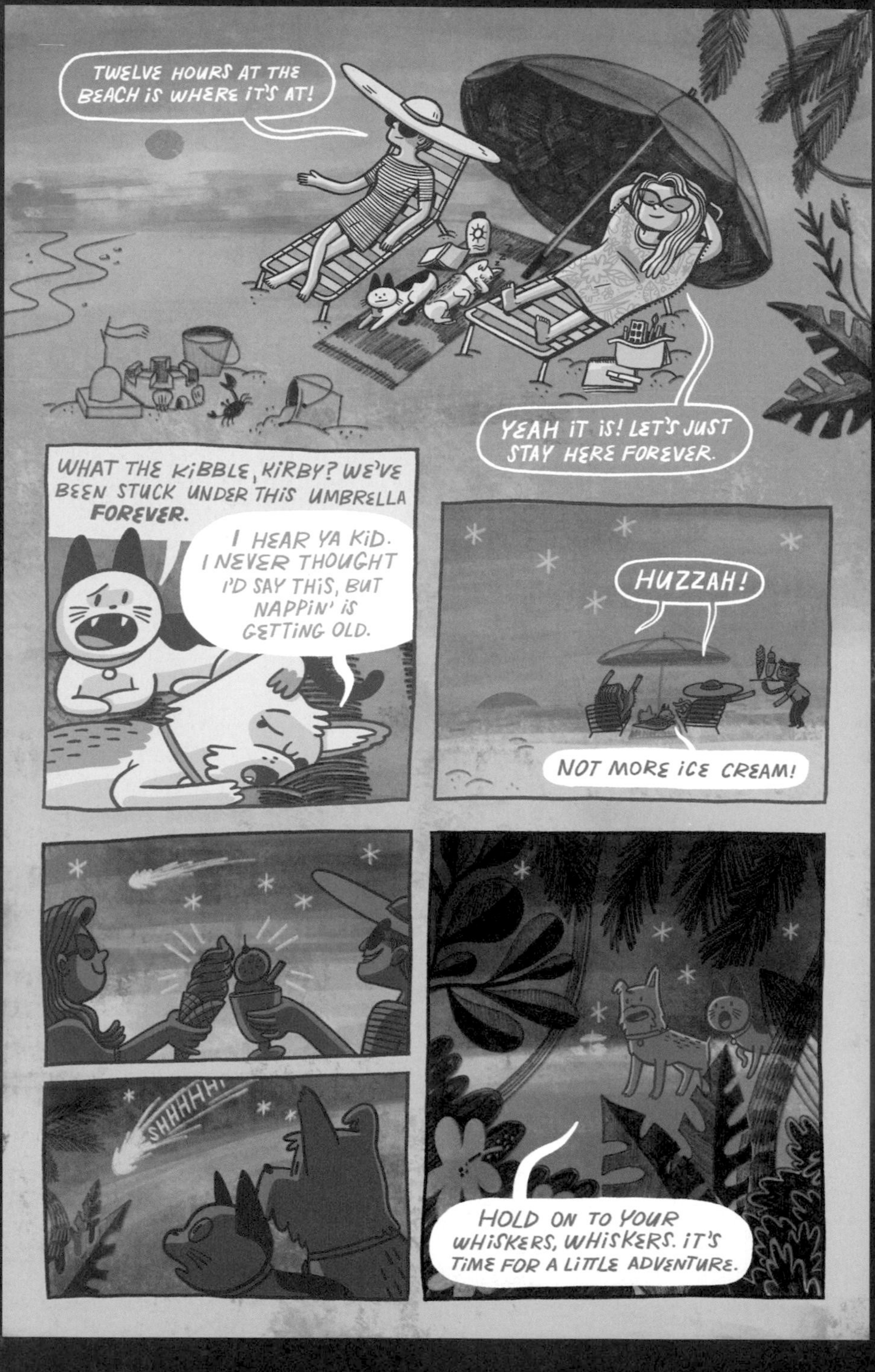
TWELVE HOURS AT THE BEACH IS WHERE IT'S AT!
YEAH IT IS! LET'S JUST STAY HERE FOREVER.
WHAT THE KIBBLE, KIRBY? WE'VE BEEN STUCK UNDER THIS UMBRELLA **FOREVER.**
I HEAR YA KID. I NEVER THOUGHT I'D SAY THIS, BUT NAPPIN' IS GETTING OLD.
HUZZAH!
NOT MORE ICE CREAM!
SHHHHH!
HOLD ON TO YOUR WHISKERS, WHISKERS. IT'S TIME FOR A LITTLE ADVENTURE.

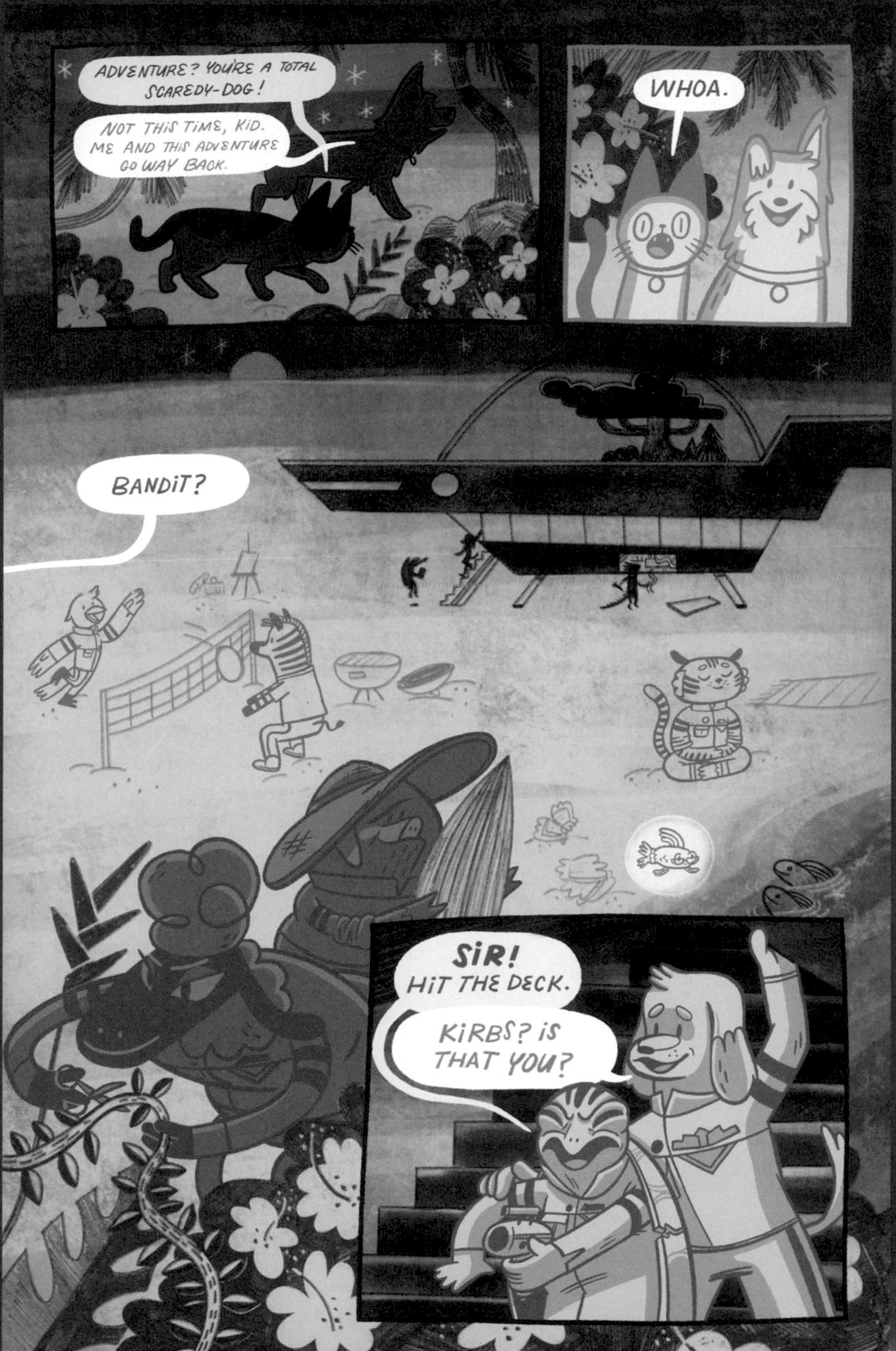
ADVENTURE? YOU'RE A TOTAL SCAREDY-DOG!
NOT THIS TIME, KID. ME AND THIS ADVENTURE GO WAY BACK.
WHOA.
BANDIT?
SIR! HIT THE DECK.
KIRBS? IS THAT YOU?

Whiskers and Kirby are Steph and Lassie's real-life pets and helped inspire *Star Beasts*.

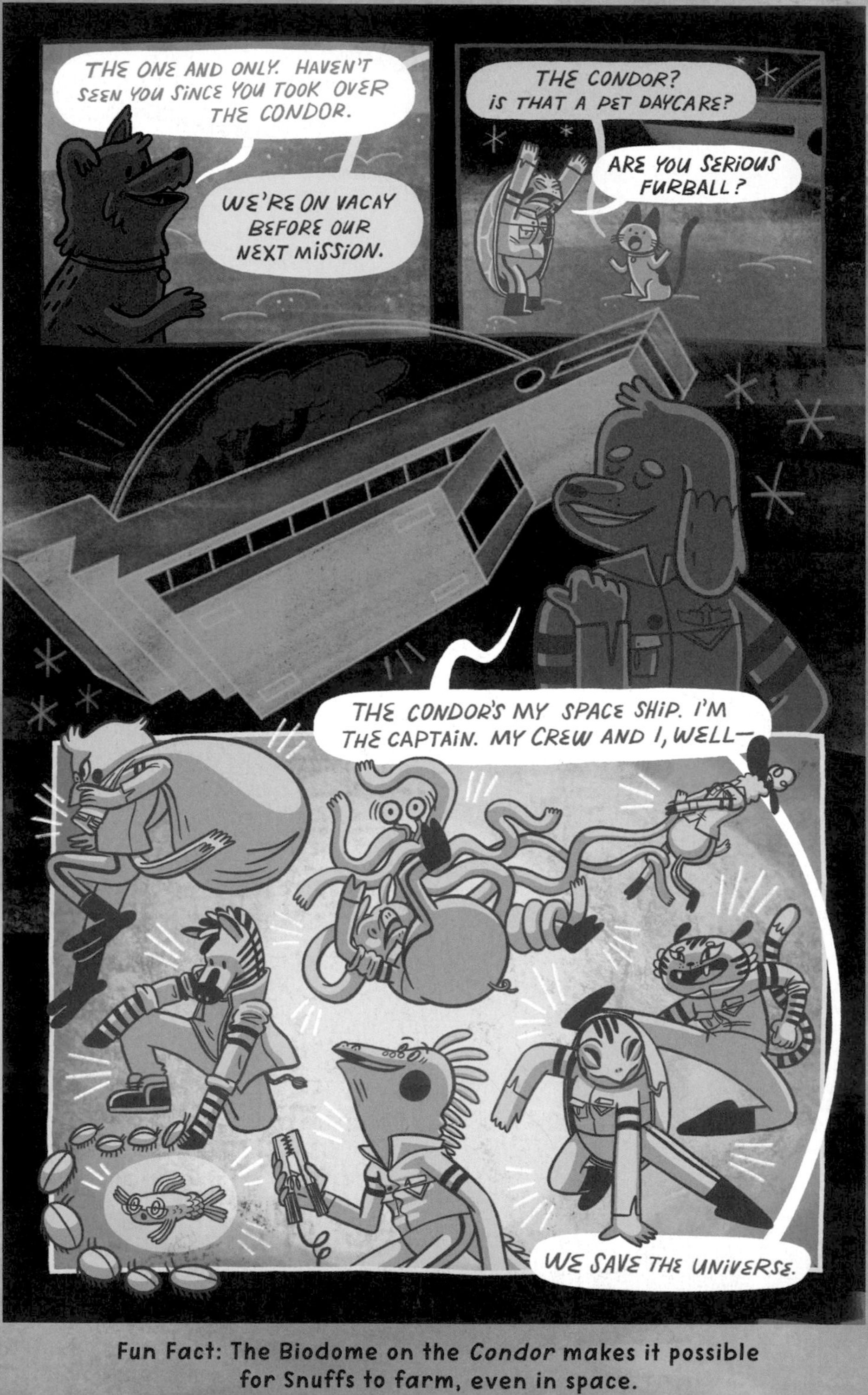
THE ONE AND ONLY. HAVEN'T SEEN YOU SINCE YOU TOOK OVER THE CONDOR.
WE'RE ON VACAY BEFORE OUR NEXT MISSION.
THE CONDOR? IS THAT A PET DAYCARE?
ARE YOU SERIOUS FURBALL?
THE CONDOR'S MY SPACE SHIP. I'M THE CAPTAIN. MY CREW AND I, WELL—
WE SAVE THE UNIVERSE.

Fun Fact: The Biodome on the *Condor* makes it possible for Snuffs to farm, even in space.

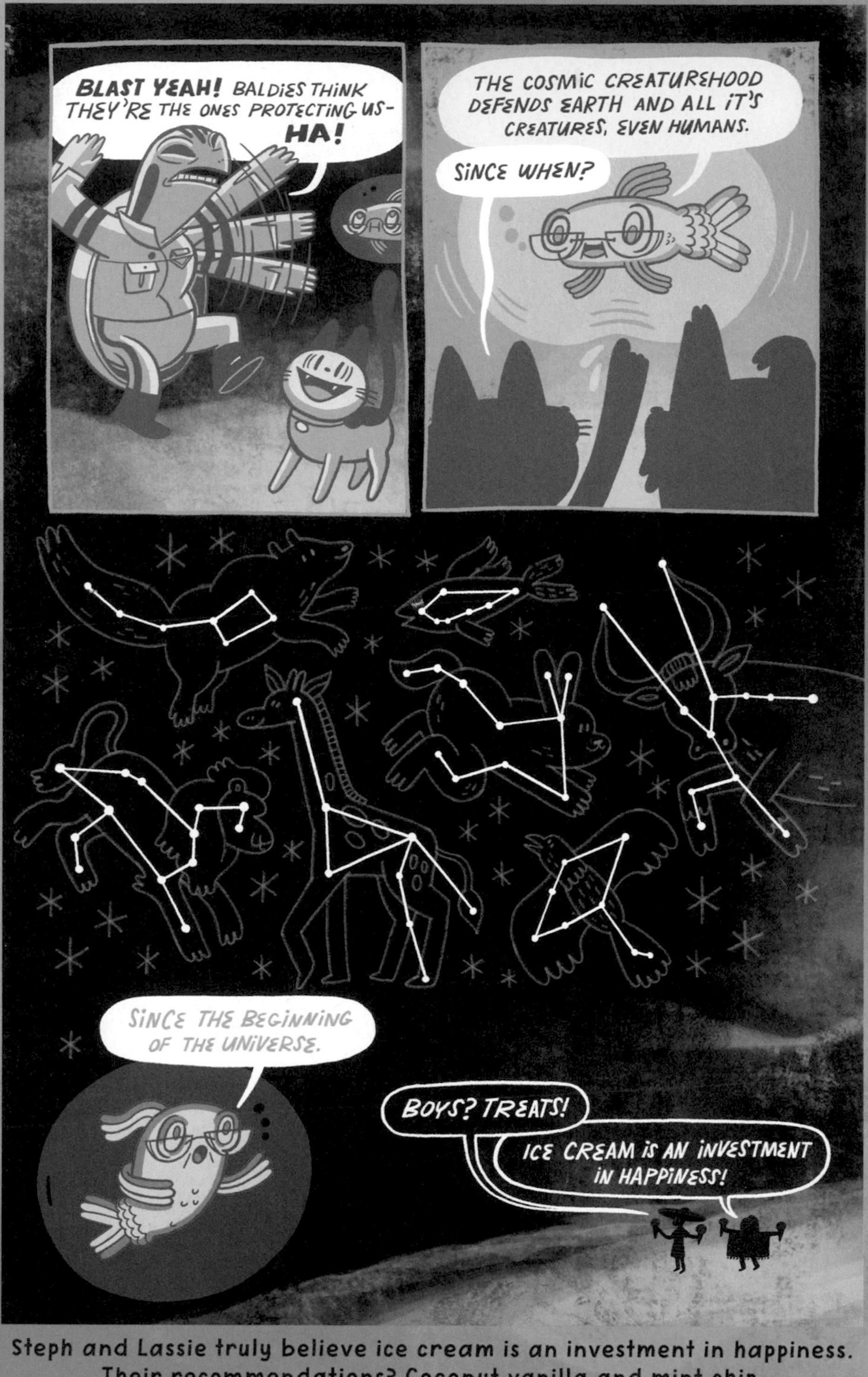
BLAST YEAH! BALDIES THINK THEY'RE THE ONES PROTECTING US- HA!
THE COSMIC CREATUREHOOD DEFENDS EARTH AND ALL IT'S CREATURES, EVEN HUMANS.
SINCE WHEN?
SINCE THE BEGINNING OF THE UNIVERSE.
BOYS? TREATS!
ICE CREAM IS AN INVESTMENT IN HAPPINESS!

Steph and Lassie truly believe ice cream is an investment in happiness. Their recommendations? Coconut vanilla and mint chip.

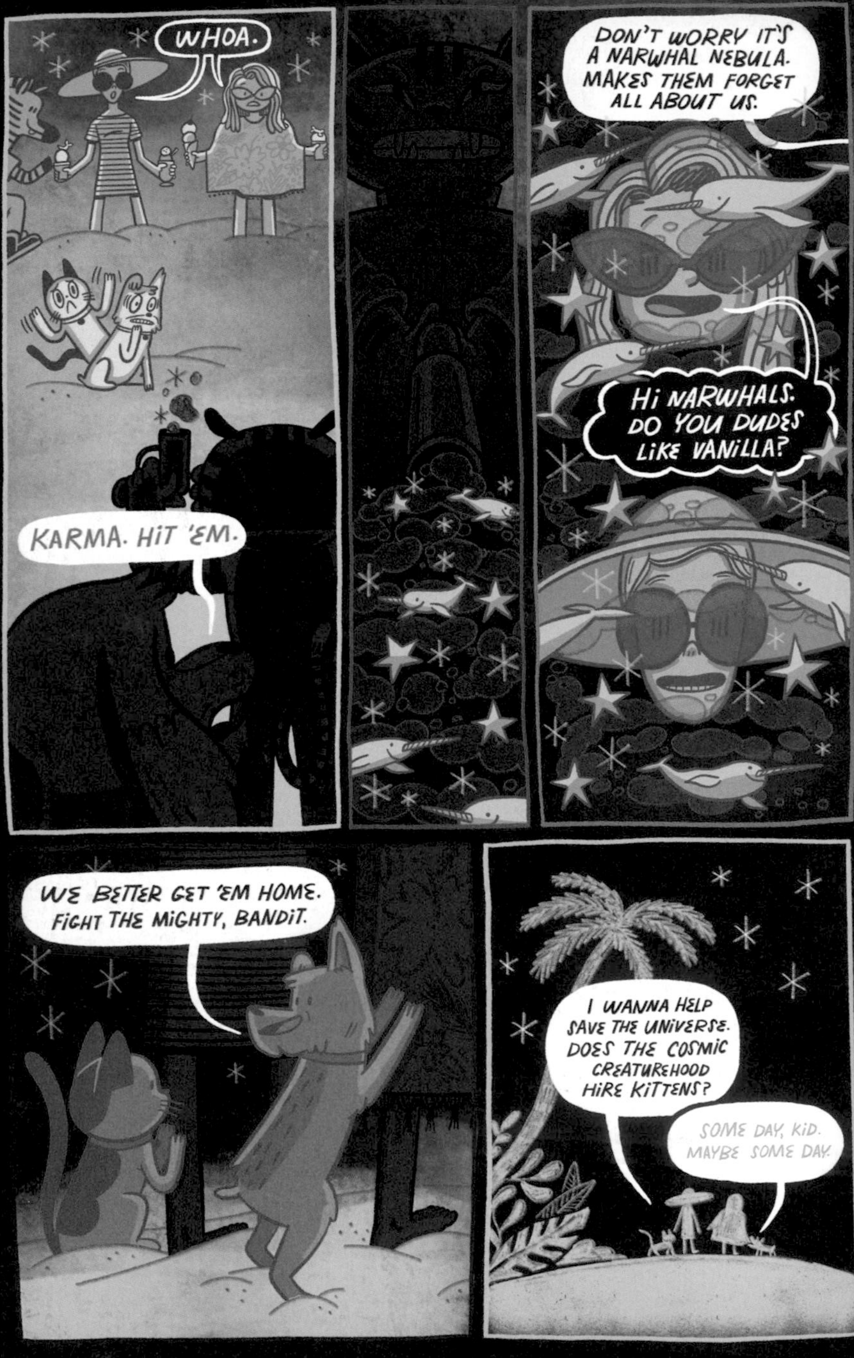
WHOA.
KARMA. HIT 'EM.
DON'T WORRY IT'S A NARWHAL NEBULA. MAKES THEM FORGET ALL ABOUT US.
Hi NARWHALS. DO YOU DUDES LIKE VANILLA?
WE BETTER GET 'EM HOME. FIGHT THE MIGHTY, BANDIT.
I WANNA HELP SAVE THE UNIVERSE. DOES THE COSMIC CREATUREHOOD HIRE KITTENS?
SOME DAY, KID. MAYBE SOME DAY.

Please notice how Karma is using the Narwhal Nebula correctly on this page.

If Bandit hadn't joined the Star Beasts crew, here are some other dogs who were almost captain.

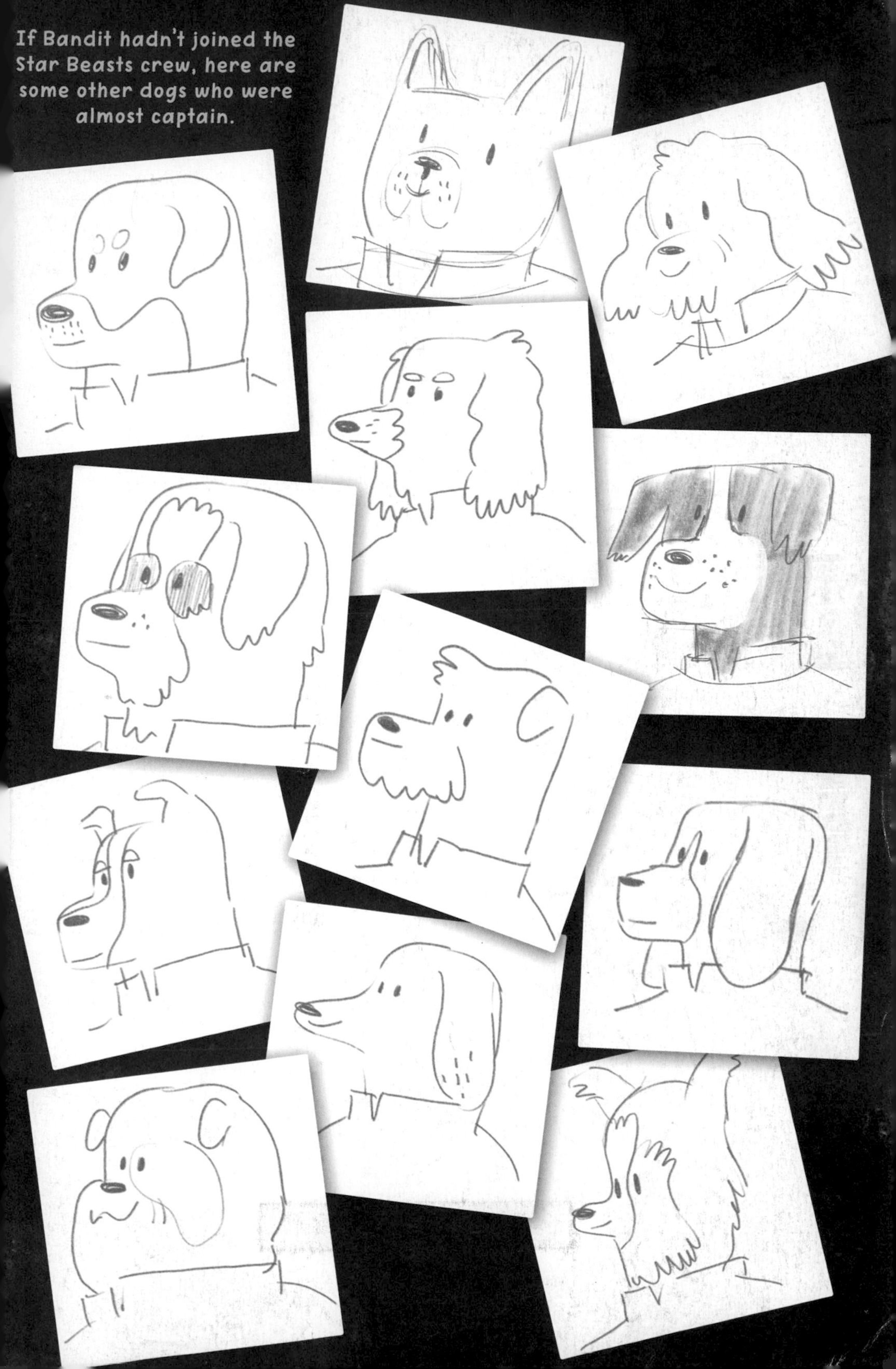